The Folly of Angels

Shelly Dixon Van Sanford

ISBN 978-1-68517-551-1 (paperback)
ISBN 978-1-68517-552-8 (digital)

Christian Faith Publishing
832 Park Avenue
Meadville, PA 16335
www.christianfaithpublishing.com

Printed in the United States of America

For Megan, Dixon, and Preston—and for
their loves, both big and small

and for Glenn, who walks beside me.

Prologue

THE TINIEST EVENT can alter the world forever—at least, that's what Ava came to believe, that everything breaks against everything else. Something moves this way, someone says that, and the sparks of electricity change, the chemicals, and sounds in the air—and most of all the people, and the path along which they were traveling. It's the trajectory of their lives that shifts; that launching point, nudged by just a degree, diverts that endpoint severely. It makes the place where they thought they'd land so far away that they never end up where they'd planned—better, maybe, or worse, but never that same hoped-for place in that same planned-for way.

She didn't know this when she was young, but there came a moment when she did: it only takes a moment to transform the course of everything there is in the world and especially one's course within it.

*Behold, he put no trust in his servants, and
his angels he charged with folly.*

—Job 4:18 (KJV)

Part I

Chapter 1

"I DON'T WANT TO get married next month."

And just like that, everything changed. The restaurant didn't look any different. The rose-colored walls still reflected halos of candlelight, and the good-natured hum of conversation still wafted above and around them. The other couples were still lifting their forks and spoons to their mouths, and a woman emitted a tinkling laugh; but Ava knew that the universe had shifted.

She didn't speak. She had been looking at him in perfect contentment until the moment he'd made that utterance, and in that next moment, her pose didn't change; she stared, motionless.

Lowering his eyes to his plate, he put down his spoon, wiped his mouth with his napkin, then leaned against the back of his chair. He took a couple of purposeful sips of merlot, taking time with these deliberations, these calculated movements, and she resented him for his cruelty.

"What does that mean, Eric?" She kept her voice calm, along with the set of her face, though the pain was visceral and strong.

He hadn't resumed eating. He leaned forward again, erect and purposeful, one hand still holding the wine glass. He looked at her. He was gauging his percolating words against her possible reactions, she thought, her brain working at warp speed. *What would Ava do if I said . . . ?*

But she already knew, and it was the worst. She knew it even as she envisioned the venue, the food, and the flowers, almost everything already paid.

"I'm not sure what's going on." He sipped again from his glass. "I'm not ready. It doesn't feel right. It isn't you, and I know you might not believe that, but you are a great person. I've always really cared for you."

Don't speak. Don't speak. If you talk now or ask questions, you will never really know.

"I was studying last week, and it occurred to me that these next two years are going to be even harder than the last two. You don't want to live in married housing, but I don't think we can afford an apartment close to the hospital—not with rent the way it is and me earning so little the first few years. I have all this debt, too, remember, which is just getting worse by the week."

She did remember. Eric's family didn't have the kind of money necessary to educate a doctor. But she made a good wage, thank God, and there was no reason to imagine they couldn't get by, even if they only had her income. People didn't change their weddings because they would have to follow a budget.

"I make a decent salary, Eric. I've been there almost two years—"

"You're an accountant."

"What's that supposed to mean?"

"Nothing." He held up both palms to her and looked around the room. His straight brown hair was deeply parted on the left, and he wore it swept across his forehead. It was too long now, and he kept raking it backward. In the candlelight, it shone like molasses.

"I guess I didn't prefer married housing, but if that's what we need…if it means we can stay together, if that's what it takes to make it, well…"

He met her eyes suddenly, with urgency. "You're great. Your job is great. We've had so many good times, but you're only twenty-two, and I have two more years in school before I can even start a residency."

She looked at him. "I know this. You're acting like you're telling me new information." He was silent, so she looked down as she moved a few pieces of chicken around her plate. A man in a white suit began noodling some music on a corner piano. "So you want to postpone the wedding because you have two more years of school, because I was hoping to get an apartment off-campus, and because I'm an accountant."

"No. You're missing the point." He took another long drink of wine and then clamped his lips together.

"I wonder if you could tell me exactly what you're trying to say without the excuses, Eric. Do you want to change something about the wedding, or postpone the wedding, or do you not want to get married at all?"

It only took twelve seconds. Twelve seconds passed before he spoke, but he didn't need to because twelve seconds of silence can speak for itself.

The restaurant crowd had gone on eating and laughing and talking. Eric had requested the check, and for what couldn't have been more than five minutes, Ava focused on surviving. In that chasm—the barest slip of time during which he paid the bill and she was able to rise with dignity—she felt another little pocket of her heart squeeze shut and die. It fell off in concealment, so *politely*, to that pit in her stomach where all the bad things always went—like fear, guilt, and rejection, loneliness, hatred, and shame.

Chapter 2

THE MORNING BROUGHT a Saturday, and she thanked the universe for small mercies. How she would face work on Monday was anyone's guess, but she would not think of that now. She raised herself in bed and stared at the clock radio; its screen glared 9:08 a.m. in ugly red light. Her eyes drifted to the calendar Harvick & Braun LLP had given her last Christmas, where—in yesterday's square, May 21, 1982—she'd written "Dinner with Eric" and drawn a little heart. Her eye took in the stock photo for the month, of an attractive blonde in a business suit smiling over a ledger and calculator while holding an elegant gold pen. Ava wondered if she'd ever been dumped.

She rubbed her eyes with their crusty mascara, then leaned against the headboard to take stock. Taking stock of what, she didn't know—the apartment? Her day? Her life? How dare he.

She wouldn't cry right now; last night had been enough. Even alone, she knew if she cried this morning, it would be hard to recover, and she needed the day to think. They were supposed to have walked down the aisle three weeks from today—three weeks! But she could not huddle down into this, could not surrender to feelings of pity. The only emotion she allowed herself was anger because this one, she was sure, would serve her well.

The apartment was a second-floor walk-up with two bedrooms overlooking a pool and two bathrooms opposite each bedroom across the hall. The hall that separated the bedrooms from the bathrooms opened into an airy kitchen/dining/living area, but Ava rarely hung out there because her roommate was messy and overbearing. And beautiful. Beautiful girls grew up thinking they could get away with anything.

Last spring, when Ava had first seen the place, and before she'd moved in, she had been overwhelmed by Chantal's décor. The walls bore shiny cream-colored paint with a sparkle finish, and fox-fur throw rugs (clearly illegal) lay beneath crystal lamps on end tables and silky gold sofa pillows with crystal tufted buttons. Ava had painted her bedroom sage green in retaliation, with an unbleached muslin quilted bedspread and her original photography. Her job at the accounting firm would be hard, she'd reasoned, when she'd agreed to move in with Chantal; she'd need a refuge not only from it but from the opium-den atmosphere outside her door.

She got up and raised her window to look at the thermometer glued to its outside sill: 72.6 degrees. Leaving the window open, she climbed back in bed and propped her two pillows behind her, pulling her knees to her chest and her covers up to her chin. She began to decide what to wear when she thought perhaps she would not dress today. Why bother? No one except Chantal would ever even know if she annihilated this whole day from the history of her life.

The picture across from her bed was one she had taken at Yancey right before she graduated. It was from the perspective of someone standing in the road—a winding sun-and-shade-spackled two-lane running through opposite rows of oaks arching into the sky. The sun, setting westward over the disappearing road, shot mind-blowing rays of radiance into the billows of clouds above it. These appeared as an upside-down frothy white ocean lit by rose, orange, yellow, and pink and surrounded by warm dove gray. "Jesus could return at a moment such as this," Madeline, her cycling companion that day, had remarked. But Ava had offered no comment. She straddled her bike and shot five quick frames with her Canon A-1, knowing at least one would be perfect—frameable and timeless—and that Jesus would not be showing up that day at all.

It was this picture at which she was staring when she heard Chantal's signature knock—*bump, ba-dump, bump-bump*, and she steeled herself for the inevitable intrusion. She didn't answer—she rarely did—for Chantal entered within a second of knocking, every time.

Her roommate had the fluid movements of a young Grace Kelly. She was slender with translucent bisque skin and watery blonde hair. In the mornings, she didn't look extraordinary—her hair lank, last night's makeup smeared, she'd wander the floor in sweats and tanks or T-shirts. But when she worked, she transformed: her makeup was impeccable, her moon-colored hair voluminous and waved like Heather Locklear's. She wore Quiana dresses or skinny Jordache jeans with tube tops and high, strappy sandals. Today she had on camo pants cut off at the ankles and a pink crop top with a heat-pressed portrait of Elvis Presley's face. She sat in Ava's desk chair facing outward and began eating a blueberry yogurt with a straw.

"Somebody had a bad date." Chantal sucked the yogurt off the straw's end.

"And who would that be, Alice? Me or you?" Ava gave as good as she got.

"Oh gosh, girl, now that you mention it, probably both of us!" Chantal laughed—a dry, cracking sound. Ava had long imagined her dates were initially surprised by her laugh, finding it incongruous. "I'm to be forgiven for mine, though. They don't have to be good, only lucrative."

She had a good vocabulary. She'd been a college student, after all, just like Ava, only falling into her work afterward and not hating it enough to get out.

"Let's see… I'll tell you about mine if you tell me why you were home before nine o'clock."

Ava chewed her thumbnail. She kept her eyes focused on the sunset and its disappearing, hopeful road.

"Okay, I'll start. A banker. Overweight, balding, but not resorting to a comb-over yet, thank God. Greasy, though. Brill cream or something, whatever they use these days. He takes me to Grand China for dinner, then orders stuff with garlic. Garlic! Like we're not gonna do it later."

Ava let her eyes meet Chantal's, and she took her thumbnail from her mouth. "Well, I've got you beat. Eric left me last night. Called off the wedding. Said it's him, not me. Couldn't even come up with a better freakin' line. So really, I'd say you had the better evening."

She got up from the bed and looked out the window, focusing beyond its screen. Along one side of the pool lay a line of musk roses, and on these, Ava lingered her gaze. It was an old trick, one she'd learned as a child: trick the mind into thinking the world was good by staring at a beautiful thing. Chantal, recovering from her initial shock, leapt from the chair and slammed her yogurt cup on the desk.

"I *knew* it! Oh man, I could have called it. What a jerk, what a completely stupid idiot."

Ava turned. "*Really?* You could have called it? Well, that's great. How would you have done that, Alice? What was your first clue?"

Chantal stared at her a moment and took a step back toward the door, leaned on its jam, and crossed her arms. "What is wrong with you? Why are you being hateful to *me?*"

Ava knew what she meant. It wasn't fair to use Chantal's real name, something she'd told her in confidence back when they'd been learning to be friends. She took a deep breath.

"I'm sorry. But honestly, here I am, having broken off an engagement to someone I love, and you tell me without a thought that you knew he was going to dump me? Like you had a secret antenna that my fiancé was a scumbag, and so when he changes his mind, you can't even sympathize for one second, you can only insinuate I picked a real lump of garbage to marry?"

Ava brushed past Chantal and went to the kitchen, poured herself a huge glass of warm chlorinated tap water and gulped it, still standing at the sink. Chantal followed her but kept her distance, leaning against the kitchen door frame, arms still crossed and one foot propped on its toes.

"I didn't mean it. Eric's a nice guy. I mean, I guess he was. Or maybe he still is. It was a cruddy thing to do, but I can see what you saw in him, at least."

The water hadn't stopped the tears. Ava turned from the sink and faced the other girl, eyes stinging, her cheeks becoming wet against her will. "What did I see in him? Can you tell me?" Chantal took her hand and led her to the white leather sofa and sat her there. She then sat on the floor in front of Ava and looked up into her face with all the kindness you would expect from a mother.

"You saw a kind, handsome man who would look at you through those cute wire-rimmed glasses and tell you everything you never wanted to know about the human body. He was serious and smart, and he had plans. He asked you out two years ago, and you must have had a good time because you went out with him again and again and again until one day last year, on your twenty-second birthday, which is Saint Patrick's Day, for Pete's sake, he said, 'Ava,' because that's your name, he said, 'Ava, I think I'd like to get married one day, so if you would think about it, I was thinking maybe summer, after my second year of medical school.' And you thought that was sweet because he was such a planner, and so unemotional, that you thought, for him, that was the most romantic proposal you could have hoped for, and you said, 'I'd love to,' and y'all were gonna live happily ever after. But now, I guess…"

Her voice trailed off. "I mean, now, I guess, there's some other plan…or something… and that's gonna be okay too."

Ava pressed her hands to her eyes and cried harder. The mascara was stinging badly, and she needed to blow her nose. "I need a tissue." Speaking between her flattened hands, she heard Chantal moving before feeling the box in her lap. Her friend sat beside her on the sofa and smoothed the top of Ava's head twice with her palm.

"You should leave." Ava raised her head to meet Chantal's powder-blue eyes, which were probably almost as blackened with last night's makeup as hers. "You should pack a bag and just go to the beach or something. Get the heck out of Dodge, as Daddy says."

Chantal—Alice Gayle Horne, as she was christened at birth—was from Dothan, Alabama. Ava was used to her scrappy Southern adages.

"And what would that do, pray tell? Besides, I have a job." Ava grabbed three more tissues from the box and blew hard.

"A job you hate."

"I do not! I fought for that job. I beat out nine interviewees and god-knows-how-many other applicants…"

"I didn't say you didn't! It's great. Let's just say it's great. But you don't like it. You know you don't. You do it because you're a good girl and you studied like a maniac for it, and you're practical, and you were saving for your magical life, the one you were going to have with Eric. But now you're not."

"I don't hate my job." Ava got up and went to the kitchen, refilling the glass with tap water.

"You do. Just admit it. I'll never tell anyone," Chantal called from the sofa. "You wanted to love it, but you don't."

"I like it fine."

"'I like it fine!' she says. Okay. You like it fine. Go pack a bag. Call in sick. They'll never know."

"I can't call in sick on a Saturday!" Ava stomped her way back to the sofa. She slammed back into it beside her roommate, throwing her arm across her eyes. Chantal's filmy white-and-gold curtains were lousy at keeping out morning light but great at creating that coveted bordello atmosphere. "You can't call in sick on a Saturday."

Chantal leaned forward toward Ava. "Sit up. Just for a minute. Listen to me." Pulling Ava up by one arm, she struggled to make Ava face her. "You're a good girl. You always have been. But it's your turn to get what you want, to take care of yourself. I don't know if you want me to think Eric is a jerk or if you still love him and want to get him back—"

"I hate him."

"Okay, well, then that means you still love him, but that's beside the point. The point is, your job has that call service. It's the easiest way to do it. You're too pure to fake it person-to-person anyway. You'd screw it up. So you call and leave a vague message that everybody's too polite to dig into when you return. You've had a bad diagnosis. Or a family emergency." She waved her hand in a devil-may-care manner, letting Ava flop backward. "You can think about it. And you won't be in the whole week, tell them that. You'll be happy to go into it when you come in on Monday, but you'd rather not talk about the medical tests or funeral arrangements or whatever you want to make up. And then you just take this week off to think about stuff and get your head on straight. Go to the beach and write Eric the letter of his life, or go have an affair. Don't go back to work on Monday. Not *this* Monday."

Ava listened until Chantal stopped. She leaned sideways into the sofa's arm and closed her eyes and began to pack a bag in her mind. But it wasn't for the beach. Nor was it full of stationery and a poetry collection to write the letter that would make Eric miss her. He would miss her soon enough, or not, and what difference did it make anyway?

She also wouldn't go home because home would be the worst—Jeanette with her constant talking, her false gaiety, and the clutter of her mismanaged life. Ava would call her mother later, perhaps Monday, from Bea's house. All she had to do was fake this phone call—a terribly risky thing to do and one that may create way more problems than it solved. But she needed it now. Just for once in her life, she needed a break from the overwhelming task of doing everything right, from trying so hard to make everything eventually go her way. It hadn't worked so far anyway. So she would make that scary phone call because she could do anything on which she set her mind. She would leave in the morning for Tarryton.

Chapter 3

SHE WENT TO bed at eight and awoke on Sunday morning a little after two. She lay there hurting until sometime after four, her veins just channels of stones. Around six, she called the service that took emergency messages from employees and told the biggest lie of her life; and at six fifteen, she went to the kitchen and poured herself a Coke, without ice, before phoning Bea. Ice would have awakened Chantal.

She would call her boss later, person-to-person, but at least the service would give the reason for her desk being empty as the troops rolled in at eight the following morning. She'd decided to call her problem a "family emergency" so that people would be less nosy when she returned in a week than they would be about her health.

She'd called Bea the night before, and Bea had understood. If not understood, then at least didn't ask a lot of questions. She supported Ava's exodus from Atlanta and all things Eric. That was her way, though. Even when they were freshman roommates at Yancey—eighteen-year-old "babies," really—she had exhibited just that marvelous way of rolling with the punches and making life look easy.

"Oh, Ava… oh, man… I'm so sorry." Bea had commiserated with everything. "You know I've missed you awful." There was a pause as Ava stifled fresh tears, but then she'd murmured a simple "Yeah," because she knew her best friend loved her. And in the last few seconds, before they hung up, Ava's mind flashed again to a thought that had occurred to her yesterday as Chantal had sashayed out of the apartment for a "date" at the Peachtree Plaza Hotel. Watching her walk to her blue Corvette, wearing black jeans, pink tube top, hoop earrings, and strappy sandals, Ava had thought Chantal tried. But Ava knew that although she considered herself a great friend, Ava wouldn't cross her mind all afternoon as she ate a luxury hotel salad and then earned the most depressing $150 there was to be had on their side of Atlanta. This stuff—people hurting and leaving each other—happened all the time all over the world, and usually nobody except the victim ever gave it a second thought.

She pulled out of the parking lot around seven, the sun having already risen—as it always did—on the blessed and on the damned. Ava drove a blue car, too, but unlike Chantal's, hers was a rusted-out VW Beetle. It was supposed to be temporary, of course. After she and Eric were married, they'd spoken of evaluating the finances and perhaps replacing it. Now, none of that mattered; all that did was getting "the heck out of Dodge."

She drove as fast as she dared, slicing through the heart of the city. Atlanta was magical and always had been. In school, she'd seen depictions after Sherman ravaged it, but to look at it now, with its majestic skyscrapers of gleaming glass, it was hard to imagine it in flames and rubble. Could she emerge victorious like that? Ava wondered. She, too, felt her life was in pieces, her dreams burning embers at her feet.

Of course, she didn't have a hundred years, either.

At eight thirty, she bought a coffee at a Shell station, which she oversugared and overcreamed, and half of which she drank standing in front of the carafe so she could top it off before resuming her journey. Somehow, she felt poorer now. Perhaps a couple, split in half, breeds scarcity.

Three and a half more hours give or take, she thought, pulling onto the expressway again. Only once in the last year had she driven the route from Atlanta, all the other times leaving from Yancey with Bea, but it was mostly just highway except for that final succession of turns as she entered the country and wasn't hard to navigate.

She drove with the back two windows down, hoping the noisy, warm air would distract her anxious mind from the suspicion she wasn't being smart. But to stay in that apartment even one more night after Eric Bankston had demolished her self-esteem, to go to the office on Monday…she couldn't see it. Just existing right then used her energy down to its dregs. And Bea would be waiting for her this afternoon—Bea and Bea's house in Tarryton.

She pictured Bea sitting cross-legged on her bed from one of the hundreds of nights they'd shared a dorm room. In the image, she wore a short-sleeved flowered peasant shirt and pastel cotton cropped pants, her heavy whiter-than-white calves peeking beneath. One of her many headbands reined back the thick and choppy bangs she often trimmed herself, and Ava imagined her eating pretzels with her headphones on while reading, not realizing how loud and annoying was her chewing.

Ava needed her. She needed her low, calm voice; her mirth; and acceptance. And she needed Tarryton, with its rolling hills and intermittent pastures; its still-majestic homes built on banking, textile, and railroad money. They would drive its backroads by rusted fences and low country houses. Around some curves, Ava remembered, would be a high-rising mansion or two gloating atop some green-carpeted hill and surrounded by twenty-thousand feet of white horse fencing.

They would go into Corinth, maybe on Tuesday, part of the half week that Bea didn't teach. Ava would welcome the distraction of grocery stores and fast-food joints, the boutiques, the mall, the clubs. Twice during college, the girls had left Yancey early on Friday and had hit Tarryton at dusk, readying themselves at Bea's house before driving north into Corinth for dancing. Bea loved to dance and was good at it, for she was more assured in her plump body and glorious robust youth than anyone Ava had ever met. Besides, Bea had her new husband Toby, who loved her and wanted her, and at the end of every day, since he'd first met Bea when they were high school freshmen, was always, always waiting.

Most of the cars were passing her. "It's okay, Rusty," Ava purred under her breath. "You're golden, buddy. You've gotten me this far…" How brazen people were, going twenty miles over the speed limit, apparently not worried about cops. "Police," Bea would have gently chided, "it's nicer to call them *police*."

It was ten thirty-two when she pulled into a rest stop. It was the same one at which she'd stopped when she made her first trip from her home in Bright Point to Tarryton almost five years ago, and she remembered that day to its last detail.

It had been Ava's first winter break as a college freshman, and Yancey had a longer break than most—six solid weeks of freedom. She'd planned to spend the first two weeks with her mother, the following two at Bea's, and to return home December twenty-second for the last two. This would be plenty of time to have the saddest Christmas in the world with her mom before resuming college on the third day of the new year.

The morning she left for Tarryton, Jeanette had tried to busy herself while Ava packed and loaded the car. She'd made her daughter a bologna sandwich and one with peanut butter and jelly, putting them in a used paper bag with a can of Coke. "You'll need to take a cup of ice at the last minute, of course." Her voice had been loud and strained over the noise of the dishes she was banging in the sink.

"I appreciate it, Mom," Ava had offered and took her secondhand Samsonite to the boot at the Volkswagen's front end. She was sorry for her mother but determined. She would not sit in that horrid, mildewed clapboard house engulfed in cigarette smoke and soap operas for every day of vacation she had.

When Ava had reentered the house, Jeanette was sitting in the old moss-green recliner, her chubby hands clutching a stained Christmas dishtowel. Ava stood in front of her, trying to think of a mollifying goodbye when Jeanette tossed the towel aside and fumbled her pack of Benson and Hedges from a cluttered TV tray. She lit one, visibly shaking, before taking a long, anesthetizing drag.

"You are going to be so homesick." She shook her head. "I really don't think you realize."

Ava stood, holding her own arms. Why did she have to make it this hard?

Jeanette pulled viciously on the cigarette before hoisting herself up and padding to what passed for a dining table but was now mounded with old magazines and their clippings, poster board, ribbons, and glue. She picked up a pair of scissors and began flipping magazine pages with a purpose and determination that Ava knew only made sense to Jeanette. She came to a slim blonde in purple legwarmers advertising baby dumbbells and began cutting.

"I'm going to be okay," Ava had assured her, "and you're going to be okay too. You need to find some stuff to do. I just want to visit my friend and try to have some fun before second quarter. I'm not trying to hurt you."

"I didn't say you were hurting me! Those are your words! But you just got here two weeks ago! Thanksgiving is barely over!" She put the scissors down and picked up the glue. Jeanette's latest hobby had been cutting out pictures and pasting them on colored posters to make theme statements for her life, which she thumbtacked on the walls of her bedroom. Ava saw she was working on an orange one (Be Brave, read the heading), a purple (Find Your Passion), and one sky blue (Seek True Peace).

Her mother was five feet two-and-a-half inches tall and two hundred twenty-four pounds. (Ava knew because she'd seen the statement on the table from a doctor's visit a few months earlier. She'd received public assistance—AFDC, food stamps, Medicaid—as long as Ava could remember. She loved the world of doctors and doctors' offices and would go to the doctor for a callus, if she could, riding the bus and talking to people she didn't know.)

That day—the day Ava was preparing to drive to Tarryton alone and from Atlanta for the first time—her mother was wearing picked-to-death, agonizingly-tight navy-blue stretch pants from which jutted ankles flaky, dry, and swollen. Her bleached hair was greasy at the crown, and her eyes were red-rimmed and puffy, like a woman twenty years her senior. Ava almost wished she could find it in her heart to care more about this state of affairs, but all she could think was, *She does this to herself.*

She had reached in to hug her mother, who had felt doughy yet solid, a rigid little canon of survival and resentment, and who'd then spouted, "Don't feel like you have to come home for Christmas, either." She'd pulled away from Ava first, and her lip was protruding petulantly as she grabbed another magazine. "They always have something at the church for people who are all alone."

*****

The rest stop was jumping, and Ava resented all the people. Why weren't they home resting from the beating they'd taken at work that week or gearing up for the debilitating (or, at the very least, tiresome) week that always, always lay ahead? What was so important that was worth leaving town for one lousy half of a weekend?

Or why weren't they in church? How could there be anyone in church, with all these chatting, milling people outside? Even Jeanette went to church and Bea and her clan. That's what normal families did, Ava thought, religion being the opiate of the masses.

After the restroom, the sun hit her shoulders like a blanket, and she was standing in front of the vending machine fishing for change when a gravelly voice spoke behind her.

"Need a quarter, sweetheart?"

She turned to face a man. He was about sixty, but a hard sixty, with a round belly sheathed in a T-shirt atop dirty jeans and short and skinny legs stuffed into motorcycle boots. The shirt read, "Ask Me for a Free Ride to Heaven."

"No, I'm fine, thanks." She turned back to the machine and slid in her coins.

"I was just wantin' to tell you, your hair's real pretty. Saw it all shinin' from over there under the trees. I'm partial to long hair, of course." There was a pause, but Ava focused on her task and didn't respond. "That's my ride, over yonder," the man continued, and as her Coke had ejected by then, she turned to see him gesture toward a huge land-cruising motorcycle built for older, out-of-shape men who wanted to impress young, tattooed women and hopefully ride some of them around.

"What's your name?" He spat out a stream of tobacco juice onto the pavement behind him.

He had not read Emily Post, poor baby…too much, too soon, and spitting…he'd never meet the truck-stop babe of his dreams this way.

"Sally. Sally Vanderkempft. And yours?" She popped her Coke tab and stood there smiling as she took a swallow.

"Al Criker. I'd love to take you for a ride before you get back on the road. Who knows, maybe you'd have a good time." He was putting his own money in the machine now and landing an Orange Crush.

"I'd love to, but I've got to beat it. Have to make Savannah before sunset."

"Savannah? You're going north, honey. You've gotta—"

"Oh, yeah, I know. Turning back around at the ramp. You have a good day, Al!" and she strode to the car with purpose.

"I like your dress too," Al called a little desperately. "Hey, if you want to just go up here to the exit and get a bite…," but the rest was lost behind her door.

She started the car and left, pulling onto the expressway heading north. Wouldn't it be ironic if he were to catch up to her? But what could he do? Make her pull over? Run her off the road with his Hog? Or better yet, creep her out for an hour, following her off the exit to Bea's at a crafty, undetectable distance, and then, *wham*! Break into the second-story bedroom window that night to make her his woman. That was all.

She got into fourth gear, then smoothed her dress under her lap and raked her hair away from her face before she relaxed. She liked her dress too—a white sundress with tiny pink sprigs, skinny straps, and a fitted bodice. She felt slim and young and hopeful, suddenly, far better than someone who'd skipped dinner, slept badly, and arose at five to drink caffeinated soda and pack. "I don't need you, Eric Bankston." She spoke it low but aloud as she drove. "Al Criker thinks I'm to die for." Of course, it was only a moment before the feeling passed because it wasn't true.

Apparently, a day and a half weren't enough to get over loving somebody, weren't enough to heal from the gutting of rejection. Once again, she felt ugly and hollow. Once again, she burned with shame as she remembered exactly what it felt like to sit across from a man who had once made her feel he'd be by her side until she died and then later reneged upon every utterance of fidelity and good feeling.

She wondered if Al Criker had ever had anyone love him. Had a woman ever thought she would eat dinner with him every night for the rest of her life? Ever wanted to take him to bed and lie close enough to smell his chest until morning? Had he ever—maybe even forty years ago—believed someone would love him without reservation, would build a life with him, and even gladly bear the unbearable act of childbirth with his genetic offering?

Probably, she thought. Probably even old Al Criker had known true love but had later lost it, and so there he was, still out there and trying.

It was a little after eleven thirty when Ava exited the expressway for Hereford and Tarryton. Through Hereford, the gray, brown, and sand-colored businesses petered and ebbed; building sites, gas stations, and restaurants melting away. The slate-colored roads narrowed and branched, their sequential thrusting tentacles passing hills and pastures, oaks, maples, and pines. She came at last to the broad, bright green-and-clay-colored town of Tarryton; and beyond its center, at ten minutes after twelve, she pulled into the weedy gravel driveway of the Mullins's old house, taking a deep breath as she shut off the engine.

"You can rest now, baby," she whispered to Rusty, though she knew she was speaking to herself.

Chapter 4

THE HOUSE LOOKED the same as when Ava had last seen it. A debutante immediately post-Confederacy, she now presented as an aging stateswoman, with a faded patina crossed between wilting daffodils and mustard.

So many years before the Mullinses had died, Mrs. Mullins had her husband paint the house sunburst yellow with white trim, along with the cottage behind it. Ava could imagine how hopeful it would have looked, with the young parents still alive and in good health and the girls and pets and the grandma all underfoot, being happy—how vibrant it must've felt, as if the house and all within it were set in perpetual motion then and would assuredly go forth and go on forever.

How many times had she come here in the last five years, ten? Fifteen? No… but they often drove up from Yancey whenever either of them was bored, had received a less-than-hoped-for grade, or to attend a wedding or baby shower for one of Bea's many friends. "Wanna play hooky this weekend?" Bea might say, playing hooky being her code for going home instead of studying, cheating a day from life, stress, and the rawness she felt from being away from her home and town for any length of time (both a first for her). This home had become more comforting to Ava than ever her own home in Bright Point had been; for although she'd never lived anywhere but the degenerate scrubbed-out suburb in southeast Atlanta, it had never been her refuge.

Ava was exiting her car when Bea, in an apron consumed with ruffles, emerged from the screened door. Stirring a mixing bowl's contents with a spoon, she let the door slam with a *bang*.

"Well, don't just sit there casing the place. Come on in and pick out what you want. We have terrible security." She wore a blue bandana folded into a triangle over her hair and tied at the nape. Her jeans—roomy-styled, high-waisted, and with little pleats—were belted below a short-sleeved gingham shirt with pouffy sleeves, and her feet sported white Converse sneakers.

"I'm not going to steal from you today—that is, unless you won't give me some tea. Then I'm going to steal some tea." Ava hiked the steps to the porch, skipping every other one.

Bea set her mixing bowl in the closest porch chair and hugged Ava hard, then pushed her back to arm's length, studying her. "You don't look bad. How do you feel? Besides the predictable."

Ava shrugged. "Just the predictable. Like a loser. A reject. And angry. But I have had a shower."

Bea grinned. "That's my girl." She smoothed Ava's hair. "You'll be okay. Besides, who's to say it's really over?" She stood with her hands on her hips for a moment, then reached to pick up the bowl. "Don't answer that. C'mon inside."

Ava followed her into the foyer. The house was cool and dark, except for scattered patches of window light, and was redolent with scents of undefinable foods. They turned to the right, through the breakfast room, then left to the kitchen beyond, where Bea began to pour the batter from the bowl into one of two muffin tins. "Missed you, Smitty," she said. "Glad you didn't die on the highway."

"Missed you too. Glad you didn't lose your toes in a cotton gin." Ava stood a moment, looking around. "Can you lose your toes in a cotton gin?"

Bea shrugged. "I haven't ginned cotton in an incredibly long time."

Ava sat on one of the red vinyl barstools that bellied up to the small kitchen island. "Why aren't you at church?"

"Because of you. Toby went. He's gonna stop off at his folks' place on the way home though, so it'll be a while before you get to ogle and paw him."

"No problem. My ogling and pawing have no time constraints."

Nothing had changed: the red range hood matched the stools and the white enameled sink matched the enamel-white cabinets, punctuated with black knobs, which was now yellowed with age and kitchen grease. Ava sat opposite the stove and countertops at the free-standing island Mr. Mullins had built with his own hands, hewn from a young oak he'd felled himself, the story went, in a time when oaks were a dime a dozen. "Oh, Kenneth," Louise would've crooned breathlessly as she watched her tall husband hack and saw and hammer, "you are the man of my dreams!" Ava was sure everything had been better in the fifties.

"I do need a drink." Ava went to the refrigerator and removed a pitcher of tea, pouring herself a glass before sitting again on the cracked barstool, tucking her dress beneath her for protection.

"You know the fam is coming for dinner, right? It being Sunday and all." Bea was bending over, aligning the two tins inside the oven.

"Crud. I mean, sorry. I just wish they weren't."

"I know. But you could take a nap first."

"No. It's no biggie. And I wouldn't sleep tonight if I did."

"Well, there's a block party in Susan's and Laura's neighborhood, so Clem is taking all the kids. It'll just be the sisters and Grandma and Greg." With their respective husbands and children, Susan and Laura lived in the same subdivision in Hereford: Susan, Clem, and their kids, Brent and Jesse, on the cul-de-sac; Laura and Greg, with Kelly and Alex, were only two houses up.

"Why Greg? Why didn't he want to go with his kids? Or why didn't he get to?

"I dunno. You know he and Clem don't hang much, and Clem would probably rather take all four kids anyway and not have to chum with Greg. Besides, you know how wrapped Laura's got Greg. Or scared, or something. Anyway, you only have to entertain him and the girls and Gram with your wit and charm."

"And ugly old Toby."

"Right, ugly old Toby." The girls grinned at each other.

"C'mere, I wanna sit outside for a minute. Bring your drink." Bea lifted her own half-empty glass and ushered Ava through the dining room to the back porch. She flopped on one of the wicker chaise lounges and shoved the other one gently toward Ava with her foot. Both faced the broad, sloping backyard—beyond which were rolling furrows of dark-red earth—which was newly planted with corn. Beyond that field were pines.

"Park it. I'm exhausted. I want to hear about your travails." Bea lay back as if she were a Zen therapist resting her arms on the chaise, one hand still holding her glass.

"Aren't you going to burn your muffins?"

"No, I have twelve minutes. I set the timer."

"Well, I'm sure I don't have twelve minutes of material." Ava settled into the other lounge chair and took a deep breath. *God, just to sit here, forever,* she thought. *Just to quit.* She leaned back and closed her eyes, then raised her head to take in the field and woods beyond. "I know I didn't tell you much on the phone, but I couldn't, you know? Like the facts, yeah, but the reasons, no."

Bea looked at her without speaking. She had a tremendous and admirable ability to sit with dead air and find peace in it.

"At first, I thought he just needed a break. Like, he was wanting to postpone it or something. I was thinking fall or winter, and then worst-case scenario, summer—which, by the way, I would've said, that's stupid. No point. Like, what would another year of medical school change?"

"Right. No point."

"Yeah. So he'd still have another year after that, and we'd be treading water, still paying two rents. And if we were married a year or two, I could go ahead and get pregnant around the time he started his residency. So again, no point. Or that *is* the point. There would be no difference in anything except I'd move into his place, or we'd get another one. One where I'd keep my job, and life would go on normally until he finished and got employed. I didn't understand how he'd want to wait two more years. Or expect me to."

"So what reason did he give?" Bea knitted her eyebrows and clasped her hands in her lap.

Ava felt the tears well up. "That's just it. I don't know if there is a good reason." She swallowed. "It was like he was searching for stuff. He goes, 'Aves, you've barely dated, do you realize that?' And I was like, 'Yeah, Eric, I had one boyfriend in high school, and we weren't that close, and a few dates in college, and well, you know how those turned out.' I mean, what does that even mean? And he's never dated all that much either, Mr. Academic. I thought that was probably a good thing."

"Phil was kind of cute. I never saw what you saw in Jason."

"Phil was cute. But you know he wasn't very ambitious. I don't think he ever figured out why he was even going to college. And Jason had a mean streak. You well remember that too."

Bea looked from Ava's face past the porch and yard to the fields. Her eyes were the lightest blue, rimmed in black, or maybe navy, and deeply set. Paired with her skin—"chalk" highlighted with hints of rose in her cheeks and outlined by the fringes of her chunky brunette page boy—she made Ava think of a ripe dark-haired Austrian milkmaid.

"I guess I don't want to ask the obvious." She looked back to her friend.

Ava waited. "You can. I want a nickel if I know what it is, though."

"You think he was just looking for an out?"

"Yeah. I think he was just looking for an out." Ava's voice cracked. "I don't know what happened. I don't know if he got tired of me or maybe thinks a little ol' accountant won't fit into his big new medical lifestyle or what. What is a medical lifestyle anyway? You still put your pants on one leg at a time, I imagine."

"I imagine you do," Bea affirmed.

They didn't speak for a moment, both casting their gazes toward the sun-hazed woods. Bea slowly rose; then opened the door that parted the broad, high-ceilinged dining room from the porch. "I'm going to get the muffins. Sit tight. I'll bring the tea pitcher when I come back out."

Ava nodded and drained her ice with one last swallow. She was grateful for Bea and for what she allowed to remain unspoken.

Chapter 5

BEA'S GRANDMA WAS short—"Four feet nine-and-a-quarter inches," she'd say if anyone asked, "and proud of it." She had thick gray hair that she chopped off about the middle of her neck, with a brake of chopped bangs that were also too short. She was a square little woman with sturdy arms and legs, well-set shoulders, and a firmly hoisted bosom; and she always walked with purpose.

She'd offered a hasty hello to her granddaughter, who was frying chicken in the kitchen, before finding Ava in the dining room setting the table.

"Ava." She said this as a pronouncement as she stood in the doorway, hands on her hips, and appraising the girl a moment before crossing the room to hug her. "You look beautiful." She then stepped back and held Ava at arm's length, just as Bea had done a few hours earlier.

"Hi, Gram. I don't know about all that, but thanks." She smiled, even as she turned back to the table to finish laying the blue ceramic plates along its edges.

"Of course," Clara said, flinging her hand outward as if brushing away an annoying fly. "Pretty girls always act as if they don't know they're pretty, but who can buy into all that?" Clara took a pile of silverware from the corner of the mammoth oak slab and began laying it around the plates. "Women haven't changed much since the 1920s if you can believe it."

"Ha! I do believe it. We're so…enigmatic."

Clara paused, looking up from the place she was setting. She was nearsighted, so she always appeared to be leaning a little forward and peering at people as if they'd imparted something particularly insightful.

"Yes. Enigmatic." She looked at her a moment longer before resuming her task. "You and your words, dear." Whatever that was supposed to mean.

Sunday dinners at the Mullins's old house—now the Phelps's, as its present-day owners were Bea and Toby—consisted of any family who could come (sisters, husbands, four children, and Gram), rarely Toby's parents, and sometimes a friend or two. This evening, Ava was glad half the usual clan was missing.

Toby sat at the head of the table, broad-shouldered and solid, his newly-tan arms adorned with hair that the sun would bleach the color of white corn by summer's end. The hair that crowned his head was the color of yellow baby chicks and still bore its ringed crease, this evening, from his John Deere cap, as he rested his forearms on the table, clutching a large piece of chicken. Ava found him, with his ordinary stability and manly Southern calm, utterly fascinating.

Susan was the oldest and always referenced by outsiders as "the redhead." She had very wide hips and full legs but was of narrow shoulders and small of bust. Ava always thought she looked as if she'd been "filled" from the head, and all the genie dust the gods had used had rushed quickly to her lower portions and settled there.

Laura, who was three years younger than Susan but almost ten years older than Bea (who'd been openly labeled her whole life as the happy accident), looked as if her genies could not decide on hair color, for hers was the nondescript and capricious color of dirt. This original color was evidenced to Ava only by looking through Bea's childhood albums, which also attested that Laura had begun dying it very young. In the five years since Ava had known her, she'd been blonde, black, chestnut, copper, and was now the orangish-yellow of tarnished brass. She also was built like the other two—solid and low to the ground—but slenderer than either of the others. Laura was the one who dieted.

"I wish you would not fry everything, Bea," she was saying now as she piled up her husband's plate. "It's absolutely not good for any of us, you know." She sat between Greg and Bea, who sat to Toby's left.

"It's great for me," murmured Bea, lifting her spoon of mashed potatoes.

"Oh heavens, Laura, it's not all fried," muttered Clara, sitting to Toby's right. "The potatoes, the salad, the biscuits, the tea…I honestly don't know how poor Greg survives over there with all that rabbit food you make."

"That's just it. He's doing fine, as you can see. And Alex has lost seven pounds since we've been going low fat."

Alex was eight, and Ava had once heard Laura call him her fat child. Ava had always had a marked affinity for Alex, with his dark hair cut like an old-fashioned Dutch boy's, his dark eyes perpetually sustaining trepidation.

"He shouldn't be dieting, Laura." This was from Susan, the thirty-five-year-old voice of reason. "Children should never be dieting unless a doctor recommends it. They need their baby fat for puberty." Ava noticed Susan's plate was not lacking in any good thing.

"Well, the doctor did say he was heavy. Right, hon? Eleven pounds, he said!" She'd finished dressing Greg's plate and placed it in front of him before turning back to fix her own.

Ava was not as amazed as she once was at the degree to which Laura managed her husband. He had always struck Ava as one of those TV husbands who had just been waiting—in his youth, minding his own business, with not a straw to chew on—waiting for some woman to come along and tell him every single thing to do with himself the minute he said his "I do's."

"Yep, that's what he said. Eleven pounds," responded Greg as he began to butter a biscuit and not looking around. Ava was pretty sure he didn't have a dog in this fight.

"Eleven!" Laura reiterated. "Eleven pounds over, and only eight years old. And not a tall eight, either." She was dipping her fork into the dressing she'd poured on the side of her plate and then spearing tiny bits of salad.

"Yeah, but"—and this again from Susan, who'd paused with a bite of gravy-covered biscuit halfway to her mouth—"don't you wonder if he'd even be heavy if you weren't so diet-conscious? It's dieting that makes you heavy, not normal eating."

"Oh, that's not true. I didn't put Alex on a diet until he was almost seven."

"Exactly! And over a year later, he's still battling it." Susan rolled her eyes and looked at Ava as if to say, *Am I right?*

"I only started coaching his eating because he was overweight!" Laura stared at her sister as if to imply she knew not the first thing about human metabolism.

"I love this dinner, babe." Toby reached under the table and patted what presumably was his wife's knee.

"It is good, isn't it?" Bea responded. Neither appeared to be paying much attention to the nutritional debate. "Ava, eat up. Next Sunday is beans and broccoli."

Laura focused her attention on her chicken, using her knife and fork to separate bits of meat from pieces of skin and bone. "Y'all can make light of it if you want. I, for one, am not going to end up like Mrs. Rhymer."

Mrs. Rhymer and her husband owned Rhymer's General Store and Mercantile in downtown Tarryton. The woman spent most of the day in a reinforced chair behind the counter and walked with a cane, though she was probably only in her fifties. Ava remembered from her visits to the store that she was seriously overweight.

Clara leaned forward, her nearsighted gaze zeroing in on the middle sister. "You could do a lot worse than turning out like Mrs. Rhymer. She would give you her left arm." Then she abruptly turned her attention to Toby. "What are you planting this year, son? Not the corn, of course, but what else?"

Toby looked up and covered his full mouth with his hand while he spoke to his grandmother by marriage. "The garden, you mean? The usual. Beans, tomatoes, peppers, squash, cucumbers…you got somethin' you want in there special?"

"No, no…I was thinking we'd do opposites though so we could better share. So many beans and tomatoes last year…of course, we still wanna bless the church…"

Clara kept a cottage variety garden at her house, the old homestead where she and her husband, Wilson, had lived and raised their two kids. Although it was nothing close to the large-scale operation that Toby depended on for income—along with the corn and the crops he planted with his daddy—it always produced far more than the widowed woman could use.

"Yeah, I gotcha, Gran Ma." Toby pronounced Clara's name with an emphasis on both syllables. Everyone knew Clara shined on Toby as her favorite male Mullins heir, much preferring him to Greg and Clem.

Toby put down his fork and took a swallow of tea before he said, "I got a lot of good butterbeans in...got some beets, cauliflower... I ain't gonna try carrots this year. Radishes do all right. You might could try spinach and broccoli, though. I know you got your squash..."

Clara nodded, intent again on her plate. Her mind must have begun wandering, for it was only a moment before she blurted, "Ava, I can't wait to meet your young man."

Ava shot a look to Clara before its quick transference to Bea. Crud—she'd forgotten—Bea's grandmother had been planning to attend the wedding with Bea, Ava's chosen matron-of-honor, of course. *Please, let their hotel room be refundable.*

Bea fixed her own eyes on Ava but said nothing, so Ava turned again to Gram.

"Actually, Gram, that's no longer happening." She paused before adding, "We're not getting married next month after all."

Susan gave a hard stare to Ava as if she thought the younger woman was trying to pull a fast one. "What? Ava, you left Eric?"

Bea broke in, "I'm not sure Ava wants to get into this right now."

Ava sat, fork paused above her plate as she lowered her eyes, saying nothing.

"Oh. Of course not. Well, for what it's worth, you probably did the right thing. Doctors do not make good husbands."

"Susan, that's uncalled for." Clara, head tilted forward, leveled her light-brown eyes at her oldest granddaughter.

"For Pete's sake!" Laura looked at Greg, for some reason, astonished, before addressing Ava and the rest of them. "Why would you break up with anyone who was studying to be a doctor?"

"Chill out, everybody… Ava didn't bring this up earlier because, my guess is, she didn't want to talk about it right now. Let's just relax a little." Bea looked from one of her sisters to the other and finished her eyes on Toby, just for good measure.

"I didn't mean it like that, Ava. I guess I'm just surprised. I would've thought you would've told us."

"Laura—" Bea began, but Ava held up her hand in a stop motion.

"I did not break up with Eric. He broke up with me. Friday night." There was a pause while everyone waited for her to go on. When she didn't, Laura took up the ball.

"I can't imagine that, Ava. I'm so sorry. Why in the world?"

Bea's sigh went unheeded.

"You want to know something? I really am not sure. He said a lot of stuff, but I kind of felt like I wasn't getting the full story."

"Like what?" Susan's eyes were dark hazel saucers.

"Well, let's see. He said I hadn't dated that much before meeting him. He said he wasn't sure what housing would be available and affordable and accessible for both his school and my job at Harvick and Braun. He said he would be *really* busy, *really* tired, and we wouldn't have much time to spend together."

"But you'd be married. You'd have more time than you do now, dating, living apart."

Ava addressed Susan, "You're preaching to the choir, missy. See what I meant about feeling like I wasn't getting the full story? Maybe more time together isn't really what old Eric wanted."

Laura was sitting with both hands in her lap, eyes focused on Ava, as were her older sister's. "How long were you together? A year, right?"

"Almost two. We met my first month in Atlanta two years ago, June. He was starting his first year of medical school."

"I thought you were in Bea's class, '81?" Laura looked from her to Bea.

"She was, but she had to show off and graduate early, remember? You knew that, Laura. She got out in '80."

"Oh, yeah, yeah, yeah, I remember now… You've been out two years. You were in Atlanta a year before Bea came back here."

"No big deal. I went summers. But yeah, I got out in three, moved to Atlanta in June of '80, and met Eric in a grocery store. We got engaged on my birthday last year."

"Yeah, yeah, I remember," Laura said again, nodding. And he's at Emory, right?"

Ava nodded back.

"So marry and live in student housing! Two can live cheaper when they live together. Greg and I saved tons of money when we moved in together." Greg nodded, his mouth full of chicken.

Susan still looked at Ava as if she'd just told them all she was having a leg cut off. "You poor baby. You were engaged for over a year! What else did he say? What could he be *thinking*?"

Ava took a deep breath, pushed back from the table ever so slightly, and sipped her tea.

"He said not to hate him. He said maybe given a little space, he could think what he really wanted. He said he would pay me back for all I'd spent on the wedding, and he said he would stay in touch. Does that tell you what he's really thinking?" Ava addressed this question, once again, to Susan.

The oldest sister looked around the table at all its many members, everyone except Greg having stopped their culinary ministrations in an attitude of repose and respect. Then she looked at her lap.

Ava smiled and rose, pushing her chair back yet further. "Exactly. Everything he said and didn't say still doesn't tell me what he's thinking." And with that, she excused herself and went to her darkened room.

Chapter 6

MAY IN TARRYTON was warm. The room Ava had been offered and had occupied every visit since her first one five years ago overlooked a generous lawn that sloped toward the road, with hills, pastures, and a couple more farmhouses beyond. This room was quaint, full of the antique cherry furniture Mrs. Mullins had loved and hoarded; a bed with a spread of cabbage roses and greenery; and on the walls, prints of happy things. Ava had long ago studied the pastoral, bucolic paintings of rabbits and English girls, so upon rising that Monday morning, she went straight to the front window and raised it to look upon nature in all its glory.

"Dear Kenneth," she murmured to Bea's father, a dead man she'd never known, "thank you for making something of yourself and for giving me this view."

The front lawn was unkempt. From some of the same pictures in which Ava had seen Laura's original hair color, she had likewise seen this vista had once been lush, green, and devoid of weeds. Now, eleven years after Louise's death, and almost nine years after Kenneth's, it was full of tufted clumps of nondescription and gangly stalks of wildflowers—all in varying patches of cream to yellow to green-emerging-from-brown. Motley though it was, it was also full of the expression of the burgeoning summer, stretching in front of Ava like a park, an invitation, and an easement. *Respite*, it whispered. *Just walk in it.*

She moved from the window to the scarred Samsonite suitcase and dressed in jeans and a baseball jersey, then slipped back into her bedroom shoes. She would borrow a pair of Bea's mud boots when she went downstairs because she wanted to walk the property and think and being still while she tried to do so hadn't been working.

Bea knocked at the door. She fluttered her fingertips against it as someone who might be drumming on a desk, and when Ava answered, floated in with a tray of coffee, juice, and toast. If observed motionless, no one would call Bea lithe, but when she moved, she was graceful as a deer.

"Hey. I heard your footsteps from downstairs." She set the tray on a round cherry table inlaid with jewel-colored stones. "You doin' okay?" She wore navy cotton pants, white boat shoes, and a white peasant blouse smattered about with tiny red flowers.

"You shouldn't have. I could've come down."

Bea shook her head. "Don't fall all over yourself thanking me. It'll be in your bill."

Ava looked again out the window. "Well, I'm planning my escape as we speak."

Bea sat in a rocker close to the small table and placed her hands in her lap. "Why, oh why, would anyone want to escape from paradise?"

Ava went to a straight-backed wooden chair that was also close to the little table and also sat, sighing. "Good point, Sherlock." Lifting one of the two coffee mugs, she sipped it. "By the way, I want to read your daddy's book. I never did, you know."

"I remember. Why now?"

"Mmmm…I don't know. Something to do the week I'm here. See, the dashing of my wedding dreams has freed up a lot of my time."

"Yeah. We'll grab you one." Bea took the other coffee mug. "Listen. I have a wicked plan."

"I have no time for your wickedness." Ava picked up a piece of toast with the hand not holding the coffee, for she hadn't eaten much dinner and felt a sudden appetite for the first time since her dinner with Eric. "Tell me only good things." She took a bite, placed it back on the plate, and looked at Bea while she chewed, dusting her fingers on her jeans.

"I want you to move here." Bea let Ava absorb the sentence a moment before continuing, "I've already talked to Toby, and, of course, he's good with it."

Ava stared, round-eyed, and swallowed. "I could never do that. Why in the world?" She sipped her coffee, still staring.

"You could live in the guest cottage. It's still in great shape, and it's barely used since Mama and Daddy died."

Ava remembered the guest cottage well—a functional little rectangle of six rectangular rooms, including the kitchen and bath. Painted yellow to match the house and cozy as a tick, it sported rustic knickknacks, handmade early American furniture, quilts, and an electric heater. An AC window unit was in each of its two bedrooms and in the common area, and both Bea and Ava loved it.

"You could get a job here," Bea continued, "and out there, you'd have all the privacy you'd ever need. Just until you figure things out, at least."

"A job? In *Tarryton?* No offense, but there aren't a lot of high-powered accounting agencies around here, are there?"

"Okay, honey, no offense to you, but you don't have to be working in your dream job right now, just two years out of the gate, do you? If you didn't have Atlanta rent, you wouldn't need that kind of salary. And I was thinking you could probably find a pretty decent job in Corinth or even Olympus if you had to."

Ava continued to stare at Bea. "That's just it. I don't have to. I mean…what're you saying, quit a very good job and move just because my engagement broke up?"

Bea sighed. "Nothing. I mean, I'm not trying to say anything other than what I'm saying, but you could *do* anything you like, even a regular entry-level job. Just until you get some stuff figured out. I already told you Toby's onboard. It's no burden." Bea's expression shifted, and she lowered her eyes to her cup. It was enough to cause Ava not to speak as she watched her friend. "The thing is, your office called."

The office—of course—but how disrespectful to call the number she'd left as an emergency contact when she'd told them she had an emergency of her own and it was barely nine o'clock.

"Who was it? Braun? Or a woman?"

Bea looked up. "It was Liz. She's the receptionist, right?"

Ava nodded. "Yeah, and an intern. She's the one training under me to be a corporate accountant. I told you—"

"Right." Bea met Ava's gaze and bit her lip.

"Well…?" Ava raised her eyebrows.

"She said Mr. Braun was looking for you." Bea spoke rapidly, then, "I told her you'd left the call-out message—that you had a family emergency—she said they didn't get it."

Ava didn't move. "What do you mean, 'she said they didn't get it'? I heard the outgoing message she leaves on the machine. I waited for the beep. Who, exactly, didn't get it?" She hesitated. "Is she saying I didn't call in?"

"Well…I don't know. Just that they didn't receive any kind of message."

"Then how in the world did she call here? This is the number I left for them. I explained the whole thing—well, not the whole thing—I said, yeah, I had a family emergency and would be gone for a week, and I was using the code. And I said I'd call Albert personally this morning."

"What code? Who's Albert?"

"Mr. Braun, Albert Braun. The code, thing, the numbers. They give you codes for stuff when you get hired, like if you have an illness, and there's one you use for vacation, paid time off, and maternity leave and stuff…all of it! So when you put in for an absence, whether it's planned or unplanned, the secretary has to log a code, for the records. How did she call here if she didn't get the message?"

Bea was speaking softer than usual. "She said when you didn't show up, she looked in your file for your emergency contact information. My name and number came up."

Of course it did. Bea was her contact. Not Jeanette, never Jeanette, and Eric was second. He didn't answer the phone half the time when he was home and said he was rarely home. What a train wreck that could be if she were ever lying on the side of the road. But then Bea spoke again as if Ava were standing on a ledge above traffic or holding something sharp.

"She said Mr. Braun said it may be time to reconsider your tenure with them, and…he would be filling your position until further notice." Ava's mouth fell open, and Bea rose and removed Ava's cup from her hands just as Ava sprung from her own chair.

"Are you kidding me? Oh my god! Oh my god!" She got up and strode to the door, flinging it open and running down the stairs. Bea went behind her.

"Ava, stop. Stop! Think for a minute! Ava! Stop!" But Ava had darted from the staircase to the living room and passed through it to Kenneth Mullins's old study. She picked up the hunter-green phone and dialed.

It was nine thirty-two when Liz Arnold answered the phone.

"Harvick and Braun, this is Liz, how may I help you?"

Ava sucked in her breath and released it. "Hi, Liz, this is Ava. How are you today?"

The briefest moment, then, "Great! Hey, Ava. How are you? Are you Okay? We missed you this morning!"

"Right. Well, Liz, thank you, but I'm a little confused about the call-out I left Sunday. I left a message and explained I had an emergency and needed 'time without pay.' I left the code, the number, remember? Now I'm here with my friend at my…emergency, and she tells me Mr. Braun, himself, actually told you I…actually, I don't know what he told you." Ava took another deep breath and continued, "What exactly did he tell you, Liz?"

There was no moment of hesitation on the other end of the line, and it was obvious Ms. Arnold was expecting this call. "Just what I told Ms. Phelps, your contact. He was disappointed you missed this morning."

This morning, this morning, and the room became overly still. She had forgotten it was May twenty-fourth. She thought fast, deeply breathing yet again. "I did not forget this morning. I had *an emergency*. And if it weren't the height of mistrust to tell you all everything, I would. But I cannot betray this confidence."

"I understand. I tried to explain to Mr. Braun, but he was… quite upset. He said he was counting on your spreadsheet, your whole presentation. He wanted them to meet you in person. He wanted you to speak to them in Japanese."

"Are you kidding me?" Her voice sounded shrill and uncontrolled. "I don't know Japanese! I learned six lousy phrases so I could greet them, tell them a joke, and break the ice. I had everything ready—he knew that!" Her thoughts popped like firecrackers, but she had to remember to breathe. She had to calm down, to be in control. "Liz…what happened? I mean, did he show them the slides? The numbers? All he had to do was show them the numbers. Did we land them?"

"Yeah. We did." And then nothing.

"Yeah? Really? So, I'm Okay, right? What did they say? I'm not sure why—"

"He just asked me to do it, Ava. He asked me to step in."

Ava felt her stomach contract. "He asked you to step in."

"Yeah."

"Step in for this week or step into my job?"

Ava waited, but nothing came from the other end of the line. "Okay. So you stepped in, then Monday I come back, and…are you filling in for me this week?"

Ava had taught Liz Arnold everything. Ava, the one with the accounting degree, had spent most of the last year, her second year hired with her first "real" job, at her first-pick agency, grooming this *temp*—who was also in charge of Albert Braun's phone line—to fill in for emergencies and to one day be offered a job at this or *another* agency, when Liz completed *her* accounting degree (which she had, just two weeks prior, graduating from Georgia State University with mostly *B*s and *C*s).

Of course.

"Ava, I think if you had been here for Sumitomo, Mr. Braun wouldn't have…" But Ava had gently placed the phone on its cradle. She could hear Bea's exhale behind her.

"She did it." Ava turned to face Bea, tears welling up. "She got the message. Of course she did. She checks them from home, even. Every night at nine and every weekend. She told me that one time. She's just that good." Then she brushed past Bea, back across the foyer to the kitchen.

Bea followed. "I'm so sorry, darlin'." She took a seat on one of the split red vinyl stools at the kitchen island as Ava strode to the refrigerator, took a Coke, and popped the tab.

"I hate her so bad." She took a long swallow. "I really do, Bea. I knew she was crafty. I could smell it. She asked for everything, you know? Phone numbers, personal information about all the customers and their companies—could *not* learn enough about the computer system. 'Oh, heavens, Ava, I just don't know how you learned so much about computers! That was my hardest course!' Sneaky little witch!" Ava began to walk to the front door, Bea following behind.

"Ava, stop, honey. Stop saying this stuff. You'll regret it," but Ava whirled around to face her.

"No, you'll regret it, Bea. You'll regret *hearing* it because you're good, and your heart is good. But I don't regret it. I hate her. And I hate little, balding, cold-hearted Albert Braun." Ava slung open the heavy front door and banged through the screened one, then walked to the faded blue Volkswagen and started the engine. Bea was immediately at its window, her face a study of concern.

"You know who I hate the most, Bea? I'll give you a hint: it's not her or Braun or even stupid Eric Bankston. It's me. I forgot the most important potential clients of my life, and I am too awful, apparently, for anyone to want to marry me after they get to know me very well. And now you and Toby have decided to throw me a long-overdue pity party. *I'm* the answer to that awful question. I hate me the most." And she backed out the driveway, vowing not to cry until out of sight while Bea stood, still watching her, resting her hands on her heart.

Chapter 7

CLARA WAS HOEING at mounds in the garden. When she met Ava five years ago, she'd bent the young girl's ear on more than one occasion, telling her the story of her and her late husband, as so many older people are wont to do. Clara had married Wilson Martin in 1926, and their homestead lay toward the back of a flat five-acre plot of fertile soil; behind which lay an acre of woods. In front of the house was the lawn; and oddly, at its foremost, was the plot they'd used for the garden, reaping its harvests for kids and animals, pantry, and church donations. Beyond this plot, at the furthest front from the house lay what had been, until a few years ago, an infrequently-traveled dirt road that, Ava knew from a teenage story of Bea's, would as soon sling an inexperienced driver into its ditch as look at you.

This plot was the same one that the eighty-eight-year-old Clara still plowed and had plowed every year since Wilson died forty-one years ago, using the same tractor he had used. As Ava pulled into the narrow, graveled drive that ran beside it, her eyes falling on the squat, gray-haired woman, her mind flashed to another image: this one, solely of imagination, was of a young, robust Clara, dark-haired and sun-reddened, with two small children frolicking around her among the hills and rows, the handsome husband dependable and solid in the backdrop. *Sometimes the slowness of time is as cruel as its surety,* Ava thought. *You barely see the coming of the end.*

Parking her car alongside the yard that lay between the house and the garden, Ava sucked in the country air. She wiped her cheeks and faked a smile to set her face in neutral, then walked back along the side of the drive toward Clara, who, hoe in hand, was standing in wait amidst the red-brown earth.

"I was hoping you'd see your way to me soon!" Bea's grandma put down the tool and picked her feet up high, stepping over clumps of tilled clay in her squat rubber boots to meet Ava at the plot's edge with a bear hug. "I've been looking for an excuse since eight o'clock to sit and drink some tea."

"Well, consider me your angel of deliverance." Ava looked over the view. "I've never tried a garden… It must be so fulfilling."

"Oh, it is! You start out just looking at the tilled earth, but when things start to grow, you just…well, I don't know about everybody else, but I have to come out every day, just to see it. It's hard to believe what all God does." She shook her head in amazement, joining Ava in overlooking the land.

"Well, I guess that's what makes Him God, right? That's His job." Ava gave a short laugh to show she was kidding, but Clara looked at her closely.

"Well, of course. But still. Don't you think about it, Ava? The miracle of it all?"

Ava lowered her head. The last thing she wanted to do was enter a religious discussion with Clara. They had connected, Ava supposed, because there was something solid and wise about the old lady and too much soggy and unformed in herself; but she wasn't ready to buy into Clara's God. If He were real, and if He ever cared, then Ava believed He had a lot of explaining to do.

"Yeah. I guess. Gram, I…" She took a deep breath and said it on the exhale, "I got canned today."

The older woman peered at her and, at first, didn't say a word. Ava always wondered how much of her squinting gazes and forward-thrusting face was nearsightedness and how much was just intent attention and listening. "What do you mean, canned? Fired?"

"Yeah. Fired. Smoked. Sayonara, baby!"

Clara still studied her face. "Come here," and she began to walk to the low front porch.

The sun was continuing its ascent over Clara's house. As they crossed the yard that held three venerable pecan trees arching their branches toward it, Ava had a strong urge to stop and lie beneath them. She didn't feel like talking anymore and thought maybe it would be more therapeutic to just crash in the yard, beneath the shade, not speaking. Of course, the grass would itch.

When they reached the open clay-reddened but comforting porch, Clara took the broad white rocker and gestured to the swing for Ava. "Sit down, child." She paused for a moment before rhetorically asking, "You've had a bad weekend, haven't you?"

Ava couldn't help but smile. "Yeah, I guess you could say that. The thing is, the receptionist, at work? She's a temp. She's been there about seven months, while she finished school, so—"

"What's a temp?" Clara sat with legs slightly apart, palms on her thighs. She wore khaki-colored Bermuda shorts above her shin-high black rubber boots, and her legs were inked with ropy blue veins.

"A temporary hire. She was working there so that when she got her degree, she could get a job at another firm, or maybe even at ours, and have solid experience. But she stole my job instead." Ava hiked one foot under its opposite thigh and began pushing at the porch with the toes of her bedroom shoe. She was tense with unreleased energy.

Clara nodded.

"And I was supersweet to her. She had only had one computer course at Georgia State and didn't have any experience with computers outside of school. So everybody is using computers now, and I've gotten to be pretty good. I showed her how ours work and taught her all about the system Harvick and Braun uses. That's my company, remember?"

"Braun…that's the big man, right? Your boss?"

"Yeah. The little man." Ava sighed. "Sorry. I'm being hateful. My boss. He's just a little shrimp of a guy, and he's the second partner. Harvick is the *real* 'big man.' But Braun is so full of himself, and he's German, and he's so cocky. He doesn't listen very well. But I could care less. I'm English and related to a king, so I should've brought that up sometime instead of always trying to be subservient and humble."

"Are you really?" Clara's voice lilted. "Which one?"

"A bad one." Ava flung her hand. "King Edward. The first. The one who killed William Wallace. That's what Mama says anyway, says it's our only claim to fame! So ha! Anyway, so he fired me because I forgot about these Japanese clients we were supposed to meet and kowtow to so we could have all their business. They're opening, like, a dozen frozen yogurt shops around Atlanta."

"Frozen yogurt! Who eats frozen yogurt?" Clara looked alarmed.

"Everybody, now. It's a new thing. Supposed to have antibiotics or something. Better for you than ice cream."

"There's nothing wrong with a little ice cream…"

"The point is, I blew it. Eric toasted my mind, and I wasn't thinking. The wedding took up so much of my brain, and it was just three weeks, you know? God, I haven't even canceled anything. Anyway, so we hadn't talked about it—this meeting—for, like, a few days at work, maybe because I had everything in place two weeks ago. But Liz, this girl, this *piranha*, she did the presentation. And get this: I'm positive she got my message that I left Sunday morning and told Braun she didn't." Ava let her head fall into her hands, then stopped the swing's motion with her toe.

Clara didn't speak for a moment. "Ava, don't use God's name like that, honey."

Ava shook her head hopefully, imperceptibly. "Sorry." *Sheesh, of all things…*

"Honey, speakin' of your mama, how *is* she?" When Ava raised her head, Clara was looking off across the yard, the garden, and the now-paved road to the tall hedge of pines on its opposite side.

"She's okay. I guess. I mean…I don't know. She's the same as she ever is. Nutty as a fruitcake."

"Oh, now, don't talk about your mama that way. She gave you life." Clara turned her eyes to Ava. "I imagine she frustrates you greatly."

"She does. And she scares me. I think there's something wrong, Gram. I mean, physically. Or mentally, to be honest. Clinically… *chemically*…is that the word?'

Clara nodded knowingly. "I used to have an aunt. Did the same stuff. Sweet as a bluebird one minute, then before you say Jack Sprat, doing just crazy, like throwing her husband's clothes in the yard if he was an hour late. Once she took all her kids' toys, I mean all of them, to the dump because she said they'd sassed her. Did stuff like that all the time. Then she'd sit in her room and wouldn't speak for three days. Then she'd be fine and wanting to pretend nothing happened. Mmmm, mmm, mmm, all the time, I tell you."

"Really?" Ava sat up straighter. "I never knew that."

"Well, we didn't talk about it! Doesn't do much good to badmouth, does it? I imagine she couldn't help her spells, and 'course nobody knew what they were. I 'spect your mama's about in the same boat."

Ava stared at her shoes. "But why? You know, I've always wondered if she ever was happy. Before Daddy died. I was only four, but maybe she was normal before that. Maybe I was just too young to remember." She shook her head a couple of times. "Mama's just a loony bin."

Clara didn't chastise the girl again. "Let me ask you something. These last couple of years…that you've been at that company…has her…problem…caused you trouble at work?"

Ava stiffened. Bea must've told her. At least about last Christmas. "Yeah. I don't mean to sound rude, but…why do you ask?"

Clara hesitated. "Bea said that's why you didn't come Christmas." She moved her gaze back to the road. "And that police were called."

"Well, alert the press! It's all true!" Ava threw up her hands to either side. "Can't get the stereo you want? Shout for the manager! Insist you were there trying to get waited on before the person who just bought the last one, but guess what? No one saw you! You weigh over two hundred pounds, you're bleached-blonde, and no one saw you!"

"Well, I didn't hear details."

"No, you wouldn't, I guess. Bea doesn't gossip. But yeah. Ended up yelling at the man who had it in his cart and then hitting him."

"Over a stereo…"

"Mmmhmm. Over a stereo." Ava began to push herself harder on the swing with both feet. "The man didn't press charges. But, yes, that's why I canceled on you guys for Christmas, that's why you didn't get to finally meet Mom, and if you want to know the truth, I was glad you didn't. I hope you never meet her now. She's a train wreck."

"So...," Clara dragged out the word, "remember when you told us you'd had some unexpected absences last year but didn't say why? Were those because of your mom? Could that be why Mr. Brown was so easy about letting you go?" She had no trouble steadying her gaze again on Ava. "Because, child, I know what kind of person you are. You're smart. You're responsible. And I know you're good at your job. But I also know your mama makes things hard for you, just like she did all those school years when you were down there with Bea."

Clara let her words sink in before she continued, "You can't blame Mr. Brown—"

"It's Braun," Ava mumbled, but Clara ignored the correction if she heard it at all.

"—for trying to run his business, for calling in a girl who was more than ready to step in the minute you dropped the ball, especially if you'd dropped the ball before. You just had one too many problems your couple of years there."

Ava felt sick. How many people were going to betray her in three days, she couldn't imagine, but Clara's judgment felt like just another tick in the stick to her. She rose to leave.

"Honey, listen," but Ava had started down the shallow porch steps.

"Ava, you stop and listen to me, now." Clara's voice was firm, and Ava stopped and turned around to meet her eyes. "You've had a hard life, baby girl. Your daddy dead, your mama sick, and your life being made hell because of it ever since you can remember. Or at least ever since I've known you. You drive out here with your bedroom shoes on, and yes, I noticed, and you just mad at the world. I'm not saying it's your fault. All I'm saying is it might be time to quit trying to fight a dust storm with a pillowcase and take stock. Do some thinking before you get back out there."

Ava lowered her eyes. "That's easy to say, I guess. Just sit down and take it."

Clara, who hadn't moved from the rocker or gotten her feathers ruffled at all, now leaned her elbows on her knees and shook her head in wonder. "That's just it, precious. At this point, I don't see you've got a choice."

Chapter 8

JIMMY WOODHAM HAD round brown eyes like pennies. He sat facing the windows of the bar he owned in Corinth, The Fox and Ale, while Ava sat facing him. Jimmy had light reddish-brown tightly-curled hair, with the graying around his temples and mild crow's feet being all that made him look over thirty. He had a pleasant roundish ruddy face and short, even teeth.

"I'm not sure what kind of pay you're used to," he was saying, flipping a cardboard coaster back and forth between his fingers. "Corrine's been doing it since we lost the last guy—he went north to start his own tax business—but she's lousy at it. Doesn't know what she's doing. She never went to school for it, of course. We've always used professionals in the past."

"Of course." Ava gave him her smooth, professional smile, the one she'd practiced all her life. "I get that. It's not for everybody."

"Right. The truth is, Corrine's not that hot with numbers. It's not a priority for her. I tell her, just keep the books, we'll have another accountant by the end of the year…but she ain't lovin' it, that's for darn sure."

He'd been glancing around the bar and out the broad lightly-tinted plate glass windows, but now he looked at her with a slight plaintive smile, looking for corroboration. "It's just math, right? Simple add and subtract?"

"Well, I guess it's not quite so simple for some people."

"Oh, naw, naw, 'course not, I didn't mean that." He scowled. "But I think if she just tried a little harder, paid a little more attention…" He began tapping the coaster on the tabletop, shifting in his chair now and then, glancing about the bar. Ava realized he was not a man comfortable having purposeful conversations with persons as yet unknown, but while he was trying to think of his next appropriate line, the swinging doors behind the bar creaked and a woman walked through, taking long strides as she approached their table and smiling.

Jimmy glanced around briefly. "Bring me a bar rag, babe. Dad-gummed night shift..."

The woman grabbed one from the bar and tossed it at Jimmy, barely breaking stride. She had light-brown hair streaked with blonde, past her shoulders and middle-parted, and feathered back in waves. The same late-morning light that splashed the insides of the place and showed Jimmy's coppery eyes was now reflected in hers as translucent emerald green. She was both rangy and full, long-limbed and supple, and she moved with the ease so typical to those who were riders—this fact Ava knew from the few minutes she'd already spent with this woman's husband.

"Hey, Cory, this is Ava...Rush. She wants to be our new book-keeper and accountant or whatever you call the person who's gonna undo all that mess of yours." He had skidded his chair back a bit as his wife approached so they might accommodate her to the table, then used the cloth to assault its sticky surface. Corrine wore straight-legged dark-blue jeans with low-heeled black sandals, and her blouse was a silky rose-colored material tucked in with a skinny belt. She reached a smooth, well-manicured hand to Ava.

"Hi, Ava. I already know. Jimmy told me I was being replaced." She directed a wide and dazzling smile toward Ava as she reached for her husband's Coke, then pursed her lips around the straw. She drew several deep swallows as she settled into the chair-backed stool Jimmy had swiveled around for her, then lay her arms confidently on the tabletop and sighed as if she'd been invited to a familiar friends' luncheon but had run just a little bit late.

"I must warn you, though, it's not all it's cracked up to be. It's not all glamour and spotlights. Your nails chip, your skin dries out, and your eyes will turn to stone. Many's the night I—"

"Okay, Laurel and Hardy, I think she knows what she's applying for. She majored in it at...where was that, honey?

Ava felt a little fazed at this term of endearment from this man she'd just met, who was probably twenty years her senior and whose wife was sitting right beside him, but if Corrine minded, she didn't show it.

"Yancey."

"Right. Yancey. Kind of a big agricultural college, isn't it?" He turned to Corrine, saying, "You know, babe, that's where that Taylor kid got his Ag degree—Bob Taylor's boy—runs that Sheepshead Farms down 53 a ways."

"Oh yeah," Ava chimed in, "it's…it's got a great Ag program, plus all the usual stuff. It's liberal arts."

"Right, right. Hey, didn't that Tucker boy go to Yancey too—Elbert Tucker's son?" He had turned to Corrine again, looking puzzled while he fiddled with the bar towel, folding it and patting it and running his fingers along its corners. Ava believed him to be as uncomfortable as she.

Corrine, again smiling easily and happily, looked from him to Ava. "I don't know, Skippy." She patted his hand and fairly popped up from the table. "I think he went to Youngstown, wasn't it? In Ohio," she called over her shoulder as she sauntered behind the bar to where the day tender—Kathy—was washing glasses. She picked up a rag and started drying. "Yeah, that's right. His mama told me." She began doing a little shoulder dance as she worked, singing "Beat It," along with Michael Jackson, off-key.

Jimmy shook his head. "Doesn't matter. Why are you here, little lady? I mean, it says here you were at some big accounting firm in Atlanta, right?" He glanced down at her resume. "Harvick and Braun?"

"Yeah, well, the mystery of mysteries!" She laughed and lightly clapped both hands down on the table. "The truth is I had a little personal situation. It's fine now, but I thought a change of scenery was in order."

Jimmy only nodded, looking down at the papers and pressing his lips together in a show of understanding. If the gods were with her, he would respect the truth.

He raised his gaze to hers. "Good for you," he said, still nodding. "Good for you. So you're here, you're living…where are you living?"

"Tarryton. My college roommate lives there, in her family home, and I just started renting the guest cottage out back. I've been there a couple of weeks." She was playing fast and loose with the term *rent*, for Bea had promised free lodging until she landed a job and was "flush."

"Eh? Yeah? Are we the first place you've looked? Just curious. I mean, is this the kind of gig you truly want, or…you know, what you'll take until you get a 'real' job?" He was trying to be light about the question but was back to torturing the coaster. Ava had the passing thought he must hate the hiring part of being a bar owner—that he probably shied away from discomfort of all kinds and was the type that would prefer to spend the day with his dog, a flask, and a sandwich while duck hunting.

"You're the second." She tossed her hair back off her shoulders and straightened her back ever so discreetly. "I just got in with a car dealership Tuesday. If I want to make a go of the freelance thing, I'll need a couple of these smaller jobs, you know, for my own place and a better car. I hope that doesn't make you uncertain. I wouldn't go for two jobs if I didn't think I could do them."

"Shoot, me? Naw, I'm sure you can do it. Straight-A student, scholarships, graduated early…I mean, it's kind of like, I need to get Corrine off those books, you know? She's got no clue what she's doing."

Corrine, seated by now at the bar, eating from a plate of fries and watching a game with her back to them, called out brightly to the side, not even turning around. "All right, Skippy, everybody's got it now. Heard you loud and clear. But you're right. Replace me before I bring the whole house down."

Ava, relieved, stepped onto the sidewalk outside the bar. The early noon was cool. The air smelled fresh after the bar's smoky atmosphere, and in an instant, she had the thought that she could start over—that the fatigue and ennui that had come from the last three weeks had suddenly stopped—that no one within 300 miles of here had ever heard of Ava Rush and her problems, except Bea and her insular family.

She could live in Tarryton: work here in Corinth, at The Fox and Ale, and also work for Arrington Ford twelve miles away until she could go back to Atlanta, get *another* great job, and begin again—her journey toward her unclaimed life.

Chapter 9

AVA STEPPED INTO the foyer. The morning had left her exhausted.

"Hey, Smitty. Come in here," Bea's voice called from the sunroom.

The sun set at the back left corner of the house, so its late spring rays cast a golden hue on the lawn outside the parlor's window. Bea, book in hand, was reclining against the right arm of the sofa that faced it, the blinds slatted to divert the glare. Ava believed that sofa was the most beautiful piece of furniture in the house—a Victorian piece in peridot-colored velvet with one thin, firm cushion for a seat and ornately carved back, arms, and legs. A tray with a pitcher of tea and two tall glasses of ice set on the coffee table in front of it.

"I knew you had to be home soon. It's almost one o'clock! How'd it go?" She leaned forward and placed the book *Mere Christianity* on the table by the tray.

"Smashingly. I got it. They could not love me more." Ava moved to sit on a cranberry-colored velvet recliner to the sofa's right and shoved it backward, elevating her legs.

"A given. Your industry and discipline inspired me to make you a ham sandwich, you know. It's in the fridge." Bea yawned, moved the pillow to the left arm of the sofa so she could see her friend, and lay back against it.

"Thanks, but they fed me, even. Well, the wife did. Did you miss me? Where's Toby? Out buying you flowers or a horse or something?"

Bea gave a short laugh. "I wish. Yes, I missed you. Toby's working on that old tractor his daddy gave us. I think we'll have to overhaul that before he buys me a horse. Or get me a better car."

Ava leaned her head back and closed her eyes. "I guess. But if he *really* loved you, he'd get us both one." She raised her head, then, and opened her eyes. "Aren't you glad to be out of school? I should've been a teacher."

"You wouldn't have liked it. I know you like kids, but you're too controlling. Kids are messy and unpredictable."

"Alas. She speaketh truth."

"Always. Tell me about the interview."

"It was fine. I told him about Arrington, the Ford dealership, and that they'd hired me on the spot, but that I could handle the two small gigs. He said his last guy did the books *and* the taxes, but then his wife started keeping the books, and he got a new guy to do taxes. But apparently, the wife's not as meticulous, shall we say, as he'd like. He just wants one person to do them both again. And do them right."

"So she's not a real accountant, of course." Bea raised and poured them both a tea before settling back on the sofa with hers.

"No, but I guess she doesn't have to be. She's kind of gorgeous." Ava reached forward for the other glass, took a long drink, and leaned her head back again. "And he showed me the books and the little office where Corrine, that's his wife, hangs out, and it's, man, a total disaster. It's gonna take a while to straighten out."

"So she just gets a pass? You're telling me now that gorgeous women don't have to work for a living? I *knew* it!" Bea pretended to slam her fist on her knee with vehemence.

"Well, I don't know, but *she* apparently doesn't. In the interview, Jimmy—that's the owner guy—said she spends most of her time riding. They have a couple of horses."

"Yeah? Where are the horses? Where do they live? In Corinth?"

"I guess. I mean, I guess they live in Corinth, but they keep the horses here in Tarryton. They've got a little cabin out here or something, and some guy lives there and keeps the horses. And get this: they hunt foxes."

"What?"

"Foxes. They go up to Virginia and do these hunts with a real fox. Isn't that gross?"

Bea stared into her tea for a minute. "I can't imagine that being fun."

"I know. I didn't ask many questions. Just trying to land the job." Ava sighed.

"I gotcha. Hey, maybe she'd let us ride the horses some time, if you tell her that we ride. And, of course, you'd have to do a good job with your little numbers and play nice." Bea had learned to ride when she was young—just another skill her wonderful parents had allowed her and her two lucky sisters to acquire. Now that she was married to Toby and teaching school, one of their hopes was to afford a horse or two someday.

"*You* know how to ride. I mostly know how to just not fall off. But she doesn't know you, and as of now, she doesn't even know *me.* Plus, she's like, in her thirties. But she's fun...and funny. She's how we're gonna be when we're old."

Bea was silent a moment. "Sometimes I wonder if I'm going to get old." She looked out the large window in front of her, where the sun was melting off the roses.

"I know. I think about that. Daddy was only twenty-nine. How do you get cancer at twenty-nine? And your mama, at...?"

"Forty-three."

They were silent a moment before Ava took it up again. "But they knew with your mama. You knew. Do you think that was better?"

Bea shook her head. "Who knows." She didn't say it like a question. "It was horrible."

Ava nodded. "Of course...of course it was. I just...with Daddy, I never even saw it coming. He was there, one day, and like, dead the next. We never had a goodbye."

"Yeah. But you were only four. And goodbyes are overrated."

"Why do you say that?" Ava had never pressed Bea for details of her mother's passing. Or her father's, for that matter.

"Because you're bawling your eyes out. And I have dreams all the time about my beautiful mother, the nightgown she wore, and the big ugly knot in her neck."

Ava looked at her lap and shook her head. "You must have been so terrified."

"I don't know. It didn't feel real. Daddy never said, 'Go in there and tell your mama goodbye.' He just pushed us to spend time with her every day. They put such a happy spin on things. And that was before she went to the hospital. I think we girls thought she was never really going to die and that she'd come home like she always did."

"Isn't it funny how kids always think that?"

Another moment of silence passed as the rhetorical question died in the air. Bea looked at Ava. "Do you even remember your daddy?"

Ava shrugged. "You know, sometimes I think I do, but I don't know if I remember him or just know him from the pictures. How much can you remember from when you were four?"

"But you told me a long time ago you don't have a lot of pictures. Wasn't that kinda why you started with the photography?"

"Yeah. I don't know. I just got a little dollar camera as a present from Mama's parents—one of their little guilt gifts, I think, since they didn't visit after Daddy died. Which is weird, right? I mean, since they were her parents and not his, and I was their grandchild, for crying out loud. Of course, they lived in New York. But, no, we didn't have a lot of pictures. Two albums. Not even full."

"Really." Bea's family library probably had over a dozen.

"Yeah. And they're sad." Ava gave a short, mirthless laugh. "Jeanette looks all right. Kind of pretty, even. It's like she had a little class back then, and of course, she was only the tiniest bit chubby. And Daddy, he was all skinny, you know, but he looked pretty handsome. He looked hopeful, I think."

Neither girl spoke for a long time. Finally, Ava took a deep breath and leaned forward, setting her glass on one of the table's several coasters.

"Can I ask you something that might hurt your feelings?"

Bea looked at her for just a moment before nodding.

"Do you ever believe that maybe your dad didn't fall off that mountain? I only ask because there was that time you said that, you know? Do you remember? When we first were talking back at Yancey, you said that people…well, that even the authorities and the people who found him…you know, the ones who came later to you guys' house…they said it didn't look like he had fallen…" Ava's voice died on the still summer air.

Bea looked from Ava's face to the front window. "It wasn't a mountain, you know. It was a cliff…just a rock face."

Ava remembered. It was what everyone called the Point, a tall cliff face that rose above Outlook Inlet with a narrow strip of rock between its base and the water where someone had seen the body. It would have been five years ago when Bea had told her the story, saying how bizarre it was that someone like her dad—the great adventurist Kenneth Mullins, with his acuity and climbing experience—would have fallen at such a spot, with its gradual slope from the side facing the trail, its relatively flat surface at the top, and the low but cautionary fence guard.

Bea looked back to her friend, her expression still pensive. "What they call the mountain was what he'd dove from earlier. That was a straight shot, of course. Into the deep water."

"Yeah, I know…"

"He wasn't climbing that day. He didn't have boots or gear. He'd just gone up to the outlook."

"Yeah, I remember, you told me that. I don't mean to open ugly thoughts," Ava continued. "I've just always wondered. I know you said he really, really missed your mom."

Bea shook her head. "It's okay. It doesn't hurt my feelings anymore."

"What do you mean, anymore?"

"I mean, you're not the first to think that. I think a lot of people wondered. Susan and Laura and I even talked about it once because… Susan said the executor guy said he'd recently 'put his affairs in perfect order.'" Bea emphasized the last two words with air quotes. "But it's only been brought up that once."

Ava waited a moment before asking, "So, no? Like, you thought of it but realized he'd never do something like that? Because of y'all, right?"

"Well, yeah. I mean, I'm sure Daddy could never have just abandoned us girls. Even if he did love Mama that much, and…you know…supposedly had depression."

Ava shook her head. "I didn't think so." She smiled in what she hoped was a reassuring way. "I just always wondered, 'cuz he was so athletic and had all that experience, and…he would have had to fall over the rail."

"No, no, I get it." Bea rose. She took Ava's empty glass, set it on the tray with her own, and picked up the tray. "It's understandable, but yeah, I don't believe he could ever abandon his children. That would be a very rough thing to do." Her gaze rested once more on the gold-tinged roses before she turned into the hall toward the kitchen.

Ava sat biting her lip.

Chapter 10

THAT NIGHT, SHE couldn't sleep. She lay in the maple double bed of the cottage's pristine bedroom as it abutted the shallow front porch that faced the back of Bea's and Toby's house. A sliver of goldenrod trickled at the edge of the curtain, and she knew this to be the back porch light Bea left on overnight. Ava rose and took the three steps to the freestanding pine chifforobe, taking from its shelf two cheap spiral photo albums that Chantal had sent with her things from Atlanta.

Ava had always believed there were vast gaps in her memory, and sometimes she wondered if it wasn't her memory so much, that told her how things had been, but the pictures—the pictures she'd found as a child in the albums under Jeanette's bed. There were no Norman Rockwell-like depictions, but there was a certain degree of normalcy in each that belied the unplanned, chaotic descent their lives had taken when the pictures stopped.

Each album had been labeled numerically on its spine in purple marker: #1 and #2. They began with a smattering of overly bright, bad wedding photos in an overly dark, cheap-looking chapel. Jeanette looked unexpectedly rosy and even pretty in a satin-and-tulle off-shoulder white dress with a simple lace at its border; and Ava's future father, John, looked gawky, wide-eared, and excitedly hopeful in his solid dark suit and skinny tie. More pictures followed of a scrubbed-out yard, some barbecues, and a sparsely-furnished living room hazed by cigarette smoke. Some women wore beehives while men sported buzz cuts or Hank Williams's pompadours, usually holding tumblers of drinks or cans of beer. In one, Ava's skinny dad in red trunks stood over Jeanette, who was lounging by a wading pool in which sat toddler Ava; he was grinning and had one hand on his hip while the other hoisted a plastic tumbler to the camera.

Interspersed with the others, only two or three pages in, were a smattering of baby pictures—the first, a cloudy Polaroid of a mewling red-faced infant with dark tufts of hair. "Ava Jane Lenoir Rush," read the caption at the bottom, "March 17th, 1959." None of the other prints were labeled, not even on the back, as Ava had, upon their initial discovery when she was seven, carefully eased one after another from their pasted corner holders.

Most were of her just being normal, like sitting in a chair with spaghetti all over her face or playing in her sandbox or blowing out the candles on a chocolate cake on her fourth birthday. In lots of these, Jeanette's round-cheeked pink face was sharing Ava's spotlight, her overly lipsticked mouth forming a garish yet carefree smile, and her teased-and-curled dishwater-blonde hair taking up a third of the frame.

But Ava's favorites of these photographs showed her dad—his face, thin and angular, in profile and smiling at his baby; his back, strong and straight, as Ava, in his arms, peered doe-eyed and wispy-haired over his shoulder; and in yet another, just one leg, one arm, and the side of his face, again, as he was reaching down from where he was seated in a chair, helping her with a piece of a puzzle. The best, the one Ava most esteemed from both albums, pictured them both facing the camera and grinning. She looked to be about three. The sunlight illuminated the pair from above, and the joy was apparent on both of their faces as they sat outside an ice cream shop, each raising a single dipped cone.

As Ava grew, she realized she had few memories of her childhood when her father was still alive except as documented in these books, and that rather than knowing her father, she had resorted to inventing him from things like a haircut, a gaze, a hand, and a pants leg. She'd then sprinkled this amalgamation of convictions with the very best father stories that she had heard in school, from movies, and sometimes from the stories and memories of friends.

If one believed the pictures, things had begun rather hopeful—a marriage, a honeymoon, a baby, and things like spaghetti and sandboxes. But one-and-a-half albums do not a childhood make, and not only the scarcity but the incongruence of the shots suggested that all was not right in the world, at least not in Bright Point, USA.

The sadness of the photos was blaring, by not only the presentment of cheapness in their lives—Ava had never known a time when they'd had money—but by everything the prints were missing: where were the dozens of pictures of the happy couple before the baby, like on early dates or vacations? There were no surreptitious shots by friends of stolen kisses, nor any performed for the benefit of the camera. (But who stands around taking pictures of other couples and gives them to them, anyway?) Also, why was there never a second or third baby? Jeanette never had reasons for any of this—it was "hard to say," or "so long ago"...but it shouldn't have been, and it wasn't.

Not only were there no happy expressions of intimacy between Jeanette and John, but there was, late in the progression of shots, a hollow expression on her dad's face when, perhaps, he'd been unexpectedly photographed. As Ava got older, revisiting the albums with increasing discernment, she noticed, even more, the ubiquity of the cigarettes and beer cans that spotted the shots of yard and living room. There was no theme or purpose to most of them—as if some addled person or another had had a Polaroid or a budget camera handy and was sober enough, for a second, to freeze that sad little wrinkle in time.

Not long after Ava's fourth birthday, in the fall of '63, all hell had broken loose, and the pictures stopped altogether. And after the last picture in the second album, one of her on her father's lap, Ava could not even remember seeing her father again—not in sickness, not in health—she couldn't even remember his dying.

It was this last that tore her up inside—and had for years—because she believed, if John could have only lived a few more years, she could have done a better job with things. She would have made sure to have been a good daughter, and she would have spent so much more time in his presence. In short, she would have liked to have made more memories. And she would have certainly taken more pictures.

Chapter 11

IT WAS THE Wednesday after she'd been hired at The Fox and Ale that she met Scott. He plopped right down into her life by fate, God, or the devil, who could say. No one could ever tell you for sure about things like that no matter how hard you try to guess during all the years after it happens, during all the years that pass as you ponder it. Just as Eric changed that first shot at happiness in a moment—all the little puffs of matter and gobs of things moving in response to that one event—Ava came to realize the road had turned again, irreversibly.

Bea and Ava had spent the first two days of her trip there—as soon as she'd gotten home that Monday afternoon from Clara's—canceling the wedding venue and all the accoutrements of which she'd dreamt her whole youth. They'd gone into Hereford for pancakes Wednesday morning and spent the afternoon walking the banks of the Tarrymore River.

Thursday, Friday, and Saturday, Bea, Toby, Ava—and Chantal, by telephone—arranged to have her few apartment possessions sent to the cottage courtesy of U-Haul and an auxiliary service; and all on the dime of Toby and Bea.

The two ensuing weeks, she'd settled in: puttering around the cottage, arranging her life, and patching her heart as inconspicuously as possible. She'd interviewed at the car dealership June tenth and at the bar June eleventh; she was supposed to have been married June twelfth.

So on her used-to-be-anticipated wedding date, having accomplished the move and the landing of two new jobs, she decided to try to rejuvenate her spirit. She read, ate, talked to Bea, shot an entire roll of thirty-six-frame film around the Mullins's old house, and then slept all the rest of the day. She dreamed of Eric, and that they lived in a hospital room with all their belongings in the parking lot below.

Everything was dirty and scattered, but no one would let her bring their stuff inside. She dreamed of looking for a dime-store ring her father had, in reality, given her and that she'd lost. She saw it on the finger of another little girl passing by, but the child's mother told Ava to go away; and the girl, obviously a child thief of some kind, had stared at Ava in wonder as Ava cried.

She awakened, hungry, at dusk. She would have called it a non-productive day by her usual standards, but life—as Jeanette was fond of saying—couldn't always be cherries and chocolate.

Arising and looking at the Harvick and Braun calendar pinned on the closet door, she crossed out "WEDDING!" on June twelfth and wrote in purple Magic marker: "Today was a good/bad day."

The following Monday emerged bright and warm. Ava spent the first three days at The Fox and Ale getting the things organized. She wouldn't start at Arrington's until the first day of July, and she wanted to have a handle on the bar.

The "office" was a disaster; it didn't deserve its name. Stacks of boxes, not even labeled, had been serving as Corrine's and Jimmy's filing system, and these lined the walls, along with dusty antique soda bottles stacked precariously toward the ceiling in every corner. Jimmy had told her the building was originally a grocery store built over fifty years ago, and hey, couldn't bottles like those be valuable? There were boxes of promotional signs and decor, cable boxes and electronic cords, and holiday decorations of all kinds. Several cardboard mannequins of models holding beers or drinks adorned various wall supports, each woman gifted with long legs, magnificent busts, and white teeth.

Ava had discarded the promotional items, telling her boss, "They don't want you to use them again, Jimmy. Every promotion, don't they give you new stuff?" She moved the decorations (after boxing each season and labeling it) to a storage room even further back in the deep, broad building; and by Wednesday, when she stopped working at precisely five o'clock, the office was clean and clear, with ledgers, pencils, pens, and a calculator, and filing cabinets galore.

"Soup's on," Kathy crowed as Ava pushed through the swinging doors from the back. She set a fried chicken sandwich in front of the third stool from the bar's left end, the one Ava preferred. The dayshift bartender had outrageously frizzed and layered blonde hair and a tattoo of an angel on one shoulder and a devil on the other. She was so light-colored and soft, with a round baby face, that Ava had no trouble imagining her as a typical American kid before she went "wild." ("Typical and boring," Kathy told her later; and, yes, she was rarely in touch with her parents, having proved a "huge" disappointment.)

"You're my hero," Ava replied and took a long swill of her Coke before sitting. "Do you have any idea what that place back there was like?" She screwed up her face for emphasis.

Kathy laughed. "Yeah. They send me into it sometimes for the decorations. But I haven't been so great at putting them back, either, so I guess I'm part of the problem."

"Well, I'll add you to my naughty list. But it's the files too. They just threw them in random boxes. And Corrine wrote in pen. There are so many scratch-outs. She wrote in different books, and I can't find all the books…it's crazy." She took a bite. The bar was still in that late afternoon lull, which Ava loved, where she could eat before it got too smoky and where she could hear herself talk. She would leave as the business crowd drifted in and be long gone before the late-night partiers.

"That's why we *hired* you, sweet cakes," she heard from behind her, and it was Corrine who spoke this time, coming up at her left shoulder and sitting, swinging her legs in front. "It is to your benefit that I'm a slacker, you know."

Ava, instantly embarrassed, swallowed before she spoke, "I guess! It's okay…we all have our weak points." She put down her sandwich and wiped her fingers.

"Oh, don't I know it." Corrine lowered her voice. "Don't worry, eat your sandwich. I only came over to tell you that you have a secret admirer." Over from where Ava didn't know. She hadn't even known Corrine was there.

It was quiet enough to hear her boss's soft voice; Jimmy didn't allow the bartenders to blast the music in the afternoons. He said that the office crowd came to enjoy a beer after a hard workday, not to drown their sorrows in liquor as they lost themselves in the throes of rock and roll. Ava instinctively turned to her left, the ear into which Corrine had whispered, and that's when she saw this…man.

He was sitting at a small table along the partial wall that jutted halfway between the main bar area and the game room on the front side of the building. He couldn't have been there when she'd come out; she would have noticed him. Even from his sitting position, she could tell the guy was tallish, lean, and well-built, with very dark-brown curly hair that he wore in a tousled, meant-to-be unstudied kind of way. He was laughing at his companion across the table, a nondescript guy in a baseball cap whose face, sitting with his back toward the bar, was obscured from Ava's view. The dark-haired man's muscular forearms—that had just the right amount of dark hair—were resting lightly on the table, and he was fiddling with a pack of matches. Ava was still looking when her line of sight was interrupted by Kathy, bouncing and grinning like a beauty queen as she took him a large mug of beer.

It was several seconds before Ava moved. She just sat there staring at the guy, soaking him in before he might cast his eyes and see her, in that way people sometimes do when they notice someone in their peripheral vision is looking at them. She loved him.

No, that couldn't be right.

She was still looking—rather, staring—when Corrine's voice cut into her thoughts.

"No, not that way. Over there…" Corrine flung her index finger to Ava's right. Ava turned and gazed upon not one but two beefy-looking guys at the opposite end of the bar, smiling in a friendly and hopeful way.

She turned back to Corrine and exhaled. "Which one, Mo or Larry?" She glanced to smile at the men but then back again, facing Corrine. The older woman twisted her stool with her legs facing out, her knees crossed, and elbows propped back on the bar. This day, she wore a turquoise wrap dress, white sandals, and a slim gold chain at her throat. Her nails were long and painted fuchsia.

"Don't be catty," Corrine said. "Some girls don't have any beaus." Her eyes were mischievous, her lashes thick with black mascara. She arched her back to pick a fry off Ava's plate.

"Oh, they're beaus, are they? What are we, girls in *Gone with the Wind*? Hey, Corrine, who's that guy behind me? The one at the second table along the wall?" Ava stole another short glance but then turned back to the sandwich, picked it up, and looked at it before placing it back on the plate.

Corrine didn't answer right away; she'd lifted two more fries off Ava's plate and was chewing. Ava had noticed she'd done that with a couple of other people, too, and with Jimmy, and had wondered why she didn't just order her own; she owned the place, after all. It occurred to her, too, that it may have been a way of establishing intimacy, so hey, perhaps she should consider it a compliment.

"That, my dear, is Scott. Only you and every other girl who walks in here want to know."

"Well, he's handsome, isn't he? You have to admit he's handsome." Ava nudged the plate gently in Corrine's direction and took a long, cold drag of her Coke.

"Yeah, nobody says he isn't handsome. That's why everybody wants to know who he is, genius." Corrine kept plucking up fries.

Scott got up then and came over, bringing his mug of beer with him. Ava sat there for a moment, realizing in a matter of seconds that she felt, again, this—what was it?—this crush. She tried to pull herself together a little bit, tried to focus on her breathing.

"Hey, pretty, how're you doin'?" He didn't say this like a question; he was calling Corrine pretty as a name. He took a swallow of his beer.

Corrine, or Cory, as Ava noticed most people called her, barely moved, leaning back a little, resting on her elbows, swinging her crossed leg laconically. The bodice of her dress was low and pulled snugly across her tanned full chest in a very appealing way. Ava wondered if she ever skipped her daily application of body lotion as she always looked somewhat dewy.

"Hey, Scottie." Corrine's voice was low and soft. "Lemme introduce you to somebody." Corrine patted Ava's arm lightly a couple of times. "This is Ava Rush. She is the latest victim of The Fox and Ale."

"I can dig it. Hi, Ava." He took the stool on the opposite side of Corrine. Ava peeked back at her two "suitors," but it appeared they had given up hopes of engaging her and resumed their conversation. Kathy plopped a fresh bowl of pretzels in front of Scott, who smiled and thanked her as he took a couple from the bowl and then didn't notice her further. He angled his barstool slightly sideways toward Corrine and Ava, and Corrine, meanwhile, had swung around to sit at the bar "properly," easing her stool back to allow them all to talk easily.

"Ava's only been down here a couple weeks, right, babe?" Now, Ava realized she was *babe*—that overworked term of endearment used by so many people in the bar business. "She came all the way from Atlanta…from some bank—"

"An accounting firm," Ava volunteered. Her voice sounded thin and childish compared to Corrine's.

"Yeah, decided she wasn't cut out for city life, kind of like Green Acres, is how I see it."

Ava wondered if Corrine was making fun of her, which would be just like most women—trying to make each other look bad in front of the good-looking guys.

"Well, if I remember that show correctly from my misspent childhood, the chick *loved* city life. It was her husband who dragged her out there." Scott looked at Ava as if for corroboration.

"Well…yeah. I liked Atlanta… I grew up there, and I'll probably go back, but…I hit a bit of a roadblock."

Scott nodded. "So…postroadblock, why here?"

"My best friend lives in Tarryton. I figure I'll stay here awhile, save some money…then go back and get on with another big firm. Or maybe even start my own business."

"Oh, cool. What kind of business?" Scott looked directly into her eyes, and it almost took her breath away—the deepest blue like a cobalt-blue ocean or agate…

"Accounting. Bookkeeping. Any kind of financial ledgers or keeping of financial documents, taxes, or…"

"Oh, gawd!" Corrine gasped, holding her hand over her mouth, then jumping off her stool. "Ava, listen, honey, tell Jimmy I didn't forget the stuff—you know, that banquet stuff—tell him I left an hour ago." She pecked Scott on the cheek and patted Ava's arm again lightly before she reached behind the bar for her purse and strode toward the door. "Bye, girls and boys," she called, and suddenly Ava and Scott were sitting with the empty stool between them.

Scott watched her go before turning back to Ava. "So you're a numbers girl, one of those girls who sat in the front in math class and raised her hand all the time. And all the other girls were jealous of you and didn't want to be your friend." He had a sexy upturn to his mouth on one side, a kind of Elvis thing going on.

He's playing with me, she thought. *Has to see what the new girl is made of.*

"Well, you know, you're half right. Not sure any girls were jealous, but the other stuff is true." She looked down into her drink, then up at Kathy still bouncing up and down the bar, her full figure shaking but contained in her tight black jeans and T-shirt knotted at her waist.

"Well, I'm telling you they were. Girls are always jealous of the pretty ones, and if you're smart…plus, I bet you were nice as hell." Again, the little upturned side of his mouth, and again, looking right smack dab into her eyes.

She felt a little easier now. She relaxed her spine a bit and crossed her knees like Corrine always did, having to turn toward him a little to do so. "I *was* nice. I still am. It's a blessing *and* a curse, I guess, but I have so many of those."

He laughed. "I bet you do." He took several swallows of beer, finishing it, and set his mug on the bar that had been so repeatedly varnished it looked as if layered with glass. He stood, pulling a healthy pad of cash from his front pocket, and from his movement, she caught a scent of what she thought was Grey Flannel cologne. He wore indigo-colored Levi's with a white long-sleeved polo shirt turned up along each golden-tanned arm and leather loafers with no socks.

"Well, I'll miss you," she said. "We get to do this so infrequently, anymore."

He grinned at her, pulling a ten from the stash and tossing it on the bar. "You're funny. You're a funny chick. Next time you should save me a place. Later, Kat," he called toward the bartender, then winked at Ava as he turned to go.

Saluting playfully, she swiveled to her watery Coke and cold, half-eaten food. She resisted the urge to turn and watch his back as he left.

Chapter 12

AVA DID HER work, ignoring the unfinished space with its raw wood two-by-fours interspersed with plywood-covered insulation as best she could. The room still—after heaven-only-knew how many years—lacked sheetrock, plaster, paint, and trim. The Woodhams had added it to the fifty-year-old store when they'd remodeled it into a bar but had never gotten around to finishing it. It's just that no one ever cared enough, is how Corrine explained it, and Ava wondered if its ease of use as a dumping ground had made the finishing off too daunting. It was an ugly, secluded spot, which was probably just one reason why the very social Corrine couldn't bear to spend much time there.

Ava, however, didn't much mind the solitude now that the smooth antique pine desk was clear and the clutter had been removed. She had asked Corrine to touch nothing and had asked Jimmy, too, to abdicate any claim to this space. Ava wanted no more beer banners or green plastic bowlers, no paper ghosts, or colored string lights piled back where she'd cleared the area of such bric-a-brac, along with the unorganized boxes of files and receipts. She'd only half-jokingly told them she'd walk if they ignored her words.

She now worked two-to-five each weekday after reporting at Arrington Ford every morning for her shift from eight-to-twelve. Both places paid her well. She'd started giving Bea and Toby thirty dollars a week despite their protests; she'd reminded them she usually ate dinner with them anyway. She'd sent fifty to Jeanette—who was calling her far too much already, Ava thought—after her first two weeks at the bar. She could manage a hundred to her mom every month and was committed to give seventy-five to her friends; that would still allow her to save for a car and an apartment back in Atlanta. Someday. Or somewhere. There were other cities with exciting people and good jobs, sprawling suburbs with clean white homes perfect for raising children. There were other nice men; there was hope. Eric Bankston did not ruin her life.

But something inside her had twisted a little when she'd met Scott, and she began to look for him. Casually, surreptitiously, she would scan the bar in the afternoon or evening, and a few days after their first meeting, she saw him. He'd come in alone, seen her standing at the bar chatting with Kathy after her workday but didn't approach or speak. Rather, he smiled, tossed up a hand, and then joined the friend in the cap at the same table as before—the one that rested beside the partition off to the side of the green-tinted-plate glass windows. The guy Ava now knew as Chet.

The men talked and laughed over mugs of beer, but Scott didn't approach or look her way again. He'd followed his beer with vodka, neat, and moved with Chet to the game room. This section was on the left side of the bar as one entered and had pinball machines, a couple of poker tables, and several four-top tables where couples or groups would play backgammon or chess. Ava had decided to stay, ordered nachos, and watched the two play pinball as she prolonged her leave, stealing glances as she lingered with her Coke.

That day, she became acutely aware of a sudden void in her—an elevated need, a mild but heightened craving. After Scott had ordered his second vodka, Ava watched his back as he played his buddy in pinball, then settled her tab with Kathy, and left.

One day when she'd come from her office about four o'clock to get a Coke, he'd breezed in. He'd smiled at both her and Kathy, then went to the section to the right of the bar. This dark, low, rectangular room was in the style of a boys' club. It displayed guns and hunting trophies behind mounted glass cases to prevent theft and dust. Two pool tables overhung with hooded lights advertising beer brands occupied the middle, and several blue padded chairs studded with nailheads bordered the walls. In the same nailhead style of the club chairs, two hunter-green sofas rested at each end of the space and four royal-blue leather recliners, in pairs, in two of the corners. Horizontal rectangular windows overlooked a parking lot, and small round pedestal tables accompanied each sofa end and chair—dark and varnished, they had become somewhat sullied, encroached upon by the nicks and watermarks of time.

She thought it odd Scott didn't speak either day—not even to Corrine, who was sitting at the bar that second visit—but headed straight to this area that everyone called the "lounge." She didn't see him again before she left and dared not ask if he was still there. (This side also was marked by two partitions, and just as the game room partition somewhat separated it from the bar area, these extended across each end and partially occluded the view, as well.) Ava sat at the bar talking with Corrine for a while but had placed her purse on the stool on her other side. Intuitively, though, she knew Scott would not be coming out to take the seat he had asked her, that first day they met, to save him.

The third time she saw him, and the last of the times during which he didn't speak, he came in around four thirty with a woman—a dark-haired girl whose name, she learned, was Lucy, because when she and Scott came in and sat in a booth beside the front windows, Kathy had poured him a draft and then called across the room, "What's Lucy want?"

Ava had taken to doing some of her "busy" work at the right corner of the bar when it was quiet. Not always but sometimes, the windowless, unfinished room was oppressive. On this occasion, she studied Lucy—of course, as much as you could study anyone while pretending the whole time not to look. The girl was slender and conveyed a reserve, so unlike the attention-seeking behavior of the buxom frizzy-haired girl who came in with him a few days later. After their first few minutes of sitting and talking, Lucy sat nursing a bottled beer while Scott carried his draft to the game room and talked to Chet, who was there playing pinball. He returned and sat with her again for about thirty more minutes while they shared about two laughs and a plate of nachos. It was pretty easy for Ava to observe all this while pretending to be engrossed by entering numbers from a paltry lot of invoices into her ledger.

The fourth time he came in, he spoke. He wore Levi's with a dark-blue Polo, and after seating his companion at a booth—a robust girl with bleached fluffed-and-teased hair like cotton candy—walked up the bar where Ava sat with her usual Coke. It was a little after five, and a few minutes later, she would have been gone. He came and stood beside her, one elbow on the bar and turning slightly in her direction, and smiled.

"The estimable Ava, rescuer of the accounting maelstrom."

She was surprised by his approach, by his playful comment, by his presence. "What? Maelstrom?"

"Yeah. Mess. The terrible tangle you walked into when they suckered you into this job."

"Oh, well, I guess I walked into it voluntarily. But yeah, it was a disaster. How did you know?"

But Kathy had popped into place in front of him with glitter-soaked pink lip gloss and sporting a lizard-skin tank top. "Beer, hot stuff?" she asked while popping her bubble gum.

"Excuse me..." He held up a finger to Ava.

He gave Kathy his order, long island tea and a vodka, and turned again to Ava.

"I've seen it. The snake pit back there. Cory's the worst."

"You've seen it? Why? Looking for the safe, probably."

"Close. Helping. They used to keep all kinds of crap back there, decorations and stuff."

She sipped her soda. "Used to? Still did until I started. Seriously, it was more storage room than business office. No wonder she had such a hard time."

"Right. Plus, not her forte. So what're you doin' now? Hanging out? Buy you a drink?" Scott held up a finger to Kathy as if to detain her as she placed his order in front of him, but Ava looked at her, smiled, and shook her head.

"Oh, no, thanks. I've got this." She hoisted her Coke for emphasis, although it was on its last dregs.

"Yeah, but you're off now. Nothing stronger? My treat."

"No, no, but thank you. I actually don't drink anything stronger."

Scott raised his eyebrows. "Really? How come, if you don't mind my asking."

Ava gave a little shrug. "I don't know. Lots of reasons. I don't need it."

He looked at her for a moment, just a few seconds, perhaps considering this concept. "Hmm. Interesting. Well, good for you, Ava Rush. Good for you."

He put a twenty on the bar. "Start me a tab, Kat," he called, then picked up the drinks and smiled at Ava. "All right, well, stay cute. Hope you've learned how to have fun somehow." And he carried the drinks toward the booth where the girl sat. Ava watched him, accidentally meeting her eyes. There was the tiniest hint of… possession, maybe—in his companion's gaze—that unuttered code between women that men supposedly didn't share, an electrically charged stare that would shock the errant female.

Kathy placed a fresh Coke in front of Ava as she swiveled back around. "That girl will drink any man under the table," she said in a low voice with just the slightest nod of her head.

"Oh, shoot, Kathy, I was leaving, but thanks." Ava shoved her almost empty glass toward the bartender and accepted the fresh one, along with a couple of napkins. "Who, the yellow-haired chick?"

"Yeah. I make a pretty strong Long Island, and she can drink four and still walk a straight line."

Ava resisted the urge to glance around again. She'd noticed the girl was stocky but shapely, wearing a black stretchy tank, black parachute pants, and boots. She looked strong and keen, her lips a slash of dark red.

"Who is she?" Ava began to fold one of the new napkins into a tiny fan.

"Some ho. No, just kidding. But she'll get with guys pretty easy if you believe the gossip. I don't know why Scottie fiddles with her, honestly."

"Mmmm. So they date?"

"Nooo, not that I know of." Kathy began pulling glasses from the shelf under the bar and stacking them on the plastic liners on top of it. "Or maybe they do, I don't know. Scott's so weird. But he does have his little menagerie."

"Like, women-wise, you mean?"

Kathy shrugged. "Yeah. But he plays everything pretty close to the vest, as Jimmy says, so you never feel like you really know him. Like, supposedly, he comes from this nice rich family but doesn't have a lot to do with them. Comes in with clients, mostly, and sometimes some ol' girl. Then there's Chet, of course."

"What kind of clients?"

"Insurance...his business? I thought you knew. His dad is Charles Divine, from Divine Chevrolet, so he probably gets lots of connections through him, especially with cars. That's your competition, of course." She winked.

"Well, I'm sure there's plenty of business to go around." Ava twirled her straw. "What's the deal on the family, though?"

Kathy shrugged. "I don't think he gets along with his dad. Not sure, though. He never talks about it. Anybody brings up his dad, he's just like, 'meh.'"

"So that dark-haired girl...she's not his girlfriend?"

"Who? Oh, you mean Lucy...no. No, she's another agent. They come in together sometimes."

"Oh. I just assumed. Is she nice? She's very pretty."

"Yeah, but...she's kind of blank. I don't mean to be mean but not super interesting in the personality department. Pretty, though. But Scottie's a weirdo anyway. Hey, you wanna eat? That lunch sandwich can't still be lasting. Barry's got a chicken wing special going on." Kathy had finished stacking the glasses.

"No, not those. But you know what, gimme a salad."

"Chef's? With chicken, right? Man, you and your chicken." Kathy didn't wait for an answer but moved back along the bar, passing in front of several more people who'd come in and taking drink orders, for they'd moved into happy hour, and a couple of the patrons had hit ice. "I'll get ya one, hon," she called back to Ava, and at that moment, Scott came up to her side again and sat. He placed two empty glasses on the bar.

"Did you save this for me?" he asked. So. He did remember asking her to save him a seat on the day they met.

"Well, you said to, right? I am ever willing to please."

"Then that makes you a rare bird, little chickie." He sat slightly turned to her and glanced back toward the front windows where another girl and guy had joined his voluptuous companion. The bar lights hit his eyes just right, turning them into sapphire-blue marbles. His lashes were black and long.

Ava glanced too. "Who's with your date?" She hoped to force him to refute the classification, but he didn't. "Just friends. She went to school with the girl. I see you're still doting on your Shirley Temple."

"Well, *doting* is a weak word. I'm putting the hurt on it. I'm on my second one." She took a long draught for emphasis.

He gave a short laugh. "Color me scared."

Neither spoke for a moment. INXS was playing on the stereo. Kat emerged from the swinging doors behind the bar with a large salad covered in cling wrap and placed this in front of Ava. She set another neat vodka in front of Scott before whisking up a tray on which sat a second tall muddled alcoholic tea and two other drinks, then veered around the bar to deliver them to the girl and the other couple. *She and Scott must have some kind of system,* Ava thought, *some unspoken agreement.* Kat returned and swept away the two empty glasses Scott had brought and reached for Ava's too.

"None for me, sweets." Ava slashed her finger across her neck in the cut-throat gesture. "Just water, please. I'll miss out on my beauty sleep." She began to unwrap the salad, but she was not looking forward to eating it in front of this handsome guy.

Scott looked at her a moment before speaking, "I'm surprised you're still here at this lousy job, you know. I thought by now you would have been rescued by some slob who did not deserve you." He began eating some pretzels, his stool still angled toward hers.

"Nah. I'm waiting on the slob who deserves me." She glanced up enough to smile at him, and he smiled back. That was the moment Ava first realized—though she wasn't sure how she knew—that some people have this "thing." Maybe a physical trait, but maybe not—that causes their lovers to forgive them for anything. She imagined Scott had ridden and would continue to ride that smile of his for years.

The neat vodka in its short glass was so full that Ava assumed it must have had three shots instead of the regulatory one, and she wondered if Scott perhaps could keep pace with the girl—wondered who could drink whom under the table. She also realized it might be polite to ask the girl's name, except that she didn't even want to know.

He took a deep swallow of drink before he spoke again. "God's sweet nectar," he said, setting the glass on the bar but still keeping his fingers upon it. "So. Who is this slob you're waiting on, Ava? The one who deserves you. Someone you already know?"

She wondered if this was his way of finding out if she had a boyfriend, and she felt a delicious little flip of her stomach. He was so confident and sexy… Wouldn't it be interesting if he really did want to know?

"Well, not now. I kind of got dumped by my fiancé a couple of months ago, so I'll have to find a new victim." She surprised herself with her candor, and she braved a messy bite of her salad, then, primarily for something to do.

Scott looked at her another moment before he spoke. "What happened?" he asked, and nothing else, while she continued to chew and swallowed. She began to realize he was one of those people, like Bea, who felt no need to fill up every silence; and in that silence, while he looked straight at her, she somehow felt the freedom to be honest.

She shrugged. "I honestly don't know." She took a sip of water, then surprised herself again with her bluntness. "I didn't sleep with him. I know you must think that's odd, that I'm waiting, that I think it's still important, but," she hesitated, "I know how that sounds to you guys."

Scott studied her face, his own thoughtful and compassionate. "How do you think it sounds to us guys? I think it sounds great. I just didn't know there were many girls around anymore who thought enough of themselves or their husbands to do that. Or you know, their future husbands."

"Well, to my credit, there aren't. I'm a rare jewel." She took another bite of her salad, and again, he was quiet. After she swallowed, she felt the need to continue. "But you know what I think is funny? You guys think it's quaint and sweet unless you want to take someone to bed. And then, if you do, you say, 'Well, baby, it doesn't matter, as long as you love each other.' Like, you try to talk them into it." She waited a moment, but he still didn't say anything, so she went on. "And correct me if I'm wrong, but you always say you do too—love her, I mean—the girl." She smiled a little and raised her eyes to his to let him know she wasn't an angry, militant type.

"Oh, do we? Say we love you?" He seemed genuinely intrigued. "Maybe we do. Maybe we do love you, and we want to add the physical to the emotional—give you, and ourselves, the whole package." He drank, killing the vodka and pushing the glass to the bar's back edge.

"Yeah. Well, that's what I call the fake sincerity line. You love us until you get us. Then you want the next new thing. You needn't argue. It's the story of too many friends." He didn't need to know that much of her opinion had also come from books and movies. "I am young, but I do know some things."

She suddenly felt a little exposed. She wasn't used to sharing her dating philosophy, usually discussing none of this, except with Bea, and made the most pedestrian small talk imaginable with the men who might try to engage her.

She felt her face get warm and realized she was upset. Eric had done this, she knew. Eric, the one who'd rejected her and her self-esteemed purity for reasons of which she still wasn't sure.

Scott sat casually, glanced a thank-you to Kathy as she set another short full glass in front of him, and looked at her. "Most men are jerks, Ava. You're right. But you're also right to not stay with one who wouldn't appreciate you. I think you'll find somebody who realizes how great you are." He didn't look away from her as he said this, not for a second.

"Well, maybe that's a matter of time," she murmured to her salad and then met his eyes again. "But do you know what the truth is? Because I don't. He left me. Six weeks ago, three weeks before our wedding. And I don't know why. If he had wanted more, you know, well, that would have only taken three more weeks! And we'd been engaged a whole year—fourteen months. I think maybe he just realized he didn't want me after all. He must not have loved me that much."

Scott held her gaze a few more seconds before lifting his drink, draining the entire thing in one gulp, and setting the glass on the bar. "I've got to get back to my friends, gorgeous," he said as he stood up to leave. "But you wanna know what I think?" He kissed his fingertip, touched it to her nose, and gave her that slight and crooked smile. "I think he's full of doo-doo." He turned and walked away.

Chapter 13

OF COURSE, THEN he did it again.

He came in three or four more times—once with a couple of friends, once with two girls—and, in essence, ignored her. Not obviously but still he would smile, say, "Hey, Ava, how're you doin'?" and go about his business, playing pool in the lounge or going into the game room; and once, sitting at one of the front booths with insurance folders and pens; and speaking in a friendly, confident way to an older gentleman who peered over everything through unrimmed tiny reading glasses.

Then toward the end of July, after she'd finished for the day, he came in and sat beside her—the same seat, for she was in the same seat, the one she'd kind of claimed for herself every day after the dealership's, and then the bar's, accounting work was done, where she sat babysitting a Coke and eating bar food before she headed to her empty little house-behind-a-house that wasn't her house at all.

That day he had on a pressed gray button-down with the minuscule Nautilus boat on it and darker gray pants with shoes that were dressy in a casual sort of way. Ava imagined he'd had a meeting with someone rather important, maybe a customer not familiar with the salesman-who-hung-out-at-a-bar type.

She watched Kathy pour his drink and now knew this to be his regular one when he wasn't drinking beer—almost three full shots of vodka, appearing as innocuous as a short fat glass of chilled water. Ava had the random thought of how different it was from water—one giving life and nourishment, the other false courage, supreme assurance, and false peace.

He sat beside her and offered his sideways smile. "Hello, gorgeous. I see you're lost again." He took a swallow of his drink, then threw a few minipretzels in his mouth and crunched them.

"I am, I guess. Sad but true." She narrowed her eyes. "Why the dress duds—trying to impress the ladies?"

"Sure. Why not?" He glanced around to both sides of the bar. She knew that wasn't it, but she liked his confidence in not explaining. "What's new in Ava-Ville?"

"Nothing. Been going to the river a little bit with my friend and her husband. Hey, sorry about all the girl talk a while back. Sheesh. Buy a psychiatrist, right?"

"Nah. You're all right. You're right, anyway, guys are wastrels." She noticed he didn't say "most." "Of course, some girls aren't much better. Game players. Teasers. Little closet floozies and such."

That was unexpected. "What does that mean?" She smiled to let him know once again she wasn't one of those bellicose "women's libbers" (as Jeanette had once called her when Ava had insisted she would never depend on a man for her income).

He laughed. "What, closet floozy? It means some girls play pure and hard to get while not being so pure with other guys, only with the fish they're trying to land. They pretend they're better than they are."

"Hmmm. Interesting. I've never heard that theory."

Scott laughed again. "Okay, sugar, but let's be honest. You admitted a while back your knowledge of life and love was a little bit secondhand, right? How old are you? Twenty-one? Two? Dated two or three guys, got engaged… I'd guess it's fair to say some of these games have been played out of your league since you're not a player. You're obviously one of the good ones."

Ava said nothing at first. She supposed she wasn't just in being offended; after all, wasn't he saying she was too pure, too clueless to know that some girls slept around while portraying virtue to their boyfriends? But that made no sense to her. If a girl was going to sleep with anybody at all, wouldn't she sleep with the boy she loved?

Scott looked at her as if waiting for a response. Maybe he was expecting her to be angry. "Again. Not saying it's you. Just saying maybe it's not honest to say all the dudes are crap and the chicks are always the wronged ones."

But she wasn't angry. For whatever reason, she felt deflated and vulnerable and took a turn at honesty once more, with only a smidgen of sarcasm and bravado.

"No, I get it. It's just a waste, isn't it? These games we play. Maybe virtue doesn't even matter. Maybe honesty doesn't matter. And like I said, in my case, anyway, it didn't. It didn't do a thing for me because I suppose I wasn't worth marrying in the first place."

If he had realized his opportunity to compliment or flatter her, he didn't take it. He took a sip of his drink and looked at her, setting down his glass and still keeping his fingers cupped around it. "Depends. Depends on the guy. They're different, you know. Just saying, all the clichés aren't true. Seems your ex was a bit of a loser, but you must still have some kind of shine for him because you don't even see it." He drank once more from his short thick glass without taking his eyes from her. "Why would you even care about someone who pulled that kind of act on you?"

Ava felt instantly defensive but also a little thrilled. He had never shown her any personal interest in her, and yet he now seemed to be stifling some small degree of irritation that she had allowed herself to be subjected to this particular kind of emotional injustice.

"Because I didn't know better." She let the words sink in. "Don't you get that? I suppose I still don't have it all figured out in the love department, as I'm sure you do." She knew how to turn the table, she thought, and get the focus off all they both knew she'd gotten wrong.

He looked at her oddly. "Yeah, I get it. But you don't have to have everything figured out to walk away with a little self-respect." And he got up and headed into the lounge.

Ava sat for several minutes. She wasn't sure what to do, where to look, whether to stay or get up and leave. She sat there with her emotions, then looking after him, while he stood by the pool table in the center of the room making small talk with a guy named Bernard. She could see, rather than hear, his occasional laugh—that she now knew to be low and relaxed—at something Bernard had said.

What is it to him? she thought. How dare he cause her to feel she was the one who had done something wrong—by what, loving someone who turned out to be unworthy?—and then walk away, leaving her no opportunity to defend herself.

She saw Kathy approach him, fill his fist with another fat glass of clear liquid, and pop back behind the bar within seconds. She sat until she'd regulated her breathing.

The bar crowd was sparse. The end-of-work regulars were just now drifting in, those who came in almost daily for happy hour, and only about ten of the thirty or so customers were hanging out in the lounge. Ava pushed out her barstool and rose, placing it gently again up against the bar. She walked with purpose to the lounge, though she had thought she was leaving for home, and approached Scott's back until she was no more than two feet behind him. He turned from where he was talking to Bernard (and now, some girl) and looked only mildly surprised. "What, princess?" he asked and took another sip of his beloved vodka.

"I just wanted to make sure that we were on the same page." She needed to come across as more sure of herself than she felt; surely, all three could hear the thumping of her chest. "I hope I'll never regret trusting somebody. And not for trying to be good either. There are excellent reasons for both." She turned on a dime and walked back the way she had come, but she heard him call her name from behind.

"Ava," he said again as he caught up to her, and as she rounded the end of the bar (so that she might go behind it and exit out the back), he put one hand on her shoulder and the other on her waist. With confidence, power, and gentleness, he guided her the few steps to the swinging doors and propelled her through them. She half-turned, mouth open, but he pushed against her with his body and hands, and she realized he could be gentle because she was letting him.

They passed the kitchen to the right, then went just a few feet down the corridor before veering left into the storeroom. It was dark, full of the heavy wood fragrance of liquor crates and the smell of freshly-bleached rags; and after pressing her to its far wall, he stopped. His mouth found hers before she realized where she was, in the outermost corner of the building, where no one could hear his murmurings, his breath, nor her pounding blood.

She pulled her lips away. "What are you doing?" she whispered. "Scott, what are you *doing*?"

But then she searched for his lips to kiss him back, for he had angled his face to the side of hers and pressed it into her hair. She swam in a murky vortex, a place where there were no thoughts except of him and Eric, careening around and colliding with each other; and it was painful.

It had already happened, she thought. This kiss had already happened and could not be uncompleted. She and Eric had gone out five times in two weeks before she'd let him kiss her, and this uninvited, unable-to-be-prepared-for nirvana was a mark on her score sheet—done at the expense of everything she had believed, up to this point, about her virtue.

Ava removed her hands from the sides of his face—*How had those gotten there?*—and placed them between their bodies, palms against his chest. "Stop, Scott. I have no idea what we're doing." And she listened to the pulse of his breath.

The only light emanated from two dirty tiny outside windows. Ava could hear Barry, the cook, raise his voice with instructions to the boy, Gil, struggling to be heard over the sputtering grease of the fryer and the clanging of both their cookware. In their tiny enclave, Ava could hear Gil responding in turn, and she felt like the child that used to hide from her mother in Jeanette's bedroom closet. She wondered if the cooks had not noticed Scott's and her odd little transit, or had they just not thought it unusual?

In the hazy light reflected against Scott's back, she could make out the outline of his face as he turned, only slightly, away from her: he had a strong but noble nose, the tiniest cleft on his somewhat-square chin. The shock of curly dark hair, she noticed, had not been cut since she had first laid eyes on him some forty-odd days ago. But what startled her most was the slackness of his mouth coupled with his silence, and her realization, as he glanced at one perfunctory window and she saw no brightness in his eyes, that he was undoubtedly somewhat drunk.

Her mind, without forethought, calculated how many drinks Kathy had served him, *Only two, right? No, there was another one—*

the one she took to him in the lounge and which he'd killed in just a few swallows by the time she confronted him. *So that would have been, good heavens—at the "Kathy-pour" rate, at least where Scott was concerned—that would have been nine "regular" shots. And not counting whatever he may have had at the business lunch he'd presumably conducted elsewhere…earlier in the day, yes, but still.*

"I don't know what that was about," she said, then moved away toward the narrow open entrance to the room; but instead of going through it, she turned right and passed between two rows of stacked boxes until she had reached the far wall. This wall separated the storage room from the bar area. If one were quiet, you could hear conversations at the server's silverware-and-prep station closest to it. Here she found a crate to sit on, one of several that had been pulled down or forward by one of the bartenders to get at something else, then left there for secret smoke breaks.

Ava sat and felt her heartbeat, trying to quiet the confused thoughts in her head. She realized without alarm that she wanted him to follow her into the passage, so she sat breathing deeply and waiting.

But he didn't. Like a shadow, she saw him pass into the light, past the opening into which she'd come, and back into the passage beside the kitchen. And then, after his greeting to Barry and Gil, she realized he was leaving.

She crept as close as she dared to the doorway and heard him beyond, calling "Later, Kat." Kathy tweeted out her goodbye to him in that loud musical voice girl bartenders so often have, and then Ava heard nothing—nothing but the gregarious banter of Kathy and the customers undoubtedly bellied up to the bar.

Ava stood listening to the singsong conversations, which she could not make out, of the customers, the cooks, and the bartender; but then she realized she was going to have to pass back through those doors herself in a moment, for she'd carried her purse out there after her bookkeeping entries, thus eliminating the option to leave quietly out the back.

She had carried her purse out there because she was done for the day and had no more business back in her dry, woody office.

Her only remaining business had been to try to wait, as usual—in an unstudied manner, with her nonalcoholic drink—for the moment when Scott might hopefully, finally walk in and find her with his eyes.

Chapter 14

TIME PASSED, AND nothing happened. Scott came in, at random times as always, making his usual rounds. The first time he came in after the kiss, he'd paused and said hello, and then had gone into the lounge with his drink. He'd smiled, as always, confident as anyone Ava had ever seen, and Ava had smiled in return.

He showed no discomfort about their awkward encounter, while she could barely function when looking at him. She wondered if he would ever engage her in conversation again, but she was not going to be pitiful enough to hang around and see. She began doing all her work, every afternoon, in her office again, with the smells of old wood and the sounds of Pink Floyd on her boom box and leaving out the back within minutes of finishing the books.

The second Saturday in August, she and Bea went to get haircuts. It was bright and hot, just the way Ava liked it. In the innermost part of Tarryton lay The Mane Event, a salon run by a high school friend of Bea's. Its exterior was lavender-painted wood with dark purple trim; an iron balustrade separated the storefront it shared with Carrie's Designs for Women and The Medicine Shoppe from a tidy brick walkway. The purple palate continued inside, fuchsia popping with hot pink and grape, and high clear-and-chrome swivel seats amidst lots of potions and posters.

Four chairs lined each side of the salon beyond the small rectangular entrance, and behind the chairs on each side hung one continuous mirror. Three of the chairs were occupied with two girls and a middle-aged woman attending the patrons with scissors or dye.

"Ava, this is Julian, a.k.a. Jude. Best biology partner I had at Tarryton High School." Bea extended one arm toward a young man in a proud teacher presentation pose.

"Oh, gosh, hold up now!" The guy laughed as he held up both hands. "But yeah, call me Jude." He then embraced Ava like a long-lost friend. "I feel as if I've known you forever, just from this one talking!" He stood back and hooked his thumbs in his hip pockets.

"Well, yes, what you heard is true. I am a rock star."

Jude laughed again, a throaty musical laugh Ava immediately came to love. "And I find that completely believable!"

Jude had shaggy honey-colored hair threaded with slender gold. He wore neat light jeans and cowboy boots with an ivory-colored shirt, a gold medallion resting above an opened button. Ava didn't feel comfortable looking long enough to determine whose robed figure it was, though Jesus would be most likely. It could have been a saint, perhaps, but Catholics were few and far between in Tarryton.

"Your hair is gorgeous, sweetie." After they'd chatted awhile, Jude had seated Ava at one of the back stations, and now he was picking up sections of her hair and letting them fall. "It's absolutely beautiful."

"Well, it covers the old head, ya know."

The best biology partner Bea ever had pumped up Ava's chair with a foot pedal. She inhaled the strident aroma of the dye chemicals a very tall girl with flaming-red hair was applying to an older woman in black stretch pants.

"That it does! So I'm assuming you're not here for a perm or a shag." His teasing smile showed very even white teeth, and his face was deeply tanned.

"No. Correct. Just a trim, if you please. Nothing fancy." She watched both of their faces in the mirror.

"You have a heart-shaped face, you know. You could wear any style you wanted." Ava did know; it had been self-determined years ago with the help of *Seventeen* magazine. She also knew she had small features, a high forehead and cheekbones, and fair skin that tanned easily in summer. Her eyes, she'd realized when she was about eight, changed from light green to dark gray, depending on the color she wore. Today they looked light olive gray, reflecting the camouflaged tank top she'd paired with dark-blue jeans and her favorite white Converse sneakers. "You'd think somebody with your body size would like clothes more," Eric had told her the first month they dated. "You'd think somebody with your brain size wouldn't say something like that to a woman," she'd replied. But it had stuck with her, nonetheless.

"Thank you, sir. It came with my body, so…"

Bea looked up from her magazine. "Don't flatter her, Jude. She's never learned how to take a compliment."

"Oh, honey." He laughed. He'd been plucking at her hair and fluffing it, but then he began to brush it. "You know, with this color, it's dark, but you've got some copper and gold in there too. You should come in one day for some highlights." He put the top section in a clip while Ava raised her eyes to the headshots above the mirror. One raven-haired girl's deep-side-parted coif was swirled to the left and then hugged the nape of her neck, and Ava studied her, staring at her smoky eyes lined all the way around in black. She looked again to her own uncontrived reflection as Jude brushed and clipped up two more sections, leaving only a thin bottom layer that currently fell past her waist. She wondered if that model was as confident in real life as she portrayed in her sultry stare.

"I don't do much with it, honestly. Sorry." Ava tried to convey apology with both her face and voice.

"That's another thing, Jude, your talents are wasted on her." Ava found Bea in the mirror to her left, and this time, Bea didn't bother to look up from her magazine. Her own straight but choppy dark-brown pageboy was pushed backward, bangs and all, by a brown swirly plastic headband a ten-year-old might wear. "And, Ava, you'll have to forgive him. He's like a frustrated artist. That's why he's so pushy with the young ones. He wants to be creative, but," she cupped her hands around her mouth and loudly whispered, "he can't do it with the little old ladies and housewives."

Ava grinned. "Well, all my sympathy, sir. You can take it up to the waist, though," she said as she met his eyes in the mirror. "That'll have to hold you."

Bea steered the battered white Impala out of the parking lot and turned right.

"I desperately need a new car."

"You could try to stop running into stuff."

"What about stuff that runs into me?"

"Yeah. That's gotta stop too. Why don't you get one?"

"I don't know. I don't superneed it, I guess. Just want it. Got a case of the want-wants."

"You think you don't deserve it because you don't work full-time. But you don't want to work five days. You want Mrs. Potts to keep having babies so you only have to work two and a half days and make pottery whenever you feel like it and pretend like you're gardening when you're really just out there killing stuff. You forget I could write your diary for you." Bea had made half-hearted attempts to maintain Louise's old flower corner at the inverted back corner of the house ever since her mother had died.

"I know. Plus, you've probably read it at some point."

"Never. Your life would bore my eyes out. I mean that figuratively, of course."

"Of course."

"Didn't your daddy make you rich? Where's all *that* money? God said share, you know."

"Nah…I wish. I mean, the book sold great, and he had the other gigs, but…you know, the house cost money, and after Mama's cancer, things just…let's just say the well got a little dry."

"Yeah. You know, Bea, don't you wonder how everybody does it? You ride around and see these great manses and realize people are keeping them up—day after day, year after year—I want that, you know? I want to be safe like that."

Bea reached over and patted her leg, still watching the road. "I know you do, Smitty. I know you do."

They drove a couple more minutes in silence.

"What did you think of the studio? And the pottery part?"

After Jude had cut their hair, Bea had shown her the back of the salon. This room, where Jude and Bea had met every Monday for almost a year to create their art and which they sold on weekends at shows and festivals for arts and crafts, was bisected perfectly into two functional halves with floor-to-ceiling shelving on each side. The left side stored hair supplies and equipment, and the right was redolent with clay powders, tools and glazes, and two free-standing pottery wheels.

"I told you. It's genius. I think you and Jude are *both* frustrated artists, just working for the man until you're discovered at some hootenanny hippie jubilee."

"I think you're right. And it could happen any day."

They drove with the windows down, meandering through the narrow streets of Tarryton north toward Corinth, with Ava clutching her pony-tailed hair in front of her and Bea's much-shorter shaggy tresses lapping about her face with no restraint. The two-lane broadened, and the houses and buildings bordering it fell backward. Bea's speed increased to the highway limit. It was hard to hear over the wind, but even though it was scorching hot, it was the sort of perfect summer-blue day in which love songs were composed, and both girls would have been reluctant to roll the windows up and turn on the air-conditioning even if it hadn't leaked out all its Freon.

Today the plan was to drop Ava off at Arrington's, where she would put in two or three hours on Steve's books since she'd bailed on work the previous day to help Bea can the peaches. Bea would shop, stop at the boutique where she consigned some of her pottery and jams and jellies, and pick Ava up around three. Then since it was a Saturday, they would head home to clean and do laundry like the good eggs they tried to be. Sunday Bea reserved for Toby and God, and Ava reserved Sunday for pictures.

"So tell me more about Jude." Ava pressed her hand against her hairline to prevent wisps of hair from beating about her face, propping her elbow on the seatback to angle herself toward her friend. In the car on the way over, Bea had told her she and Jude had been good friends since seventh grade, and up until two years ago, Jude had dated men.

"Well, the short version is that he pretty much keeps a low profile. He doesn't see his parents much anymore after telling them when he was in high school that he was gay. And they live here in town, of course, so it's odd and sad. Most people don't even know his situation or act like they don't, but everyone loves him. He does a good business here."

"So his parents cut him off?"

"Not really, I don't think, not technically. But it's not like he visits them a lot at home, and you never see them go to the salon even to say hi. But you know how it is. They don't understand. They're hurt and ashamed...even though he's not in the lifestyle anymore. I think they're just confused." Bea gave the tiniest shake of her head, then reached to roll her window up halfway.

"What does that mean 'not in the lifestyle'? Did he decide he's not gay after all?"

Bea laughed. "Not exactly. He just...it's hard to explain, but he just left that life when he got saved a couple of years ago."

Ava ignored that last sentence, even though she was intrigued at how that had happened. She wasn't any more in the mood for an exploration of the topic of salvation than she'd ever been, even if it were cloaked in some interesting narrative about somebody else.

"Were you really that close of a friend? Like, in middle and high school? I mean, what did you even have in common?" Ava rolled her window up halfway too. She wouldn't have to hold her hair now, and she settled into the crook of the car door and the seat.

"Oh yeah. I think...well, I guess it's just our personalities or something... Jude's the best. He's funny and sweet... He'd do anything for anyone."

"Did you know? How he was then? Or did he know?"

"Heavens, no. I didn't know there was such a thing. He hung out with us girls mostly, and you know, as we all got older, he dressed and acted a little differently from other guys. But he didn't tell me until he was sixteen. And he still never told the others. Then when I came home summer of sophomore year, he told me he had a boyfriend."

"So y'all were, what, nineteen?"

Bea looked thoughtful, then nodded. "Yeah, guess so. That sounds right."

"How'd he get the salon?"

"He'd started cosmetology classes in high school, then went to Braden's. That's where he got his degree. After he passed the exams and got licensed, he leased the salon the same year."

"At nineteen? Wow. Pretty young to start a business. Where'd he get the money?"

"Bryan's parents—that was the boyfriend. I guess you could say they were financially comfortable."

So. Jude was smart—and nothing if not charismatic. Ava could see how a "comfortable" couple may have been persuaded.

"And he does well?"

"Oh yeah. And you saw the others. Those women know their stuff, and Jude works hard. I'm pretty proud of him myself."

"Where'd he meet Bryan?"

"Olympus—that was where Julian would go to, you know, have this 'other' life—and I guess Bryan, too, and Bryan was from Corinth—so I guess this would have been toward the end of high school when he was doing all that. And they lived together for a while, too, in Corinth, but I think they just presented themselves as roommates. Anyway, Bryan's parents loaned the money as an investment and didn't know they were romantic until Jude left him. He was doing well, so he was able to get a bank loan and pay them back."

Ava sat for a moment and looked out the window before asking, "Were you okay? I mean, when you found out, were you accepting? Because if you buy into God and Jesus and everything like you do, you're supposed to condemn it, right? I mean, I don't know, but that's what I thought." She squinched up her face. "Why were you such good friends with a gay person?"

Bea looked at her friend, smiling but shaking her head.

"No, I'm just saying! I don't mean it to sound ugly, but you know what I mean. How come you were...I mean, like, your mama raised you all 'Little Miss Jesus,' and then, you're like, friends with this guy, who's so different from that."

Bea, who'd returned her eyes to the road as they were approaching the turn-off for the city, nodded her head. "I know what you're trying to say—and I know what the Bible says—it's not in the creation story and it's called an unnatural act. But you don't reject somebody because they have a sin struggle. We *all* do, even when we're not consciously battling it."

"You don't."

"Oh, mercy, Ava, are you crazy?"

"Yes." It was a moment before she spoke again, "And you think God loves Jude as much as normal people?"

"Yes, goofball, because he's 'normal' too! We're all fallen people, so all fallen people are 'normal.'"

Fallen people. Huh. Ava didn't believe people were fallen so much as born right into the thick of things, right down in the muck and the mire.

"I don't have everything figured out…but I don't know if I'm supposed to. I *have* read about it in the Bible and thought about it, but the best I can come up with is that God made each person, and each has to figure things out for himself. I just don't think we're capable of determining out each other's answers." She hesitated for a moment, and Ava didn't speak. "I think we're all sinners in need of a Savior."

Bea had witnessed to Ava soon after meeting at Yancey, but when Ava had expressed her rejection, Bea had let it lie. Ever since that first moment, when Bea proclaimed or referenced God, Ava had politely ignored it, and Bea was smart enough to have never pushed it.

"You know I don't buy that, Bea." Ava looked at her lap, shaking her head and toying with her hair pulled over her shoulder. A god dropping people willy-nilly into hardship and mayhem sounded like no god at all, and even if he were real, and everybody was a sinner, it was because Bea's god had made them that way.

"I know, sweetie. But I do. And even though I try to be 'good'—you know, walk the good walk every day—I fail all the time."

"You do not! Bea, you're the most—"

"No, I'm not. Ava, I'm fallen. I'm at least as fallen as Jude. At least that's what I believe, just like I told you five years ago."

"Right…when I found out I was living with a Jesus freak."

"Exactly. But you fell madly in love with me anyway."

"So…how is he different? If he's not gay anymore?"

"It's not like that, dollface. But if you ask him, he'll tell you about it. He met Jesus on the highway to death, he says. Just like the Damascus Road..."

Ava had no idea what that meant. She rolled her window down again because they had slowed coming into Corinth. Other cars were stopping and starting in front of them as each navigated turns or yellow lights and the random pedestrian crossing. A couple of turns had them facing south again as they neared Arrington's, and Ava twisted to the sun filtering through the oil-soaked pavement's haze at her window.

Bea inhaled slowly and sighed. "I love Jude. I'm so glad God chose me for one of his friends. He goes to our church now, by the way, for two years. That's where he got saved." She suppressed a smile and glanced at Ava, whose eyes rounded in wonder.

"How does *that* work?" Ava had never been to Bea's church, and she could only imagine that the ignorant country people would judge Jude's gold medallion and highlighted honey hair.

"Good. It's really good." Bea replied, but she didn't offer more.

They would soon be at Arrington's, and Ava sat for the remaining minutes saying nothing, listening to the soft cicada hum of the city. She thought back to a day in fourth grade when she sat at her usual table, eating her peanut butter and honey sandwich, wearing a red-and-green plaid dress with a white collar and white knee socks. She remembered her dress and lunch because that was the day a little girl named Sandra had looked at her pointedly and asked, "Why don't you have a father?" to which Ava replied that he had died.

"You're the only one in class with a dead daddy," Sandra then observed, looking around the table for corroboration. "If there was a bunch of you, you could've all just sat at your own table."

There were wounds everywhere, Ava thought. She could imagine how lonely it must have been for Jude and how much confusion he must have felt when she'd endured plenty just by being a fatherless child living with a slovenly, poor, and erratic mother.

Traffic opened before them, then, and Bea increased her speed once more. A comfortable silence crept between the two girls, and after a few moments, Bea began to sing "Joy to the World" by Three Dog Night, of which she knew all the words. Ava listened to her tuneless voice until they reached Arrington's and also to the passing wind.

Chapter 15

STEVE ARRINGTON HIMSELF was on the showroom floor when Ava entered. He was a slight man with a straight posture, whose hair curled high on top and in back, and who wore slightly elevated soles. Ava found him likable—complimentary only when he could be sincere, generous, and persistent without being pushy. When Ava had first responded to his advertisement, he'd scanned her resume on the spot. Then with a smile as broad as the Nile, he'd told her, "It's time we had a smart girl around here. I hope you won't feel slighted by a short interview that's merely a formality." This job was the first of the two for which the proprietors felt no need to call Harvick and Braun, so maybe there was a god.

"Morning, Mr. Arrington," Ava said that day, flipping her hand up awkwardly before turning to the coffee station opportunistically placed just inside the door.

"Hey, hey, hey, little lady! Say, did you cut your hair?" His voice was bright and pleasant.

"I did! I can't believe you even noticed. I'm not very daring, I'm afraid," she spoke over her shoulder as she ministered to the cup with her usual excess of cream and sugar.

"Well, when you're married as long as I've been, you get trained!" he said with a short laugh. "It looks great. But it did before, too, you know that."

Ava pivoted to face her boss, too-small cup in hand. He stood with his hands in his pockets, feet apart, tipping up and down on his toes. He fairly beamed in his approbation of her.

"Well, you're to be commended." She lifted her coffee in the move of a toast and sipped. Arrington continued to grin.

"What are you doing here on a Saturday, for heaven's sake? All work and no play will make Ava Lou a dull girl."

"Well, I wouldn't call it *all* work. In case you haven't noticed, I played hooky yesterday." One of the things Ava liked about both of her jobs was that as long as she had the books done in a timely way, nobody gave a rat's whisker about when she was there—not Steve nor Jimmy at The Fox and Ale. She needed to be disciplined, but that was easy for her, and part of that was keeping a schedule for herself.

"Yes, I noticed, and so did all the other poor peons around here who count on you to bring in that purty smile. Say—" Arrington kept pace beside her as she began walking toward her office at the back of the showroom—"there was a boy in here looking for you this morning. Good-looking fella, kind of tall, dark hair. I told him you probably wouldn't be here on the weekend, and he said he'd try to get you at home."

"Really?" *Home*? Her wheels turned as she opened her office door. "Did he leave a name?" She knew of only one tall good-looking fellow in all of Corinth, but did Scott even know where she lived? She was pretty sure she'd mentioned she rented the guesthouse behind Bea's, but he didn't know Bea, did he? She knew also that *he* knew she had a second job in the mornings at this dealership. But why would he ever come to this job? And on a Saturday? Or why even look for her at all when he practically ignored her those days at the bar? If he'd wanted to apologize, he could have done that at The Fox. Lastly, Scott was hardly a "boy"; he had to be approaching thirty. But still, Steve had to be almost sixty; he probably called lots of young guys "boys."

"No. But I didn't ask. After I told him I probably wouldn't see you today, he didn't stick around." He patted her shoulder. "Sorry, honey, I figured he was someone you knew. Hope I didn't miss my chance to stop a stalker." He winked at her, hands back in his pockets, hovering near the door.

Ava sank to the worn leather chair, immersed in the sea of banana-yellow walls, and confronted by the knicked and fake-veneered desk that sat opposite the papery-looking air fern that made her sadder than if the space had been void of greenery altogether. She fiddled with some folders and papers.

"Well, me, too, Steve. But you know what they say, negative attention is better than none at all." She turned her palms upward and shrugged her shoulders, smiling, raising her eyebrows.

"Yeah, heh, heh. I guess so. Well, don't stay too long, Miss Ava. It's hot but gorgeous out there. We need to enjoy these glorious summer weekends." He strolled out to the showroom, hands still in his pockets, whistling as he walked toward a couple circling a Crown Victoria. She supposed he didn't mind spending his gorgeous summer Saturdays in the air-conditioned business, as long as he was making sales.

It was mere seconds before Jack Levinson appeared in her doorway. Jack was a salesman—tall, stoop-shouldered, and very thin, with wispy black hair that Ava knew he dyed because of its matte appearance and the graying of almost every other visible hair on his body. He combed one wing far over from the side in the pitiful way insecure balding men do. Ava sometimes abstractedly imagined herself rushing him and pushing it back on his head with both hands and yelling, "Stop it! You're not fooling anyone, and I can barely talk to you! Now leave and don't come back in here until you've combed it normally." But she always tried to listen to him instead with a tight line of expression to her lips that she hoped conveyed a genuine smile of interest.

"Hi, Jack. Happy Saturday."

"Hey, Ava, hey. It's good to see you." He nodded repeatedly, smiling with closed lips, his arms crossed against his chest. Ava noticed his jacket sleeves were too short. "You doin' all right today?"

"I'm great, Jack, how're you? Just have a lot of work to catch up on, but that's cool."

"Yeah. We missed you yesterday. I hope you're not getting tired of us!" He gave a short laugh.

"Oh, heavens no, there's nowhere I'd rather be. The glamour, the money…I'm pretty sure I'll be here until I die." She pulled some ledgers out of the top desk drawer and reached for a pencil from the coffee cup that read "Mr. Right" in bold black letters that Steve had provided as part of her supplies. She always meant to bring a few of her things from home.

"Ha! Well, I hope so! We would sure miss you if you left. Have you got plans later today?" Jack had asked her to do things with him before, even though he was married. The pretense was always as "just friends."

"Oh, yeah, well, I wouldn't even be here, but I'm behind. I'm going to try to catch up a little bit, and then I've got a whole list of things to do." She opened one ledger purposely, then removed the lid from the box where Steve and the front desk clerks put all the paperwork. She cleared a space, then lifted the papers out and began sorting through them, sighing dramatically.

"Oh, good, okay. I was going to take that '75 Mustang out for a test drive in a couple of hours. That restored one. Thought you might want to go. It's a pretty sweet ride… I don't know if you've checked her out, but she might not be on the lot long."

"No, not really. You know me, not much of a car person. But sounds like fun! I wonder if your wife might want to go? You should call her and surprise her—get an ice cream or something—women love that! Is it the yellow one, with the sunroof?" She continued sorting the receipts and bills of sale, a few carbons of recent orders, and copies of customers' financial documentation, glancing from them to the salesman.

"Um, yeah, that's it. Okay, well, another time!" He threw up his hand and walked out into the showroom, where Steve and the couple now stood by a light-blue Ranger. Jack sidled up to them but glanced over his shoulder toward Ava, where she'd moved to close the door behind him. Accidentally meeting her gaze, his face registered surprised pleasure.

Darn it, she thought as she sat back down to her work.

She tried to be nice; she felt she had to be. But even though she couldn't encourage him, she felt terribly sorry for him just the same—wearing his persona of insecurity, ineptitude, need, and loneliness like a mantle, marching cluelessly toward middle and old age.

She couldn't concentrate, but she couldn't leave yet, either. For the first time, she wished her office had some décor, some color, some place to rest her eyes. She had done absolutely nothing to it. There was not even anything on the walls except a "Car of the Month" calendar that saw fit to pair each car with a scantily-clad girl who appeared to be barely pushing eighteen. One had nothing to do with the other, of course, except each resided in most men's fantasies and were usually nowhere within their reach. The August photo featured a red Mustang GT, upon the hood of which was a pig-tailed blonde in cut-off jeans shorts with a red-bandana halter top and fake freckles adorning her cheeks. *Men are perverts,* Ava thought. *Why we bother, I don't even know.*

She stood and removed the calendar, curling it to place in the wastebasket atop the cups and paper wads. Closing the open ledger, she put it and the others back in the drawer, put the receipts and other papers in their assigned box, and then replaced the lid. She'd tell Steve she had a splitting headache that she'd been trying to power through, only to have spontaneously decided it was too much. Not to worry, she'd tell him, she'd catch up the books on Monday. She had to see if Scott had somehow found where she lived, and she had to know why he was looking, even though before now, it had been so clear to her he considered there was nothing at all between them and nothing at all to say.

Chapter 16

THE COTTAGE SAT low, with a narrow front porch and two windows on opposite sides of the faded yolk-colored door. The windows' bottom sills rested about level with a person's hips and were white-rimmed and cross-hatched atop the panes. The small brass knocker that rested against the door was tarnished green, and the rose bushes on either side of the steps were unpruned and chewed by the June bugs who'd called them home for heaven-knew-how-many summers.

It was into this cottage that she walked that Saturday afternoon after she'd reached Bea at the consignment shop, by luck, and after Bea had abandoned her plans and come to pick Ava up. Ava had walked in with her newly trimmed hair and a mildly bilious stomach replacing her fake headache after the shock of seeing that it wasn't Scott's car in the driveway at all; and it was this, about which, she didn't even know how to feel.

He sat on the loveseat, his knees apart and elbows resting on them, leaning forward and toying with one of the pens she kept atop a notepad that lay on an end table. His eyes met hers when she walked through the cottage's door, his eyebrows raised slightly in anticipation of her reaction.

"Eric." She imagined her voice sounded as flat to him as it did to her.

"Hey, baby. Surprise." He rose and hugged her uncertainly, then remained standing and faced her, his hands in the pockets of his jeans. "You cut your hair." It wasn't a question, so she didn't address it. "And you look great, as usual."

"Thanks." She moved to the cane-bottomed chair at the small writing desk and sat. "I have to say I'm surprised you're here."

"Yeah. Well, Chantal told me, you know. Where you went." Eric sat again, too, erect and nervous, gently rubbing his palms a couple of times on his knees.

"I know, she told me." He'd called twice the Saturday after he'd broken their engagement, but she'd refused, through her roommate, to speak with him. In the weeks since Ava had moved, Chantal had said he hadn't called again. "How did you know the directions?"

"You gave them to me, remember? Last summer, when you came and wanted me to join you later."

"And...you saved them?" He didn't answer, just looked at her.

"Okay. And how did you know about the dealership?"

"Your mom. She misses you a lot, by the way."

Ava ignored that. "And you just assumed I'd be around?" He could have called the house—she'd given him Bea's phone number last year as well—but they'd been gone. "Did you call? Did you talk to Toby?"

"I called. Nobody answered. I came here first, then the dealership, then here again. Jeanette mentioned the bar, too, but I figured you had to come home eventually."

"So you just walked in, or did you see Toby?" She'd seen Toby's truck under the shed. Sitting on the narrow little chair and focusing on her breathing, she wondered if Bea, who'd gone into the main house almost wordlessly after they'd seen Eric's car, was watching from one of the house's back windows.

Eric took a deep breath. "Good to see you, too, Ava." And he began looking at the walls while Ava watched him.

Who did he think he was? She said nothing while he looked at the pictures.

These were her rescuers, her salvation, the fillers of her soul. She'd been taping pictures to her walls ever since she was a child with her first camera, and now prints and collages in handmade frames adorned almost every wall of the little house—her only homage to decoration.

The dollar camera Jeanette's parents had sent her for her birthday had not only given her a hobby but led to better cameras which, surprisingly, then gave her a life rope—a release from her existence by shadowing the existences of others. Every photograph offered a way to find a story, a way to explain the world.

The photographs were in all different sizes, some in color and others in black and white. The frames were cobbled-together manifestations of the creative explosions of her brain—white-painted birch limbs, broken tile mosaics, flea market frames wrapped with strips of fabric or covered in miniature shells and stones. She used putty to make a picture border around a frameless mirror and had bordered a collage with peacock feathers. Her creations littered the nail-hole-speckled walls that Louise and Kenneth Mullins had painted a golden cream so many years ago, no doubt with the same ardor and expectation with which they'd painted the house. They were young; they were "making it"; and everything was going to be okay.

Ava loved the overpowering, haphazard, incongruous collections of photos; sometimes, she believed she almost hated what others would call tasteful, or perhaps she was passively rebellious. After she shot her photographs, developed them, and boxed them or hung them on the walls, something in her would mellow. The churning would ebb, and life felt less importunate, more controlled, now that it was recorded and organized. Inevitably though, the calm would pass, and the chaos and life's propensity for disharmony would supervene, bringing her attempts to make sense of life's purpose back to the theoretical drawing board: *How could anything matter much,* she thought, *anyone's life matter at all, when so many lives were competing?*

She would gaze at these prints, at random times and for random reasons, and feel that although she and the other members of her species were "all in this together"—living in those spaces and realms common to all humanity—the journeys were all persistently and ultimately calamitous. The fact that Ava could find little purpose in it and that it would all end in death and nonexistence caused her to perceive life the only way she knew how—a collage as figurative as the photo collages were literal, just random moments of comedy, tragedy, or neutrality, passing immutable but meaningless into eternity. Just random slices of life.

Yet still, she strove toward the capture and control.

She was in charge of the small black box, her hands and eyes and posture working together to reduce each scene, once so active and multidimensional, to flat expanses frozen in time and allowing no untruths. Honesty was a given. Time had been caught, willingly or not, and every captured act, expression, and feeling—implied or imagined—was hers.

Sometimes they caught in her throat. And always, she knew she harbored that secret wish that she would someday be able to understand the world through these. If she looked hard enough and long enough and shut out all the other noise, maybe then, she imagined, she could—at least when she was better at life—explain to her heart how things were.

"You're amazing, Ava." Eric didn't turn around but murmured this low, almost as if to himself. His head was thrust forward to where he was studying a 5" × 7" of an old man, overalls smudged with corn dust, grimy cap bearing the name "Standard" overlaying a torch. He sat on the bench outside Gary's Gas and Auto Repair, his face creased a million ways, his eyes faded but still noticeably blue. They were why Ava had decided to develop him in color.

"I am what I am." Which meant nothing, of course, but what was she supposed to say?

He turned to look at her and again sat on the loveseat. Above his head rose a three-feet-by-two-feet array of black-and-whites, and in his red Izod sport shirt and blue jeans, he looked a little out of place, like a young man sitting in front of a school project and as if he was waiting for his turn at presentation.

"I came because I missed you. And I wanted to talk to you." He'd spoken this to his fingernails but then raised his eyes to meet hers. "Is that okay?"

Ava shrugged, glanced away, then back again, but wordless.

"After we got engaged, it felt like we started growing apart. Like, when we talked, it was sometimes hard to think of things to say. Except for maybe plans about the wedding."

"Huh." She kept her eyes steady. "Well, I'm pretty sure I had things to say, sometimes, other than wedding talk, and then I guess sometimes I didn't. Just like real people." She began picking at a fraying strip of cane from the chair bottom, knowing that was the last thing you should do with something that old. "You know what they say about medical students' relationships." Her voice sounded cold and sarcastic.

"No, what?" He looked at her intently, but she had no idea what anybody said, so she had to wing it.

"That they're not easy, I guess."

"Right." He sat hunched forward a little, hands dangling between his legs, looking at her.

"Why are you here, Eric? Didn't you say everything you had to say back in Atlanta?"

He shook his head. "I'm not sure. I felt bad. I'm not sure I have said everything I wanted to say. Have you?" He waited a few seconds for the response that didn't come, then stood and passed the bedroom entranceway to peer at the prints scattered across its wall.

Several shell-covered frames contained small prints arranged in a butterfly-shaped collection—a child's face in profile, wearing a knitted cap and looking down at her palm; a close-up of a branch, with ever-out-sprigging, veined and sun-splashed leaves; a woman's face staring intently at the camera but half-covered with a shield of blonde hair; and then a kitten's face, half-shadowed, half-sunlit, looking upward and sideways…at what? Eric's gaze stopped on a glistening surface of water droplets. "What's this?" he asked, again not bothering to turn around.

Ava's eyes found the direction of his stare. "Skin," she answered. "On the back of a child's calf, fallen asleep on a raft by a pool, on her tummy, before she even got dry." She got up to look at the picture. "Look how smooth. How utterly smooth and perfect. Now, look at this one." She turned to a collage over the heater, framed in pine bark and moss, and pointed to a woman's face, looking over a hundred years old. The fissures went everywhere—transverse, vertical, angled toward and away from her mouth like rivulets of water coursing through dirt and strong, repeating hourglass patterns emanating from the center of her brow. Even her nose, bulbous and elongated, so surely changed since her youth, was crisscrossed with the ravages of time. "She's dead now, you know." She took her place back on the chair.

"I never completely understood why you take these." Eric turned. "I mean, I know you must enjoy it a *lot,* but why?"

Her first inclination was to deflect him. It would sound stupid to say out loud that she thought they were helping her figure out how things were, *why* they were the way they were, helping her answer all the questions she had about how people related to each other and to the world, and where God—if He were real—may be in it all. But when she spoke, it was the most honest thought to come to her mind without yards of explanation in front of it.

"I'm not sure. I feel like I have to. Everything's out there, for just a fraction of a second… And I have to capture it…or who will?"

He stood there a moment, looking at his shoes before he brought his eyes back up to hers. "Will you lie with me, Ava?" And without waiting for an answer, he went into the tiny bedroom that rested just behind the wall of the cottage's front porch, where she heard the old bedsprings creak softly, then stop. She followed him, quiet as a cat.

He was lying on his back, hands on his stomach, one hand holding the wrist of the other, fingers folded under. Eyes closed, head straight and slightly back and looking as if he were practicing for his final respite, there was no frivolity about his mouth. She eased her body straight beside his, and again the old bed made gentle protest, though even less than when he'd laid his slender runner's form upon it.

"I know I've hurt you." She imagined, even without looking, that his eyes were still closed—his posture was immobile as death. "I don't know what's wrong with a lot of us, and I mean us guys, because ever since I met you, I thought you would be enough for me." He paused, and she did nothing to ease the silence.

One minute, then two—and although it felt like a lifetime, she knew it wasn't more because she was watching the electric clock on the dresser, her head turned slightly from his. This watching she did on purpose: she did it to keep from speaking. *Why?* she wanted to yell. *Why did you think you could do anything close to what you did and have it not matter?*

He removed his glasses and turned on his side to face her, his eyes open and searching hers. "Ava"—he took a deep breath—"the truth is, I don't know what I'm doing." He paused. "Sometimes we'd talk, and I'd feel we weren't connecting. Sometimes I worried we were too different. You don't give two flips about medicine, and I live for it—"

"And?" She felt herself getting angry. "You don't give two flips about accounting. You never even tried to understand what I did all day—"

"Exactly! And…I just felt like we were growing apart."

"Whatever, Eric." She lay rigid, staring at the ceiling, but she felt the stirring of guilt in her gut because she knew what he meant. She remembered when he proposed—how he'd admitted he'd prefer to start by living together but knew she'd never agree to that. He talked about how hard it would be to save for a house with his debt and while he was still becoming a doctor. During the serious discussions of their dating life, they'd disagreed about where to live: He'd wanted a condo, while she'd wanted a large home in suburbia. And he'd confessed he never wanted more than one child. The conversations had meandered on, eventually floating out into nothingness, and she must have convinced herself they would ultimately agree somehow. It was after the proposal she remembered that growing unease had begun. Feelings in her stomach that defied classification as butterflies of anticipation for the wedding were settling hard and sour as fear, instead.

But she'd never retracted her "yes." She'd said yes because she had carefully and methodically chosen Eric over time. She had weighed his degree intentions (medicine, with a specialty in cardiology), his family heritage (Scotts-English, with many bankers and financiers), his posture, and the tenor of his voice. She'd chosen him because he was tall and serious, smart and determined. There were so many logical reasons she chose him, and these were the foundations on which she'd laid her life's plans.

And then...if she were honest...if she looked deep, deep in her heart...she knew it was because he had selected her. The brilliant, determined, physically acceptable American boy had chosen her—a fantastically un-choice specimen.

Eric had risen on one elbow to face her. She lay supine, still rigid, clutching her waist with both arms.

"Ava, I need to tell you something..." And then she knew. Just like in the restaurant, nothing more needed to be said, but it was, and nothing could make it unsaid again. "I had sex with a girl when we were engaged."

The words from his mouth entered her ears and coagulated. It was only a couple of feet from the bed to the dresser, but she rose and stood against the dresser, at the bed's far end; she crossed her arms. Eric remained propped on his elbow to face her. "I'm sorry. I'm not trying to hurt you. I just want you to understand."

The room was hot, the air too stale to breathe. Ava's heart beat wildly, and although this had never once occurred to her, it now felt old and known.

"I barely know her. I haven't even seen her again, except... around. I mean, we don't talk. I don't even know why I did it, but I did. And it was wrong." He paused. If he were waiting for her to speak, he waited in vain.

"It started out, we were just studying. But it went further. It was like I just was on autopilot, you know? I think it was exams, and I'd had a couple of beers, but—"

"Spare me, Eric." Her breathing was heavy but controlled.

"I'm sorry. I'm not trying to hurt you."

"You said that. You want me to understand. So you're saying all the right things that you think you need to say, to get me to understand, even though no words exist that will ever make that happen." She looked at him hard, uncrossing her arms to hold onto the dresser.

"Well, I guess I'm trying to, but you're not giving me much credit here. I'm confessing to you. I just need to be honest."

"Why? Why, Eric? You already broke up with me! Is this how you get your jollies? 'Let's track the poor reject down and twist the knife'? This is how you, oh, I don't know, 'do the right thing,' absolve your conscience by making me want to blow my brains out?" She was on overload then and couldn't stop.

"Why were you drinking with a girl, anyway, when you're supposed to be studying? You don't study with drinks, you know? Alcohol? And how convenient your study partner was cute! Why would you invite her to 'study' in your room? You never invited any ugly girls to your room, did you, Eric? And I bet she was *so* needy. In medical school, just as smart as you but just needing so much *extra* help. You probably had to sit *really* close to her, too, right? And I bet the top she wore to study in was just oh-too-easy to look down."

She stopped herself; she could have gone on, but there was no point. He was just a guy—a boy, really, or a man, or just a hybrid man-child; but it didn't matter what society called him because age didn't change that garbage. He'd only fallen for what they all fall for, succumbing to the balm of a woman after the combination of school pressure, fatigue, and alcohol had proved too much for his mettle.

She stood still and held herself again with both arms. Her stare was ripe with malice. "You don't joke much, do you, sweetie?"

He'd risen, sitting against the headboard during her diatribe, and he sat searching her face, his expression slack and bewildered as her question caught him off-guard. "I don't know, Ava. What's that supposed to mean?"

She put her face in her hands and smoothed her eyebrows with her fingertips a couple of times with her eyes closed, then raised them with a world-weary look in his direction. "I'm just glad this ship has sailed, that's all."

And just like that, she lost him, again, but forever—or, one might have more accurately spun it, that she gave him away—and let him pass through her, body and soul—a live sacrifice for her karma.

Chapter 17

THE REST OF August passed uneventfully. Bea and her teaching partner, Karen Potts—raising her very young children—both reportedly loved their two-and-a-half-day workweek, and since their shared class of kindergarteners had achieved on grade level, administration had approved the requested job-share for the upcoming year.

Toby pulled in his harvest and was rarely seen except at the dinner table; every spare minute he didn't work on his farm and animal husbandry, he spent working at his daddy's on their big-money crops. They harvested the corn and tobacco from mid-to-late summer, cotton in late September, and soybeans late in the fall.

Time's passage was marked as much by Sunday midday dinners at the old Mullins house as by the turning of the seasons. Most Sundays included the other Mullins girls with their husbands and children: Susan and Clem with Brent and Jesse and Laura and Greg with Kelly and Alex. Brent and Kelly were ten, and Jesse and Alex both eight—kind of like the Bobbsey Twins in the old children's series but cousins instead of siblings.

While Brent, Jesse, and Kelly sat at the kids' table in the breakfast room, Alex—the shy and chubby Alex—would take his place to sit at the main table beside Ava and talk with her about his collections of frogs, tadpoles, and turtles, and the occasional wounded bird or errant dragonfly. The insects, he insisted, he only kept for a day—for "research"—for, as he told her with the solemnity of a minister, "Wild things are always happier in the wild."

The other children, also, would eat and run the property like untamed Indians, but Alex, an old soul, would join the proclivities of the adults—the sitting, the small talk, and if truth be known, the company of Ava.

The Sunday dinner before Labor Day hosted the usual suspects.

"I'm telling you, Ava. You need to bring out your eyes." Laura looked around the table for corroboration.

"My eyes are already out. Been out my whole life. See?" She made wide, crazy eyes and flashed them about, making Alex giggle.

Laura pretended not to notice. "Makeup can do so much these days. My nose looked so much slenderer after my makeover. I don't *ever* want to go without contouring powder again."

"Do you have it on now?" Susan held a bite of mashed potatoes to her mouth but paused to peer at her younger sister.

"Well…yes! And I think it looks—"

"I think it looks the same." Susan took the bite and continued before she'd finished chewing. "I mean, I'm not trying to be mean, but I totally can't tell."

Laura looked mildly annoyed but replaced the expression with her cosmetic seller's smile. "It shouldn't be obvious, Susan. But I think if you saw a picture of me barefaced and then one with the contouring, you'd think my nose looked slimmer."

"Why would you want your nose to look slimmer?" Clara sounded genuinely puzzled.

Laura let out the tiniest puff of air in disgust. "To be more attractive!"

"Well. You know, back in my time, you were lucky to bathe every other day and have a little bacon grease to rub on the callouses of your feet at night. We had no way or time to worry about putting some brown powder on our noses."

"I think it's great, Laura. I know a mom of one of the kids who uses Mary Kay, and the only reason I even know is because I told her I liked her lipstick one day. She always looks great."

The defensiveness on Laura's face softened.

"Thanks, Bea. I was just saying, Ava, if you don't mind sitting for a makeover—" But Ava was already shaking her head.

"I don't know, Lar… I don't like to mess with that stuff. I've never learned how to put it on very well."

"I'll teach you! I'm a trained consultant! I did Susan, and I could show you some pictures of some friends I did."

Ava hated how hopeful she looked. Were they hurting for money? She knew after the makeover Laura would try to sell her a lot of products she'd probably rarely wear.

"I still have a stash I bought for the wedding..."

"I'll treat you, Ava. You and Bea. Y'all can go together." Susan sold real estate all over Corinth, Hereford, and even into Olympus. She gestured with her fork at both of them, then went back to cutting her steak.

"That's sweet. Really." Ava met Bea's eyes—she was intent on her ear of corn—and they both began to giggle a little. Bea's wedding day was perhaps the only day *she* had ever worn makeup, either. "We'll think about it."

"Oh, for heaven's sake!" Laura, exasperated, looked from one to the other. "You'd think I was asking you girls to shave your heads!"

Ava was still giggling as she passed a bowl of butterbeans to Alex, but Laura intercepted it and dashed a very modest amount onto her youngest child's plate.

Ava, glancing at Alex, saw his embarrassment. Clara, too, had noticed.

"For Pete's sake, Laura," she chided. "They're beans."

Laura looked at Clara with exaggerated offense. "I know what they are, Gram. They're full of carbohydrates." Alex ate a mincing bite of beans from his fork tip as if afraid of offending his mother further. Clara looked away in disgust.

"I read good carbohydrates are way different from bad ones, Lar," Susan chimed in. "I'd be really careful about limiting stuff like beans at his age."

Before anyone else could speak, Alex had put down his fork and looked at his hands in his lap. "May I be excused?" he asked of no one in particular.

"No, you may—" Laura began, but Clara interjected with authority.

"Yes, son, go ahead. Go look at Toby's new ducks, he's got, what, now, Tobes, sixteen?"

Toby nodded, mouth full, glancing at Clara, then Alex.

"Thereabouts. Fifteen, maybe. One duckling passed away last night."

Pain overtook Alex's face.

"C'mon, mister." Ava put her napkin to the side of her plate and rose. "I know where Toby keeps the mash." Alex rose, pushed under his chair, and followed her.

"Not too much, Aves!" Toby said as she strode toward the back porch, holding the screened door for Alex.

Alex smiled at Toby as he passed him. "Don't worry, Uncle Toby." He patted the large man's shoulder. "I won't let her go crazy."

It was a hundred yards to the duck pen, a wire enclosure between the house and fields. Ava filled two tin cans with ground corn and feed pellets from the bin inside the ducks' sleeping quarters and handed one to the boy before taking a seat on an overturned fifty-gallon bucket.

Alex sprinkled a little on the ground amidst the swirling squawking ducklings, exclaiming with delight at their enthusiasm and trying to pet various ones before they waddled away. After a few minutes, he perched beside Ava on another overturned bucket, his dark-brown hair straight and shining in the sun. They spoke of the ducklings and their colors, laughed at their ineptitude as they fell over each other in attempts at the mash, and, after a few moments, fell silent.

Then, he asked, "Ava? Were you ever fat when you were a little girl?" His eyes were the color of cane syrup, holding at bay the beginnings of the questions of the universe.

"Me? Gosh, no. Skinny. Skinnier than a snake and hated every minute of it."

"Really? That's funny. I have a real skinny friend. But I don't think she hates it."

"Well, boy, I sure did. Knobby knees, pointy elbows…picked last for a sixth-grade softball team one day. Still remember how that felt."

Alex was sifting a small puddle of mash through his fingers while the ducklings scrambled below his feet to claim it. "I don't get picked, either."

"Right. You want to know something, though? Something nobody told me that I wished they had?" She turned and leaned close to the boy's soft face. "It doesn't really matter that much." She began to pluck fingerfuls of mash from her can and fling it across the dirt.

The kid turned his face upward to hers, eyes squinting. "Why not?"

"I don't know. It just doesn't. One day you're going to get to spend almost all your time doing mostly what you want to do. All the games they make you play in grammar school, and the kids you knew back then, won't even matter. For example, you're going to be a forest ranger."

"A biologist."

"Oh. I thought it was a forest ranger."

"It was. I changed it last year."

"Okay, that's cool. See, I like math. I can look at how businesses spend and earn money, make sure they're putting it in all the right places, and earn a living. And I love to take pictures, as you know. So that's what I do. And I don't ever play softball because I don't have to."

He was quiet while he considered her words. "But Miss Pauley says I have to."

"Yeah, maybe now you do because schools want kids to have to try new things. But one day you won't have to. And one day, your mom won't be there to tell you everything to eat and not eat, either, even though she only does it now because she loves you and wants you healthy and thinks it's best."

"I guess. I guess your mom did that stuff too?"

"Oh, sure. Moms are the worst."

He looked up at her and grinned, even though he was squinting because of the falling sun, while Ava thought back to her childhood with its persistent overlay of loneliness.

When she'd been Alex's age—eight or so, after her daddy died and she and Jeannette had been on their own for a while—she'd felt engulfed by a sense of otherness, different, she imagined, from all the other children in the world. She would lie in her bed, curled on her side like a baby, putting her head under her scratchy polyester blanket and trying to feel safe.

Jeanette, who had taken to wandering the house clutching an increasingly-present plastic tumbler, becoming more reticent, more distant, and who would sometimes sit in the living room playing heart-wrenching songs by Patsy Cline or Tammy Wynette, forgot to tell Ava they were going to be okay; forgot to remind Ava that she, Jeanette, wouldn't die soon, as well.

As she entered junior high, Ava would dream of a day when she would not be there in the cluttered little house with its stacks of unread newspapers and stinking ashtrays; its piles of clothes in every corner of Jeanette's room; the horrible, broken plastic corner-étagère and fake-wood-veneered end tables—everything imitation and embarrassing, everything filling the spaces behind Ava's eyes every night as she consciously tried to sleep. She was the only twelve-year-old insomniac she knew.

Her world then, as well as she'd been able to understand it, was missing the requisite proper people but was simultaneously full of meaningless things—a tiny cavern of debris that had outlived or lost its purpose, things rotting or fossilizing in her presence. Ava imagined if strangers saw their squalor, they would wonder at the family who lived like that. They would never know it was barely a family at all but rather, a collection of two humans related only by blood but not joined in spirit, tethered by fate and need. Jeanette was stagnant and broken as her house, and Ava sullied and stunted by association, a fearfully-mannered, overly polite child who spent an inappropriate amount of her girlhood time trying to be brave, hoping against hope she could still turn out good.

Ava dumped the remainder of her can's contents and managed a smile for the boy.

"You hang in there, buddy." She rose and brushed the seat of her jeans. "Your life is gonna be *choice*. Especially if your old Aunt Ava has anything to say about it."

Chapter 18

ON LABOR DAY morning, Jimmy mentioned Scott had once worked at The Fox and Ale.

Everyone was getting ready for the crowd that would predictably be larger than usual: those who'd start the trickle at ten to begin their day of drinking; the surge in the late afternoon of the mildly drunk who'd spent the day on the river; and the ones who'd started partying on Sunday and were committed to keeping it going through Monday night.

Corrine had spent the morning hanging red, white, and blue crepe paper streamers across the ceiling and tying bouquets of red, white, and blue balloons to various items; and the place looked valiant and festive. Jimmy and Kat were stocking. The bar owner lifted assorted liquors to the cheerleader-gone-rogue, who alternately crouched and stood atop the counter, placing them on the shelves lining the tall mirrored wall behind her.

Ava, who had the day off from Arrington's, was also not going to punch the clock at The Fox. She sat at the bar looking through *Things You Need,* a small advertising paper of businesses, events, for-sale items, and personals that she'd lifted from the rack by the front door; and Corrine, having finished her preposterous festooning of the place, now sat two chairs away, thumbing through her own choice from the publication rack, an issue of *Horse & Rider*.

"He worked here a couple of years, I guess…but, like, four years ago," Jimmy said to Ava. "And he used to date one of the other waitresses…a redhead… Remember her, babe? Lorraine?" He looked down the bar to his wife.

Without waiting for a response, he said, "Lorraine, she was a looker," this time addressing Ava. "Right, Cory?" He looked again to his wife even as he handed up a bottle of Courvoisier to Kat.

Corrine was still studying her magazine as she said, "Yes, she was. They were quite the pair." Then she flipped the pages closed and propped her arms on the bar, folded as a guy would do. "Scott had already worked here about two years, but when they broke up, Lorraine quit, then Scott quit a week later. But he felt ready to go full-time with the insurance business by then, I think."

Corrine looked extra pretty that day—her hair feathered back as perfectly as Farrah Fawcett's, and she wore tight tan riding pants and a skinny white tank top under a riding jacket, her lips pink and icy-looking. Just last week, when Ava had emerged from the back through the swinging doors, Jimmy had been encircling his wife from behind as she'd been keying out the register before they opened; he'd been murmuring and smiling into her hair against her neck until she swatted him away but laughing as she did so. *What is that like,* Ava wondered, *to have desire for someone you'd been married to for years? Didn't familiarity kill that sort of thing?*

Corrine pushed her magazine away and leaned conspiratorially across the bar toward Ava's seat. "Lorraine was gorgeous, Aves, but she was trouble. She was like a wild horse. Jimmy can tell you." She flitted her eyes briefly to Jimmy for corroboration. "She was a dancer, and she rode a bike. Like a motorcycle, I mean. She was very erratic, that one," she said, rolling her eyes. She sat back and fiddled with the corner of her magazine but kept her little smile as she looked back to Ava's face.

Kathy hopped off the counter and spoke to Ava, "This was before my time." She had on purple lip gloss, tight purple jeans, and a black tank. She'd tucked a miniature paper flag into each of her back pockets.

By now, Jimmy was shoving beer in the ice from a case he'd also brought up from the back. "Yeah, well, you're lucky, Kat, if you ask me. Lorraine was stockyard crazy." He laughed and shook his head as if he were remembering stories. "She came in here once, remember that, babe, when she called him out?" He'd paused and turned to Corrine, laughing. "She called him all *kinds* of names, and—"

"Oh hush, Jimmy, don't tell other people's garbage," Corrine said, opening her magazine again and not bothering to look up.

Jimmy still looked at his wife, smirking. "What, what's the problem?" he asked. "She was literally crazy if you ask me."

"Yeah, but you needn't gossip about it. Honestly, you're worse than a woman. She just loved him, that's all. Everybody acts a little crazy when they love someone and it's not going well."

Ava glanced away. So…she'd loved him. A redhead with a cool name and a spirit that sounded like Scarlet O'Hara's had *loved* him, but it hadn't gone "well."

Here was yet another exemplar to whom Ava could feel inferior—in addition to the dagger-eyed spiky-haired girl; the demure, classically beautiful, and undoubtedly sweet-natured Lucy; and several others Ava had witnessed through the months. But this one was a *vixen*—a she-devil—with (Ava imagined) thick coppery tresses, a hair-trigger temper and *passion*. She recognized the hollow in her stomach as jealousy.

Still looking at her magazine, gazing from page to page, Corrine spoke again, "I'm surprised he hasn't tried to hit you up, Ava."

Ava felt the hollow space deepen. "For what? Insurance?"

Corrine glanced up, first at Jimmy, then Ava; her eyes glistened with mischief. "You know for what. For romance."

Ava looked at her. "Um, no. Not once. He barely speaks."

Corrine studied her. "That's surprising. Well, somebody's gonna scoop you up." She casually turned some pages.

"Scott's strange." This was from Kathy. "I told you, Ava, nobody knows much of his story." She'd begun pulling stir straws from a box for the dispenser.

"Cory does. Don't you, babe?" Jimmy looked at Corrine with a half-smile, and Corrine looked up at Jimmy.

"Sure do." Then, turning to Ava as if on cue, she said, "His daddy has the car dealership, of course, which you know, and the old man kind of got him into it when he was young, after college. Scott worked with him a couple of years there. I don't think he could stand it very much, though."

"Is his family here? In Corinth?" She *had* already learned that his daddy owned Divine Chevrolet, from Kathy, of course, and after realizing weeks ago she was crushing on him hard, had half-wished that that was where she'd gotten her first job, even though now it sounded as if he never went around it, anyway.

"Just beyond, out in Olympus, you know, the froufrou part. One dealership's there. It's called Divine North, but the one where Scott worked is here in Corinth. I think that's why he moved here after college. Anyway, when he realized he didn't want any part of his daddy's business, he started bartending for us and managing nights about six years ago…and started selling insurance too."

"What he does now."

"Right. Does pretty well with it, too, by all accounts."

"What did he want to do? I mean, what was his major, do you know?"

Corrine smiled and said with mock seriousness, "English and Business—a double, supposedly."

"So…I guess he *wanted* to sell insurance…?"

"I don't know. I guess so…but yeah, anyway, he was working here and building a clientele for a couple of years, then left us after the whole Lorraine thing and went full-time. Like I said, I think he's good at it. He used to live in a condo over there off Lee Street, but after he quit here, he sold it and moved into our cabin, out in Tarryton. Did you know that? Keeps our horses for us, so…so, yeah, all that was like, four years ago."

Ava just stared at her for a moment.

"What? He never told you? Might be close to where you are, but who knows. Tarryton's bigger than it looks."

"No, I told you. Scott doesn't talk to me much."

"Yeah, well, he's moody. But he keeps the horses and grounds up, and he goes up with us sometimes to Virginia. Goes on the hunts with us… He loves to ride."

"That's crazy." Ava had no idea Scott lived in a house owned by her bosses.

"You should let him take you out, Ava," Corrine spoke as if to her magazine. "Spend some of his bounty on you."

What was her game? Ava wondered. She'd already said they barely spoke, twice… Surely, Corrine didn't know about the kiss?

"Well, insurance can be pretty lucrative. Back at Harvick and Braun, we managed clients worth millions and millions." She hoped she didn't sound braggadocios.

"Right. Well, he always seems to have plenty."

There was a lull, then Ava said, "I wonder why he'd move from a condo in Corinth to your cabin in Tarryton, though, if he had a job where he was always meeting with people. You'd think he'd want to be in the hub."

By that point of the conversation, Jimmy had finished with the beer. Polishing the bar in front of the women, he said, "He likes to ride, and he don't like people as much as you might think. But other than that, I don't know. You oughta ask him. He'll probably tell a pretty girl anything she wants to know." He winked at his wife.

"Oh, that's okay." Ava gave a little laugh. "I think I'll mind my beeswax."

Corrine looked at her. The smile still hovered on her lips.

"Really, little missy? You afraid to talk to him because he's pretty? Although I get it. Plus, his name—"

"What—Scott?" Ava gave a little laugh.

"No. Divine. Scott lucked out if you ask me. He could probably get a girl to marry him just for his killer last name." She laughed, stood, and, hiking her purse onto her shoulder, pushed her stool under the bar. Ava knew she'd made plans to avoid the holiday's drunks and go riding. "A pretty face and named Scott Divine… funny, smart, family has money—"

"Aw, leave her alone, Cory. She's not trying to start up any conversations with guys right now." They all knew at least the skeleton of her story as the jilted fiancée. Jimmy shot Ava a supportive look. "Corrine likes Scott. She likes to mention how good-looking he is in my presence about once a month just to keep me on my toes." He leaned over the cooler and kissed Corrine, who was leaning over the bar, goodbye. Then he grabbed one forearm with his other hand, flexed, and twisted his hips in a body-builder pose. "As if I should worry, ya know?" His voice sounded strangled from the hard sucking in of his stomach.

Chapter 19

THE FOX AND Ale wasn't packed because it was Thursday. Bea had switched her workday with Mrs. Potts. She'd worked last Monday to have this Friday off so she could stay out later to celebrate her birthday.

"You could have picked anywhere, you know." Ava surveyed the room. "You can ask for all kinds of royal treatment on your birthday."

"Yeah, but I want to meet your friends." Bea stood behind her while Ava looked for a table.

She saw some of the usual suspects, looking, looking away, and then looking again, with no human coda for manners. And then she saw Scott, who sat in a booth along the front wall with two women and another man (all of whom she'd never seen before), who looked at her and didn't bother to look away once, who drank his drink and set it down and continued still to watch her for almost a full minute, who knew he was making her uncomfortable but smilingly did it anyway.

She found a booth toward the right, in the corner closest to the lounge, and nudged her friend into one side so she could face the area where Scott sat. Gwen, one of the night servers on duty, was talking to a group at one of the center tables; but as Ava caught her eye, the waitress nodded in her direction. Gwen was probably thirty or beyond and had black curly hair so high on top and puffy at the sides that she looked like Eddie Van Halen. She wore a skinny gold belt with her jeans and a black off-the-shoulder top with no bra, though Ava believed she could've used one.

Ava had never mentioned Scott to Bea.

In moments, Gwen had slapped down a couple of napkins and a bowl of pretzels in front of them. "Hey, chicks!" She smiled at Bea.

"Hey, hey, Gwennie, this is Bea. My homegirl. My old roomie from Yancey and now my landlord. She's a beast."

Bea grinned at Gwen, wiggling her fingers from shoulder level in greeting. "You have been sufficiently warned."

"Ha! Well, you look harmless to me." Gwen held her pad and pencil poised. "I know this one's poison"—she gestured with the pad toward Ava—"but what can I get for you?"

"I am just as easy as her. Coke is good." Bea reached into the pretzel bowl to her left and began munching.

"As she," Ava corrected, "I'm just as easy as *she*." She rested both arms on the table and sighed. "I can't take you anywhere."

"And yet you keep asking. Begging, in fact. Here, I'll get the tape, it's in my purse, somewhere…" Bea began rummaging in the shoulder bag at her hip until Ava flung a pretzel at her face.

"Stop it, you're an idiot."

"So Aves says it's your birthday? The big two-three?" Gwen put up two fingers, then three, like she was calling a game score.

"Yeah. And since nothing infamous probably ever happened on September ninth, we have to make it happen tonight."

"Hey, show me, don't tell me. Let me go get your drinks. And what? Burgers, nachos…?"

After they gave their order, Gwen whirled away, stopping long enough to scoop up empty bottles and glasses as she worked her way back to the bar, her loud voice and New York accent jabbing the air above Tom Petty and the Heartbreakers and the blended Southern voices of the crowd.

Ava was flipping through the jukebox menu when he appeared at her right.

"Hi, Ava," then turning, "I'm Scott," and he held out his hand to Bea. Ava got the faintest whiff of Grey Flannel.

"Hi. Bea. Ava's old roommate."

"I've heard." He turned to Ava, smiling. "Cory told me. Said you were coming in tonight to celebrate this one's birthday."

"Caught me. She wants to see where I make my fortune, so—ta-da!" Ava gestured with a broad sweep of her hand.

"It's true." Scott nodded to Bea, then took a long swallow from his bottle. "Also, at my dad's competition, of course. And not even sorry about it." He gave a killer smile, radiant, as he raked his hand through a wave of his dark hair. When he pushed it back, Ava watched his arm, just a forearm, but beautiful, tan, and sinewy. His white shirt sleeves were cuffed and rolled, and he wore faded jeans with loafers. His belt, she could tell, was expensive.

Bea scooted over in her seat. "Here…sit with us if you like."

"Thanks. I have a booth over there." Scott gestured in the direction of his friends, who were standing and gathering their wraps and jackets. "Why don't you guys join me? No use staying stuck here in the corner."

Ava looked and caught the eye of the girl beside whom Scott had been sitting. She had fried dirty-blonde hair, a low-cut red shirt with ruffles down the front, a short black skirt, black fishnet hose, and black boots. When their eyes met, she didn't turn away fast enough, and Ava realized that, like Ava herself, the girl probably had no idea what was going on.

"Your friends are leaving? But you're staying?" Ava looked at Scott while Bea continued to busy herself with the pretzels. "Isn't that your date?" She nodded toward the girl as she exited the door the other guy from Scott's group held for her. The second girl followed, who also looked sideways to steal another glance at Ava and Bea.

"Nope," Scott answered, appearing neither nervous nor apologetic. "Only a friend of a friend."

Gwen came over with their Cokes. She must have popped into the back for her customary two-drags of cigarette, for, though the place was smoky as usual, she brought with her a fresh draft of tobacco. "How are you doing, baby?" she asked brightly, addressing Scott. "You need another drink?"

"Yes, please." Scott fished a fifty from his front pocket, placing it on the tray she held in her hand. "Add them to my tab, Gwennie. They're going to join me back at my table." Without waiting for a response, Scott stepped back, laid his hand on Ava's shoulder, and gestured with the other one. "Ladies."

Bea glanced at Ava and shrugged, rising. She grabbed her denim jacket and began walking toward the empty booth, Ava following.

"That's very nice of you," Ava offered as she stepped past him, following her friend. "You must have heard the rate of my salary."

She had to raise her voice a little to be heard over the raspy cries of Rod Stewart.

"No. But it wouldn't matter." Scott put his fingertips gently in the small of her back, guiding her to where Bea was already settling. She could feel the pressure of his fingers through her blouse.

Bea had no sooner taken her place than she rose again. "I already have to go to the bathroom. Save my seat." Sliding out of the booth, she turned to the side toward the game room, where a "Restrooms" sign overhung its entranceway. Scott sat opposite Ava.

"You cut your hair." He took a sip of his drink.

"You're a genius, detective. Except a real genius would've noticed it before this."

"Who says I didn't?" He had leaned back in the booth but never shifted his eyes from hers.

"Because a gentleman would've mentioned it."

"Well. Perhaps I'm not a gentleman." That smile that danced just *around* his lips…

"Okay, touché. Let me know when it's time to critique your looks."

"Don't get mad. It's beautiful. But it was perfect how it was."

She averted her eyes because his comment felt like a criticism, and that was stupid because what did she care? Someone had played The Pretenders' song "Back on the Chain Gang," on the juke, and Ava tried to focus on the words.

"I want to apologize to you for the day I kissed you." Ava felt her nerves go taut. Her eyes found his again. "Maybe you weren't expecting me to follow with that."

She wanted his face on film. "Well, actually, no, I wasn't." She took a sip of the Coke she'd brought with her to the table. "But you want to hear something funny? They said some guy had stopped by my work at Steve's one day, and the only person I could imagine it being was you. Coming to apologize on neutral turf."

"Really? Huh. Did you ever find out who it was?"

"Ha! Yeah. My ex. He just came to do a little knife-twisting." The comment hung between them.

Then, he asked, "So. What does Ava want? If it's not the hateful boyfriend and the big-status job in Atlanta."

"What do you know about my big-status job? What do *you* want?" She looked toward the game room, after Bea.

"You're not going to answer me." Scott looked into his glass, ran his thumb down its sweaty side, and darted his eyes around the bar before bringing them back to her.

"Because I don't know what to say." Ava looked into her own drink before looking again at him. "Because I am adrift. I'm saving money. I'm trying to get back to a real city, somewhere, into a place of my own." She looked away, but she could feel Scott's gaze pulling her back to his eyes. "I'm assuming you've guessed my current status was not my life's ambition, or you wouldn't have asked."

"No. But you could do worse. What do you want to do? And why aren't you doing it?"

"I am. I mean, I will. I just need to make some money and think for a bit." Ava smiled. She knew she sounded defensive. "I can't believe you don't think The Fox and Ale and Arrington's aren't worthy of all my passion."

"No, I don't. I think they're way beneath you." His expression was deadly serious.

Bea emerged from the game room and pushed in beside Ava just as Gwen brought nachos and plates. They ate in an easy manner, making small talk and small jokes as various other patrons stopped to say hi to either Scott or Ava and to be introduced to her friend.

Bea finished first, wiped her hands, and began digging in her purse. "My kingdom for some Chapstick."

Along with a collection of other items she placed upon the table was a miniature spiral notebook, opened to the tiniest of garden scenes, complete with penciled elves and fairies.

Scott picked it up and began to glance through it. It was full of detailed tableaus. He raised his eyes to Ava.

"She does that. When she's bored."

"Most excellent." He turned it over in his hand. "Do you ever draw at home? Or to sell?"

Bea didn't look up, still pawing. "Sometimes. Not to sell. I make pottery, though. I sell that."

Scott held up the notebook. "What do you do with these?"

Finding the tube of balm, she began running it over her lips. "Nothing. But you can buy it if you want. A thousand dollars. Or a quarter for the payphone."

Scott fished a quarter out of his pocket and laid it on the table in front of her. "Why don't you sell them? Put them on quality paper, add color?" He raised his eyebrows in Bea's direction, who shrugged.

"I have a bit going on as it is." She finished applying her Chapstick, tossed it back in her purse, and picked up the coin. "But thanks for the quarter. And my husband thanks you. I'll give it back when I break one of these hundreds."

Scott looked at Ava, then at Bea. "You're married?" he asked.

"Yep. To the luckiest man in the world. Thanks again." She tipped the quarter to him, scooting again from the booth.

"*If* she does say so herself," Ava added. "But he is, and he knows it. He's at a tractor convention with his daddy, so now she's going to call him and let him whine to her about how lonely he is and how he can't wait to take her out tomorrow night. Blah, blah, blah. It's sickening."

"I see." Scott looked at Ava. "And you're not jealous at all."

"Me? Of course. I think we've already established I am not living the life of my dreams."

Scott waved to Gwen and pointed to his glass. She tipped her pencil to him in acknowledgment, and he turned back to Ava. "Do you miss him? Mr. Wonderful?"

She was irritated. "Why do you call him that? I never called him Mr. Wonderful. Why do you have to be sarcastic?"

Scott shrugged, unfazed.

Ava looked into the game room where Bea stood propped against its wall by the phone, one ear against the receiver and a finger pressing her other ear against the sounds of The Police. Her face looked as if she were talking to a long-lost friend.

"You know what's funny? I don't miss him as much as I thought I would. It took two days for me and Bea, and even my roommate back in Atlanta, to cancel all the wedding arrangements, but after that? And after he came to find me at the house?" She pooched out her bottom lip, shaking her head. "Not really. I miss the idea of him. And the life I thought we'd have."

He sat, this very handsome guy, just sat there, steady as rain.

He had leaned back against the booth with his fingers holding his glass and was watching her. His eyes were blue crystalline agates. His lashes were black against his cheeks as he glanced down, and the bar lights made his hair look almost black as well, instead of the dark, hickory nut brown she knew it to be from the daylight.

She found herself thinking how she didn't want to notice these things because she was also aware of how he sometimes rubbed her the wrong way. And she especially did not want to remember that every couple of minutes since she had first laid eyes on him when she walked in the door that night, she had thought about the kiss—the incredible kiss over two months ago with its perfect mixture of pressure and gentleness, of wet and dry, of force of body and drift of air between them; and how, against all reason, she was incredibly attracted to this guy who, by all appearances, circled in a maddeningly self-satisfied orbit, disregarding his impact on others.

Scott raised his lashes, then his face. "So. I shouldn't have kissed you without your permission. I'm sorry."

She pursed her lips, looked down, and wondered why wasn't she?

"Why have you never called me out about what happened, anyway? I've been expecting it."

Ava looked around the bar. Bea was still in the game room, now slamming on a pinball machine, her arms working quickly, her body turning one way, then the other. A guy approached her, and she turned, smiled, and shook her head. *Married*, Ava thought. *Out of the race forever.*

"I don't know what you want me to say."

Gwen set a new drink before him; Scott acknowledged it and took a sip. He leaned forward on the table, arms resting crossed in front of him as if he were about to negotiate a delicate deal.

"Would you like to go somewhere?" He looked at her full-on, without blinking.

"I am going somewhere. We're going dancing." Jude was going to meet them.

Scott leaned back again, and again, picked up his drink. He drained it in a few swallows; turned to meet the eye of Gwen, who perpetually watched them, and shook his head; then set his empty glass close to the edge of the table. "I don't mean today."

Ava watched Bea making her way back to the table. She sat down by Ava a little breathlessly and sucked down several swallows of watery Coke.

"I killed it. Pinball *wizard!* One game only, of course, that's my limit. Absolutely cannot develop an addiction, no matter how darn good I am. That's how the disease gets you." She took another swig and pushed her glass toward the edge of the table. "Here, cowboy." She placed a quarter in front of Scott. "I got change, so I'm paying back my loan. Call off your dogs and forget my name and number."

"Fine." Scott picked up the quarter. "But you've obviously been overserved. You're aggressive and overly confident."

"Not gonna argue that one with you, Smitty. So what have y'all been talking about? Me?"

"We were talking about you," Ava said, "and how we both wish we were you because you look *so* good, *and* you've perfected the art of lying about your pinball skills."

"Um, I was not talking about any of those things," Scott interjected. "I happen to not want to be a woman, and I don't have to lie about pinball."

"Oh, okay, I see how it is. Come on. You and me. And bring your wallet." Bea stood up beside the booth again.

"No, no-no-no, we're not starting this. We have to go, or it will be too late, and only the alkies will still be out at the club. And Jude will probably be there by now." Ava edged her way out of the booth and reached in her purse for her wallet, but Scott, having also stood, laid his hand on hers and shook his head. "I told you, I've got it."

"Well, lucky break, kid." Bea made a gun with finger and thumb and jabbed Scott in the arm.

"Yes." He gave an understated bow to Bea. "Point taken. I *will* be honing my skills, and meeting you was my extreme pleasure. I hope this was the first of many birthdays we'll share."

Bea gave some retort as she headed for the door, but Ava couldn't have repeated it; Scott pulled out his wallet and waved it toward Gwen before turning to Ava. "You should go out with me." He reached for his black leather bomber and began pulling it on, standing at the end of the table.

Ava glanced away before speaking. Even after what he'd said earlier, she was in no way expecting that. "I…I think I'm confused. Don't you date somebody? That girl who was here earlier, maybe? And last week, that other girl…you came in with that tall girl, remember? I thought…"

"Yeah. I date. Nobody serious, and I would like to take you out. Is that a big deal?"

"Is what a big deal?"

"I don't know. That I date. That I want to take you out. You know, we're not supposed to have communication problems until at least we've been out a couple of times."

He had the *most* incredible smile. It was sometimes a smirk, that crooked smirk, but sometimes it was full-blown like a beam of sunlight that hit you when you raised a window shade, and you were taken aback for a moment, full-force, by the impact.

"I guess I could. I mean, I would like that. I just, you know, don't want to step on anybody's toes."

"Hey, I'm fine with it, I am." Bea, realizing Ava hadn't accompanied her to the exit, had meandered back in time to get this gist. "But I'm going to wait in the car."

Ava nodded to Bea, grateful for the break in the tension. "I only ask because…I mean, I just need to make sure there isn't a girl somewhere out there who thinks you belong to her."

Gwen came over with the check, and Scott gave her a fifty without looking at it.

"You already gave me that one fifty earlier, so—" Gwen began.

"I know, just keep it, we're good." Scott didn't look at her as she expressed profuse thanks before heading back to the service area but kept his eyes on Ava.

"They all think they belong to me." He rested his hands in the bomber's pockets.

Ava returned his gaze but stood there, uncertain.

"Find me when you're ready. I think you're pretty cool." And then he left without looking back but flung up an arm at a buddy toward the lounge as he passed through the heavy front doors.

The club was full of sparkling people, mostly young. Jude, Ava, and Bea all danced together; and toward the end of the evening, Jude danced with Bea while Ava accepted other proposals. The music beat down upon her, saturating her senses; and for two hours, she felt alive and busy and full. She knew men looked at her as she responded to the percussion and rhythm that had been exacting an elemental euphoria since man first discovered his jungle drums. And as her breath became heavy and her heart beat with the ecstatic mania of movement done to music, she felt so exhilarated and adored that she believed she could dance forever. The only thing missing was a person—a man who would not only watch her and dance with her but who would one day leave and make a home with her, a man who would love her forever.

Chapter 20

THE HOUSE SMELLED like old food, old cigarettes, and old people. Jeanette wore a pink sweatsuit with its pants bunched around her ankles, her decolorized hair raked back by a white headband and showing its graying roots. Her eyes were bright, even manic-looking, but her heavy tanned face was tired and lined. Ava noticed her hands looked dry, tight, and swollen. She bent down and hugged her mother.

"Hi, Mom. You look good. You remember Bea?" Ava stepped aside, and Bea followed Ava's hug with one of her own.

"Oh, my gracious, well, of course I do! Beatrice!" The older woman stepped back, beaming.

"Hi, Mrs. Rush. Thanks for letting me come down."

"Well, good grief, my pleasure! It's been, what"—she turned to Ava—"three years?"

"I don't know…yeah, three and a few months."

Three summers ago, Ava had left Yancey to visit her mother for two days before Bea had come from Tarryton to pick Ava up; they were taking the Impala to the beach in St. Petersburg, and it was the only time Bea had met Ava's mother.

"Well, it's good to see you again. Come in, come in," Jeanette flapped her hand as she led the girls from the entryway into the living room.

There was clutter everywhere. Even old dishes were on the floor, pushed against the walls, and to one side of the room on a large-but-cheap folding table were stacks of magazines and construction-paper scrapbooks. Clippings were scattered everywhere, with markers and scissors and glue.

"Whatcha got going on here, Mom?" Ava stepped to the table and picked up a scrapbook. Bea took a place on the sofa.

"Oh"—Jeanette waved her hand dismissively—"don't look at all that. It's a little project I've been working on. Are you girls hungry? I'll get some snacks, hold on." She walked through the door to the kitchen.

Ava caught Bea's eye before opening the scrapbook to its first page. At the top, in Magic Marker, with a different color for every letter, was written, "A Dress for All Occasions," and Jeanette had pasted six styles of cocktail dresses below.

The second page showed different dogs, and the heading, in elaborate orange script over them, stated, "Some of My Favorite Breeds." The third page, labeled "My Ideal Man," showed six typical studs, two without shirts and with rippling stomachs, all with lush locks and white teeth. One man wore a suit, and one was walking on the beach in jeans and a T-shirt, looking over at nothing and smiling, his arm outstretched, hand missing. Ava presumed he'd been holding hands with a woman, but she had been cut and discarded. In the fantasy world of Ava's mother, the woman never even stood a chance.

Ava replaced the scrapbook as her mother returned from the kitchen. She sat in a woven-nylon and aluminum chair one usually buys for one's yard while Jeanette set a tin baking pan on the coffee table with Triscuits, Fig Newtons, and Oreos in three mounds. A return trip to the kitchen brought forth a cookie sheet with an old juice bottle filled with purple liquid and three plastic fast-food cups of ice. Ava recognized it as grape Kool-Aid on first sip, though Jeanette had written a "J" on hers with a permanent marker to ensure she got (Ava knew) the one spiked with vodka.

"I am so glad you girls finally came to visit." Jeanette passed them each a paper plate and pulled a plastic lawn chair of a different design from Ava's (the kind made for substantial people) to the table as Ava scooted up her own. "I have been busy, but I miss my girl." She smiled at Ava as she piled up her plate, and the girls each helped themselves.

"I missed you, too, Mom. I knew you'd be okay, though, you always are." Building Jeanette's confidence was second nature to Ava now, believing it helped stave off her potential to spiral into crisis mode.

"I don't know why you don't move back here, Ava, now that Eric left you. It's only forty miles from downtown and would be rent-free, too, of course."

Ava sighed. "You don't need to keep saying that, Mom, you say that almost every week—"

"You don't even call every week!"

"Mom, please. I missed one week and called three days later, and you still had a cow."

"You said when you moved that you would call every week."

"Okay. Okay, but I don't need to come back. I need to move forward. I'm saving money, and I'm sure I'll have a plan by spring."

Jeanette looked miffed but stoic. Ava knew how much it would hurt her mother to know she'd do anything not to get sucked back into the depressing vortex of Bright Point, that she was never, ever moving close to Bright Point again, and so she began to backpedal.

"You're doing okay, Mom, right? Who knows what the future holds! Let's have a good visit. Bea and I thought we'd help you get things tidied up a little before we go home tomorrow."

Jeanette brightened. Her emotions were as transient as a child's. "Oh, that can wait." She took a drink from her Burger King cup before turning to Bea. "Now, Bea, you live at home again, right?"

"Yes, ma'am, but with my husband. It's my parents' old house, where I grew up."

"Right. Tobias."

"Right. We just call him Toby."

"And I remember your parents are dead, of course."

Ava rolled her eyes, and a smile played on Bea's lips before she responded, "Yep, dead as doornails. Mama died when I was twelve, and Daddy when I was almost fourteen."

Jeanette chewed vigorously, listening, and Ava wondered if this overload of sugar and chemicals was what was supposed to pass for lunch.

"I remember. Ava told me your mama had neck cancer and ended up with just this *huge* ball on her neck that they couldn't operate on and that your daddy fell off a mountain."

Ava had leaned her head back and was looking up at the ceiling with its dark Rorschach water stain, the result of one-too-many bathtub leaks and very lousy caulk along the floor.

"Well, not a mountain. It was a rock face—an outlook…where people would go to look out over the river. He just lost his footing."

"Just fell right off…" Jeanette was shaking her head, her face a reflection of complete sorrow, except for her mouth, which was full of Triscuit.

"We've already established that, Mom. Bea, don't—"

"'So'k. That pretty much sums it up." Bea took a bite of an Oreo.

"And your daddy, I remember, wrote that book when you were—"

"Not even born."

"Really?"

"Yep. I'll tell the standard story if you wanna hear it." She wiped her fingers on her lap and leaned back on the sofa, hiking her legs beneath her but still holding her Kool-Aid.

"Daddy and Mama married young. I think it was twenty-two and eighteen. But Daddy had gotten drafted for World War II, first, when he was only eighteen, and he'd never been what you'd call superbrave. Those were his words, by the way. Said he'd been an anxious child."

"Ava was an anxious child."

"Hold on, Mom. Let her talk, no one cares."

Jeanette looked offended but was silent, so Bea continued.

"So he was part of Operation Neptune. Part of the troops landing in Normandy Beach. And not to go into detail, but it's in the book, but Daddy was all traumatized by it because he survived, and so many of his friends from home didn't. Plus, he did it, he said, by hiding when he got ashore while his friends were fighting and getting killed—just hid until he got rescued. And then he was so screwed up that after he and Mom married, she insisted he get help, or she was leaving."

"Well, who would blame her?" Jeanette's eyes were round. "If he was that screwed up, I mean."

Bea nodded her affirmation. "So he went to therapy, and they had a daughter. And in the midst of all that, I'm not sure how, he had what he called an epiphany."

"I've heard of those." Jeanette turned to Ava, nodding. "I think I've had those too."

"So," Bea continued, "this epiphany was that he decided to do one thing after another that he was afraid of—stuff that was dangerous. And he began writing a book about it. He was like, twenty-four when he started doing this, right before their second child was born."

"What did he do?" Jeanette was spellbound. Ava, having heard the story, enjoyed watching her mother.

"Well, everything. You name it. He walked a tightrope—right in Tarryton, between the upper window of Miller's Feed and the roof of the filling station." She looked to Ava. "It was Edward's then, but it's Gary's now. You know. Same place."

"How in the world…" Jeanette murmured.

Bea nodded again, reaching for another Oreo. "I know, I know. Said he learned how to string it from a visiting carny. And my mom said she remembered him practicing for hours. They set up the apparatus in the backyard."

"What else?"

"Bull riding. Diving. He had to research the deepest part of the Tarrymore, and he was pretty scared he wouldn't be able to swim to shore before the current carried him out. He did other stuff too. He went to Olympus when they had a visiting circus and got in the ring with the tiger trainer, which was pretty risky because the tiger didn't know him, and it would stress the tiger out." Bea's eyes fairly sparkled in the retelling. "He had to work everything out, ahead of time, of course. And then he did the other stuff…mountain climbing, riding a motorcycle off a barn onto a plank, stuff like that. But he broke his leg on that one."

Bea sat forward again and filled her glass from the bottle that contained the Kool-Aid.

"Unbelievable. And then he fell, right? Dove off one big mountain but then just fell right off that little one, even though Ava said it had a little fence—"

"She already confirmed that, Mom. Geez." Ava shook her bowed head into her hand.

"But a fence!"

"Yes, ma'am, a little parapet. So it was a border, but you know, people could get over it if they chose, and apparently, Daddy chose to."

"And Ava said nobody understood how he could have fallen, as athletic as he was."

"Mom, it doesn't matter, nobody knows." Ava watched Bea's face.

"Yeah…it was an accident."

"Did you read his book? Surely, you read it."

"Oh, sure, of course. Before he died, even. It's great. He started off talking about how he'd been this scared kid and how he got messed up in the war, and then, of course, he wrote it while he was doing all the crazy stuff and recorded how he was learning it all, and his fears, and how he was overcoming them. And how he did overcome them, I guess."

Nobody spoke for a moment.

"And then he got rich? Ava said it made him rich."

Ava lowered her head back into both hands. "Sorry, Bea. God, Mom."

Bea gave a small laugh. "I don't know about rich, but it made a little money. He bought us a beautiful turn-of-the-century farmhouse and restored it, and we got a little land. The thing is, they started this sort of adventure club and this foundation and all these chapters of people who were, I guess, little scaredy-cat weirdos who used all that stuff to get over it. They helped kids and war vets, and he would give lectures and stuff, with psychiatrists and psychologists, even. He did well."

"Who took care of you? You said you were fourteen?"

"Almost. It was August…my birthday's in September. My grandma came. My mom's mom. She only lives five miles away, so she just migrated over and went back home after I went to college. We kind of lived both places. Susan and Laura were already on their own, but none of us was ready to lose the house."

"And you went back there after college."

"Yeah. And Tobes and I live in the house now. I teach part-time, Toby farms. His folks live down a ways. He farms with his daddy, too, who's got a bigger thing going on."

"You own that house now?"

"Mom, don't ask personal stuff, please."

Bea threw Ava a dismissive wave. "Well, us and the bank. My sisters didn't want it, so I bought them out last year. It's a lot to keep up, but we love it. I could die there and be happy."

No one spoke for a moment. Ava recognized the familiar gut burn of jealousy that Bea so easily and quickly had almost all she'd ever wanted while Ava was left renting the cottage behind her, in a "home" town not her own—alone, starting over, and working two part-time jobs.

Jeanette got up and closed the blinds against the afternoon sun. "Ava's daddy's dead." Her eyes were wide with solemnity as if she wanted them all to observe this moment of not only shared tragedy but also the warmth of commonality between her daughter and her daughter's old friend.

Without a beat passing, Ava concurred. "Dead as a doornail too," she said, and they'd all laughed for a moment—three slightly broken women sharing a macabre joke, some cookies, and Kool-Aid.

Chapter 21

THE GIRLS SPENT the rest of the afternoon cleaning. In the kitchen, they washed dishes, cleared counters, and purged the refrigerator. They tossed boxes of open, stale cereal; withered carrots; and moldy peanuts. "Every time I come," Ava had whispered to Bea, for the distance from where they worked to where Jeanette was sitting at the table with her scrapbooks—just through the open doorway—was not far.

"I know," Bea had mouthed, nodding her head in sympathy.

In the living room, they stacked three piles of newspapers, tying them with twine and placing them on the curb. Ava knew Jeanette didn't read the paper and believed she subscribed because she liked the *idea* of being a newspaper reader. They placed two garbage bags of what could only be described as litter beside the papers and then moved upstairs while Jeanette, protesting, went to the curb and opened them both, pawing through each, one at a time. She salvaged a plastic watering can, brittle from the sun, three dollar-store vases, a broken transistor radio, and a plastic table lamp with a frayed cord. Having moved to the second level, Ava watched her mother from her childhood bedroom window.

"Hey. Don't worry," Bea said from behind her. "We'll sneak them back out before we leave. We just have to find where she puts them."

Ava had brought flattened boxes from The Fox in the Impala's large trunk, and the girls had reconstructed these with packing tape. Setting them in her mother's bedroom, she called down to Jeanette, whom she could hear banging the front screened door as she hauled back in the contraband items.

"Mom, we need you up here. I want to help you clean out your closet."

"Not today, honey. There's nothing in there I need to get rid of."

Ava and Bea exchanged glances. "Expecting that," Ava said.

Then she had a thought: "Okay!" she called down, "then we'll just straighten up my room so we can sleep there tonight!" Both twin beds in Ava's old bedroom were piled with books, curlers, clothes, picture frames, dried flowers, crafts supplies, a can of outdoor paint and more; but Ava decided to work in her mother's closet before they got caught.

Quietly, she began placing shoes into a box—white patent-leather chunky heels Jeanette probably wore as a young woman in the sixties; go-go boots; moldy suede mules, orange gladiator sandals, and pink vinyl heels, in which Jeanette, today, would probably break her neck before she made it down the stairs.

The girls moved on to the clothes. Ava's heart raced; Jeanette could decide to come upstairs any minute. She eyeballed what Jeanette could still wear, what could pass for style within the last five years, and realized that though probably half could go, she'd aim to cull a third. The pair placed shoes in a reconstructed box and stuffed the jettisoned clothes into two large Hefty bags.

Bea snuck everything back into Ava's childhood room, then both worked to clean off the beds, filling more bags and boxes of everything Ava hoped Jeanette would not remember she owned. That evening, everyone ate delivery pizza with milk Bea had fetched at the Kroger then crashed into bed around ten.

"What did you tell her?" Bea had been in the shower when Jeanette had gone in to tell them good night. "Did she ask where all the stuff was?"

Ava was exhausted from the drive and the work of the day. They could hear Jeanette's soft snores from across the hall.

"I know you're totally going to judge me because you have principles and such, but I told her we were going to put a few things in storage."

"Ava Rush—!"

"Oh god, Bea—gosh—good grief, you know how she is. She hoards things. She won't even remember she owns most of this stuff."

"I hope not. How often have you had to do this?"

Ava sighed. "Clean? Or sneak stuff out? I can only get rid of a few things at a time because when I've tried to do a big overhaul, she has a hissy fit. I mean, did you see those *shoes*? That's why I brought you, by the way, for distraction."

"I thought you liked me and couldn't stand to be apart from me."

"Not at all. Your sheer perfection and beauty are a pain in my side."

"I understand. But please continue."

"Every visit, I have to do this—clean and organize and throw away just pure garbage. But I've done it since I was a kid when I started realizing how twisted we lived."

"I get it. But you said you'd never gone through her shoes and clothes… Aren't you afraid you may have gotten rid of stuff she still cares about?"

Ava's felt instantly defensive. "I don't care, Bea. She'll be okay. You forget Miss Depression Era 1935 will start a whole new crapload."

Bea didn't say anything in response, and it was only seconds before Ava spoke again, "Sorry. I know you hate that word. You know what I mean. I'm so frustrated with her. All the time."

Bea's voice was gracious. "It's okay. I get it. You have a lot on your plate, potty-mouth. What's 1935?"

"Nothing…the year she was born. But her parents didn't have that hard of a time in the Depression, so I don't know where she gets her need to keep a bunch of worthless…junk. See what I did there? Totally avoided the C-word. Just for you, little flower."

"My deepest appreciation. What do her parents do again? I mean, for money? I know you must have told me a long time ago, but…and I still don't get why you don't see them. Or talk to them, even."

"They own land in New York. They have railroad money. And I talked to them a couple of times when I was a kid, but it was weird. They're like, my grandparents in name only. Like, they don't even care if they see us or not. Mom won't talk about it, just says she doesn't 'know,' or a bunch of stupid stuff that I know isn't true. Like, 'they're busy' or 'they're too old to travel' or 'they're too old-fashioned to talk much on the phone.' She's only talked to them a few times in almost twenty years herself."

"And you really have no idea why?"

"Nope. Supposedly, they'd visit a couple of times a year when I was a baby and a little girl, but not after Daddy died. Like I told you before, not once. But I don't remember much, and I've seen a couple of pictures. Grandmother had this big silver beehive, and Grandfather was all skinny and sour-looking."

"You call them Grandmother and Grandfather? Really?"

"Yeah. I don't know if I remember them a tiny bit or just the pictures, but they've sent a couple of gifts and notes, and that's how they referred to themselves. And that's what Mom calls them. It's always like, 'Your grandfather used to have this beautiful Cadillac,' and 'Grandmother was so beautiful as a girl.'"

"So weird. They're still alive and still have money, I guess, but Jeanette lives on welfare. Or AFDC. Is that what you called it?"

"Yeah. It's all welfare. The *public dole*, I believe, is the term I heard at school."

"Sorry. And they never came down, all these years after she lost her husband, and they never call?"

"Once in a blue moon, like I said—but it will be, like, years… but then, too, they've always paid our rent, at least as long as I've been old enough to remember."

"Wow." Bea was silent for a minute before she asked, "Is that why you didn't invite them to the wedding? Cuz they take pity on you, but you don't think they love you? They might have sent you a nice gift or some money or something, you know." Her voice sounded playful even though Ava couldn't make out the expression on her face.

"Yeah. I mean, why should I? I don't want their charity. Even if they still have money—and I assume they do—who cares? They're just not interested in me. Or their daughter."

Neither girl spoke for a couple more minutes.

"But they bought you that camera."

Ava couldn't help but smile. "Humph! Right. My dollar 'Diana' camera. Made me the famous photographer I am today. Of course, they mailed it to me."

"Look out, Ansel Adams."

"Ahh…I'm a little bit of him… I don't do that many landscapes. I'm a little more Margaret Bourke-White."

"Well, of course you are!" Bea paused. "Who the heck is she?"

"Look her up. Or just look at my stuff. We're practically identical."

Ava heard Bea's soft laugh in the other bed, then another moment passed.

"What are you gonna do about your mom, Aves?"

"What do you mean, do about her?"

"Well. So tomorrow, we go to church, and you sneak everything to Goodwill or the park dumpster or the trunk. And we go home until it's time to do it again. And you're moving in a few months, you say, but not back here, and I don't mean to be rude, but you say it yourself, your mom is kind of 'off.'"

"Not 'kind of.' She is 'off.' You're not being rude. She's *One Flew Over the Cuckoo's Nest.*"

"So this housekeeping thing and all the posters on the walls and the scrapbooks and the rotten food…you know it's going to get worse. And it seems her parents are done with her."

"I guess." Ava felt her heart race again. She was too young to have all this anxiety. "I don't know, Bea. I'm so stuck by her."

"You're stymied."

Ava smiled in the dark. "Very, very stymied."

In a moment, Ava asked, "Why are you going to church with her? Doesn't it bother you that she's desperate to take you to church but she's such a hypocrite?"

"Well, part of your evil plan, if I remember correctly, was to sneak her belongings away while we were gone. But I'd go anyway. She wants me to. She wants *us* to, but you know that."

"Of course she does. But she just wants to show off to her friends. And I hate to even say this, but I think she has a crush on the pastor. She didn't start going regularly until four or five years ago when Pastor Carl came. I met him, you know, after we had our little stereo-at-the-department-store incident, and I can see how she'd think he was handsome in a white-American-suburban-dad kind of way."

"But is that so bad? To want to show off her beautiful, successful daughter, to have a little something going on outside of church and being shut up here all day? I can't speak about the pastor crush, though."

"It's her choice to be shut up here all day. She could work. She could go to the library. She could have a little garden, take up cooking real food. She could volunteer."

"Yeah, maybe. I think she's overwhelmed or something. There have to be reasons she's turned out like this, don't you think? Her parents apparently abandoning her, her husband dying from cancer, her only child leaving home."

"Okay, so, speaking of that dead husband, what's up with that? Just try asking her about that. 'Hey, Mom, can you tell me about when Dad passed away?' 'Oh, Ava! He had cancer! What else do you want to know?' Well, gee, more than that!"

"I still don't understand, either, why you know so little about him. Haven't you ever looked into it?"

"I don't know how to do that with him being an orphan."

"What was his full name?"

Ava took a deep breath. "John Lawrence Rush. And that's about all I know."

"Maybe we could research him. I know we could. There are records everywhere, you know."

"I know. I also know that maybe I just don't want to know. He's dead, I'm not, that's all I know." After a long pause, she added, "You know, it bothers me how smug Mom is about you going to church with her."

"Ava Rush, what's wrong with you? Do you have trouble seeing your mother happy?"

"Oh, good grief. I just hate this fake God stuff. If she wants to be so godly, she should go get a job, or go volunteer at a homeless shelter."

"Maybe. You just seem so angry at her."

Ava sighed. "Maybe I am angry at her."

"And also angry at God."

Ava was wide awake. "So? What if I am. Why shouldn't I be?"

"But why should you be?"

Ava sat up and turned on the bedside lamp, the one they'd found when they raked everything out from under the beds.

"Because I have no reason not to be." Bea was squinting, shielding her eyes as if in pain, so Ava turned off the light and flopped back into her pillow.

"Where are all the blessings, Bea? Where is all the love God is supposed to be showing to His children? I have no grandparents to speak of. I never got to know my father. I have no brothers or sisters or cousins. I grew up like white trash. My mother is going crazier by the month, and the only chance I had at happiness, that I could see, dumped me in an Italian restaurant three weeks before I was supposed to walk down the aisle." She took a breath before she said, "Which is actually, probably, a blessing, since my side of the church would have had exactly one family member." She could still remember the night, not too long after her engagement, that she had shared with Bea her fear of embarrassment that almost every one of her attendees would be friends from school and work.

Her heart was pounding, and in the moment of silence that followed, not only did she become aware she needed to keep her voice low, but also that Bea had not had the most charmed life, either. But she wasn't broke, and she had a family and Toby.

"You're beautiful, Ava. I don't even think you know how pretty you are, and you're smart, a college graduate, and you're funny, and you're my best friend. You could do or be anything, and everybody loves you."

"Huh. Not Eric. And the only reason I'm a college graduate is because of my own hard work and my grants and scholarships. Jeanette didn't have a dime for my education."

"God loves you. Whether you believe it or not."

"That's what you always say, Bea, but you know I think if there were a God, He could be doing a much better job than this."

The black air hung heavy between them before Bea said, "I love you, Ava," to which Ava responded she loved Bea too. A million hours later, Ava slept.

Chapter 22

THE DRIVEWAY LEADING to the cabin from the paved road was long and winding. It was lined with paper bags scarified with jack-o'-lantern faces, their visages glowing from the votive candles placed within. There was a night breeze, and some of the eerie casts had gone out. A giggling girl wearing shorts, high-top Reeboks, and a motorcycle jacket, and a guy in a cowboy hat were stumbling in the dark, trying to light the darkened sacks. Paper ghosts flapped in the lower branches of the trees. Ava hated Halloween.

Gwen went through the front door without knocking, and Ava followed. About fifteen people in varying arrays of costumes were inside, some of whom Ava recognized from The Fox and Ale.

Gwen called out hellos but made no great effort to introduce Ava to anyone; instead, she made a beeline for the kitchen, so Ava followed again. The counters were cluttered, and amidst the typical kitchen accoutrements were all the makings for cocktails—liquor, juice, limes, lemons, and glasses. A large ice chest rested on the floor to the side.

"Hey, Gwennie? I'll be out here," Ava said, gesturing back to the front room. At that moment, only half-hearing Gwen's response, she saw Scott enter from a door on its opposite side.

He didn't say anything at first, looking at her and holding his glass and a cigarette. He wore a dark flannel button-down shirt, an unzipped sleeveless gray vest, and dark jeans with hiking boots. When he spoke, it sounded both deprecating and pleasantly surprised.

"Little Ava Rush. As I live and breathe." He came up to her, took her elbow, and maneuvered her through the room from which he'd just emerged, then through another, and out the back door to a set of narrow rustic steps. He sat, took her hand, and guided her down beside him, then stubbed his cigarette out in a bucket of sand one level below them. She didn't know what to say.

"I didn't think you'd come." His voice, close to her ear, had a low, musical timbre, and she shivered from it as much as from her quick reemergence back into the almost-November cold.

"I didn't think I would either. But my social calendar for tonight was shockingly lacking."

"I'm glad. Here's to social awkwardness." Scott toasted the night air before he took a swig from his glass. "Of course, this points up the embarrassing situation that you are drinkless. How gauche of me. What's your poison?" He stood, looking down at her. "Screwdriver?" he asked, tipping his own gently toward her in question.

"Um…soda water? With lime?" She raised her eyebrows.

"Daring, but I'll allow it." He left and returned with a highball glass, passing it to her as he sat down.

"Thank you. You should have coffee."

"I do have coffee. And Kahlua. And Baileys. You seriously never drink anything?"

"Nope. I told you that already. Seriously. Jokingly, stupidly, smartly…nada."

He smiled; his head cocked as he turned to look at her. He had an unnerving yet attractive habit of looking into one's face with intent, with focused interest…or was it just hers into which he did this? No.

"Amazing. Well, good for you. Can I ask why not?"

"You can. I don't know. I never thought about it much. When kids started drinking in high school, I just didn't, but I didn't socialize much in high school either. I was one of those annoying smarty-pants kids who was trying to earn ways to go to college. So, of course, I didn't lean into the drinking crowd when I went to college."

"For accounting."

She nodded. "Yep. For accounting. Or something. I wasn't sure what I was going to major in when I went, but yeah. I was good in math. And it's good money if you get in with the right firm."

"But you could be a drinking accountant."

"I could. But it never appealed to me."

"Not even to loosen up? To have a little fun?"

She shrugged. "From what I see of drinking, it never looks like that much fun." She took a long drink from her glass.

"Oh, you're one of those. Child of an alcoholic."

Ava smarted. There was a line she had subconsciously drawn, she wasn't exactly sure when, that prevented her from considering this title could ever apply to Jeanette—church-going Jeanette, her mother, her only family—even though Ava knew she always kept something around to "take the edge off," help her sleep, help her "get up and moving," help her think, help her "get out of the house."

She shook her head. "I don't think so. I have a mom, my dad's dead, but Mom isn't an alcoholic."

Scott nodded, sipping his cocktail. "I understand. My parents are. Mostly my dad, but Mom is right there, every night, every social gathering, holding her own. And yet, here, also, am I." He held up his glass in her direction before drinking again.

"But you don't have a problem."

He shook his head. "Let's hope not." Then he smiled, looking deep into her eyes again. "I think it has its place. Life is stressful. If I didn't unwind and have a little fun, I don't think I'd even see a point in being here."

"Huh. So do you know the point in being here?"

He tossed back his head as he laughed, and his hair shone thick and lustrous in the light coming from the window at their backs. She noticed again the sinewy, tawny muscle of his forearm and that even his hands were proportioned, smooth, and tanned. Eric had had nice hands, but his fingers were a little too long.

"No, Ms. Rush, I do not."

They didn't speak for a moment, and he lit another cigarette. Some guy from the screened door behind them asked Scott where his *Let It Bleed* Stones album was, and Scott said stolen, but of course, there were plenty of others.

"So what do you do for fun?" Scott asked, turning back to Ava, asking it without being lascivious, as other men in her past had done.

"Not a lot, right now. In college, Bea and I and a few friends would go dancing, and…well, you know we went a few weeks ago, but now they're doing all that Western stuff, the line dancing. Bea loves it, but not me."

"Ahh, yes. *Urban Cowboy.*"

"Right! It used to be all *Saturday Night Fever,* and now it's *Urban Cowboy.*"

"Do you ride?"

"Not seriously. I used to go with Bea at school, and I can sit a horse, but not like her. I never had rich-white-girl lessons."

"But you aren't bitter," he said with humor, not accusation.

"Oh, deep down, I am." She gave a small smile.

"You know Corrine's and Jimmy's horses are out back. I could take you."

"Oh, I couldn't do that. What if something happened? Corrine says they're pretty pricey."

"They are. They're professional fox-hunting steeds, and Jimmy and Corrine are sinfully proud of them. But it's up to me to keep them exercised, and they're well-trained, and I'd appreciate the help. It's more fun to ride with a buddy in half the time than to take them out separately and alone."

"I hope you get a break on the rent."

"Actually, yeah, I get free rent. For them and the upkeep of the whole place. But it's a little more work than it looks to the average Joe."

"Are you calling me Joe?" Ava asked, and Scott laughed.

"So you don't drink or ride…I can't think of anything else to do in life, can you?"

It was Ava's turn to laugh. "I keep busy with work. I eat dinner with Bea and Toby most nights and help her cook. I go to see my mom every third weekend. I clean up."

"Where's she live?"

"A little suburb about forty miles south of Atlanta. Bright Point." He shook his head. "No, you wouldn't have heard of it."

"Still. None of that sounds like fun."

"We have Sunday dinners at Bea's every week after church… I visit with her family."

"You go to church?"

"No. I don't really get all that stuff."

Scott looked out into the sooted woods beyond the back stoop. "Me neither, if you want the truth."

She took a drink of her soda water. "I take pictures."

"Really? What kind?"

"All kinds. I'm not super serious about it now, but someday I plan to have a dark room."

"What kind of camera do you use?"

"Mostly a Canon. The A-1. I also just bought a Kodak disc and the New F-1."

"Well, that's Greek to me. Don't even know why I asked."

"It's okay. They're just simple thirty-five-millimeter cameras." She pulled her jacket closer around her and lowered her chin into its collar.

"Come on. You look cold." Scott stood up and reached for her hand.

What old-world manners he has, she thought.

Inside was smoky and loud. Bruce Springsteen's album *The River* was playing, and when they entered back into the main room, Corrine was sitting on the floor with a young guy Ava didn't recognize and the girl in the bomber jacket. They were going through a stack of LPs.

She looked up to see Ava and Scott and hopped to her feet, beaming, kissed Scott on the cheek, and hugged Ava briefly but hard. "I can't believe it! Gwen told me she was bringing you, but I said, 'When pigs fly!'" She smelled like flowers, citrus, and candy.

"Well, goes to show!" But after that, Ava was speechless.

Corrine gestured to the guy on the floor with the records. "Guess who?" He had on a dark business suit, and his hair was parted and slicked.

"Um…an FBI agent?" Scott ventured.

Corrine swatted his shoulder. "JFK! I never noticed, but he looks just like a young JFK, doesn't he? Can't you see it?"

Cory and Scott made small talk, and Ava left for the kitchen. She was helping herself to some Bloody Mary mix when Corrine appeared by her side.

"Well, this is fun, right?"

"Yeah." Ava hoisted her glass. Corrine began refreshing her gin and tonic, then took a couple of surprisingly big gulps of it before leaning back against one of the kitchen counters. "Look at this place. I swear, Scottie didn't even think he should do dishes before having this thing."

The double sink was empty on one side but full on the other. The counters held not only the constituents for drinks but also pantry items, more dirty dishes, and dishcloths. Even tools were strewn amongst the usual canisters, toaster, and paper towel holder.

Corrine looked at Ava as if she had an idea. "Wanna help?" And without waiting for an answer, she grabbed the dish soap and began to fill the sink with water.

They'd been working ten minutes or so, with guests coming in and out, each making small talk and drinks when Ava asked about Jimmy.

"Mr. Responsible is home in bed like a good boy. You know he's got to open in the morning."

"Yeah. Must be rough being married and having to party on different nights."

Corrine laughed. "Kind of. He's a lightweight these days anyway…an old man… He'll be like, 'Stay home and watch TV with me!' Crazy. I may be forty-two, but I'm not dead. I get tired of same old same old."

Ava was surprised but tried not to show it. She would have guessed thirty-seven, thirty-eight at the outside. Corrine had the tiniest of lines at the outsides of her eyes and mouth, but most of her face (and all of her body) appeared smooth and toned. That night she had on a shell-pink off-the-shoulder suede shirt over what looked like a pink bra top paired with rose-colored jeans. In the kitchen light, her green eyes were vibrant, luminous. Her lips shined with an iridescent pink gloss, and her hair feathered back in soft, loose waves.

"Yeah, I get it. Does Jimmy *ever* go out?" Ava was drying, opening every cabinet door to find places to stick things.

"Not much. We go out together, of course, but between the bar, coming out here to ride, and the house, it's like…no. There's always so much to do."

"And then you hunt."

"Right. In season, of course… I can't believe it's coming up again so soon! That's a whole other thing."

"Where do you go in Virginia? To hunt?"

"Back home." Corrine paused in her washing. "I guess you don't know about all that?" Her statement sounded like a question.

"Not really. Gwen mentioned you met in Virginia, and Jimmy's daddy owns an old plantation. And you told me you guys go riding up there."

"That's all true. A thousand acres, thereabouts, passed through generations. His daddy says it's never been sold since they ran off the Indians."

"That's unbelievable."

Corrine nodded. "The old families used to grow tobacco, mainly when they had slaves. Supposedly, it'll pass to Jimmy when his dad dies… Jimmy grew up spoiled, in case you couldn't tell." Corrine rolled her eyes but smiled.

"What does his daddy do?"

"He's what they call a gentleman's gentleman. He likes everything comfortable, and between you and me, he doesn't much like work unless it's the thinking kind. So he pretty much uses the plantation to keep the tobacco going, and, so the story goes, by paying these pitiful people the most pitiful wages—kind of like his own granddaddy did with the sharecroppers—*after* slavery. *And* so the story goes again, like his daddy did after him. You know, after the granddaddy, I mean."

Ava smiled. "Age-old story. The rich get richer, and the poor just keep on scraping by. You can see why Marx and Lenin wanted to switch things up."

"Yeah, but it never works, does it? Anyway, so Jimmy's like the little prince, and his mom and dad just let him grow up doing whatever his little curly-headed-self desired, and that was pretty much just hunting and fishing. And his daddy buys him this gorgeous roan from my daddy, so he becomes kind of a big deal in the Virginia fox-hunting scene."

"Yeah? I have to say I did not know there was such a thing."

"Oh, yeah, just like in England. His old man sent him over there—to England—for his high school graduation trip. He didn't even start college until the winter term so he could make that trip that fall, and it was a real hunting expedition and everything with all these big wigs."

"How did you guys meet?"

"When his daddy bought the stallion—Whistler—from my daddy. I started crushing on him pretty hard." She laughed. She had a rather raucous laugh, Ava thought, for a woman. "I set my cap for him, but I was smart about it so I wouldn't scare him off. Like, I'd just happen to be where he was sometimes. Make myself available but not too available, if you know what I mean." She raised and lowered her eyebrows like a different Marx, the one named Groucho, smiling.

"What did you do? I mean, back then. I just assumed you met in college."

"Oh, heck no, I didn't go. I mean, Jimmy went, like I said, and he dated some girls, but I think it was hard for him to get interested in any kind of career. His daddy has that hateful tobacco business, and Jimmy practically already had everything he wanted. But when he came home that first summer, see, there I was, and we just went riding everywhere, every chance we got. Then the summer after that too. His junior year, he just quit." Her mien was smug as if she had accomplished a remarkable feat, getting her dream man to drop out of college.

Ava wrinkled her brow. "And did what?"

Corrine pursed her lips together in a bit of a smirk and looked at Ava mischievously. "Married me."

"Huh. So…where did you guys get the bar?" Ava's drying had caught up with Corrine's washing, and she started putting boxes and bags of food in the corner pantry.

Corrine stopped washing, dried her hands, and sat in one of the folding wooden chairs at the small kitchen table. She lit a cigarette from a pack on the table, crossed her legs, and reached for her drink. "Well, don't tell Jimmy I told you because I think it digs at his pride, but it all came from me. It was a country store my aunt owned."

Ava's eyes widened in surprise, and Corrine nodded as if she was finally getting to share a delicious secret.

"My aunt left me an inheritance when I was sixteen. She never married nor had kids. It's a long story. Anyway, when she died, my brothers and I were the heirs." Her face clouded over. "I was given my share when I turned eighteen. My two brothers had already gotten their money, but they didn't want the store. It wasn't in our state, of course, and they saw it as a burden 'cuz they were older and were both doing pretty well on their own. But I did—I wanted it—even though I felt so horrible."

"For what?"

Corrine shook her head. "When she was alive, I never realized I was gonna get any of her stuff or money or anything. And I was not very good to her. None of us called or visited her much, and she was down here all alone, family-wise. So when I realized I had this money and I was so young, I felt like some kind of demon." Corrine looked up at Ava, waiting for her reaction.

"I get that. But you were a kid." Ava paused in her task and sat in the other kitchen chair. "I hate going to my mom's, but I try to visit and hang out with her because I already think about that stuff—how I'll feel when she's gone, how I messed up her life by being born, blah, blah, blah—and then, when I go, after about two hours she gets on my nerves so bad I have to leave or go hang out in my old room. I don't know why we don't love our family more."

"I know. And it was like I couldn't wait to give it to Jimmy. He proposed that Christmas after I turned twenty, and I'd never told him about the money. And, of course, his family would never give him money to speak of while his dad's still alive...things, yes, but money... Anyway, he had no clue what he was doing with his life or what he even wanted to do, but he used to talk about owning a little pub somewhere, somewhere warmer. He wanted this hunting-scene kind of thing and close to a city, but he didn't want to live in the city because he still wanted to have horses. He just *loved* the riding and fox-hunting scene." She paused. "And then, well, you know the rest of the story."

"Not really."

Cory shook her head. "Well, we just moved here and turned the store into the bar. My aunt had bought the land and built this little place on it"—she gestured around the room with her finger—"and owned everything outright when she died. I bought out Ned and Victor, and that was it."

"Who're—oh, your brothers?"

"Yes, ma'am. And we lived here, of course—you knew that—while we renovated the store, and so we could keep a couple of horses. When we got more money, we bought the house where we live now. In Corinth."

"It must have been a pretty lucrative little store."

"Oh, it wasn't just the store. She bought some of the early Coke stock and Johnson & Johnson too. Mama claimed she was a smart little cookie."

"So Jimmy got lucky. A beautiful wife in love with him and rich too."

"I guess. Maybe." She picked up a salt shaker and began to tip it back and forth, dribbling crystals onto the table.

"Why'd you want to do it? Give him the money and the store, I mean."

"Well, I was in love with him, first of all. And he didn't know about it. I mean, I was just training horses—practically penniless as far as he knew—and he wanted to marry me anyway. I didn't know what I was going to do with the rest of my life either, just like him. My parents breed horses, but they aren't rich. They'd tell you they're still just getting by." She rolled her eyes, shook her head, and pulled hard on the cigarette, squinting.

"So you both just up and moved to Corinth from Virginia. Even though the hunting scene is there."

"Oh, gawd, I couldn't wait to get away from the town I grew up in. And Jimmy had no desire to stay around his parents. He felt like he was never going to be anything but his Daddy Martin's little boy, and I had a falling out with my family because of an abortion."

Ava watched her face, but Corrine didn't slow down; apparently, there was no shame or regret in the telling of that. She hopped up, stubbed out the cigarette, and began washing again at the sink, so Ava got up to dry.

"We got married the June after we turned twenty-one, and we just 'went for it.' Took almost two years to get the store converted to the bar, but it will have been opened twenty years in September." She paused and looked out the tiny window in front of them even though it was nothing but a rectangle of black. "It's funny where you end up, isn't it? I thought I'd be in Virginia my whole life. And never thought I'd be a bar owner."

Chet, Scott's friend from the bar, came into the kitchen and began making two drinks from the laden back counter.

"Tell Scottie he owes us," Cory called over her shoulder and nodded toward Ava.

"Later, maybe. He walked down to the stable to show Lonnie and Theresa your horses."

"Oh, he should let them be. It's not good to mess with them at night."

Ava guessed Chet's costume was a lumberjack, for he had on a safety helmet with his plaid shirt and hiking boots and an inflatable ax shoved through a belt loop. He and Corrine talked while Ava tried to finish clearing the counter clutter, hoping she wasn't misplacing items too badly. She watched Corrine toss her hair, having paused in her washing to turn to Chet and laugh at some prattle from the heavily-bearded young man.

The glaring kitchen light shining on Corrine's face during the conversation showed the slight lines around her eyes but also some kind of magical vitality behind them. Her gloss played upon her lips, and the yellow-gold streaks in her hair were more visible than they usually were in the smoky haze and muted lighting of the bar. Ava looked at her for a moment, and Corrine met her eyes, giving her a smile and a wink. Other people came and went, mixing their trademark cocktails.

When Chet left, as Corrine and Ava were finishing their last ministrations to the cozy, cluttered kitchen, Ava ventured, “I hope you don’t beat yourself up about your aunt anymore.”

Corrine, as grave as Ava had ever seen her, paused from wiping a counter and shook her head. “For what purpose? You know? You can’t get any deader than dead.”

Whatever that was supposed to mean.

Chapter 23

HE DIDN'T SEEK her out.

The night of the party, he'd come back from the stable with the other two—Lonnie and Theresa—who were supposedly dressed like Duckie from *Pretty in Pink* and Deborah Harry. He'd mingled around, going into the back room a couple of times, sometimes alone, sometimes with one or two guests. His eyes were very dark, and she had caught him looking at her more than once. He hadn't made an effort to avert his gaze.

During the two weeks that followed, she'd gone to Arrington's and suffered through the excessive engrossment of Jack Levinson, and she'd gone to the bar and seen Scott come and meet with clients, drinking a beer, pointing out clauses, and assisting with policy signatures.

One afternoon he'd asked about her latest photography as if he were merely polite; on another, he'd offered to pay for her nachos and, after she'd declined, found out from Kathy that he'd gone ahead and paid for them anyway.

On the third Monday in November, he asked her about her plans for Thanksgiving. She replied she didn't celebrate Thanksgiving. (After that melancholy celebration with Jeanette during Ava's first college year, Jeanette cooked and ate the holiday meal at her church with the homeless and divorced. Ava had enjoyed the next two Thanksgivings on a virtually empty campus and spent the last two dining in Atlanta with Eric and his parents.)

"That's perfect," Scott had said, sitting beside her at the bar that day and giving her the only real attention he had since that Sunday night of Halloween. "No one's expecting you. So you can come this year and eat with us."

She was so close…so close to saying, "This is the oddest friendship I've ever had. Are all your relationships based on only your terms? You barely speak. You engage me in conversation only every couple of weeks, but when you choose to shine on me, you treat me as more elevated than anyone else. How many of your 'friends' will be there? And how will your lovers be celebrating?"

But she said none of that. Instead, she'd made modest protestations that it wasn't necessary, she was sure she'd be eating with Bea, et cetera. Then it only took him about three sentences more to arrange it. He'd meet her at the bar at ten Thanksgiving morning. His parents' house in Olympus was only thirty or so minutes farther out from there.

"How well do you know this guy?" Bea had asked her later that day. She was placing boxes of clay powder into her front seat to take to Julian's studio, for it was Monday, their weekly afternoon crafting date. She turned to where Ava was standing behind her and put her hands on her hips in mock exasperation. "And why is any guy worth missing the Mullins family Thanksgiving? My pies alone are worth more than that." She circled to the driver's side. "Plus, Gram and Alex will be crushed. Your first Thanksgiving here as a resident."

"My *first*? I'm not settling here!" Ava had waved her hand. "Never mind. We're just friends. He's known Jimmy and Corrine forever, and he knows lots of people at the bar." She looked at the sun splashing its afternoon favor along the lawn. "I think I need a change of pace."

*****

"Ava, this is my mom. Marilyn Beaumont Divine." Scott gestured to his mother and made a reserved bow. "Mom, this is Ava Rush. She works at The Fox and Ale." Why Scott felt he needed to introduce her that way was beyond Ava, but it occurred to her that this was about all they had in common.

Mrs. Divine was trim, petite. Scott must have inherited the wave and color of his hair from her, for hers was also dark, almost black, as were her eyes. The smooth pageboy curved along her collar bone, accenting a squarish chin that was also like Scott's but attractively scaled for a woman. Her nose was straight and very small, with a pinched look to it around the nostrils like a Barbie's, and Ava realized with a start she was one of the few women who were not celebrities or famous who had had "work" done.

"Ava, I'm delighted. Come in, come in!" Scott's mother ushered them across the marble-tiled floors, through white French doors, and into the living room.

The walls were wide dark planks, like mahogany, bisected by towering windows. Two white sofas faced each other, divided by a large oval coffee table of stone and glass, and two brown leather club chairs flanked the ends of the sofas. Above the marble mantle were two oversized gold crystal sconces flanking a gargantuan mounted buck's head.

Marilyn gestured to a sofa and took her place on the other one, smoothing her red pencil skirt beneath her with well-manicured hands tipped by red nails. She wore a coral-colored silk blouse, pearls, and black pumps; and her lips were also darkened red.

"The others should be in from the barn soon. I told them be in here by twelve." She placed her hands flat on her thighs and sighed. "Ava, I'm so glad you could come. Scott tells me you're an accountant."

Ava threw up one hand. "Guilty. I worked in Atlanta the last couple of years, but I've been here, I guess, about six months now." She took the punch cup Marilyn offered her from a tray.

"Scott says you don't drink? This is just a simple punch I make—cranberry, pineapple, ginger ale." Marilyn passed a cup to each of them and took one herself before settling back on the sofa.

Ava had barely emitted her thank you before she heard voices and scuffling from the hall to her right. In moments, the room was occupied by—of all things—Scott's family.

A very athletic-looking girl entered first. Robin, Scott's younger sister, had wavy blonde shoulder-length hair with egg-beater bangs and wore jeans with a gray long-underwear-style shirt and riding boots. Peter and Starr came behind Robin.

Peter—Scott's older brother—was very tall, 6'4" or so with a long neck; an angular, pensive face; and short slicked straight brown hair. Starr had rusty, cocoa-colored hair, thick and waved, but unattractively blunt cut as if she could not care less. She was plump and wore a placid expression above a white-and-blue short-sleeved blouse with a string threading its waist and blue knit pants a housewife might wear. Peter wore jeans and a flannel shirt.

Chuck—Charles Divine, of Divine Chevrolet and Divine North—was behind them all. He was a large man, as tall as Scott but not Peter, with blonde hair ashing to gray, combed straight back and receding. His deep-set brown eyes lay under a heavy brow, accompanied a heavy girth and a loud voice that, Ava came to believe as the afternoon went on, had become habitually loud over time as it appeared he would not accept not being the center of attention. This need was tolerated but possibly resented by his family, as everyone but Peter—to some degree—participated in a polite but sometimes condescending or tributary conversational dance around the patriarch.

"Don't even sit, people!" Marilyn waved her hands in front of her as she rose to shoo the gathering back the way they had come. "Dinner is ready, and I don't want it cold. Go wash up and let's eat."

The dining room was as elegant as the living room with white upholstered Parson's chairs surrounding a marble-top table. A pewter chandelier set off the grisaille wallpaper. Robin and Marilyn brought out the turkey and all its appurtenances amidst chatter and shared jokes as everyone assumed their places: Chuck at the head of the table, Peter to his right, then Starr. Scott guided Ava to Chuck's left, then sat on her other side. Marilyn sat opposite Chuck at the end of the table, and Robin sat to Marilyn's left and beside Starr. Ava was wildly uncomfortable.

Chuck carved and began serving the plates without asking who wanted what kind of meat or how much. Marilyn passed peas and requested Ava begin with the sweet potatoes until she'd created a musical, cyclical rhythm whereby everyone was served. Ava noticed Peter took no meat and was offered none and that Starr's plate was filled to bursting.

Chuck wore a perpetual smirk. Once, after he'd made a joke, he poked Peter in the shoulder with his fork. With affable pestilence, he teased Starr about her portions and Robin about her lack of a "date."

("She's too smart for any of them. It's her own fault, but you can't blame her.") Ava jumped in with what she hoped was the appropriate amount of deference and interest to ask about each of the guests.

At one point, when they were discussing Peter's job, Marilyn interjected, "He's being modest! So modest!" She shook her head. "Tell her what you found yesterday in that one slide," she said to her oldest son.

Peter didn't look at his mother and only glanced at Ava before looking back to his plate. "A filarial worm. It's a parasite caused by mosquitoes."

"This woman comes in with the beginnings of elephantiasis," Marilyn effused. "I'd seen it, you know, on TV. That's the kind of stuff he does."

Robin addressed Ava, "Peter's our resident genius. He could have been a doctor, but he likes to work with blood and microscopes instead of people."

"Robin's our resident smart-aleck." Scott looked from his sister to Ava. "She could have been a contender, too, but she'd rather shovel horse poop."

"Yes, I'd rather train horses than suck up to you guys' froufrou career ambitions. I just *have* to shovel horse poop as part of my job."

"What's your job?" Ava asked.

"Well, I help train the horses people board with us, but I want to be a professional. I have six right now, and I train for riding, dressage, and sometimes for racing if I'm lucky."

"You only had that one," Scott teased.

"So? I'm still getting my name out. I'm young, but I'm still a 'contenda.'" She pronounced it all New York-Italian, the way Stallone had in the movie *Rocky*.

"Scott and Robin are both excellent riders. Don't ask how much we spent on that little hobby."

"Mom. Hobby? *Training*. Her *career*. How many times does Robin have to tell you she's going places?"

"Oh, Scott. Well, for whatever reason. Peter never had a speck of interest, of course." Marilyn shook her head but smiled as if to say, *What're you gonna do?* "And Scott sells insurance, of course."

Radiating a mother's pride, she paused a tiny forkful of sweet potatoes midway to her lips. "Does quite well with it too."

Scott nodded. "I'm fascinating." He took a bite of turkey.

"All the children have done so well." Marilyn looked to Ava with a closed-mouth smile that continued to bespeak her satisfaction in her children. "Scott is also trying to be a writer."

Scott shook his head at his mother. "That's barely worth mentioning, Mother."

"Oh! Well…I know…I just thought that since you…" Marilyn stopped and sighed.

Scott put his fork down and took a drink. "I'm just getting started," he addressed Ava. "I want to travel. And I want to write about it. Also, maybe sports or adventure writing. I wrote an article for *Fox and Hound* last year, and it got published. But it's hard to break into all that."

Ava was spellbound. "I think that's wonderful. Do you…not want anyone to know you write?" She'd never heard anyone mention this side of him, especially not him. The table was quieter than it had been.

"No, it's okay." He paused. "No, not really. If you mention it, people ask about it a lot, and they expect a lot. I'd like to have a little more success before putting it out there."

"You live with Bea Mullins, am I right?" Chuck asked. "I sold Ken Mullins a car years back. He's the one wrote that book."

"I do! She's Phelps now, but yeah, I rent her guesthouse."

Chuck nodded to his plate. "I remember. White Impala. He died, like, not long after."

No one spoke for a moment.

"I wrote a report on that book *Eat Your Fear Like a Sandwich*. Remember, Mom, you read it?" Robin looked to her mother. "We had to research a local celebrity."

"Yes, of course I do. You wrote a beautiful report. It made me want to read the book…very inspiring."

"Yeah. I wished I could have interviewed him. He was already dead, though. He and his old lady both."

"Robin…"

"Sorry, Mom. He and his estimable wife."

"That title. So odd!" Starr mused, looking around the table as if for confirmation.

"He talks about that in the introduction. He was going to just call it *Eat Your Fear,* but after his editor read why, he made him add the *Like a Sandwich* part. He was just sick, he said, about the war. And he had to go to therapy..."

Chuck snickered.

"The therapist had told him he had to face his fears...any and all of them. And Kenneth was eating a sandwich when it occurred to him that he had to—and was going to—do everything he was afraid of, methodically, just like taking bite after bite of food. Because facing your fear constantly, daily, was like eating, and you couldn't negotiate it all the time. You had to accept that you just had to do it, continually, to survive."

Peter looked sideways toward his sister. "Then why did he do all that extra crazy stuff? Why didn't he just face the normal fears that came into his life like the rest of us?"

Robin's eyes widened, and she leaned a little toward Peter for emphasis. "That's the interesting part. Because he was in overkill mode. He felt tragic about the war and had to make amends to everybody...and to prove to them, and himself, too, I guess, that he could be brave."

There was a lull, a space for chewing before Marilyn shook her head and murmured, "I wonder if it was ever enough."

The meal progressed. Ava noticed Peter nor Starr spoke much. Robin joked during the whole dinner, and though Scott deflected a lot, he could give as good as he got. Marilyn auditioned for the cameras that weren't there for an episode of the not-yet-created TV show *Happiest Family Ever*, and Chuck continued to use his conversation skills to tease and badger, barely sidestepping the risqué like a pubescent boy. After dessert, Marilyn and Robin began clearing, but when Ava stood and reached for a bowl, Marilyn waved her away.

"Go, honey, we've got this. Let Scott show you around a little bit."

Chuck bellowed parting words as he retired to a game in the den, and Peter and Starr, almost wordlessly and hand in hand, left out the front door for a walk across the front lawn and then to who-knew-where.

Scott led Ava out the back, and after crossing the veranda, they began to traverse the sweeping back lawn in the direction of the field beyond.

The stable was painted red with white trim, with two mighty doors sporting a jumbo padlock. Scott took out his keys, and on the ring, Ava noticed a tiny gold spoon on a chain. After he opened the lock and removed his keys, she reached for it.

"What is this?" She laughed openly. "A charm?"

He looked at her as if to determine that she really didn't know. "It's for blow. A little bump now and then."

She fingered the little spoon, about the size of an eighth teaspoon. "You mean cocaine?"

His sexy little smile. "Yes, ma'am. Cocaine."

A moment passed. "I didn't know you did that."

"Well, to be fair, miss, I imagine there is quite a bit about me you don't know. I think we're just getting to know each other now."

Thanks to you and your weird, distant ways, Ava thought.

He pulled open one of the heavy doors, and they entered the shadowy dark. Two rows of stalls allowed seven horses to occupy each side, although, as Robin had said, only six resided there now. An atrium cathedral ceiling rested above the passageway that separated the rows.

"Why do you do it?" The question surprised even herself, but she wanted to know. She'd never known anyone to use cocaine.

"What, the coke? I'm not sure. It started in college. It just heightens everything. To party, too, if it's that kind of night. Mostly just to put a good spin on a bad day."

"And it doesn't bother you? Does your family know?"

"First, no, my family doesn't know, to my knowledge. It isn't a problem. But they were adults in the fifties, remember…pretty closedminded about what's available today. Dad's just always drunk booze and smoked, and Mother…well, you saw she likes her wine. And, no, it doesn't bother me. I just have to be careful."

By now, they'd stopped at a stall where Ava rubbed the muzzle of a blazed roan mare. "Your family is very nice." The mare butted her head against Ava's hand.

"All families are nice when you first meet them. We have our disgraces and misconducts." He walked to a tin garbage can, took off the lid, and withdrew a wide shallow cup full of grain. He offered the cup to Ava, but she shook her head.

"I don't know of what you speak, but I'd go against you any day."

Scott flashed her his signature sideways smile, then offered the cup to a bay stallion to Ava's left. "Tell me what you find nice about my family."

Ava cocked her head. "Well, your mother is beautiful. What's her heritage, anyway?"

"French, with a little black bastard Spanish, my dad says."

Ava was silent a moment, then continued, "Okay, well, and she's like a lady of the highest order, manners and all. Robin is kind and also pretty, but she favors your dad, I think. Very funny. Looks like she works out or runs or something. And Peter is quiet, but I can tell, very bright. And Starr, I couldn't quite get a handle on, but let's see…dependable…devoted to Peter…am I right? Just the way she looks at him and stuff."

Scott returned the cup to the can, took Ava's hand, and started walking toward the back doors of the barn.

"I notice you didn't mention ol' Chuck, who divorced his first wife, Dora, who didn't take his crap, to marry my aristocrat mother, who does. He sleeps around on her. She pretends she doesn't know, and so do we, except for a huge boxing match he and I had when I was sixteen.

"Peter is different. He's like the opposite of a retarded person. He's superbright. He really could have been a doctor, but he doesn't like being around people, so he became a medical technologist so he can look at slides and test tubes of people's blood all day and barely have to talk. And he could give two whits about money. Starr's very simple, too, but likes to be around people and doesn't have half his brains. She runs a gift shop."

"In Jacksonville?"

"Kind of. In Jacksonville Beach, about forty-five minutes out. They've been together about six years, and we still don't know much about her. They keep to themselves. They come for Thanksgiving and for the big fat Fourth of July party where everybody but them gets drunk at the river. They don't celebrate Christmas, supposedly. And, yeah, they're just as scintillating at the summer party as they were today."

"I know what you're trying to do." She stopped walking. After exiting the stable, they had crossed the pasture, and, without conferring, had headed to an enormous loan oak. Ava leaned back against it.

"You're trying to make your beautiful, rich, witty, brilliant family look damaged so I won't go blow my brains out."

Scott stopped in front of her and bent down to pull a long-stemmed weed, then fingered its seeds to the ground.

"You shouldn't joke like that, baby." And her blood quickened. A breeze had picked up, and his oh-so-soft curls blew, and he had called her baby.

She looked away toward the border of trees at the property's edge. "I know."

"And as far as sweet Robin, you probably don't know her preference for dating women is our family's best-kept secret."

Ava was almost speechless. "I can't believe that." She pictured Robin with her tousled bangs and honest brown eyes; her ready laugh; tennis-girl figure; and shiny, glossed lips.

"Well, join the club. My parents can't believe it either."

"How do they know? Did she just tell them one day she was gay?"

Scott shook his head. "Not sure. I was away at school. She's quiet about it. She has a friend she sees in Corinth. And, you know, she lives here, she trains here, she rides here, but she pretty much keeps her social life out of Mom's and Dad's faces."

"But…she's so feminine." Ava looked down, then back into Scott's face. "She doesn't look like I always thought they looked. But I don't know any gay people." She brightened. "No, actually, I do now. Bea has a friend. But you can kind of tell."

"Ava." He smiled. "Sweet Ava. I know Julian. I get my haircut there…you probably know Fran."

Of course, Ava thought. *The pretty stylist of Jude's three hires.*

"You do know gay people… You just haven't known they were gay."

"No, I honestly don't think I do…"

"But Robin's gay. And you didn't know. You don't think you've ever met anyone else that was, but you just wouldn't have guessed it?"

"I don't know. Maybe. Jude is…kind of different. Not to be mean. But Robin isn't like a boy. She doesn't act like a boy, I mean."

Scott reached down and snapped up two more weeds. "I know what you mean, even though I think you're confused, little sheltered Ava Rush."

Ava rolled off the tree trunk and began walking again, this time toward the house. She'd taken only a few steps before she realized he wasn't following her but was looking toward the western horizon. She walked back to the tree trunk and this time leaned her shoulder against it. "Why don't you have a girlfriend?"

He looked hard into her face before answering, and she could only hold his gaze for a moment before looking away and looking back again.

"I have never deserved any girlfriend I've ever had." And still, he didn't avert his gaze.

The wind stirred, and she pushed at the hair that had blown across her face. "Why haven't you tried to change that?"

Scott threw the stems down and closed the few steps between them, placing his hands on the trunk on either side of her. "I'm trying as hard as I can, right now," he said and leaned in—pressing her against the tree—placing his lips on her waiting ones—and changing her destiny again.

Part II

Chapter 24

AVA FELT LOVED. She felt pretty and noticed and nervous as people milled around and chatted. Crystal and silver shone as a low hum of conversation and laughter reverberated around the seasoned wooden walls of the converted pole barn. Ceiling-high windows, long-ago reinforced with iron crosses and hung with creamy taffeta sashes along the top and sides, let in the evening light. White roses juxtaposed with lavender orchids were springing from vases, chair slipcovers, and ribbon-bound torchieres. Crystal hearts hung from the ceiling, and tablecloths in a replete range of purple from lilac to amethyst were draped and swirled to the floor.

Her dress—her dress! She was a queen. It was a pale lavender satin sheath, cut on the bias and pierced with a thousand crystals. Its back half-moon grazed the boards behind her as she walked and the lights caught the crystals in her hair. Scott—her husband—sported thick glossy hair above a black tuxedo, along with the most stunning smile Ava had ever seen on a man.

"You haven't said hello to Uncle Arthur," he teased her. Chuck's brother had not attempted to hide his infatuation.

Ava sipped her sparkling cider and lifted it with a smile toward Arthur. "Hello, Uncle Arthur," she murmured, where only Scott could hear, and turning back to her husband, said, "I will go talk to your weirdo uncle if you stop feeling like you have to babysit my mother. As sweet as that is."

"Your mother is as nervous as a cat and is drinking too much. But c'mon, I'll introduce you to Uncle Art. He's shy, so he's going to need my help to even talk to you."

Ava glanced over to where Jeanette was seated. "I am worried about Mom, but Bea's got her now. Okay, let's go see your freaky uncle and get it over with."

The reception had been Marilyn's idea. Valentine's Day was a Monday, so she'd arranged the reception for the twelfth. Beaufort Vale was 103 acres of pastures, wooded hills, and an ancient homestead, complete with the original pole barn the owners repurposed for a wedding and reception venue. A myriad of white lights overhung the wide cedar ceiling beams, and the crowd was polished and convivial.

Ava had been married less than two months.

Almost an hour passed while she worked the crowd before pleading hurting feet and sitting with her old Atlanta friend.

"I can't believe it." They were seated along one of the tufted brocade sofas lining the walls, and Chantal's eyes shone. "Why didn't you tell me sooner?" She wore a midnight-blue dress bedecked with dark-blue beads and a twenties-style headband with a spray of tiny blue feathers on its sequined border.

Ava leaned in. "We didn't know. Honestly…*I* didn't know." She shook her head. "I can't explain it, but…he proposed, and he wanted to elope, so…" She shrugged.

Chantal nodded, smiling behind her cherry lip gloss. "I get it. And after the last thing, and all—"

"Yes. Yeah, see, I knew you'd get it. His mama was kind of hurt, but that's what all this is about. Throw her a bone, he said."

"Oh yeah. But it doesn't exactly hurt to be queen for a day, does it?" Her former roommate's smile was genuine, and Ava was touched. By all appearances, though Ava's rebound was even better than Chantal's secure, orchestrated, luxury lifestyle, the girl could still be happy for her friend.

"I can tell he's wonderful, Ava. So handsome. But…how did you know?"

"That I loved him?"

"Well…how do I say this…you said you dated three weeks." Chantal looked apologetic but curious. "It's very romantic, but… weren't you scared?"

Ava threw her head back and laughed. "Yes! And no. I told you, I can't explain it. I knew him, a little bit, before we dated, of course, but…he's…." She looked across the room to the man she realized some would believe she barely knew, and although maybe, just maybe, they were right, all she said was, "He's magical, Alice. Pure magic."

Chantal pressed her lips together as if she were suppressing a smile and nodded. "And he sells insurance?"

"Yeah. But he's kind of weird about this, kind of private, but he writes stuff too. He just started submitting last year."

"What kind of writer?"

"Travel, sports…events…? Like, we live in the cabin my bosses own…and Scott exercises their horses because they're fox hunters—I'm not kidding—and, every year, for the last few years, he goes with them up to Jimmy's daddy's old plantation to hunt. Then last year, December before last, he wrote about it—the hunt—and it got published. Something else too. So he's excited about that. He'd never submitted to a magazine before."

"Oh, gosh! Who buys that stuff?" Chantal's eyes were wide, and she took another big drink of champagne.

"*Fox and Hound* is the magazine that published his article. It's a whole thing"—she waved her hand—"like, in Great Britain, it's a big deal, and Jimmy, my boss, you met him earlier, remember? He even went over there after high school to ride in one of their hunts. His daddy gave it to him for his graduation present."

"So his daddy has a real plantation?"

"It used to be, yeah. In Virginia. So now, Jimmy and Corrine have this club. And they go up a few times a year, every season."

"Man. Well, that's exciting." Chantal sat with one arm across her waist and her elbow propped upon its wrist as she held her champagne aloft. Ava saw a shadow pass over her eyes as she scanned the room, and her eyes rested on Scott. "I'd like to meet a nice guy. You know, for real, not in the business." She turned back to Ava. "Chet's pretty cute."

"He is, but I think he does too many drugs. I didn't know, but Scott told me he just lost his job over it last week. He was, like, a pole climber or something…for the electric company."

"Wow. Okay. Of course, almost everybody I know does something, but...I envy you. It's like, there aren't that many guys in Atlanta...which sounds weird, doesn't it?" She shook her head.

"Maybe you've got to get out of that business, babe. It's not where all the good guys are hanging out."

Chantal looked at the floor. "I know." She raised her head to meet her friend's eyes. "It's hard to go back, though. Especially now. I don't have any skills. And I'm hooked on the money."

"I thought you wanted to be a singer."

"Please. I might as well have wanted to be an astronaut."

"Still, I bet if you thought about it, you could come up with a plan. And it would be worth it. You don't want old Chet. Plus, he lives in Tarryton. You'd have to move out there to Hicksville." Ava gave her a mischievous smile.

"But you live in Hicksville. And you're happy. And you have *two* jobs."

Ava hesitated a moment before responding, "I don't plan to *stay* in Hicksville."

Chuck had to raise his voice a little, as they danced, to be heard over "Sweet Caroline."

"You look beautiful, sweetheart." He was beaming.

"As do you, sir," Ava said, and they both laughed. She could see Scott glancing back and forth at them as he talked with Jeanette at the table.

"You're a welcome addition to our little clan of misfits, you know."

"Well, I had to find me some misfits because I wouldn't fit in with any normal people. Good thing you guys were around."

Her new father-in-law laughed again. "Marilyn told me you were worried about your mama. How's that going?"

"She's drinking too much. I'm sorry." Ava looked to where her mother was talking and flailing her hands for emphasis. Marilyn, Scott, and the rest of the table appeared to be listening.

"She's a different bird. But don't worry so much." And he maneuvered her through and under his arms in a circle.

Chuck had obviously been around a dance floor. He twirled her, waltzed her, and even dipped her at the song's end before walking her back to the table at which Scott, Jeanette, and Marilyn were seated, along with Chuck's brother Arthur, Robin, and her "friend," Naomi, a girl with an exotic American Indian look. (Peter, supposedly, oddly, had to work, a reason which Scott, also oddly, said was not a problem.) Behind them was another table for Toby, Bea, Jude, Clara, and the sisters and their husbands, and beyond that were Jimmy, Corrine, Gwen, Kathy, Chet, and three other workers from The Fox and Ale, including Barry the cook. Chantal's chair had been squeezed beside Bea's at Bea's kind insistence, but her chair was then empty, as she was at the bar chatting up the bartender. Friends and acquaintances from Tarryton, Corinth, Olympus, and a smattering of Scott's relatives from near and far filled the rest of the room. Ava winked at Bea as Chuck seated her back at their table.

"I didn't approach her with the dirty deed," Chuck said to his wife as he sat. "My excuse is that I couldn't hear over the music."

Marilyn shook her head as if to say she expected as much. "Ava, Chuck wants you to work for us. Same job you're doing for Steve. A little more pay. We like to keep things in the family as much as we can, and it would be a wonderful opportunity for all of us."

Jeanette was seated by Marilyn and wore a shiny orange dress and coral lipstick that made her teeth look yellow. She clasped her hands together like a delighted child. "How marvelous that would be!" She turned to Ava's new mother-in-law. "Ava is the brightest girl. It's why I never had another. Couldn't top her, that's why!" Three empty champagne glasses were still cresting her place setting, though no one knew the true number she had consumed.

Ava didn't know what to say. She couldn't help but wonder if she were being offered a position because Arrington's was the competition or to help her and Scott financially or both. Chuck must have read her mind.

"We could pay you a little more. What's good for the business would be good for you, and what's good for you would be good for business. Scott's onboard, right, son?"

Scott offered a slight shrug. "Yeah. Of course. But it's really up to Ava. She should do what she wants."

At least four pairs of eyes were on Ava as she answered, "Well, of course, I'm flattered. I might feel bad about leaving Steve's, though. But then, I don't know. I hope you don't mind if I think about it. He's been good to me."

Just for a moment, Chuck's pleasant expression hardened, only to return a second later.

"Nah, sweetheart, I wouldn't expect nothin' less. We ain't goin' nowhere."

Whitney Houston's "I Wanna Dance with Somebody" came over the speakers, and Jeanette asked Arthur to dance with her. Naomi went to grab Jude while Robin nabbed Chet, and the four navigated to the shoe-worn dance floor. Ava took a sip of her cider and noticed Chantal bouncing lightly to the music as she hovered at the bar, reluctant to find a partner if it meant leaving the striking tall bartender in the back.

Scott leaned close to the ear of his wife. "You've made me very happy, Mrs. Divine."

Ava turned to look at her husband, eyes round. "Oh gosh. That still sounds like you're speaking to your mother."

Scott grinned and took a sip of champagne before answering, "Nah. You've already made it your own. And I never call my mother Mrs. Divine. Marilyn, maybe."

Ava looked again toward the center of the pole barn where Bea—in a shin-length, ill-fitting blue knit dress with black tights—and Toby had joined the others. Ava knew Toby only danced under duress from the wife he loved, this fact belied by his clumsy and self-conscious moves. Robin waved and flailed her arms dramatically while the brass studs along the length of Jude's belt caught the lights.

"Robin looks happy, doesn't she? Do you think she is?"

Scott plucked an orchid from the vase, kissed it, and put it in the cleft of her sweetheart neckline. "As happy as anybody, I guess."

Ava sipped her drink and picked at her triangle of cake, crusty with the lightest-of-light purple frosting flowers.

But *she* was happy. And Scott seemed happy. And for the last fifty-five days since they had eloped to Elkland Falls—for the just-under-two months they'd been moving her things from cottage to cabin, riding Duke and Wallis, and she'd been learning to be a wife, lover, and a roommate to a man, she had been very happy—and felt pretty and loved, and noticed, and confused—because sometimes Scott didn't come home.

Chapter 25

"I WANT YOU TO know I appreciated that reception. Your parents are pretty great."

They were in bed. Scott was watching the last episode of *M*A*S*H*, and in Ava's lap was a folder Chuck had given her to prepare her for her job at his dealership. Tomorrow was to be her first day.

"They're all right." A commercial began, and he turned from the TV to look at her. "Did you want to take that job?" He nodded toward the papers in her lap.

Ava hesitated. "I guess. I think so. It is more money. And I'm sleeping with the owner's son, so I'm hoping to get special treatment."

"But I'm serious. I know Dad can be pushy. Sometimes I think he makes people feel like they don't have a choice when he wants his way."

"Yeah. Why would he want me to work there, though? I mean, what bad reason? Besides the money, it's a little closer. It's family. And there's no Jack Levinson." She had told Scott about the salesman, who had made her uncomfortable until her very last day.

"You should've been harsher with that guy. You're too afraid of hurting people's feelings."

"Not really. Maybe. But not everybody needs their feelings hurt. You grew up handsome and smart. You don't know what it's like to be shut down your whole life."

"How do you know Mr. Jack's life story so well?"

"I don't. But I can guess. You know I didn't grow up being invited to every ball."

"That was more because you were shy and because of your mom. And your house. And your dad, probably."

"But see, it's all the same. It can be because your house is trashed and your mom is drunk or your dad is dead or your leg is missing or you just don't know how to talk to a girl. He's just awkward. And probably lonely."

"An awkward guy who would sleep with you and thereby cheat on his wife if given a chance."

"You don't know that."

"Okay. I'm sure you're right. He'd probably refuse you if you offered. He's a saint."

"Don't do that! I didn't say that."

He sighed, then reached up and pecked her cheek. "Sorry. Pretend I never said a word."

Scott's show was back on, and he turned to it. Ava couldn't concentrate on the paperwork—which was a packet of the dealership's partner accounts, the companies from which they bought, and a couple of tax reports from the last two years—so she put it aside. There was nothing she needed to know that she couldn't learn as she went. She opened her nightstand and took out the letter. Although she'd read it two times, that was days ago, and she wanted to read it again.

Scott reached over and placed his hand on the envelope. "Why do you want to look at that again?"

The tension from the earlier moment had vanished, but she felt on the edge of unrest once again. "I don't know. It's a great gift, but I still don't get it—I still don't understand what's wrong with me. Maybe I'm just trying to figure it out." She slipped the envelope out from under his hand.

"There's nothing wrong with you. It's what's wrong with all of them. But you do have $35,000 you didn't know you had three days ago, and you can make a down payment on a house now. We can."

"I know. And you have twelve, and I have the other seven in savings. Unless Jeanette needs it."

Scott rolled over on his side, propped on his elbow, and faced her. "Listen. Every time Jeanette doesn't pay a bill or buys something on credit or goes to a medicine man you didn't know about that she gets billed for, you don't have to rescue her." He nodded toward the letter she had taken from the nightstand. "You see that now, right?"

Ava nodded, removed the letter from its envelope, and began to read. Scott leaned back against the headboard. "Read it out loud," he said and turned off the TV.

"Don't you want to see how it ends?" Ava asked, looking from him to the set and back.

"Nah. Don't really care. Never followed it much anyway."

> February 21, 1983
> Dear Ava,
>
> I heard of your marriage from your mother when we called at Christmas. As you may know, it had been a few years. I want to congratulate you, and also tell you I am sorry for a number of things and more than you can know.
>
> You should know your grandfather is the main reason I'm writing this letter. He has always felt badly about you. Of course, we both do, but your grandfather has carried it with him your whole life.
>
> You also should know we both believe Jeanette has made her bed. She was a popular girl but always ran a little heavy, always disrespectful of the laws of nature. She eats what she wants, and now I suppose she drinks what she wants—I think that's a fair assumption given the few phone calls we've had; that she has hedonism as an ideal. She has always lacked self-discipline, and although we haven't seen her since you were just a small thing, we know her whole life has just been a pursuit of pleasure with no regard to its consequences of type.
>
> I don't want to write too much, and I don't want to make you feel bad. But this has been burdening me, and I'm old now, so I want to make sure you know it is not your fault.

Your mother had everything handed to her. She had a temper, and although she could be very sweet and was always a lot of fun, she never wanted to work for anything, and if she couldn't have her way, she made everyone miserable.

She didn't want college. Nothing we said or promised could make her go. She wanted to get married and have babies. When she met John, she only wanted John. It makes me sad to say she wanted him much more than he wanted her. And that's my own child.

I'm sure you know by now we have paid her rent since John died. Elbert insisted. He was afraid, because of how she couldn't keep jobs, her tantrums, her spending and drinking, that she would lose the house and you would be homeless. You didn't choose your circumstances.

However, I must now unburden myself on another account. I am old, as I said, and I have to make my confessions while I can. Elbert wanted to pay for your college, but I did not. You were bright. You are bright. I knew from Jeannie you got scholarships and grants. (You may remember we called when you graduated high school, but you declined to speak to us then.) I knew they, along with your gumption and occasional campus jobs, would serve you, though I can't imagine working and graduating in three years as you did. I knew the struggle would make you stronger.

But that's not the only reason I opposed him. I was having a hard time with the whole situation that has existed since your mother and father met.

I am grateful you have turned out well, and you only have yourself to thank for that. Your gumption, as Elbert calls it, is why he wanted you to have this money. There will be more when we die—only God knows how much—and we are not as well off now as he and I once were. But you are not to use this for Jeanette. I know you pay for most things she needs and bail her out when she gets in financial binds because she has, shamelessly, told me.

We will continue to pay her rent as long as we are alive. The rest of our estate will go to the New York Adeline Lowenstein Home for Children and, as I said, a small amount more to you.

Jeanette, perhaps, cannot help whatever it is that is wrong with her. And you cannot help being born into the situation in which you were. Elbert insisted that we give you this when you married or reached age twenty-seven, whichever came first, and it is even in our will. He has always regretted not getting to know you.

Your Grandmother,
Eloise Draper

P.S. Jeannie has provided me the address of your college friend. If this letter is not received, I assume it will be returned to sender, the check will remain uncashed, or both. If the check is cashed, I will assume all is well. You may write me, but please don't call, as I believe we are incapable, at this point, of establishing a normal or comfortable relationship with you.

Ava put the letter down. "You should probably go deposit this." She handed the check to Scott but not before reading her name upon it in spidery script: *Ava Jane Lenoir Rush Divine*. Her eyes were blurry. On the line after "for," was written, "Your future."

Scott rolled her unto himself and stroked her hair. "They don't know what they missed."

"Can we really buy a house soon?"

"Of course. A big house with an extra room for your pictures."

"You mean a dark room?"

"Of course…what else?"

"Yikes! And we're going to fill it with babies. No 'only' child. Dozens and dozens of babies."

"Otherwise known as four."

They were silent for a while. "Don't let my dad bully you, Ava. When you go in there tomorrow, act that you've been around the block a time or two."

"What's that supposed to mean?" she spoke into the hollow of his T-shirted chest. "Do I look like a pushover to you? He called me feisty at the reception."

"He calls people a lot of things. He flatters, and he denigrates. He manipulates the people he can."

She pulled away and lay back against her propped-up pillows. "Well, you guys turned out okay."

Scott lay back as well and folded his hands behind his head. "Not really. And my dad hardly has one kind thing to say about any of us." He expressed this to the ceiling before turning his head toward hers, "you've never noticed that? 'Robin doesn't know which end is up,' he'll say, 'Peter could be making five times the money he is,' and 'Scott'—that's me, baby—'has no idea what it takes to make it in the real world.'"

"Because you didn't want to take over the business."

"And other stuff. To try to write. 'Who wants to read about doing stuff instead of just doing stuff?'"

"But you're making a go selling insurance. And writing is very important. People need writing! Not everybody can just go out and do all the stuff they read about." She shook her head. "I don't think he even knows what you're trying to do."

Scott's face softened. "It doesn't matter. We kids learned a long time ago to shut down the noise, but you haven't. He can cut you. And he can try to sleep with you."

"Scott—!"

"Yeah. He offered once to an old girlfriend."

"I find that hard to believe. Did *she* tell you that?"

"Actually, she did."

"And you believed her?" She used her most incredulous voice, a cross between a scoff and a laugh.

"You think this is all a joke," he said, his face set and sober. "That's what's hard to believe."

He got up and began to move toward the bathroom leaving her with her thoughts.

Chapter 26

DIVINE CHEVROLET WAS somewhat nicer than Arrington Ford. Still, except for a grander lot, flashier showroom, and a few more bells and whistles, they were both similar to dealerships everywhere in America.

Chuck gave her the tour himself with his usual booming voice, glad-handing personnel and customers alike as he introduced Ava to mechanics, salespeople, and clerks. Though the building was not spectacularly above par compared to Arrington's, her office was quite beautiful—much different than her previous small antiseptic box. The walls were of the palest tangerine imaginable, with plants, a beautiful desk, a large sunset (or sunrise?) landscape painting, and a couple of smaller ones. Ava admired the art.

"Marilyn did those," Chuck said, looking at the walls with Ava. "She's a talented lady."

Ava's eyes widened. "I didn't even know she painted!"

"Oh, she doesn't much anymore. She keeps busy. She gets bored, easily, too, so…"

"Wow. Well, these are good. I painted a little in college."

"Huh. I thought Scott said your hobby was pictures."

"It is. Probably my first love. But my art professor wanted me to keep painting, to take the upper-level courses, and I never did. Kind of wanted to, though." Ava walked closer to one of the smaller canvases, a mountainscape with rivers, trees, and rocks.

"What stopped you?" Chuck sat in one of the two padded leather chairs placed in front of the desk and gestured to Ava to take the other. He rested his arms on the chair rests, legs relaxed, in a display of ownership and complete ease.

"A couple of things. Every class costs money, as you know, and I was focused on my core classes so I could get out and earn a living. And any spare time I had, I just went on little picture-taking adventures."

"Right. Well, why not now?"

Ava shrugged. "Time. Space. Money."

"I get it. Marilyn has a whole room with that crap."

"I'd love to see it." Ava wondered why she never had, remembering that when Scott had first shown her the house, there had been a locked room he'd referred to as his mother's junk room. That had to be the one.

About that time, a very tall young woman with curly pouffy jet-black hair entered the office, wearing a navy pinstriped suit with a white tailored shirt unbuttoned relatively low. Chuck stepped to the woman and placed a hand on her shoulder.

"Ava, you remember Kimberly De Luca." Ava accepted the other girl's outstretched hand, recognizing her as a guest at the reception whom Scott had introduced as a Divine Chevrolet employee.

"Kimberly is kind of a checkpoint for us. She'll be the one that gets all the paperwork and then passes it off to you."

"I'm sorry? She's…I'm sorry, she does what?"

"She gets the invoices and payments, goes over it, and makes sure the numbers look right before she passes it all to you."

Ava didn't know what to say. "So…another accountant? Or office manager?"

"Well, not really. In a way. Never hurts to have two sets of eyes, though." Chuck was smiling from one to the other.

"It's so nice to see you again, Ava." The other woman extended a hand studded with two jeweled rings and tipped with long red nails.

Ava shook it. "So…what exactly is she…are you…receiving? And then giving to me?"

"The usual. Everything. Sales, services, parts invoices. All the payment receipts, you know, again, parts, cars, overhead…she'll pass it on to you to record in the ledgers and put it into our computer system. And then it's your show for the taxes."

"Oh. Okay, but Mr. Divine—"

"No, honey, it's still Chuck. I'm still your father-in-law."

"Okay. But, Chuck, I can—I mean, that's all kind of part of my job, isn't it?"

"Of course it is, sweetheart. It's more about two sets of eyes, as I said."

Kimberly, who had said nothing after her initial greeting, reassured her too.

"After today, we'll barely see each other. I'll show you everything Greta was doing before she left and where everything is, and I'll be around to answer any questions. But I'm not any kind of threat, so please don't worry about that."

"No…don't be silly…it isn't that."

But what it was, she wasn't sure. If Chuck was confident of her abilities, why have another accountant, or "set of eyes," as he called it? And if Kimberly was around when Greta was the accountant, why had he needed two then, and why had he hired Ava? But maybe it was just what he said it was, and sometimes businesses hired one accountant to check up on another's honesty; although, if that were the case, Kimberly should be checking the books after Ava, not before.

Ava let it go. She spent the rest of the morning with Kimberly, the latter explaining procedures and showing her where everything was. Ava left at noon. Starting tomorrow, she would work the morning at Divine instead of Arrington's and eat lunch before beginning her work at The Fox and Ale at two o'clock, just as she had always done; and just as she and Chuck had agreed she would continue to do now that she worked for him instead of Steve. But today, Marilyn had invited her to lunch—a celebration, she said, of her new job—but also, she said, to get to know each other better. Life was moving on, but now with more money, a new husband, and a new family. What did she care about Kimberly De Luca?

Chapter 27

MARILYN GREETED HER at the front door. "You don't need to knock anymore, dear. You're family now." She turned and led her guest to the living room, the same one in which the Divines had first entertained Ava when she'd come to the grand house the previous Thanksgiving. Marilyn wore cream-colored flannel pants, cream leather flats, and a silk blouse of cobalt blue. Her not-quite-black hair was smooth as glass, her almost-black eyes bright and heavily made-up to match her red lips. Ava felt mousy in her earth-colored pants and jacket.

"We should have done this sooner! Here, sit down." Marilyn sat as well. "Have a little of this. It's delicious." Marilyn lifted what looked like a flute of champagne in Ava's direction.

"Oh! No thanks…remember? I'm sorry." She smiled. "I'd love one of these, though," she said, taking a deviled egg. "Thank you."

"Oh. Well, I knew you didn't drink normally, but I thought if it was a special occasion—"

"No"—Ava shook her head and said with a laugh—"there would be too many special occasions, I think."

Marilyn's face pleasantly froze. "Of course!" A beat or two passed before she said, "Actually, honey, I thought maybe that was because, at Thanksgiving, we were all new to you. I thought you were playing it safe."

Ava nodded and swallowed. "Oh, sure, no, I get it." She smiled to show her understanding. "But no, I…I never do."

"Well…good for you…good for you." She squinted her eyes at her guest. "May I ask why you don't? I mean, it's fine, it's great, but you have to admit it's unusual in a young person today."

Ava shrugged. "I don't know. I haven't given it a lot of thought. I just never wanted to pick it up."

"Is it because of your mother?" Marilyn's head was tilted. Ava stiffened.

"Perhaps. As I said, I never thought much about it. It seems to take a lot away from people and without adding very much back. And I don't like the idea of anything controlling me."

Marilyn studied her a moment and sipped from her own champagne flute before responding, "I certainly get that. But it's nice too. It's nice to relax and to have fun, I think."

"Well, sure." Ava took another bite of egg, and there was a pause until she swallowed. "Those are delicious, by the way." She wiped her fingers on a napkin.

They made small talk and, twenty minutes into the conversation, moved to the breakfast room for their lunch, Marilyn having retrieved a soda from the kitchen for Ava. She told Ava she and Chuck met when he was a salesman at a parts store, and he had begun selling cars after they were married but hadn't bought the dealership until after Peter was born. And (ala Jimmy and Corrine) he'd bought it with Marilyn's money.

"He was quite the persuader," Marilyn said. She pursed her lips playfully and, holding her second glass of wine after her two flutes of champagne, leaned toward Ava and lowered her voice. "In *many* ways."

"I imagine. He *can* be charming. Weren't you scared, though? To put so much money into something he hadn't done before?"

"Kind of. But—and this isn't anything to be proud of, but—my folks had money. Still do. It wasn't like I was going to go hungry. And Daddy never got angry with me, so even if it didn't go well, it wouldn't have been so awful." She took a long swallow. "And then, it did go well, so there's that."

"Did you ever want something for yourself?" Ava thought for a moment she may have overstepped, but Marilyn answered without hesitation.

"You mean, with piano?" She looked out the window. "Maybe only for a moment. But after Peter…" She shook her head. "He was a hard baby."

Ava remembered how, at Thanksgiving, Chuck had said Marilyn played piano and could have been—wanted to be, but not really—a professional pianist. Marilyn had brushed it off.

"How was he hard? He seems so quiet. And smart. Like he would have been easy."

Marilyn toyed with her chicken salad. "No, just the opposite. He cried constantly. Hated loud noises, hated anything unexpected. Sensitive to everything. Chuck didn't have any patience with those sorts of things, so I tended him myself."

"Did he mellow out?"

"You mean as a child? No, not really. He stayed so distant. And he was always, always troubled and irritated and traumatized by the slightest things. It didn't take me long to give up piano."

"Scott was easier, I guess. And Robin."

"Well, yes, but…I still always loved Peter more. The harder children always need more love."

Ava was shocked, staring at Marilyn as she nibbled at her salad. She'd never heard any parent admit they loved one child over another.

Recovering, Ava said, "Chuck said you painted. I saw three of them in my office."

"Oh, those! Yes, I painted. Still do, sometimes. I have a room upstairs, but I don't have the patience anymore to stick with anything long enough to make it good."

"Well, I think the ones *I* saw were…so multidimensional and detailed…all the nuance, just like nature. I'd love to see more."

Marilyn shrugged. "Why not? But finish your lunch first. I made a crème brulee."

The room was packed—canvases on easels, folding tables covered with palettes and cups of brushes, sponges and rags, and what looked to be completed pictures along the floor, stacked against the walls. Ava felt chills mixed with envy mixed with passion. *I could do this,* she thought. She walked over to an acrylic portrait of a horse.

"Oh, don't look at that. Horses are incredibly hard for me."

"I think it's marvelous. Its eye looks as if you were trying to capture fear."

Marilyn looked at her in wonder. "I was. Do you paint?"

"I dabbled at Yancey. I spend more time on photography now."

"You should come out here sometime. I mean, I know you're busy with work and all, but if you ever get time...I have so many materials." She made a lame sweep of the room with her hand.

It had been about two hours, and Ava made the appropriate comments to prepare to leave.

"Ava, before you go...sit on the veranda with me, will you? It's not too cold, and anyway, you have your blazer."

When they had settled, Marilyn placed her hand on one of Ava's. "Now that you're part of the family and working for us and all, I just wanted to share or perhaps reassure you about a few things."

"Of course. I'm very grateful—"

"Hush, no, I'm not looking for gratitude." Marilyn removed her hand and looked across the pasture toward the stables as if to consider her words before looking back to Ava.

"Chuck is...basically, a good man. He is a good provider, and what he cannot accept, such as some things in Robin's life and the fact he and Scott don't get along well, he just let's go. Or tries to."

Ava nodded. She wondered if the problems between Scott and Chuck were more serious than she realized. Scott had disappointed Chuck by not staying on at the dealership and preparing to follow in his father's footsteps, but that was acceptable, wasn't it? Lots of sons disappointed their fathers that way.

"Chuck doesn't always do things the way other people do. He's a little selfish, and he got his way too much growing up. He doesn't take well to people telling him no or trying to restrain his impulses."

"Marilyn, I would never—I mean, whatever he says, I'm just there to do a job, and—"

"I don't mean you, dear." She looked again to the field.

"If you see things aren't done exactly by the books there at DC, and if you think perhaps his relationships are a little odd, I don't want you to be concerned. And don't feel the need to tell anyone, not even me. Do you understand?"

Ava hesitated. "I'm sorry, no. Not really."

Marilyn studied her daughter-in-law's face a moment. "Come with me." She moved back into the house and led Ava back upstairs into her painting room.

On one wall hung a tremendous but tasteful nude Ava had admired earlier, a lithe woman with cascading auburn hair sitting on a rocky precipice, head turned over one shoulder and looking down at her hand trailing through the water.

"Help me with this," Marilyn said, gesturing; and with some effort, the women lifted it from the wall to reveal a safe. This the older woman opened, revealing stacks and stacks of money, some manila envelopes, and a small carved chest that she removed, lifting its lid.

"This is the jewelry too valuable not to keep locked up."

Ava saw pearls, brooches, rings, necklaces, and bracelets, some garnished with jewels of startling proportion; but in a split second, Marilyn had closed the lid and put it to the side on a table. "These"—she gestured to the envelopes—"are stocks and bonds certificates. And this"—she picked up one of the stacks of hundreds—"is the money Chuck gives me."

Ava was silent. "Why? You mean, you guys' savings?"

"No, not 'our' savings. My money—money he began giving me when I realized he wanted to do what he wanted to do and that I insisted on to ensure I would be okay if he left me or if I decided to leave him so I would never be dependent on my parents or children. He's been giving it to me for over twenty years."

She waited a moment, then replaced the stack amongst the others, all of which were neat as pins. She was about to speak again when the phone rang, a black corded extension resting across the room atop a corner table with a chair beside it. Marilyn excused herself to answer it.

"Hello? Yes! Well, no, I was going to call you this afternoon, my daughter-in-law—no, Ava—yes, Scott's wife, but—well, no, not much longer, I just—"

Marilyn chattered on, but Ava was looking at the safe's contents, spellbound. Behind the stacks of unlabeled, rubber-banded hundreds were more stacks still bound by their paper bank sleeves, each labeled "five thousand." And then, before Marilyn hung up, Ava's gaze fell upon the inside door panel and the pasted laminated paper that relayed the make, model, and serial number of the safe. At the bottom, below the printed information, was a blank line where the owner could record the combination after it was programmed into the safe. In red ink, someone had written 4-29-54. Scott's birthday.

Marilyn finished her phone call and recrossed the room, waving a hand. "I'm so sorry. Mrs. Delacroix, her son, Louis, he's doing the landscaping this year, but—it doesn't matter, I just wanted to show you." She closed the safe, and Ava helped her rehang the painting.

"You don't understand this, I know. You're young, you're in love, and I don't even like to talk about unpleasant things. And I don't need to go into detail. But I just want you to know that when you work with Chuck, when you see or hear things that don't seem right or savory, I want you to know that I know. And, as friends, I don't want you to feel bad for me or worry or feel we need to discuss things. I have protected myself, and I will continue to do so, and as far I'm concerned, we can pretend this visit was all about girl stuff." She smiled and pressed herself into Ava for a hug.

In the drive, Ava waved bye with a forced smile and a wave of relief. She had the sense of something sad and dirty falling from her shoulders as she drove away, but what stayed with her—all the way back to the cabin—was just the smallest nugget of fear.

Chapter 28

SHE DIDN'T KNOW what to say. The house was gray and was set back from the road on a low, flat plain that nourished five strong trees—two oaks and three elms. The structure consisted of two rectangles that appeared as if they'd been set side by side but one slightly back from the other and then fused. A low-hanging porch (roofed in tin, as was the rest of the house) overhung five thin but ornately carved pillars standing shyly behind five nondescript shaggy bushes. Seven windows blocked along the house's two stories, the seventh being from a single-story appendage to the left. Stone steps led up to the porch, and brick stacked as latticework barricaded a narrow crawl space. The house's aura as something once loved but now forgotten was reinforced by missing shutters, peeling paint, and overgrown grass.

"So? What do you think?" Ava and Scott were standing back in the front yard after walking the perimeter of the house. He had driven her here for her birthday surprise a day early. Now he looked hopeful, but there was also a look of defense about his features. He knew this house was a betrayal.

Ava pressed her fingertips to her mouth, then spoke from beneath them, "And you're telling me you bought it?" She formed a fist and pressed it to her chest, holding her elbow with her other hand. "You filled out the paperwork, took the money from the bank, and signed the papers so that it's nonnegotiable? You *purchased* it?"

His face hardened. "I told you that. Yes, and I thought you would love it."

To be fair, she could see why he may have thought so: it had once been a great house, if not a grand house, and still, beneath its injured facade and lifeless patina, it could yet be a very good house.

But that was beside the point.

"Isn't that a little bold? A little risky? I mean, you took the money, my money, and a tiny bit of yours, and put a down payment on a house with a mortgage, for Pete's sake, without asking your wife?" Her heart thrashed behind her ribs. How could this be real?

"Your money? We talked about this. In the mountains, you were adamant we would share money—that a supportive wife always let her husband take the lead."

That was true. But that was in theory. And that was when they had eloped to Elkland Falls just a week before Christmas and when she only had a few thousand dollars. It never occurred to her that after Scott deposited the $35,000 check into a bank account they'd opened together, that he would look at houses with a Realtor, take the bulk of the savings, and acquire a mortgage, in only his name, and without her knowing. But how could she tell him she felt differently after she had the majority of the capital?

She walked to the porch and sat on its uppermost step as her husband moved to stand before her in the struggling grass pathway, arms crossed.

"What's wrong?" he asked, and she sighed.

"What's wrong?" She looked at her feet and shook her head, then up at him. He looked like a child who knew he should be in trouble but was maintaining his innocence anyway.

"I don't know what to say. I thought we would live in Olympus, maybe—or Corinth—in a nice neighborhood, in a house that didn't need any work. You just committed me to thirty years of living where I never even…even…in a place that I never…oh, man."

He reached his hands to his head and coursed them through his hair before holding them out as if to explain something to a confused child. "Listen, I get that. But, Ava, listen to me. Tarryton has good schools. Olympus is full of braggarts and snobs. Don't forget I grew up there, and I hated it. Corinth is only slightly better. And I know you're still a few hours away from Jeanette, but as often as you have to go there, you're still forty-five minutes closer living in Tarryton."

"That's not the point, Scott! You bought a house! With the only money I've ever had to do anything with!"

"I didn't use all of it! And I thought you'd like it. I thought it would be fun to surprise you."

"Did you really? You really thought I wouldn't like to be in on this decision? You surprise a wife with flowers or a piece of jewelry. And I'm not even on the mortgage!"

"Well, it was supposed to be a surprise. And you wouldn't be liable if we lost it either."

"Lost it! I work two jobs! I would never lose a house! I'm *really* good with money, babe. If it weren't for Jeanette and that college loan, I would be more than flush. Which is more than I can say for you."

His face was cold. He turned and walked back toward the car.

"Scott, listen…stop! I didn't mean that." He stopped and turned toward her. "I don't want to fight, but…I have to admit I've wondered where your money went sometimes."

"What's that supposed to mean?"

"You've lived at the cabin rent-free for several years in exchange for taking care of the horses. You have lots of clients and make a lot of insurance sales. I've seen that since we've been preparing our tax return. Your car payment, I get that…but I guess I don't understand why you only have a few thousand dollars."

"I'm only twenty-eight."

"Right. Twenty-nine next month."

"Whatever. I live life. Same as you."

"You…spend a lot. Drinks and food and your little weekend trips. Cocaine. That's expensive."

"I don't do that much blow. I take you out, too, Ava. I've got car insurance and other expenses. Clothes. I've always bought stuff for the cabin's upkeep too, and the horses, in case you never noticed."

"I know! And I've always thought Jimmy and Corrine should have been paying for that."

"I'm not going to niggle them for every dollar when they let me live there for years rent-free."

"The deal was to exercise and take care of Duke and Wallis. Not buy their stuff. Not work on their house." She lowered her head. "I thought we would save up a while longer. And get a better house. In a better place. Especially while we still had free rent."

He looked away from her, across the road, then walked to the porch, hiking it but standing away from her. "Ava, I want to write. I want to travel and write articles. I don't want to sell insurance for the rest of my life. I sold two of the only three articles I submitted last year, so I'm pretty sure I can make a go of it, now that I've started to take it seriously…but if we got the kind of house you were hoping for, I'd be obligated to kill it in sales, and I don't know if I'd ever make it with the writing. And you'd be obligated to work those two jobs or maybe even have to get one better-paying job just to keep up. And I thought you wanted to start a family."

This was true. They'd never even used birth control since the wedding in the tiny Elkland Falls Chapel because she wanted a baby as soon as it could happen, especially since Bea had told her four days before Christmas when Ava returned that Monday after eloping that she was already two months along.

Scott came and sat beside her on the step. "I don't want to argue this stuff with you. I can add you to the mortgage. We can always sell it in few years. And I thought it would be fun to fix it up ourselves. Bea knows about it, and she said she's 'dying' to help." Scott made air quotes with his fingers. "Chet already said he would, too, especially until he gets hired again. Even that grandma, Clara, wants to. You know how she's always trying to ingratiate herself into all you guys' lives."

He fell silent, but she didn't speak right away. She felt deflated and sick. When she finally raised her head to look at him, she expected to see a look of contrition, but it wasn't there. She wanted to go back to the way they'd looked at each other that morning when, in bed, he'd told her he wanted to take her to see her birthday surprise.

Ava spoke to her shoes, "Bea's not going to want to paint since she's pregnant."

"Whatever. She can do other stuff. And nobody has to do anything. I can fix the whole place up myself."

She took a deep breath, stood up, and turned to him. "Well, I guess I don't know how to fix everything right now, but I'm sorry. I want us to be okay."

Scott stood, too, and his face softened. He pressed into her, and she eased into his strong arms, his crisp shirt, and his warm chest. She breathed deeply of his Grey Flannel cologne.

Chapter 29

THE CALL AWOKE Ava only. The clock radio illuminated 3:21 a.m., and she didn't recognize the caller's voice.

"I'm so sorry, is this Ava Rush?"

"Yes, Ava Divine, but yes—"

"Right. Right. This is Pastor Everly. Your mother goes to our church."

"Oh! Pastor…Carl?"

"Yes, yes. I don't want to alarm you, but on the slim chance you'd want to talk with your mother before I got a chance to call you at a decent hour, she's here at my house. I'll try to be brief if you'll allow me."

She took the cordless phone to the cabin's darkened kitchen, and as she left the room, Scott stayed gently snoring.

By six o'clock, she was dressed and had breakfast ready for them both. (Scott always awoke at 5:45, and they ate together.) She would pack after they ate and then call into her two jobs. It didn't take long to tell Scott everything the pastor had told her.

A neighbor—the only one who had any semblance of a relationship with Jeanette—had called the police out of concern, she said. Jeanette had spent the day emptying her house, not into a moving truck as one might expect but into the yard and along the street. The neighbor also said Jeanette had worked most of the night, and it looked to be almost everything one might own. Lastly, the woman added, Jeanette had worked alone, in her pajamas, talking loudly to herself and wildly gesturing.

When the police arrived around one in the morning, Jeanette told them she was going to an ashram; she would be helping to care for the commune's children. She had seen it on *60 Minutes.*

The police told her she couldn't abandon the things in the yard or on the street. Jeanette told them she was donating them to the church, which is how they'd learned of Pastor Carl. He'd come to get her, taken her to his house, and called Ava.

Scott ate, listening to her story without much comment. She hurriedly talked as she ate, then moved to the bedroom to pack with Scott following.

"I'm going, too, Ava. You can't handle her alone."

She turned. "Oh, baby. I would never ask."

"I know. Little Miss Independent. But you don't even know what to do with her."

Ava's eyes filled with tears. "I don't. I really don't." And he held her.

"Don't you think we should figure this out? For the long term?"

"Sure. I know. But I can't think about that right now. I can't imagine what that poor man is already putting up with." She wondered if Pastor Everly was married.

By seven, when Scott went to take care of the horses, and after he'd called Corrine to say they'd be gone a couple of days, Ava had called Bea.

"I'm coming too," she'd said. "And Toby. Toby can come." Ava felt limp with gratitude and relief; in an instant, she'd amassed a posse.

They were on the road by eight thirty, and by twelve fifteen, with Scott driving the Chevy Blazer far too fast, they were there, parking along the street. Ava exited the car, staring, and walked to the yard's edge.

The small dirt-scrubbed patch was a surfeit of goods. Many things Ava recognized and some she did not, but she wandered around the piles as if she were looking at objects from another planet. Most small items were in open boxes and untied trash bags, while larger ones lay about in abandon. There were canisters and dishes and shoes and magazines, the round breakfast table and its chairs. Pillows and blankets and trinkets and books mingled with towels and washcloths, sheets and end tables, lamps, notebooks, and paint cans.

Bea came up beside her, linking her arm through Ava's, and leaned her head on Ava's shoulder.

"Mama's gone and done it now, Smitty," she said, and Ava couldn't help but smile.

"What am I gonna do, Bea?"

Bea motioned Toby and Scott, who were hauling up the sofa and an overturned dresser from the street, to follow them as she pulled Ava by the arm toward the house. They entered the front door, spellbound.

It looked like an eviction scene, and then, as if—a couple of days later—a squatter had moved in. Trash littered the floor, and a pillow was propped against the living room wall with a half-gone quart of vodka, a Solo cup, and a pack of Benson and Hedges arranged in a tribal semicircle. Beside the ashtray was a pencil and a composition book opened to its first page, which Ava picked up and read:

> To Do:
> Get rid of all stuff except personal stuff for trip
> Clean out the house
> Call the ashram
> Call *60 minutes* to find out the name and number of the ashram
> Buy a bus ticket
> Call ava
> Call pastor carl
> See if Franny will take the cat

Ava passed it to Bea and sank against the wall, after which Bea sat beside her and read the page as well. Toby and Scott stood in the middle of the room, Toby looking uncomfortable and Scott lighting a cigarette.

"Hey, Superman," Bea directed to Toby, "start getting the stuff back in the house, please. There should be two big cans out back for all the trash." She put the notebook down and sighed. "Hopefully, they'll have been emptied." Both guys went out the door.

Ava cupped her face with both hands, elbows propped on knees. “Should we look for a cat?”

“I guess we’d better.”

“Maybe she will have found it a home. It’s not like the list is in any particular order.”

“Maybe.” Bea put her arm across Ava’s shoulders. “Ava, you got to roll with this, darlin’, or it’s gonna getcha. Go in the kitchen and call the good preacher. Ask him if he can keep her caged up until seven.”

Ava and Bea picked up the litter within the living room and kitchen and vacuumed before the guys brought in the furniture. Luckily, Jeanette had been unable to haul any of the second-floor appointments down the narrow stairs, or at least not before the police had apprehended her, so it didn’t take long for both men to return the house’s contents to its inside.

The two women pried open the bags and peered into the boxes, each chock-full of a random assortment of items to the degree that they needed to be dumped in the living room floor and sorted: bath linens were mixed with the contents of kitchen drawers, lingerie with bathroom cleansers, and bric-a-brac from the mantle dumped onto scrapbook supplies.

They hadn’t worked long when Ava straightened, dropped her hands, and sighed; and Bea, stepping quickly to her good friend’s side, whispered into her ear, “Don’t worry your pretty head about this, okay? Even now, I’m hatching a brilliant plan.”

Ava turned and questioned this with her eyes, but Bea only smiled, shook her head, and walked toward the kitchen.

“I *said*, I’m *hatching* it. You’ll be the first to know.”

Pastor Everly brought Jeanette back to the house at seven thirty, declined a fast-food dinner, and left. “Please call if I can help,” he’d told Ava and looked as sincere as anyone she’d ever known. “Jeanette is valued by our congregation.”

Ava watched his slim form in its khaki pants and soft cotton shirt give Jeanette a chaste hug, then slip into his car and pull away. She couldn’t help but wonder what her mother could possibly bring to the good man's congregation except for a lot of need and chatter and chaos.

Fifteen minutes later, they were all in the living room with their fast-food meals. Bea, who had already discussed her idea with her husband, had ridden along with Ava and Scott to McDonald's to talk it over with them while Toby mowed Jeanette's lawn. Jeanette sat smoking in her overburdened green recliner, her chubby legs crossed at the ankles.

"It's very important to be able to live small if you go to an ashram." She pulled deeply on her cigarette. "They don't want you attached to your stuff. You can barely take anything with you."

"Mom, you're not going to an ashram. Do you even know what an ashram is?" Ava and Scott sat on the two folding lawn chairs with Bea and Toby on the sofa, everyone eating except Jeanette.

"Of course I do, Ava." Jeanette's eyes flashed with anger at her daughter. "You go to do good. And you get closer to God." She took a drink of the Sprite she'd already laced with vodka.

"Yeah, but they don't worship Jesus there, Mom. Most all ashrams are Hindu. Are you going to be a Hindu?"

"Oh, you sound like Pastor Carl! You don't know what they do there!"

"Okay, but, Mom, do *you* know what they do there?"

"Did you watch the show, Ava? Did you? No, you did not." Jeanette heaved from the chair and picked up the cat, whom Bea had found upstairs with nothing, whose very litter box Jeanette had relegated to a mound in the yard. She settled back down in her seat.

"Where did you get that cat, Mom? Is it yours?"

"Yes! Do you think I'd steal a cat?" She buried her face into the fat gray tabby's neck. "They were giving them away at the supermarket. They were on death row." Her voice, muffled from the tabby's fur, cracked at the end of the sentence.

"Jeanette, do you miss Ava?" Bea's voice was soft.

Here it comes, Ava thought.

It took only a moment for Jeanette's eyes to well with tears. "Of course I do. She's my baby."

"So did you really want to go to California, or have you just been so lonely without Ava that you didn't know what else to do?"

The older woman bowed her head. "Ava doesn't need me anymore. The ashram has children, and Mike Wallace said that the older women take care of them all day while the young women worship and meditate."

Bea nodded her understanding. "I think that might be hard after a while. You'd have a lot of children to tend, and I wonder if you would ever get a break. I only teach twenty hours a week, and those kids drive me crazy."

Ava thought of the unborn baby about the size now, Bea had said, of a butternut squash resting safely under Bea's sun-bedecked smock top. She bet Bea would never tire of her own child.

"I'm sure I'd get a break!" Jeanette spat it out as if everyone in the room were clueless except for her. "I think Mike Wallace would have mentioned if they never got a break!"

Toby laughed but not unkindly. "I don't know, Ms. Rush. I'm not sure us men even think to ask those questions. Those women might be mindin' those crowds of young'uns day and night, just wonderin' what they got themselves into."

For the first time, Jeanette's face showed uncertainty. "I never had a lot of children."

"I know, ma'am. But my mama did. Believe me, there was a lot o' times I thought she'd trade the whole pack of us for a nice new car if she'd ever got a chance."

Scott, who had stayed silent, got up and collected the food trash. "I'm with you on that, Tobes," he said. "Kids are overrated."

Ava shot him a questioning look, but he shook his head, smiling. *I love you,* he mouthed and carried the bags to the kitchen.

"The thing is, Jeanette, Ava and Scott and I were talking… before Pastor Carl brought you home…we thought, you know, that you might not really want to go to California. We thought you might want to move closer to Ava."

Jeanette looked from one person to another. "I…I would love to live with Ava."

"Well, you wouldn't exactly live with her. I mean, she's married now, and they have their own place...but Toby and I have a beautiful little guesthouse. You know, it's where Ava lived before she and Scott got married. And it's so close to Ava's and Scott's, and it's close to their new house too. I think you would love it."

Jeanette looked wild-eyed but hopeful. "Well...I would need my stuff. And I don't mean just this, but all that other stuff, too, that you girls put in storage." Bea and Ava exchanged glances. So she wasn't crazy enough to have forgotten that after all.

"Well, we thought you were getting rid of everything forever... you were, weren't you?"

"No! I mean I was, but I wasn't sure I was going, so I think I was going. But I'll need my stuff if I don't, though." She struggled out of the chair again, tossing the surprised cat beforehand, and began pacing. She stopped at one of the blackened windows, staring as if she could see out, but she couldn't. "I do need my stuff." She then turned to Ava. "Is it still in storage? Can we get it tomorrow?"

"Mom, you don't ever need anything we put in storage *ever* again. You were just ready to abandon everything, remember?"

"Well, Ava Jane, you don't know! You *do not* know."

Scott had returned and was standing in the doorway between the kitchen and living room. "Jeanette, you'll have what you need." He lit a cigarette and smoked it while Jeanette paced and looked at each of them with a caged animal stare.

"I don't think I do. I don't think I do."

Ava looked at her mother for minutes without speaking, while Bea, with interpositions from Toby, tried to talk her down from the proverbial ledge. For all the time it took for Bea to get up and gently nudge her back to her chair, for Toby to bring her a glass of water and her McDonald's dinner, for Scott to stand and watch Ava, Ava looked at her mother. *How did this happen?* she wondered. How did a woman like this ever lie with Ava's handsome dead father, make a baby, and raise it and then slowly, or not so slowly, lose her ever-lovin' mind?

By morning, the plans had been laid.

Jeanette, who had to have been beyond exhausted, had passed out in the recliner around nine. Bea and Toby had blown up an air mattress they'd brought from home, along with its pump and some bedding and pillows, and slept on the screened back porch. Ava had been all too ready to crash on one of the twin beds in her old room, and Scott offered to sleep on the sofa to keep an eye on his mother-in-law rather than wake her and risk her resisting going up to bed.

But Ava realized in the morning that Scott had never gone to sleep, and he was standing in the open doorway staring at the street when Ava went downstairs around six. His eyes looked vacant and were darkly circled, and his mouth looked tense and set.

Ava had questioned his face wordlessly.

"Your mom wanted to talk." He reached his pack from the kitchen counter and flipped it open for a cigarette.

"You don't look like you slept at all. Did you?" Scott clicked his lighter to its flame, his face and silence answering for him.

"I'm going to get coffees," Ava said and banged out the screen door. Jeanette couldn't have talked all night.

When she returned, Bea had invited her to sit on the cement stoop overlooking the yard, its patchy grass still bruised from its burdens of the day before. They sipped the precious coffee they had rewarmed in a tiny steel pot on the stove and discussed how they would help her mother transition.

Jeanette would live in the guest cottage; everyone agreed she needed people available to keep an eye on her until more permanent arrangements were made. The possessions she didn't need that would have to be left behind would be offered to the landlord or taken, as was the last batch, to Goodwill. Ava would reach out to her grandmother in a respectful attempt to receive the money she currently paid for Jeanette's rent, some of which could go to Bea and Toby for "rent" or the cottage's maintenance, some to be given to Jeanette for spending, and some to go to Ava to save or buy her mother's essentials. Jeanette's welfare checks, hopefully, could be transferred by showing proof of residence, and they would find her medical care by starting with Bea's family's physician. Then with Jeanette still sleeping, Bea had asked Toby and Scott outside to run everything by them, and a little after eight thirty, Bea called the landlord.

"Well, there's good news and bad news," she told the little crew after hanging up and rejoining them in the front yard. "I told him as much as he needed to know about what happened and asked him what it would take to get out of the lease, but he said it's up in June anyway, so we'll just to pay it till then. It's cheaper than paying the fees. He also said we could leave any furniture or decent stuff she didn't need, and he'll use it or find it a home." She turned to Toby. "Just rent the smallest U-Haul you can. I think that and Scott's Blazer can do it, especially since it'll have two people less."

"Where ya gonna put it all, doll?" Toby stood with his thumbs hitched in his pockets. "I reckon it could go in the shed, under some tarps."

"Yeah. Exactly. We can do that. Perfect, baby."

Bea waved the men off from the front yard, giving last-minute instructions, then reentered the house with Ava. The two girls began bagging an assortment of toiletries and pantry items that had been dumped back into the living room floor, working quietly, even though Jeanette, still snoring, proved to be as sound a sleeper as Ava had promised; they could sort through the hodgepodge in Tarryton.

When they'd filled two bags, Ava stopped and sat down amid the clutter. "Why are you doing this?" She peered upward at her friend, realizing Bea didn't need her to clarify.

"You can't imagine?"

"Not really. I mean, when you offered me the guesthouse, I was surprised and, of course, grateful. But, you know, I planned to come back to Atlanta in a few months. Or maybe move to Florida, even—you can't imagine how much I've thought about that—but now you're moving in my psychoid, broke mother, with no plan. And I don't have a plan either. I have no idea what to do with her."

Bea sat down too. "I know. Me neither. But I think it would be a bad idea to leave her alone down here again."

Ava stared at her. "Then what the heck, Bea? I mean, don't get me wrong, it's like a gift from the Magi, but this could blow up in your face big time. And Toby's. And God—I mean, man—you're expecting a baby, for cryin' out loud. I would never do this."

"But you're agreeing to it."

"No, you don't get it. I'm agreeing to it because I have no answers. You're helping *me.*"

Her eyes welled, and her voice broke. "I just don't think I would ever do this… I don't think I would ever even think to do this…for you." And then she began to cry, full-on.

Bea scooted over to hug her. "Oh, baby, come on. You're under so much stress. It's okay if you wouldn't. I'm not doing it because I think you'd do it for me. It looks kind of unfun, to be honest."

Ava pulled away. "Then why are you doing it? I'm so ashamed. I'd like to be the kind of person who would invite your crazy mother to live on my property, but I don't know how you get to be like that." She found a washcloth in a pile of dumped linens and blew her nose into it.

"Gross. Now, what're you gonna do?"

"I don't know. Burn it. I'll probably make a funeral pyre in the front yard with all the self-help posters still up there on her walls. Do you think she was going to haul those out to the yard or try to smuggle them into the ashram?"

Bea gave a short laugh. "Maybe she hadn't thought that far." They sat without speaking for a moment.

"This is one of those Jesus things you try to do."

Bea smiled, stood up, and pulled up her friend by the hand. "Maybe."

Ava stuffed the used washcloth into a bag of trash. "Well, just so you know, I'm gonna plan to not be around when it all goes south."

"Ha!" Bea grinned. "Me, too, probably, for that matter." They started again with the bags.

Chapter 30

AVA SAT IN her beaten-down car, feeling its pain. She stared at the house in front of her—a sad large gray mistress, the object of someone's long-ago fantasy. Scott had relayed its origins, that it had been built seventy-five years ago by a mill supervisor who had left his wife and who had thought, foolishly, his five children would want to move with him. When all had opted to stay with their mother, he'd sold it three years later, moved to Florida, and bought a boat, opening a deep-sea fishing business. *Irony*, Ava thought, *my constant companion.*

Bea's Impala was already there, but Ava just wanted a minute.

She didn't hate the house; she didn't hate Scott for buying it. She had already decided she would claim it as part of her dream because otherwise, there could be no reconciliation between what she had wanted and what she now had.

She'd never believed she wanted too much, just her share—one husband, some kids, a few friends, a great job. The downside to this plan was that as each person or thing disappointed her, the dream cache began to feel too small.

Maybe *she* was too small—always striving, but always, too, pulling ever inward, being careful, being watchful, being good. She was storing it up she sometimes felt like tinder in her soul awaiting a match, combustible but unlit; she was waiting for the moment she would break free, make her move, and be happy.

It hurt her that some people were born right into happiness—with a family, with money, with both—but others, like herself, had to struggle. And she wasn't going to settle for false and stupid happiness, like Jeanette, who thought happiness was sugar and cigarettes and something good on TV. Those people all broke down along the way, and she would not; she wouldn't settle for the mundane. Everything she did was to shore herself up against the tragically mediocre.

The sad thing was that sometimes, she believed it was imminent—that elusive joy and peace she thought was happiness. Sometimes her work and her clamoring brought this new scent right to the cusp of her nostrils, but then, just around the corner, some new event would flush the victory, just as had happened with Eric. The whole world would turn on a dime.

Well, no more. Ava loved Scott. She would make this place her dream home. Soon, she may even be expecting a baby.

She heard the gravel crunching behind her and saw the two cars in her rearview mirror. *Right on time,* she thought. She stepped out of the VW and stood there, shading her eyes as they emerged from the vehicles—Susan, Clem, Brent, Jesse, and Clara in one, Laura, Greg, Kelly, and Alex in the other. Clem went to the back of their Oldsmobile and unloaded two large picnic coolers from the trunk.

"I can't believe y'all came," Ava said, and she moved in to receive her requisite hug from Clara.

"Well, good time, honey, of course we came!" the girls' grandma declared. She squinted as she looked toward the house. "I remember this place from when I was a young thing. Henry Berger built it. Remember him to this day."

The kids, except for Alex, had rushed into the house. Alex shyly hugged Ava's waist, then pulled away. "I have a terrarium." His eyes shone with pride.

"Get outta town!" Ava gently punched his arm. "You're the coolest kid in fourth grade. I never had a terrarium. I had some flower pots with worms. I'm guessing a terrarium is cooler than that, though."

Alex just stood there, smiling.

"I remember this house too." Susan peered at the upstairs windows. "I was on the cheerleading team with a girl who lived here. Ninth grade."

"That would have been one of the Akers' kids," Clara said. "They were the third owners. Dolly Akers ran that flower shop, Laura, you remember that?"

The grown-ups talked amongst themselves while Alex remained beside them, shining and hopeful. Ava hadn't seen either of the girls or their families since the wedding reception and had only seen Clara when the older woman arranged to meet her to give Ava some plants for her birthday—a potted mum, a Meyer lemon tree, and a philodendron in a whiskey barrel. Laura's hair was now bleached platinum blonde, and Greg, who sported a mild sunburn, commented he wasn't going to stand around outside as he made his way to the door.

"I'm grateful, you guys. It's a mess, but it has potential. That's what Scott and I keep saying to each other." She laughed.

"Well, of course. You get a better deal this way. Don't pay somebody else to fix up what you can do yourself." Clem proclaimed this as if he were imparting unknown wisdom that it would behoove them all to remember. "Sure does need a new roof, though, I will say that."

"I know. But it's supposed to be structurally sound."

"Oh, it's a great house, a great house!" Clara declared. "Mr. Berger had money. There was no need to scrimp. I bet by the time it's painted and the floors refinished, and you said the plumbing needs updating—"

"We don't have money for plumbing yet, Gram," Ava interjected.

Clara waved her hand. "Oh, no, not yet, that's okay. I mean, in my day, people did what they could, when they could. Nobody dreamed of taking out a loan, just did the best we could, and—"

"I've got a buddy. He's done plumbing for—"

"Clem, she just said not yet—"

"I couldn't live with a grody bathroom, though." Laura offered a pinched face to Ava. "Are they just outdated, or are they gross too?"

"Laura, my land, that is too rude. You girls were not raised—"

"I have a turtle, Ava. A big one. Mama said if I played outside for one hour a day—"

The group moved toward the house. Ava retrieved a cooler of ice from the boot of her VW and went inside. Bea was taping off the living room, surrounded by stacks of paint cans and cleaning and painting supplies. Radiating hospitality in Ava's stead, she greeted everyone and began filling cups with the ice from Ava's cooler and tea she'd brought from home. Her belly looked perfectly round now, but Ava knew she still had almost three months to go. Her bangs fringed her blue bandana, and her face was luminous, happy.

Everyone was given tools for their trade of the day—tape, rags, brushes, rollers, paint, and trays; or buckets, rags, scrub brushes, ammonia, and soap. Bea had, of course, devised a plan, and everyone received working orders. Bea even assigned the children as personal assistants to each of the parents—little step-and-fetch-its. Ava, embarrassed by this collective gift, tried to go unnoticed to the kitchen, her rags, bucket, and cleansers in hand, her boombox already on the counter.

"They've been informed." Bea's voice, low, came from behind Ava, and she turned to see her friend standing in the kitchen doorway, clasping each doorjamb with a look of mock seriousness. "There's no turning back until the dirty deeds are done." She walked on into the kitchen.

Ava laughed. "Imagine if the sellers hadn't already supposedly cleaned it. It could have looked like my mother's when we moved her out."

"Yeah. Hers wasn't too bad. And it was small. I think we did the best we could by her landlord."

"Me too. I don't suppose you saw her today." Ava felt an odd twinge, as she already had several times, remembering she'd grown up in that run-down home, and she would never stay there again.

Bea nodded. "I did. I went out to see if she needed anything before I left. I told her Tobes was working around if she thought of anything before Jude picked her up."

"Poor Jude. Does he know what he's getting into?"

"That's just it. Ever since she went with us last Saturday, they're like big buddies." Jeanette had gone with Jude and Bea to an arts-and-crafts festival and had been "no trouble at all." Now Bea gave her a knowing look. "I told her she would have to work extra hard all day if she came with us today, but that, of course, she was welcome to come. I think she liked her chances better with Julian."

Ava nodded, a smile playing about her lips. "You're good. You know her, Bea. She'd come out here and talk to everyone and not do anything."

"I know. I told her how much I was dreading it, how it was the worst, how you were going to owe me big time—"

"Yeah, yeah, yeah. Just don't let her drive you crazy while she's out there."

Jeanette had lived in Tarryton for one and a half weeks. They'd gone to Bright Point on Monday before last and had her settled in the cottage by the time Bea had to start her midday workweek Wednesday afternoon. This Saturday, the twenty-third of April, was the last one before Scott's birthday, and Ava would concentrate on what to do with Jeanette after that.

"She's all right. I should've adopted her a year ago though, 'cuz the entertainment value is priceless."

Ava cut her a look. "You don't need entertaining. God knows Toby doesn't either."

"No. But she's fine. On the mornings I didn't work this week, I went out there to see if she wanted to have coffee with me, and she did—all three days. And now, of course, we have the phone hooked up again."

"With no long-distance."

"With no long-distance. But wouldn't it be great if this job works out? And I'll take her to church again. She liked it."

"And she loved the festival."

"She did. I know she has those weird episodes, Ava, but normally, she's not that bad. Talks a lot. I think she's desperate for attention."

"Well, there's a news flash for ya."

"Yeah. I know. It's not as hard on me because she's not my mother. But she did, she talked to everybody. Jude told her though, more than once, that she helped him sell."

"What…what did she help him sell?"

"A planter. It was gorgeous—I know he would have sold it anyway—but your mom, she's a people person. She's going to have to be around people."

"So you keep saying." Ava was taping off the doorjamb while Bea had begun blocking off the backsplash. "If she works at the salon, what did he say, afternoons?"

"That's what he's thinking—afternoons to evening, just cleaning, restocking. He couldn't pay her much, but I don't think she'd even mind."

"Probably not. Plus I could get a new car out of it. Scott already said we could give her the Bug. And since we'd need a minivan, eventually, anyway, with kids, we thought, why not now? Like, we're already trying for the first one, and if we got it now, we wouldn't have to lose money on a trade-in when we had the others."

"You know I'd be super jealous, right? Even though I'd allow it. But we're gonna get rid of the Impala by baby number two, anyway, hopefully."

They worked a couple of minutes without speaking. Ava heard the rise and fall of a car pass on the road beyond them.

"Bea. Do you think—I mean, you've seen her now—can she do that, do you think? I mean, do a decent job at the salon?"

Bea nodded right away. "Of course. Don't worry about that. Worry about something *when* it happens, not before."

Clara and Clem came in to find out what color went in the upstairs master bedroom. Laura came in a few minutes later to ask if either of them had a Band-Aid.

When they were alone again, Ava asked, "When you said it was hard with your mom, why was it? Did you ever not get along? Or did you just say that to try to make me feel better?"

"Oh, heavens, no. I mean, it was hard, but not as hard as for you, I'm guessing. But I was younger too. And I think it's harder when you go through those teen years together, but I missed that. Mama used to try to get me more interested in clothes, for one thing, or just to care how I looked in general. I cut my bangs once, and she sobbed like a baby." Bea shook her head. "Like it was just the biggest reflection on her. She always made me write letters and thank-you notes, and I thought it would kill her when I didn't want to learn to sew. You know how she loved to sew."

Ava visualized the drapes that still hung throughout the old Mullins house, the needlepoint pillows, and the pictures she remembered in the albums, showing Kenneth in a light-blue handmade leisure suit and the three girls in matching seersucker dresses.

"Did you…were you ever ashamed of her?" Ava stayed focused on the straight edges of the wood.

"I don't know. No, I guess not. I just remember being very afraid of whatever the thing was that was changing her because at my age, she was still the biggest part of my world."

They were quiet a moment. Kelly, who at ten looked even taller than when Ava had last seen her at the reception, bounded in, almost breathless. "Brent and I are having a contest."

"Why are you sweaty?"

"Daddy and Uncle Clem said whoever works the fastest and best and hardest can stay home with Grandma tomorrow." Ava knew Clara would not work on Sundays, but the others had already committed to coming.

"That's sad, Kelly. I think helping me and your Aunt Bea on my house would be all the fun you'd ever need."

The girl shook her shaggy short blonde hair and licked her lips. "No, Ava, we don't like it that much. I want to stay with Grandma."

The girl didn't get the joke, but that was okay. "So I will cry later. I'm busy now. What can we do for you?"

"Daddy says clean off the table on the porch so we can eat out there later. But Brent wants me to have to scrub it, and he wants to use the hose, but that's not fair."

"Well, tell Brent—"

"I'll handle it," Bea interposed. "You don't need a hose. Go get a bucket and two rags, and I'll give you each a little squirt of Palmolive. Nobody needs to be squirting a hose out on the porch before lunch." Kelly gave an exaggerated sigh but bounded off again like a young colt.

Bea paused to scan the room, hands on hips. "What color are you doing in here again?"

"Egg-yolk yellow." Ava stopped working too. "We should have brought stools or something."

Brent, who had just turned eleven and could have been Kelly's brother instead of first cousin, appeared at the door with Kelly, holding a bucket and a handful of rags. His face looked sulky, but Bea ignored it and began filling the pail at the sink, infusing it with a dash of dish soap.

"Bring this out when it's full," Bea said to Brent, gesturing to the bucket, then nodding to Ava, said, "C'mon," and led the way to the back porch. A picnic table rested within its torn screens, with benches aligning each long side, and they pulled these to the edge of the porch so the kids had room to work on the table. The girls had just sat side by side on one when the kids tumbled out the back door, each then splashing a rag on the grimy wood surface.

"We're gonna get fired when the others find us out here." Ava leaned her head against one of the porch posts, and it was bathed in sun.

"Nah. You're the boss."

"Of a crew of volunteers. Who will quit when they see us. Pretend you fainted and I brought you out here."

"Got it."

Ava raised her head; they sat without speaking for a moment as they watched the kids, listening to them argue about sections and who was doing the best.

"Scott will be here tomorrow."

"I know. I told them."

"Did they ask?"

"No. I told each of them when I called to ask if they could help. They all love you, Ava. They were happy to come. We can imagine what's it like to live without family close by."

"Well. He's really busy these days. And I told you he just sold the Masters article. We couldn't believe it. They want him to go to Texas in a couple of weeks for the Houston Coca-Cola Open."

Bea's mouth gaped. "That's fantastic, you! So he's gonna do sports? I thought he wanted to do travel."

"Well…we don't have enough money yet for him to do a lot of travel. But, yeah. He says golf, adventure, travel, plus health, which he says is easy. Those are what he calls his markets. But after he sold that article to *Fox and Hound* last fall, he hit up some other editors about sports, and especially golf, which he knows a lot about. And, of course, he'd sold that one to *Men's Health.* He even heard back from *Horse and Hound,* you know, the British magazine? He'd asked them about covering the American fox-hunting scene for next season."

"That is so great. I can't believe he sold an article about the Masters. I mean, no offense, but with no experience."

"That's one of the cool things. I was going to let Scott tell it, but he probably won't care. You don't know golf, I know, I don't either. But he struck up this conversation with this guy on the sidelines, this old dude, and he happened to be the uncle of the winner, Ballesteros. All these other journalists and sportswriters were there, but Scott started a conversation with this guy in a camp chair, and turns out, it was Ballesteros's uncle. None of the other writers must have known…or they didn't care."

"Ballesteros was the winner guy?"

"Yep. Course, he hadn't won yet. But this guy, he's old, and Scott sits on the grass beside him and gets all this inside scoop information about Ballesteros as a kid and an early golfer, and so when he wins, Scott pitches this to *World of Golf*, and they ate it up."

"Man! So he didn't know Ballesteros was gonna win…and then, if anybody *did* know who the uncle was, he probably couldn't have even gotten close to the old man after it happened, right?"

"Exactly. It was like nobody knew who he was, or they weren't trying to talk to him. Scott got lucky. Plus he's mega-observant, you know. He was kind of on the prowl."

"So let me ask you…are y'all okay? Moneywise? For a while?"

Ava smiled. "I hope. I think so. You know Scott would love to leave insurance altogether, one day. Cory and Jimmy were going to pay him to exercise the horses, still, when we move because—I think I told you—Gwen was going to live there, and she doesn't ride, but now Robin and Naomi are going to do it."

"Oh, yeah. And Robin trains for a living."

"Yep. So she'll do it and get the free rent. But Scott says that's cool. He's just going to sell insurance and write. And we can still go ride for fun, anytime."

"As long as your money's going to be okay."

"I'm sure it will. My two jobs, the writing, and insurance… we've still got my college loan, anything extra for Jeanette, this house, the baby fund, but right now it's our time I'm worried about."

"I get that. Same with me and Toby. Can I ask you something, Smitty?"

Ava nodded.

"Are you taking care of you? Cuz, you work two jobs, you're visiting your mama most days when you get home, *and* you're working out here. You're a wife and trying to be a mommy. Have you had any fun lately? Taken any pictures?"

"Gosh, no. I think about it. I haven't gone out shooting since the reception."

"I thought so. Well, Jude and I were talking. He and I are making frames now."

"What kind of frames?"

"Picture frames, photo frames…from clay. It was his idea, and I immediately thought of you, and when I started to mention it, it was like we had the same idea at almost the same time."

"Which was what?"

"You go to shows with us sometimes and market your photographs. We showcase them together. We can price prints and frames separately and also make a discount for what's bought together. You'd match the photograph to a frame that 'went' with it—you know, it would be your own aesthetic—or people could pair up their own."

Ava thought for a moment. "I would love that…but I don't think I'd have time."

"Listen…you make time…just like Jude and me."

"I think it's Jude and I."

"Oh, hush. Please? For you. For *me*."

Ava leaned her head back to look at the dirty, cobwebbed ceiling. "You're annoying, you know. As heck. But I'll try it."

Bea raised her arms in the air. "Ah! You're kidding!" She brought her hands down in a slap on her rounded tummy. "I thought you'd give me a harder time."

"Well…I've thought about trying to sell some before…some that were in the cooler of the frames…but my frames are pretty bootleg."

"Are not. Do both." She gazed into the woods. "See, we women…it's easy to let the men go for their little joys and extravagances and be left behind the curtain, but…ya gotta do your thing, little missy, or you end up sad."

Ava stood up, smiling, and moved toward the door leading into the house. "You're so uncool."

"I know. But you're so in love with me anyway."

Chapter 31

SHE HADN'T PLANNED to do it. She wasn't nosy by nature, and it was none of her concern. She fell into it; she told herself later. And she would pretend she didn't know.

It was Thursday, the day before Scott's birthday, and she was taking Friday off. The new house had been cleaned and painted in only five days, and Scott and Ava had moved in most of their things. "It's lipstick on a pig," Ava would joke—the outside, and the real work of the inside, would have to wait.

The plan was that she and Scott would picnic and hike at the river on Friday and then come home to a surprise party. Marilyn and Bea and all the Mullins women would set it up while Ava and Scott were gone, and after the celebration, the couple would spend their first night in the house—one that had started to feel like Ava's own. She felt good, happy, and she couldn't wait to end her work at the dealership and the bar before the start of the long weekend.

The dealership that morning was bright with overhead lights, the cars inside immaculate, and a silver Trans Am sat angled in the middle of the showroom floor. Chuck and Kimberly were standing at the room's far end talking to someone at the greeter's desk, and Chuck's hand rested poised in the small of Kimberly's back. The girl's raven-colored hair was juxtaposed against her dolman-sleeved turquoise dress, buttoned down the back and rakishly set off one shoulder; around her waist, she'd cinched a wide black belt that matched her hair and heels.

Chuck must have seen Ava pull up, for she was just unlocking her filing cabinet when he tapped at the door and entered.

"My favorite." He gave her a light hug. "How's that son of mine?" Chuck's deep-set chocolate eyes were hooded, and his lips were somewhat thick. Ava wondered if that was one reason he perpetually looked lascivious but then decided it was probably less the physiognomy than the constant predatory expression he wore.

She gave him her warmest smile. "He's good. I don't think he has any idea about the party. And I know he's looking forward to the river."

Chuck nodded. "I remember my twenty-ninth birthday… It was not so chaste or wholesome. I'm glad the kid's done better than his old man." His eyes bore into hers with the attentiveness that felt so intimate and that she found so disconcerting. Abruptly, he looked away.

"So. I'm going to be leaving for the morning, and I'm taking Kimberly with me. Her paperwork is on her desk, so after you grab it, just pull her door closed. It will lock behind you. I don't think we'll be back by the time you're done, but leave it all with Franny, as usual. I'll see ya at y'all's house tomorrow night."

"Okay, sure…no problem," Ava said as he turned and went out the door. "Have a great day!"

Ava could see Kimberly standing by the front entryway with her handbag, and when they pulled off, in a midnight-blue Trans Am almost identical to the one on the showroom floor, she was the one who was driving.

It had been so easy, but her heart hammered anyway. What did she hope to find? It was just that the label on the bottom drawer had intrigued her: PRIVATE, it read, in red underlined letters. If it hadn't been there, who would've even cared?

She had finished recording the sales invoices—new and used cars, parts sales, service. She'd counted and recorded the cash and credit sales, recorded payments made on leased vehicles and equipment. She'd written checks for parts and car invoices, service contracts, and a bank loan. She had filed everything in the appropriate folders and finished a cold cup of coffee.

She hadn't completely closed the door after retrieving the papers and folders from Kimberly's office, and she could easily see the entrance while she worked. So after finishing her books, she swooped up her stack of the morning's paperwork and strode briskly but quietly back into Ms. De Luca's office as if on a mission—just one professional's business melding seamlessly into the realm of another.

It was around eleven thirty when she reentered Kimberly's office, which was even nicer than hers. How did a woman who—of her own admission—possessed no accounting degree or specific job description merit the heavy polished desk, soft recessed lights, and expensive potted plants?

Her windows were fractalized and frosted, too, unlike Ava's transparent ones; and after locking the door behind herself, Ava knew she was safe from scrutiny. She didn't think any of the salesmen or the front desk receptionist had seen her enter, and she only wanted a minute.

The filing cabinet key was actually in the lock itself. And in those drawers, and because of the trust Kimberly had placed so naively with Ava or Fate by not bothering to conceal it, she saw what Kimberly did.

The top two drawers of the cabinet didn't yield much—"closed" files that Ava, and the accountant before her, had passed to Chuck at the end of each month and that she knew were moved at year's end to the storeroom's fireproof safe. There were also a few new receipt books, ledgers, and other office supplies. But in the bottom drawer, Ava found what she could only describe as duplicate files labeled by the same months and years.

The tab in front of this row of monthly folders was labeled "Unreported Sales." Ava's heart pounded even more furiously as she pulled a couple from the row and saw they contained invoices and receipts for cars, parts, and services she didn't recognize.

She quickly opened the second-from-the-top drawer, and pulling the most recent folder—for March—she recognized its ledger as containing all of what she remembered reconciling and recording for that month. It also held the sales invoices and payment receipts for cars, parts, and services. Then looking back into the March folder in the Unreported Sales row, she confirmed what she already knew: It held receipts and invoices she'd never seen.

In the main desk drawer—also labeled Private, and locked, but whose key Ava easily discerned was the one that had opened the filing cabinet—was what Ava then understood to be the "working folder" for April 1983. This was the original folder for which Kimberly had left the dummy folder on her desk that morning for Ava. April was to be closed out on Saturday, the thirtieth, and then this folder, too, would be placed in Kimberly's filing cabinet under "Unreported Sales" while Ava would naively give her own "legitimate" handiwork to Chuck. He or Kimberly would, presumably, place this behind "March" in the second drawer from the top; and Mr. Divine would, no doubt, produce this one to an auditor, should the request ever be made. The writing was on the wall, she thought. The receipts, invoices, and cash Ava received each business day could have more accurately been labeled "Reported Sales."

Two more folders in the centered thin drawer of Kimberly's desk were labeled "Tax Deductions," but one—with a skull-and-crossbones doodle on it—contained bogus write-ups and receipts for work such as upkeep and repairs that Ava realized—just by her albeit-recent frequency of time there and proximity to the everyday machinations—had never even occurred.

And then there was a manila envelope full of cash labeled "Cash Sales." Ava perused the sales folder she had worked from that morning, the one she had carried back into the office with her. Within only a few minutes of cross-checking, she'd confirmed her suspicion that very few of these, with the corresponding amounts of cash, had been reported in the "Sales" ledger at all. Ava knew, also, that those few were recorded only for the sake of the appearance of authenticity—to Ava first and then, ultimately, to the IRS.

She left no trace of her perusal; she repositioned everything as perfectly as she'd found it. She exited as stealthily, she hoped, as she'd entered and calmly walked into the showroom. She placed her folders in the safe behind the reception desk for Chuck to retrieve in the morning; this was her last task before she left each day to make the deposit before heading to The Fox and Ale for her self-determined shift there. She managed a smile in the direction of Franny, who wished her a great weekend and please tell Scott happy birthday! Ava called out something in return, but it was something banal and rote, as she couldn't even look the girl in the eye.

She was still agitated when she pulled into The Fox and Ale. Inside, Scott sat at a table in the middle of the main room; they had agreed to eat lunch together. Corrine, wearing a blue-and-white striped sundress, sat to his left, with Jimmy beside her. They all were laughing.

"Hey, babe." Scott rose to pull out her chair, again using the old-world manners she had found so attractive from the beginning. "Jimmy wants to tell you a story."

"Well, I need a laugh. Shoot, Jimmy." But Jimmy waved his hand.

"Nah, it's not for ladies."

"Um, excuse me," Corrine said, "I'm here…"

"Exactly." Jimmy laughed again. "C'mon, leave the lovebirds alone." He rose from his chair as had Scott. "Don't forget, Scott," Jimmy said, pointing an index finger. "Memorial Day." Then he walked toward the bar and through the small door to the back.

"You can come, too, Ava." Corrine also rose to go. "Scottie has to remember he's not a bachelor anymore." She winked.

When they were alone, Ava asked, "What's Memorial Day? Let me guess, another party. They love to party, don't they?" Kathy set a Coke in front of her.

"Nah, not this time. It's another trip."

"Huh. For…what?"

"Memorial Day. It's a PGA event in Ohio." He was tearing little strips in a bar napkin.

"Oh."

"I ordered you a sandwich."

She nodded. "That's cool."

"You can come, Ava. As you heard, Jimmy is, and Cory, too, I think."

"Why? That's a busy weekend around here."

Scott shrugged. "I don't know. For fun."

She hesitated. "I don't think I could go, Scott." She wanted to remind him he had just gone to Georgia for the Masters and was about to leave for Texas for the Coca-Cola Open, but she knew it would sound argumentative. He knew those facts, anyway, of course.

"I don't see why not. My old man's not *that* strict, is he?"

"No, it's just…it takes money to travel, and if I go, it…well, it's a lot just for you. And we're trying to have a baby, and there's the house—"

"What does a baby have to do with anything? Or the house? And I sold that article after the Masters for a good price. Not a lot of people with so little experience could do that, you know."

"I know. And I'm proud of you, I am—"

"And you could have come."

"No, I couldn't. That was five days before tax deadline, and I was pushing it at both places, you remember? And then Jeanette decided to go crazy right in the middle of it. I'm lucky your dad didn't fire me. He just trusted I'd get done on time."

Scott shook his head and wadded up the scraps of napkin that littered the table in front of him. "He wouldn't ever. Plus he still has his main squeeze who could cover for you for a few days. It's not like you're indispensable."

Ava didn't know if he meant to hurt her, but he did.

Kathy set down a chicken sandwich in front of Ava, nachos and another beer in front of Scott. They murmured the appropriate gratitude.

"I assume you're talking about Kimberly."

"Who else?" The food provided a distraction while Ava chose her words.

"She can't help with the taxes, you know—she's not a real accountant—and I wouldn't let her anyway. It's too risky."

Scott said nothing but took a bite of nachos.

"Do you even know what she does?" Ava sought out her husband's face until he'd swallowed, wiping his fingers on another unmutilated napkin.

"Besides my dad?" And Ava just sat there, dumb.

"He could afford to let you go rescue your mom because little Kimmy could 'mind the store' for a while. But right, she can't do the "real" accounting, and she has another job you don't. Making Big Daddy happy."

"But…you know she does other stuff too." Ava waited a moment. If he knew, he may still have been assuming she didn't.

The afternoon sun, as it had first fallen across that very table where Ava had interviewed with Jimmy Woodham and illuminated his copper penny eyes, now fell into Scott's. And there was so much color there—now the Atlantic Sea, with so much storm and bitterness, so much hurt and hardness in a heartbreakingly beautiful amalgam—that Ava wanted to hold him in his white Izod shirt, with his hard chest and soft, floppy hair and his heart full of family shame, like hers.

He cast his eyes to the game room and held them there a moment before he responded, though no one was even in view. "I know she does other stuff too."

Chapter 32

IT WAS NIGHT, and Scott was packing.

The last few days had been warm, and for a couple of weeks, Ava nursed May's unspoken promise they wouldn't turn cold again. For almost a month, she had basked in the awareness she was a homeowner, and even though she sometimes awakened with a heart that careened in anticipation of everything that needed to be done before she got pregnant, she relished the undertaking.

The house was a hodgepodge of fresh indoor paint and an outdated heating system, refinished hardwoods, and tired bathroom linoleum. The roof was rusted, the outside peeling, and Ava didn't even know where to start to landscape the yard into something resembling real borders around a cared-for lawn. The only room that was satisfactory was the bedroom, and this was where her husband's dark, gleaming head was then bent over an alligator "overnight," jaws agape on the bed.

She didn't feel well. She didn't feel sick, but she felt tight... wired...edgy. She recognized this for what it was and decided to own it: she didn't want him to go. It wasn't reasonable, for she had plenty to keep her occupied, but maybe that was the problem—maybe he didn't have *enough*, and she didn't understand why.

"I'm going to miss you," she said, but he didn't turn around. "I don't feel good right now," she said next, and with that, he did.

"I'm sorry. I'm somewhere else." He held out his arms, and she made her way into them. "What's the matter, baby?"

"I guess I just don't want you to go. It doesn't make a lot of sense."

"And why don't you want me to go?" He bent low and spoke the words into her hair.

"I...feel like there's so much to do, and you've already taken several trips this year. And when you're not on a trip, you're off with clients or riding the horses, and even when you're home, it feels like… you're not." She felt his body stiffen by the smallest degree, and then he released her.

"I'm not blaming you for anything"—*God, look at his face*—"but I feel like I'm getting up so early and working the two jobs and then spending the rest of the evening working on this place or visiting Mom, and…you're always just…somewhere else."

He turned back to the bed where he had various clothing articles laid about and began placing some, with much care, into the yawning bag. "And where do you think I am? That is, that I'm not supposed to be."

"I didn't say that. I know you like to exercise the horses, but that's Robin's job now. And there were those two days you had to go morning and night to feed them, the days Robin and Naomi went camping, but I don't know why Jimmy or Corrine couldn't have done that."

"They don't live out here, Ava."

"I know, I get it, that's fine. But did they pay you, even?"

He turned to her, his face set. "You want me to ask them to pay me? They let me live rent-free the entire time I lived there."

"You took care of the place and the horses!"

He stared at her for a moment. "You don't do favors for anybody?"

"It doesn't matter. It's not about those two days. But you go to meet clients, I guess, and it's always at the bar. And you always seem to have a few drinks, and you eat lunch there, or dinner sometimes, to meet people, and then the trips—that money adds up—and then when you're home, you kind of hole up in your office, and…I'm not trying to make you mad, Scott, but it seems like a lot of your writing time or maybe just alone time or, whatever you want to call it, involves drinking. And…coke."

He crossed his arms, face hard. "So just to get this straight: you resent me going riding, feeding Jimmy's and Cory's horses, conducting business at the bar, eating lunch and having drinks at the bar while conducting business, going on trips to try to get writing gigs for the PGA, working on articles or clients' files or making sales calls at night, in my office, and even more so because I might be drinking or using coke."

She didn't like the way it sounded, as if she found fault with almost everything he did, but she couldn't argue it well because too much of it was true. She did have a problem with all of it, but she couldn't be sure she was justified.

"You're trying to make it sound bad."

"What did I get wrong? Is there anything I do that is okay with you?"

"Of course! I love you. I just feel…I get lonely, Scott. And I get really tired. I thought we might work on the house more together, even though I know we need help with the bathrooms…but we could do stuff like that moulding."

"The house is going to take a long time, Ava. That's why we got a good deal on it."

"Yeah, but the stuff you could help me with—like refinishing that armoire—why am I doing most of it alone, at night, while you're upstairs or away?"

"That's your decision, isn't it?" His voice was cold. "I make sales. My clients don't chase me down to offer me their insurance business because they're too busy using their hard-earned money to ensure the wives they don't even love anymore will be able to keep their snotty-nosed kids in soccer practice—"

"You don't have to be crude—"

"So I have to be jolly and wonderful all the time and invite them to lunch, or even dinner, and buy them drinks and even kick some of them a little blow now and then, and then I have to even, sometimes, unbelievably, call them at night because they couldn't *quite* see fit to work me into their day, and because they asked me to… And then, yeah, sometimes, I try to write something interesting or do some *research* I need to do to write something interesting or plan a trip so I don't have to die just some stupid tool, just another crooked, cheating salesman like my father."

Ava was quiet and then because she could think of nothing else to do, she went to his highboy—through which he had been rummaging earlier—and began removing and refolding T-shirts and pullovers into neat, symmetrical rectangles.

"I'm not trying to criticize you. And I didn't want to fight before you left."

His voice was softer, then. "So what exactly *are* you trying to do? What do you want?"

She shook her head and pursed her lips. "I don't know. I thought we'd do more together."

"We do things together, Ava. We had that great birthday you gave me. We went to dinner at Bea and Toby's that Sunday."

"That was two things. Literally two things in a month. And I had to beg you to go to Bea's. I hadn't even gone by myself since the reception."

"Beg me or not—and I would've called it 'persuaded'—I still went."

"Well, just so you know, it's not fun when you act like it's such a sacrifice."

"If I don't act according to your expectations, then I guess I shouldn't go anymore."

"Why would you not want to go anymore? And why was it such a sacrifice? I've been to your parents' house, what, ten times since Thanksgiving? Do you think they're some kind of great carnival?" Her voice felt tremulous and weak.

"What is your problem? Seriously? Because you seem to be looking for one."

She took a deep breath as she sat in the corner chair; she formed a "church steeple" with her fingertips and pressed it against her lip before answering. "I don't know. It's everything. Sometimes, when you're in the bar with clients or even talking to Jimmy and Corrine or Chet or Kathy or Gwen, you're all relaxed and happy and funny. And then when you're with me, you...kind of aren't. And I feel like I'm not enough for you. Or like you'd rather be somewhere else." She didn't look at him but decided to keep going. "And I wonder if you care about having a baby as much as I do."

He sounded calmer when he answered, but her heart sickened just the same. "No. I don't care as much as you about having a baby."

The tears stung, but she didn't let them fall. She pressed her hands against her eyes so she wouldn't see his face and he couldn't see hers. He hadn't even denied, much less addressed, the accusations that had come before.

"Ava, why do you want a baby so badly?" When she opened her eyes, she saw he had sat upon the bed facing her, pushing the travel bag to its furthest edge.

"You said…when you asked me to marry you, that very night, we talked about all of it, and you said we could have children. A baby. Several babies."

He looked at his hands before raising his face to hers. "Yes. I did. We can, that's fine. But really…it's mostly you."

"How can you say that, Scott? How can you say that now like you don't care?" She heard her voice grow shrill and louder.

"I do care. We'll have kids. That's fine. But I don't understand how, when you came from such a mucked-up childhood, and God knows I did, how you could want kids to come take part in this wasteland of a world."

She stared. She felt like she was seeing a new person. He inhabited Scott's body, but this person was too calm, too cold, and too raw, even if he was just trying to be real.

"Is that why you…is that why, sometimes, when…I want you… you kind of aren't there?"

He sighed, but instead of angrily denying it as she expected him to, he said, "I don't know. To be honest, I haven't thought about it that much. But we have so much life ahead and so much we could be doing, but you're just obsessed with going to work, working on the house, saving lots of money, and having baby-making sex."

She was hurt again. "And what do you want?"

His eyes were sad. "I just want a different life. I want to tell great stories about adventures I get to have or cover great sports and have fun. Travel, and share the world with you too. And not be a used-up salesman at forty who wants to blow his brains out."

"Your dad acts happy."

"He isn't happy. Unless he's deluded himself because he railroads everyone and always gets his way. Is that happiness to you?"

"Of course not."

Scott stood again and clasped the case closed. "You know I love you, Ava. We've only been married five months. Nobody gets it right at first."

"Scott."

"Yeah." He had moved into the bathroom and was going through the medicine cabinet.

"Why do you have to drink so much?"

He turned again to face her. "What is 'so much,' Ava?"

"Don't get mad. But when you're out or down the hall working or whatever, why do you feel like you always have to be doing something?"

"Doing something."

"Yes. I mean, I know you're working or say you're working"—his eyes bore holes through hers—"I mean, I know you're working, I guess, all that time, but it's weird that you're using stuff or drinking while you're working. Especially as much as you do it. Do you feel like you need it?"

"And are you making a point? I'm assuming you know exactly what I'm doing and how much."

"No, not at all. I don't. But…sometimes you're ill and out of sorts, and maybe even a little mean or grumpy, and I just wonder if it's the stuff you do all the time."

"All the time?"

"Don't pick on my every word."

"Okay, well, let's talk about the fact that I drank and did a little coke now and then when you met me. When did it get to be a problem? I believe my insurance-sales checks still clear, as do the ones I get for the articles."

"Your sarcasm isn't going to help."

"No, really, let's talk about that. Or maybe about why you *don't* have a drink now and then just to loosen up or have fun for once in your life instead of looking down your nose at everyone who isn't as perfect as you."

Her heart was crashing against its cage. This was awful, but she steeled herself to face him and steadied her voice. "I don't drink because my mother has done nothing but stuff her face with hamburgers and cake and swill vodka and beer and wine and gin and bourbon and whatever she can get her hands on ever since I can remember, and I'm better than that. I'm better than all of you."

And she went to the den and stayed there, madly wishing he would follow her and horribly aware that he didn't.

Chapter 33

THE BABY WAS born three days early, and Bea was thrilled because she was born on the Fourth of July.

She was one day old, and she was beautiful, even though the syndrome showed. Her eyes, upward-slanted and widely spaced, were the color of the darkest, wettest quarry rock. Her head was perfectly shaped and nearly bald, with the faintest yellow duck-down imaginable, and her lips were the edges of rose petals.

Bea looked wan, exhausted, and happy while Toby hovered, his strapping, overall-clad presence in the room as incongruent as a doctor in white coat would have looked standing in one of Toby's cornfields. Clara squeezed Ava's hands and beamed at her before rising to head for the door; only two visitors were allowed at a time.

"She knows her Aunt Ava is here. She hasn't kept her eyes open all day." Bea sat in the bed with the baby cradled but tilted so that Ava could get a good look. "Did you see her little hands?" Bea unswaddled the baby just enough to lift a fist with her finger, exposing a tiny pearl-colored cockle shell.

Ava stared. "God, Bea...and I don't mean 'god' in a bad way. I mean, just...god. You have a baby. I guess God gave you a baby."

Bea laughed. "Well, of course He did! Oh, Ava, I can't stand it. I knew, just as soon as they said she had Down's, that nothing could touch my happiness. I don't even know why. I would have thought I would have been wrecked."

Ava nodded. She didn't have enough words. "So...I thought they knew these days. Before."

Bea shook her head. "Not always. And they don't usually test in young mothers. Plus, it wouldn't have mattered."

"No, of course not." But Ava wondered, just for a second, if it would have mattered to her. How would she have felt if the doctor, with his pink bald head and manner of being omniscient, had placed a defective baby in Ava's outstretched arms?

"One day, I want you to tell me about the labor. Not today, but…you know what? Maybe not. I don't know if I want any horror stories before I go through it myself."

"I know. Toby can tell you." Bea grinned in Toby's direction.

"If you want to hear how it feels to watch someone you love yelling like they're being crushed while you stand by and know you can't do nothing about it, I'll tell it," Toby offered, "but otherwise, I'd skip it if I were you." And they laughed because they could, because it was over.

"Don't worry too much, it does end. It's just we didn't get here in time for the epidural. I was asking for it, and they were like, 'No, sweetie, no, it's too late,' and I was like, 'You animal! You sadist!' Cause it did hurt like the dickens."

"Oh, now, Bea, don't be dramatic. 'The dickens' are pretty strong words."

"Yes. Well, sorry, but it hurts like the most dickens I've ever felt."

The baby began to mew; she squinted her eyes and squirmed her little body. *Just a tiny oblong of such pulsing life,* Ava thought, *full of cells and vessels and muscles and bones!* She stared again. She knew, or imagined she knew, that Bea's whole spirit life was contained in that one little shell; and that was so frightening and tenuous to Ava because…well, how easily it could be snuffed out—lost, misplaced, even stolen. How horrid a world where whole people could be so fragile, so easily ruined, or become adrift, leaving those who loved them, who had invested every atom of their being in them, so easily smattered and smashed.

Bea had adjusted her robe and put the baby under one of its flaps, draping a thin nursing cloth over her shoulder. In the minutes that followed, Ava could hear the infant nursing, and like a harmonious bass accompaniment, Toby—who'd lain on the narrow studio couch to the side only minutes before—began a sonorous snore.

"She is beautiful, isn't she?" Bea wasn't looking for confirmation. Everything in her gaze relayed supreme confidence in this gift that been bestowed in its perfection and in God's providence; in His goodness, mercy, and grace. Everything Ava knew about her friend, this woman—now, and since they had met and bonded six years ago—told her everything she needed to know about where Bea's heart was then. She was in love with God, in love with Toby and Heidi, and no number of birth defects, no amount of bad luck—if birth defects were even bad luck at all—could change it.

"She's perfect, Bea," Ava answered, and she meant it. "She's absolutely, unequivocally perfect."

The cafeteria was too bright, as Ava and Clara found a table in the corner and placed their trays on opposite sides of it. The older woman's spread was sparse, with an egg salad sandwich, a bag of chips, and a tea. Ava, who'd spent the morning at Divine before heading to the hospital, was ravenous—a burger, fries, and pecan pie accompanied her soda. Cory had told her to take the afternoon off.

"I'm exhausted." Clara settled her stout frame into the plastic and metal chair. "But so relieved." She then said, "Excuse me, dear," and bowed her head.

After the awkward silence, during which Ava bowed her head but did nothing, Clara raised her own and took a large bite of her sandwich.

"What are you so relieved about?"

"Oh, everything! So much can go wrong, you know. But now, well…I guess they have it pretty much under control." It amazed Ava that Bea's grandmother didn't express any sorrow over Heidi having Down syndrome. It was as if nobody was factoring this into the day's events or what it might mean for the future.

"I'm sure. It's all over now except for eighteen years of fatigue and drudgery, worry and screaming matches." She chuckled and tried to catch Clara's eye so her companion would not misread the lighthearted intent of the comment.

"Oh, gracious, yes, isn't it just so much," Clara said, without inquisition, and Ava knew the humor had landed. "I remember when Louise and her brother were small. So much to do on the farm all the time and not a minute's rest from those two. And Louise was the worst of the two!"

"I bet. Did Mr. Martin help?" Ava made small shrift of her burger as they talked.

"Wilson? Heavens no! Oh, my, in those days, there was no asking the daddy to do with the young'uns. So much farmwork, and he did carpentry and mechanics, too, just to survive. You have to remember we were still young and in the Great Depression. We had the place, and always we had to keep things growing. We tried to keep a hog or two—a cow and chickens… One year we had peacocks! And ducks, yes, he tried his hand at ducks."

"So you were like a single mom, huh?"

Clara had been focused on her plate but shot her eyes upward. "Oh, no, no, it was not like that. But it was hard… We all just had to do our part. I sewed everything and mended patches upon the patches of mine and Wilson's clothes. Made the kids' clothes from flour sacks, jackets from burlap, one year, stuffed with cotton and lined with flannel." She took a sip of her tea. "In summer, we picked berries, and we had to cut wood all the time. We canned. We made every speck of our own food, and we slaughtered our own meat. Oh, that was hard on the kids, I'll tell you what." Clara wasn't letting the memories of slaughter or toil diminish her attack on the sandwich or chips, and she had finished in just a few minutes.

"You can get something else, Gram. I've got money."

"No, no, I'm good. You get to be my age, you don't get so hungry."

She wore a polyester tunic of red, white, and blue. Although Ava first thought she would have worn it on the day before, the actual Fourth, she quickly realized Clara had worn it for Heidi, had saved it for her trip to the hospital. Her headband was blue, and her bangs were raked back from her forehead just as Bea's often were. For just a nanosecond, Ava was struck by how much she looked like Bea if the younger had been done up in old-lady makeup, her silver-gray bob framing the same cherubic face, solid and strong above a solid and stocky body.

"I admire you. I wonder if I would be so strong in like times."

Clara didn't hesitate for a moment. "Of course you would. Of course you would! You'd fight to survive, and mamas and daddies will always fight for their broods. Even nature will tell you that."

Ava didn't respond but ate her fries as Clara continued.

"You know that little baby that Bea's got wrapped up in her arms right now? She will die for that little baby. And she doesn't even know her yet. You could've laid another baby in her arms yesterday morning, one she'd never seen and hadn't birthed. You could have played the biggest trick. And she would still die for it. God changes you when He uses you to make life, even if you didn't even make it after all."

It was another moment before Ava spoke, "Gram, can I ask you something? Or tell you something?" Her hands were clammy as she anticipated releasing her cache of burdens.

The woman's watery brown eyes sought hers.

"I feel like I really want a baby."

"Well, of course you do! That's only natural, that comes from our good Father in heaven."

"I know, but…I mean, it's all I ever think about anymore, and we even have the nursery finished, but…it's been almost seven months. How long does it take?"

Clara looked at Ava as if she were trying to figure out if there was a hidden question. "That depends, child. I'm sure you know by now what it takes to bring about the condition."

"Oh, well, of course, it's not that. In fact, that's why I'm asking. We…this is embarrassing—"

Clara waved her hand in front of her face. "Oh, shaw…you listen to me. Are you all right? I mean, all right in the bedroom?"

Ava looked at her plate. "Yes. I mean, as far as I know. It doesn't take anything special, does it?"

Clara shook her head. "No, ma'am, it does not. You give this to God. You love your man, and you give this to God. Babies are part of what God does."

Ava felt lighter, then. She thought of the new life down the hall and had the fleeting evil thought that the odds of her having a disabled child had somehow lessened since it had happened so close to her realm of existence. Surely lightning would not strike twice so close to the same vicinity.

"You have such a healthy appetite, sweetheart," Clara said. Then out of the blue, she added, "But you seem just as thin as ever and tired. Maybe you and Scott could go away for a while." She drained the last sips of her tea.

Ava smiled and wondered what to say to that as she ate the last few crumbs of her pie. It was all she could do not to say, "Scott goes away all the time."

Chapter 34

THE NURSERY LAY perfect. After the bedroom, Ava had focused on it, painting the second coat of buttercream yellow over the one applied months ago by Susan and Clem. She'd coated all the mouldings and baseboards with white enamel paint and used any spare money to put toward the shiny white crib, changing table, cradle, and dresser.

The rocker Bea had given her—one that was half of a pair, both having sat all of Bea's life in Louise's old sewing room—occupied a corner by the window, its green back and seat cushions splashed with lemon-colored lilies with darker green leaves, and Ava had purchased bedding and curtains to go with it. All of this—every bit of renovation, purchasing, and decoration—had occurred before they'd even ripped the sticky linoleum off the bathroom floor or replaced the pungent, outdated refrigerator. Creamy panels fluttered in front of the open window, in shades of Sunlight, Mist, and Frost.

Bea stood with her arms encircling the sleeping Heidi, swaying as she surveyed everything, making all the appropriate "oohs" and "ahs."

"It's incredible, Ava. You should be so proud. I can't believe you put together that crib yourself."

"I know. I am proud." Ava allowed herself a moment to bask in Bea's praise. "Scott said he'd do it, of course, but I'm so anxious. I can't explain it. I just wanted everything done."

"Yeah, but be patient. Remember, the house is perfectly livable even though there's a lot to do. You'll just have to do a little at a time. That's how Tobes and I look at it. You'll always feel like there's something you need to fix or update or make better. What are you gonna do for art? As if I couldn't guess."

"Oh, hush, you don't know. I did think about using my own photos, of course...like, maybe everything in black and white, even. But I also thought about trying to do a couple of paintings."

Ava had told Bea about the lunch at Marilyn's and how seeing her studio had stirred something in her—something drowsy but persistent, not too deeply buried, a yearning to work again with paints. Canvases sat, even then, and sequestered even from Scott, in the bottom of the laundry room closet—acrylics and oils; watercolors and chalks; a bare smattering of brushes, palettes, and solvents.

"I could try a landscape, maybe...they're forgiving...or do, like, one perfect tree, or a baby, even, but...babies are hard...it would have to be almost impressionistic, probably..."

Bea nodded her head over and over. "Yes, honey, yes! That would be so perfect. Mama's artwork. Little baby girl would love it."

Ava laughed. "It might be a boy, you know. That's the second time you've done that."

Bea shook her head. "Speakin' it into truth, darlin'. Just leave it up to me."

They ate lunch in the dining room, which was just the right side of the wide-paneled great room. Hired hands of Mr. Berger (the mill supervisor Clara remembered from her childhood) had hewn the walls and floor from white ash trees that had ranged behind the pines past the yard, but that land—that glorious untamed timberland—had been raped and sold long before the property had passed to Scott and Ava.

Heidi, who, at two-and-a-half months still slept the sleep of the innocent, lay in the cradle Ava had bought for her own baby and which she had moved downstairs for them to use today. They ate hot dogs with relish, coleslaw, and beans; Ava had even made a chocolate cake to celebrate the occasion.

"Tell me what Scott said when you told him." Bea's eyes sparkled as she took a spoonful of beans.

"Who, Mr. Suave? Mr. Ruffle-Me-Not? No, he was excited. But he stayed cool." Ava grinned. "I do think he's happy. Not like me, but...he did bring me home some roses."

"You're kidding! Yikes. Toby gave me nothing but a crushing bear hug." She shrugged. "To each his own."

"I wish I could go to the doctor tomorrow. How do they tell the due date for sure?"

"They can't, exactly. I mean, they use the dates of your cycle. And it helps if you know all the times you made love since the last one, but who keeps up with that? Then when you get closer, they can kind of tell better. I don't understand it all that much to tell you the truth."

"Well. I think it's about three months."

"I can't believe you didn't go to a doctor in the first place."

"You know I've never been to a doctor. That kind. We never paid for that. And this place was free because I told you, they're trying to get you to not have an abortion."

"I know, I know. But you know what kind of makes me mad about Jeanette? That she never took you. When you first started."

"Why would she? She didn't go herself." Ava squinched her eyes at her friend. "When was the last time you thought my mother had it together, anyway?"

"Well, you should've gone. All those times in college. It's not supposed to hurt that bad every month. And you better tell Dr. Montal. You'll love him, by the way."

"Everybody has cramps, Bea."

"Not me. Never like you, and hardly ever, at all. But especially not like I'm trying to die."

"I know. I hate it. It's been so nice. But I still feel tight."

"What do you mean?" Bea's mouth was full of hot dog, and she covered it with her hand as she spoke.

"I'm not sure. Like, too stretched, or too full or something. Did you feel that way?"

"I don't think so…just tell Dr. Monty. You will *love* him."

"So I've heard."

Heidi began to mew, and Ava jumped up. "I've got her. Hold on, don't get her. Finish your lunch."

She peeled around the sharp corner to the kitchen and washed her hands at the sink.

"Well, she'll want to eat..." Bea got up slowly, putting the last few bites from her plate in her mouth before she replicated Ava's actions and then took Heidi from her, settling with the baby on the sofa across the room. She unbuttoned the top two buttons of her shirt, which looked like one of Toby's well-worn chambray button-downs. She still carried extra baby weight, and she had deep circles under her eyes.

Ava sat on the other end of the sofa, curling her legs under her. She wore canary-colored leggings and an oversized turquoise-and-yellow plaid shirt, her abdomen already somewhat distended. "How's mom? I'm almost afraid to ask."

Bea lowered her eyes. "She's okay. I wanted to tell you, just last night, I got her to agree to go to the doctor."

Ava's eyes widened. "You didn't! I can't believe that! How?"

"I told her we'd pay for it."

"We who?"

"Me and Toby. I think we need to see if she needs any kind of extra help or medicine or something. Once we know, we can go from there."

It was Ava's turn to look down. "That can't be your responsibility, Bea. Although it would be nice to figure out what's wrong with her, wouldn't it? I'll talk to Scott."

Bea shifted Heidi a little and began to stroke the blonde down above the baby's forehead before she spoke, "Yeah. But here's the deal, peaches. It has to be done. She's...she's in distress a lot of times."

"What does that mean? More than usual?"

Bea shrugged. "She's come to the door a few times. Wanting a drink. Or for us to give her the keys." (Ava's Volkswagen had, indeed, been bequeathed to Jeanette when she'd begun working at the salon for Jude, but only on the condition she would drive straight there and back and leave the keys with Bea and Toby every evening after work. It had taken her four tries to pass the driver's license exam.)

"You're kidding! To where? To get booze?" Ava bought her mother two six-packs of beer every week on her grocery runs, but Jeanette went through it like water. When Bea had questioned it, Ava had responded she was afraid of what would happen if Jeanette were forced to stop; she had drunk as long as her daughter could remember.

"Who knows? I've told her, Toby and I don't drink, that we don't have anything, and she's…gotten a little upset. Like, even, like I was lying or something. And Jude—he didn't want to bother you—he says most days she's good and acts like she loves helping out at the salon, but she took some cash. About a week ago. After we all got back from that show."

Ava was spellbound. Bea adjusted the delicate pink blanket around her baby's feet.

"He said it wasn't much, fifty bucks—"

"Fifty bucks!"

"But he was more concerned because she didn't come in the next day. She still doesn't know he knows about the money, but he called her, and she sounded drunk even though she said she was sick, so he guessed that was why she wanted it."

Ava sat silent and ashamed.

"I don't want you to worry. We know she has a drinking problem, but it also might be something else. They're finding out a lot about hormones these days, especially at her age…women get screwy. Or she might have blood sugar issues or mental problems. Something like, if she got some kind of medication, she wouldn't crave the drinking or be so emotionally unstable. She might even not eat so destructively."

Ava gave a short dry laugh. "Destructive eating. Manic eating. How about this one, 'diabetic thievery' or 'hormone-induced put-all-your-stuff-in-the-yard-in-the-middle-of-the-night' disorder. I guess the best we can do is hope she can take a pill and not be such a waste of a person."

"Stop. Don't say that about your mother. You'll regret it, Ava. You don't mean it."

She left Bea on the sofa and went back to the luncheon table for her tea. "You need to finish up there and let me hold that baby. And we need to cut this cake."

"She has to nurse the other side. And I'm going to refuse to eat cake if you don't say you love your mother."

Ava sighed. "I will force you to eat cake. And you both need to hurry so you don't bore me." She sat back on the sofa and took a long drink of tea.

"I'm waiting…"

Ava squinted at her friend. "I love my stupid mother."

"Ava…"

"I love my mother. But if they don't give us some good drugs, I'm sending her back to Pastor Carl in a cardboard box."

Bea hefted the infant to her shoulder. "We'll cross that bridge when we come to it."

Chapter 35

MONDAY—TWO DAYS AFTER Bea came for lunch, the third week in September—Ava received two letters amidst the coupons and flyers and bills. She recognized the distinctive handwritings of both, and both caused her stomach to flip-flop. One had been sent to her current house, and one had been forwarded, having been originally mailed to Bea's house from the months when Ava lived at the cottage. On its face, she recognized Bea's handwriting: *No longer at this address. Please forward.* Ava dreaded opening either.

Her nausea was infrequent and not overwhelming; but when it occurred, it rested awhile, making her feel lethargic, out of sorts, and impatient. She felt so early swollen, too, but excited—for that was what babies did. She could imagine it being twins.

She grabbed a Coke from the refrigerator and sat down to read the letter that had come to this house, with its spidery script and cream-colored envelope.

> August 27, 1983
> Dear Ava,
>
> I am sorry it has taken me so long to write you back. I have had much thinking to do. I do thank you for writing me telling me of Jeanette's new living arrangements. I have been long aware that her situation was precarious at best. Isn't it ironic that a daughter—who I had so late in life and is therefore so much younger than I—is already incapable of living alone?
>
> As you can see, I have noted your new address. As you can also see, I have deliberated some about the prudence of continuing Jeanette's

> support now that she is living in the cottage of your friend. Still, if, as you say, the money will help your friend—Bea, you called her—and you keep a roof over your mother's head and pay for her incidentals, I will continue to provide the same amount as I was before.
>
> Our financial advisers assured us as recently as last year that we are in good standing and should remain so for the rest of our lives. Since you were honest and responsible enough to tell me the money could also go towards your mother's incidentals due to the unselfish nature of your friend, I will assume this is a beneficial situation for all. I do have utmost regard for my daughter's well-being, though her choices have made a mature, enjoyable, and reciprocal relationship unpalatable.
>
> I will send all further checks for Jeanette's "rent," etc., to the new address you provided. Congratulations on the purchase of your new home.
>
> Your grandmother,
> Eloise Draper

What was it? Ava wondered. What was it that made communication with this woman so distasteful? Did she really believe that she had "utmost regard" for her daughter's well-being? Would it have been that "unpalatable" to have a relationship with her daughter just because she had physical or behavioral issues or maybe even mental ones? And did she actually believe that Ava believed her "regard" was of the "utmost"?

As usual, Ava wondered how a woman who had had one child and one grandchild could turn her back so thoroughly on regular contact with either—on visits and calls, on letters or notes, or pictures. Where was her happiness? Did she have a soap opera she liked or a book collection? Was she part of a garden club, or did she sit in a rocker with a cat? What was it like to have one's genes pass into the watery abyss of all the earth and voluntarily bid them adieu?

Even worse, what had she, Ava, ever done to lose the only other family she had? Her mind wandered back to canceling the guests of hers and Eric's wedding and how only friends from college and work and a few miscellaneous others had had to be canceled on her side. Jeanette, practically speaking, was her only remaining family.

Ava crumpled the letter and threw it toward the hall. "What do I care?" she muttered. At least she was helping with money.

The second letter was in a white legal-sized envelope, was a little thick, and was emblazoned with Eric's strong, angular, heavy-handed penciled words. She felt her stomach roil again in anticipation. Part of her was curious as a cat, but the other part just as soon wished it had been returned to sender.

She tore open the envelope. Inside was what looked like a newspaper clipping wrapped in a single sheet of notebook paper. On another sheet of notebook paper, Eric had written:

> Dear Ava,
>
> I hope you are well. I won't bother you with news of me as I'm sure it wouldn't interest you. I am sending this because I think you would want to know, and it's possible you don't. I know you were friends.
>
> Please get in touch if I can ever help you in any way.
>
> Love,
> Eric

Ava unwrapped the folded newspaper clipping; two side-by-side photograph copies faced her. The first copy was of a wallet-sized photo of a smiling Chantal in what looked like a high school senior picture. Her hair, winged at the sides, fell in two long panels hanging over her shoulders as blue shadow embellished her eyes, and her velvet drape showcased a silver cross. The other photograph copy was a

4 × 6 of five police officers and some bystanders in a parking lot in front of a high-rise building.

Above the picture were the words, Top Story, and the headline:

Hotel Housekeepers Find Murder
Victim at Downtown Plaza Hotel
By Clarence Barton
August 29, 1983

Below the pictures was the following caption:

Police respond to a call from Peachtree
Plaza Hotel in downtown Atlanta after
housekeepers discover the body of a young
woman during morning rounds.

And below that caption were the ensuing words:

> Atlanta—Police are investigating an apparent murder after the body of a young woman was discovered in a room of one of Atlanta's upscale hotels late Sunday morning. The victim was found by two employees who had come to service the room and who wish to remain anonymous. A family member has positively identified the victim as Alice Gayle Horne, age 23, from Dothan, Alabama.
>
> The hotel room in which Ms. Horne's body was found was secured the previous evening by a man whose driver's license bore the name Willie Earl Francis. No staff interviewed at the scene could recall having seen Mr. Francis previously, but several employees knew Miss Horne, who went by the name "Chantal" as a prior guest. The same family member who identified the body confirmed Chantal was a name the victim

> occasionally used after moving to Atlanta from Dothan six years prior, hoping to establish a career as a singer.
>
> Police immediately put out an APB after Mr. Francis's identity was confirmed, as he is a suspect in the murder and his whereabouts are unknown.
>
> Guests in an adjoining room remembered hearing arguing around 4:00 a.m., Sunday, but didn't think it was unusually loud or suspicious. No other suspicious sounds were noted.
>
> Police have released no other information concerning the crime but are requesting any persons with information that may lead to the whereabouts of Mr. Francis immediately report such to one of the telephone numbers below. Witnesses describe Willie Francis as a black male, about 40 to 50 years old, with a medium-length Afro hairstyle. Records show Mr. Francis checked out at 6:26 a.m. on Sunday and was wearing a dark-colored business suit. Reports from valet parking at the hotel listed his vehicle as a '75 Lincoln Continental, hunter green, and a valet staff member noted it has a green velour interior.

The license plate information and contact numbers for police followed, but Ava's eyes had blurred. She barely moved and, after finishing the article, realized she'd also been barely breathing. Hot tears were streaming, but she hadn't made a sound. She sank to the floor from the sofa, first kneeling, then curling fetally, burying her head in her hands. *God, god, god,* she murmured. *Sweet, brazen, clueless, smart, lost, beautiful Chantal.* Ava had no place to put it and eventually fell asleep on the floor.

Chapter 36

SHE LOST THE baby four days after Thanksgiving.

Dinner at Scott's family's had been festive, and Ava was more relaxed than she had been the previous year. She enjoyed hearing the family news.

The medical lab supervisor had promoted Peter, who now had three clinicians under him. Starr had reorganized a section of the novelties store she managed to showcase original crafts and offered to take back some of Ava's photographs and even some of the pottery frames of her friends. Most everyone enthused about the baby-to-be.

She and Scott had also joined Bea's family for dinner three days later, and again, everyone exclaimed about the new addition expected in April and what a good playmate she would be for Heidi. Ava caught Alex looking at her tummy twice, and Susan and Laura pestered her for names. 'Surely you have some ideas!' Susan had insisted. Laura, looking wistful, said, "I wish I could have another girl—I always wanted to use the name Amy." Not much more was mentioned before Clara told them to leave Ava alone, and that if the mother-to-be did have ideas, she would do well to keep them to herself, that someone would be bound to not like them, or they might be passed to another and used for that one's own child first.

She'd been tired, so very tired. She'd dragged herself to the office at Divine, conscientiously doing her work while avoiding the unpleasant thoughts of Kimberly's tax evasive skullduggery. Ava kept to herself.

On one occasion in October, she'd heard the dark sounds of two people in private communion behind the dark-haired beauty's door and seen Chuck emerge later, looking heinous yet sated. Her subsequent nausea had taken her to the bathroom, but she hadn't gotten sick, finally realizing the cause was simply emotional revulsion.

Corrine and Jimmy were happy for her, of course they were! But Jimmy confessed he'd never seen the appeal of being a parent, and Corrine had seemed—on more than one occasion—to be faking it. One moment she was flip or cavalier, another guiltily overobsequious. "How wonderful," she would coo, "how marvelous and utterly delightful for you both."

Evenings, after her work at the bar was done, Ava went home to make dinner for herself and Scott. More frequently than ever, though, she served up fast-food burgers, tacos, Chinese, and country-style take-out plates. Sometimes they ate together, and sometimes she heard him, late at night, or in the wee hours, coming home—after they'd talked, or not—and quietly crack the refrigerator door.

Dr. Montal had been kind and calm, as Bea had assured Ava he would be. He'd chastised her for taking too long to come in, had listened to her concerns, had gone over her history, and examined her. When he'd confronted her with his findings—even coupled with reassurance—she had cried. But there was no need to panic, he had said. She would just need to be very careful.

Scott knew nothing of endometriosis. Ava and Bea knew very little more.

Dr. Montal classified it as between stage 2 and 3. It would have been best if she had been seen years ago; a laparoscopy may have helped had it been done before she had attempted conception. Hormone therapy could have been tried as well, but now they would wait and see.

No, no, it would do no good to blame herself, he'd said. All was not lost; they would just "take it from here." No, no need to cry. Take it easy. "I want to see you every two weeks"; "Call if anything begins to feel wrong—cramping, bleeding, et cetera."

Dr. Montal was a really great guy.

Monday, at ten forty in the morning, it had begun.

Scott was out of the office, and he wasn't at The Fox and Ale. Corrine wondered if everything was okay because Ava's voice sounded weird. Just tired, Ava had lied. Just tell him to give her a ring if he stopped in.

Bea didn't work on Mondays, of course, but she didn't answer her phone at home even though Ava let it ring twelve times, twice. Jeanette didn't answer either. *Where could she be on a Monday morning?* She tried Scott's office again, and again the front desk secretary said the only agent in the office was Lucy.

Lucy. The pretty girl who had come in the bar with Scott that day—that day a hundred years ago when Ava was crushing so hard but wouldn't admit it—the girl she had been so, so relieved to find out had not been Scott's girlfriend.

By noon it was happening in earnest. She moved from her bed to the bathroom, spread a towel on the floor, and lay curled, knees to chest. Why hadn't they replaced the linoleum by now? It was uncleanable, disintegrated to a state of tackiness, from layers of ancient hairspray.

She would lie down until the cramps subsided, then try and use the bathroom; maybe that was all she needed. She was four-and-a-half months along, and the good doctor had reassured her the dangerous time was over.

The whole process did not take long.

It was a relief, actually, as the cramps crescendoed in their culmination of loss, as her yells then groans died after spewing forth her heart's rage. Her body calmed in a moment, and she felt almost dizzy from the lack of pain and undoubtedly from loss of blood. Feeling as if she were spiraling into a state of unconsciousness, she forced herself to look before she lost the will. The cordless phone she had brought into the bathroom with her lay within reach on the floor. She dialed the number of The Mane Event, hoping this wouldn't be one of the times it would fail to make a connection.

The rest of the day was a blur.

Jude had answered at the salon—thank God—and, before Ava told him what happened, had said Jeanette was given the afternoon off for her doctor's appointment and that Bea had driven her.

Alternating between a whisper and a cry, Ava informed him of the morning's events. Jude's passionate concern was almost more than she could bear, but she realized how badly she needed him, that there was no other person besides Scott that she had in the world at that moment; and Jude had no idea, of course, where her husband was.

He was there in minutes. Ava had moved the towel to a corner of the bathroom, covering its contents as best she could without looking further. She took a shallow bath, dressing in the ways necessary after this occurrence and doing everything on automatic pilot. The male high school friend of her now best friend in the world, meanwhile, sat outside the bathroom door in her bedroom—this handsome young man, this man with whom she had so little in common, but who now was her lifeline to sanity.

He wore jeans and boots, along with a leather cuff, wide and branded with a cross. His eyes found hers as he took one of her hands, sitting beside her on her marriage bed; and before rising, he kissed her hand like a supplicant, his face bearing the kindest expression she had ever seen.

He readied her for the trip to the doctor's office and asked for her address book. He called the insurance agency again, The Fox and Ale, Robin's and Naomi's cabin, and Scott's parents' home, but no one knew the whereabouts of Ava's husband. Jude found a bag for the towel and its contents, placed it in the car without comment, and then carried Ava to its passenger side.

They were getting ready to leave when Scott came home. He'd been playing golf with Chet, and he'd had "a few beers." With as little conversation as necessary, it was agreed Jude would drive them all to the hospital, and Ava rode between Scott and Jude in the cab of Jude's truck

The emergency hysterectomy was performed at 2:44 p.m. The endometriosis was extensive; the miscarriage substantially incomplete. The dilation and curettage—routine after "spontaneous abortions"—was reportedly, typically, no cause for concern; but the resultant bleeding had been, also reportedly, unpredictable.

Ava's blood pressure—always naturally low—had dropped by the second, and her heartbeat was alarmingly slow. The bleeding was excessive, persistent, unrelenting in its progression; and Dr. Montal ordered an attendant to locate Scott, who met him outside the operating room doors. It had taken less than a minute for the doctor to inform Ava's husband that there was no discernable origin of the inordinate, unreasonable bleeding; that a surgeon was already prepping; and to present Scott with his only two options: a hysterectomy to potentially save Ava's life or a written refusal, which would force them all to try to stave the blood flow as best they could, the consequences being anyone's guess. Scott signed on his chosen line.

Chapter 37

THREE WEEKS OF anything is a very long time; three weeks of nothing is longer.

The hospital released Ava after three days, and she lay in her bed for seventeen more. Fourteen days in, Scott had tended her, only leaving for work as necessary and coming down the hall from the office several times in the evenings to give her water or food or company. On the fifteenth day, he asked her to go for a "tiny" walk, but she refused. They had argued, but just a little, for he didn't have the heart for too much remonstration, and she didn't have enough care to respond.

It was December seventeenth when he boarded the plane for Cancun, the day before they'd wedded a year ago. The airline, understanding the situation, had refunded the cost of Ava's nonrefundable ticket. A first anniversary, superseded by a lost pregnancy and emergency surgery—the agent had wished them well.

"I didn't think he would go." Ava sat propped in their bed, and Bea and Jeanette sat in upholstered club chairs they'd pulled to the bedside.

Jeanette looked at Bea first as if she might be waiting for permission but then barreled ahead anyway. "Honey, I can't understand why you didn't go too. The doctor said you're fine to move around and that you could travel if wanted to… It was your anniversary trip, after all."

Ava gave the woman a cold stare. "I don't feel good, Mom. And I still hurt."

Bea sat silently, but Jeanette sallied forth. "But he did say you could travel, and—"

"Oh, I'm sorry. Well, okay, Mother, if the doctor said I could travel, I guess I should travel! Who cares if I can never have kids? Not my husband, that's evident. I mean, seriously, I'm sore, exhausted, oh, and yeah, barren, but I should have traveled. I'm sure I would have had a great time."

"Oh, Ava, why do you have to be so sarcastic? You said yourself Scott's been great since this happened! Men don't go about moaning and groaning like us women, and you have to remember he's got feelings too."

"Right. What do you think his feelings are? He doesn't seem that upset to me." She put her thumbnail in her mouth and began to rip it with her teeth.

Bea reached over, scooped her purse off the floor, and began rummaging.

"Stop that. Here, I have clippers. Ava, I'm not trying to take Scott's side, but Jeanette has a point. Men aren't wired to just shut down in crisis, even when they're grieving. It's like they're programmed. They keep going. And they don't talk about it a lot or cry as much as we do, but I'm sure he's very stricken."

Ava dropped her head back on the pillow, let out a long sigh, and rolled her head, looking again toward Jeanette; her mother balanced in the overstuffed chair, rigid and defensive as a wounded bird. "I'm sorry, Mom. I don't mean to be a jerk." She raised her head, accepted the clippers, and cut the nail as far down as she could, to the quick, then sucked on its little bit of blood before continuing.

"He hasn't cried at all. Not that I've seen. And I don't see how going on a trip he planned for *us* could have made him feel much better."

Bea didn't speak for a moment. "This might make you mad, but I think he probably didn't want to go. He may have done it just to show you."

"Show me what? That he's in charge?"

Bea shook her head. "To show you life goes on. That *he* has to go on. To give you a bit of a wake-up call."

Jeanette piped in, "That's right, honey. You're gonna have a great life, even if you don't believe it right now."

Ava turned over in the bed, facing the flowing dusk.

"No offense, Mom, but I can't see how anyone can predict that. It just looks like one big crapshoot to me."

Bea gestured to Jeanette to let it rest. She watched Ava watching the pines, whose branches were swaying in the cold gray breeze; they were supposed to have a storm that night. She rose, took the glass from Ava's nightstand, and filled it with cold water from the bathroom tap before placing it back on the coaster and sitting by her friend on the bed.

"I love you, Ava. And I know you have a hard time with God—with Jesus, even—but He loves you too. And you feel really sad right now that something's been taken away from you, and I understand that. But you will be better, by and by. If you could only reach out to Him sometime, darlin'. What do you have to lose?"

A minute passed, but Ava lay recalcitrant, watching the tall black-water pines as their needles danced ever so slightly. She then turned on her side away from the women and curled her hands under her chin. Another minute passed before Bea beckoned to Jeanette, and they left.

The church was decorated in the inexpensive way of a thousand other poor Southern churches. Four live poinsettias sat atop the raised semicircle platform, and behind them sat a manger scene constructed of plywood painted mud brown. There were cardboard cutout animals but a real-live shepherd in robes, with staff.

The small white pulpit had been moved stage left, off-center; and slightly to its right sat a worn pastor's chair, with a small bald smiling pastor seated in it. Two small imitation trees flanked the baptistry at the rear, and two large imitation wreaths were on the walls on either side of that, glistening with white twinkling lights.

Scott had come home from Mexico the twenty-third—sunburnt, drink-logged, chagrined, uncertain, and expectant. They had lain together that first night, huddled like war-stricken children while Ava dreamed. She dreamed of Chantal, babies, her almost-faceless father, and Eric, who was always, always distant, cold, nonplussed; the incalculable, unconquerable Eric. Once, during the night, the back of her hand had brushed against Scott's cheek, and it felt like there was dampness upon it—but then again, there were just so, so many dreams.

"I want you to take me to church," she had told him in the morning. "That's all I really want right now."

It was the Saturday night Christmas Eve service, and they arrived late, which was fine because Ava had told Bea they weren't coming. The interior of the small, low building was dim, except for candlelight lining the walls in sconces at the end of every pew and one buttery-soft spotlight on Bea, who stood to one side, enshrouded as Mary. With her chopped dark hair straggling from the edges of her headpiece and pink-and-white complexion, Ava had almost no trouble imagining her as Jesus's mother. A tall dark young man, heavily bearded and clasping his hands in front of him, stood beside her, displaying a different physiognomy than Bea. It was as if he alone were prescient; he alone bore the countenance of someone fully aware of his newborn baby's fate.

The organist, far recessed on stage right, played a nondescript soothing song while a boy of about eleven, nervous and thin as a reed in a black suit appropriate for a man at a funeral, began to read:

> And in the sixth month, the angel Gabriel was sent from God unto a city of Galilee, named Nazareth, to a virgin espoused to a man whose name was Joseph, of the house of David; and the virgin's name was Mary. And the angel came in unto her, and said,
>
> Hail, thou that art highly favored, the Lord is with thee: blessed art thou among women.

Bea's face, uplifted to the filmy light, shone radiance, and "Joseph," who had been standing in shadow, now wafted into the spotlight as Bea stepped back and the angel began to speak to him. He bowed his head and received these words:

> Then Joseph her husband, being a just man, and not willing to make her a public example, was

> minded to put her away privily. But while he thought on these things, behold, the angel of the LORD appeared unto him in a dream, saying, Joseph, thou son of David, fear not to take unto thee Mary thy wife: for that which is conceived in her is of the Holy Ghost. And she shall bring forth a son, and thou shalt call his name JESUS: for he shall save his people from their sins.
>
> Now all this was done, that it might be fulfilled which was spoken of the Lord by the prophet, saying, Behold, a virgin shall be with child, and shall bring forth a son, and they shall call his name Emmanuel, which being interpreted is, God with us.
>
> Then Joseph being raised from sleep did as the angel of the Lord had bidden him, and took unto him his wife: And knew her not till she had brought forth her firstborn son: and he called his name JESUS.

Ava was barely breathing. Scott sat motionless beside her.

More of the story was told—of Cesar Augustus sending out the decree that all people needed to return to their homeland for the census; of Mary riding on a donkey and of Joseph finding no room in the inn. While this part of the story was told, "O Little Town of Bethlehem" coursed from the organist's pipes. A woman two rows up had her hands uplifted toward the ceiling.

The first spotlight ebbed as Bea floated into a second one that bloomed above the manger, and from the shadows behind the manger's cardboard backdrop, Ava saw a woman in regular street clothes, crouching, pass a baby—a real baby—into Bea's waiting arms.

Bea looked upon the child with pure love as she placed him into the manger. Joseph stood solemn beside her.

"O Little Town of Bethlehem" segued to "Away in a Manger," and after a few moments of little movement while Bea adored the baby, three apparent wise men appeared where Bea and Joseph originally stood, just paces from the little family. The spotlight over them beamed back to life while the young narrator (who looked to Ava more like a mourner) read further:

> And, lo, the angel of the LORD came upon them, and the glory of the LORD shone round about them: and they were sore afraid. And the angel said unto them, Fear not: for, behold, I bring you good tidings of great joy, which shall be to all people. For unto you is born this day in the city of David a Savior, which is Christ the LORD.
>
> And this shall be a sign unto you; Ye shall find the babe wrapped in swaddling clothes, lying in a manger. And suddenly there was with the angel a multitude of the heavenly host praising God, and saying, Glory to God in the highest, and on earth peace, goodwill toward men.

Bagpipes, from some faraway recording, formed the backdrop of "Silent Night" as a sweet, pure voice emanating from shadows behind the scene lifted and crested toward heaven. Ava watched as the shepherds gathered to worship the baby, all from angles to the side, to ensure the audience had an optimum view. The spotlight, no doubt unwelcome to the drowsy child, caused him to squirm—to gesture with his doll-like arms and legs extending from his tiny white gown. Ava took a sharp breath inward, but Scott, beside her, remained inanimate.

This baby, Ava knew, was a mistake. His mother was fifteen, living with the youth pastor and his wife after being kicked out by her parents. She had refused to "summer in Europe" or to abort the baby while there was still "time."

Within the main light that was not candlelight, that spotlight of buttery yellow, Bea picked up the two-month-old infant. She cradled and rocked the little boy, his face a mere moon drop in linens, and continued to do so while the shepherds alternately knelt and stretched their arms to God and while the wise men stepped forward in reverence having come by a singular star.

The baby mewed, and when placed on Bea's shoulder, found his fist to suck on. Ava felt a cry arise in her throat.

Because they had sat in the back, it was not hard to get out without disturbance. She pushed by Scott's legs without warning, holding her own fist to her mouth as she stumbled, and reached the dirt road in front of the church before he grabbed her. She crumpled against him and he sank with her to the grass, hidden from view by the cars.

"I couldn't hold him…I couldn't…I couldn't hold on to him, Scott!" she wailed. Crumpled in the grass, racked by sobs, she pulled his arms further around her as he whispered, *Baby, baby, baby*, into her ear.

He held her crushingly, and she could smell the alcohol on his breath. It was comforting and angering and solid and true, and she thought how hard it was for him to face the world stone-cold sober at the same time thinking she could not bear her sterility even one more day. What would become of them, she wondered, amidst her sobs and tears. All she'd ever wanted was to be happy.

Part III

Chapter 38

IT WAS THE last Saturday in August, and they lay in lounge chairs. Bea's was under the umbrella; Ava's just outside its fringe. Bea was forbidden to swim, but Ava knew she didn't want to. She wore maternity shorts from her last two pregnancies, even though this time she was only four months along, and a red "JESUS SAVES" T-shirt. Her left breast was present in its usual bra; Ava knew the cup had been cut from the right one.

"Tell me if you want something. I am the keeper of the cooler after all." Ava had been smearing herself with tanning lotion that smelled like coconuts but now leaned her head back and leveled her eyes at the pool.

It wasn't too crowded: Jude's apartment complex had two, one at either end of the property, which helped spread out the residents. Kelly, thirteen; Brent, almost thirteen; and Jesse, eleven, were in the big pool. They had come to swim and help with Heidi. Gram and Alex—who was also now eleven—were with Wesley, who, at eleven months, splashed around in a dragon float in a shady area of the kiddie pool. Ava noticed Bea's gaze alternated from one area to the other, rarely deviating to any other view.

Ava leaned forward and grabbed a tube of sunblocking Chapstick, running it around her lips. "You didn't tell me what the doctor said yesterday. I shouldn't have to ask, either, since I'm your soulmate and all."

"Well, technically, I think Toby's supposed to be my soulmate."

"Yeah, but we both know that's not true."

Bea was shading her eyes as she looked out at the big pool, where Heidi, with a broad pink canvas sun hat strapped under her chin, was squealing as Brent "whooshed" her through the water in her swan float.

"Well, Larimore said the scar is healing as expected. He said keep it greased up to help with itching. And then I put the gauze over that."

"And what did Goober-head say?" Dr. Larimore was the oncologist who had performed the mastectomy, and Goober-head—Dr. Garvin—was Bea's obstetrician for this third pregnancy, Dr. Montal having retired. Ava knew them both well as she accompanied Bea often on her appointments; and Garvin—overly tall, wide-hipped, and even wearing that particular style of glasses—couldn't help but remind Ava, on each visit, of Mr. Peanut.

"I told you don't call him that! Just because you were born beautiful." Bea shook her head in a "what am I to do about you" manner. "He's very kind. And goofy, I get it."

She started to reach for the cooler, but Ava stopped her. "No, I told you, Larimore said no stretching. What do you want?"

"Orange juice, please. So okay, Dr. Garvin said that everything looks good. I've gained twelve pounds. The baby's heart rate is good." She trained her gaze to the kiddie pool. Alex was holding Wesley in a chair, giving him a bottle with Clara sitting beside him, messing and fluttering over them to make it all go okay. "He thinks it's going to be another big one, just as large and painful as the last two."

"You give birth to little Toby clones."

"I know. Hopefully, I can get the epidural again this time… I thought Heidi was gonna kill me."

They had reached a spot of synthesis between them: a place of Bea's easy fertility in détente with Ava's incapacity to conceive or bear another life. Ava would walk around the edge of the pool in a few minutes to slather more sunscreen on Heidi—to remind Kelly and Brent to put on more as well—and more than one man, or almost man, or old man would watch the movement of her lean legs in her black high-cut maillot, her long sun-streaked hair, and her strong brown arms as she raked it backward. They would take her for another carefree poolside beauty, and some would wish they could leave their own lives, with no concern for the repercussions, and join hers; but others were content to look at her merely for the moment. None would've guessed the carefree effect was a ruse.

"Ava...I don't want you to worry about me. I know you pretend you don't, but I know you do because you wear more on your face than you know."

"Do not. I have my own fish to fry."

"Whatever." Bea took a drink from her bottle. "Larimore wants to start chemo as soon as possible. I told him three or four weeks because it's safer in the second and third trimesters."

"But you're four months...why can't he start it now?"

"He's willing to, but I'm not. I thought, if it's safer the further you get, I could wait another month."

"But, Bea, if he thinks—"

"I know, listen, I know. I'm being aggressive, I am, and you know I let them take the breast because it was too early to wait that long for radiation. So the plan is to start the chemo in about a month and start radiation after I have the baby."

Ava played with the Chapstick in her hand. "You know what I wish? And maybe you'll think I'm evil, but I wish I could be the one pregnant this time. And that you hadn't even gotten pregnant, and they could have taken just the lump and the nodes and given you all the chemo and radiation and cured you. Because you already have two kids. And I don't have any. And you wouldn't still have this sucky disease."

"Stinky disease."

"Sucky. Sucky, sucky, sucky disease."

They didn't speak for a long time. Finally, Bea said, "I don't think that's evil. I think that sounds lovely." And she turned her eyes from the kiddie pool, looked at Ava, and smiled.

It was after four o'clock. The sun had shifted, as it always does, and Bea was no longer completely shaded. Ava had just arisen to adjust the umbrella when she saw Jude walking toward them with a short dark-complected woman by his side. She had long, thick wavy hair, iron-gray and black, and braided over one shoulder; she wore dark-blue Bermuda shorts topped by a red sleeveless blouse, and her feet sported red canvas boat shoes. They were laughing, and she slapped his shoulder; he pretended to be hurt.

"Hey, y'all." Jude wore the grin of the Cheshire cat when the pair stopped in front of Ava and Bea. "This is Harriet. She's an artist." He told Harriet each of the girls' names.

The woman reached first toward Bea, then Ava, and shook their hands as the girls murmured their hellos. "I paint. It seems to keep the bogeyman away." She had deep-set black eyes, faded lips, and weathered skin.

"We met at Gooden's," Jude said. "She had, like, a million canvases in her cart. I told her you painted, too, Ava, and then, of course—" gesturing "—Bea's the one that does the pottery with me. We do the shows."

Harriet smiled and nodded. A breeze blew, bringing closer that glorious chlorine smell that Ava loved so well, and ruffling wisps of hair.

Jude continued, "Ava won't call herself an artist. She's good, but she won't admit it, so that's why I had to trap her by bringing you over."

Harriet laughed. "I'd love to see your work sometime."

"I don't have a lot. I mostly shoot film, but not seriously—"

"And yet your stuff always sells when we go to market…" Jude rolled his eyes toward Bea before speaking again to Ava. "I told her you did photography but that you'd been painting for a couple years now, too, and taking classes. I also told her you won't take any to shows, so I want you to show some to her." He nodded in Harriet's direction. "She can tell you if she thinks you could sell."

It was true; Ava had taken up painting in earnest over a year and a half ago, right after the botched surgery. She'd started painting and going with Scott to ride the horses some weekends, and she'd started lying—to almost everyone—and stealing.

"I have a gallery in Corinth. It's mostly my stuff, but I take in some stuff from others. I'd love you to stop by sometime," Harriet offered. "And don't worry, it's not intimidating. It's tiny, and it's in the slummy part." She looked at Jude as if he were familiar with it and agreed, and laughed.

Ava shaded her eyes with her hand as she peered into Harriet's shadowed face. "Well. As long as it's in the slummy part."

The following Monday, the afternoon Jude routinely closed The Mane Event at three, he brought Harriet to Ava's house. Bea had gone to work in the back section of the studio as usual, and Jeanette had stayed to do the weekly deep clean, but Jude would skip sculpting with Bea that day and "happily" do paperwork and ordering of supplies later.

Now Ava and her company stood in one of the four rooms upstairs that traditionally would have served as a bedroom but instead now served as Ava's studio. Finished canvases lined the walls, paints and palettes rested on a folding table, and another table held framed and unframed photographs—the framed ones leaning against each other, stacked like records in a file, and everything sorted by size.

There were twenty-two finished paintings. Harriet clasped her hands behind her back and began to stroll the room as Ava moved to sit on a hassock. Jude tried to convince her to take the rocker, but Ava twice refused. This was the rocker Bea had given her—its lily-covered fabric matching the one Bea still owned, both reupholstered by Louise Mullins and moved to this room from the nursery months ago.

Ava had planned nothing. Perhaps it was because Marilyn's studio had stirred something in her, or perhaps it was the loss. Maybe it was simply that things seen with her naked eye and captured through light and angle on film had, ultimately, felt inadequate.

Each painting had oozed from her psyche like an infection and, once expelled, dwelt tangentially on the fringe of her life while she continued her ordinary days. They'd clamored in her roiling mind—morphing, advancing, retreating, and morphing again until she satisfied the compulsion to transpose and transfigure them to the helpless receptive canvases. Gravely, she had laid down her offerings, in jabs and streaks, in pointillism and lines, in shadow, in washes, in curves. Psychic turmoil not explored but merely expended, in catharsis, offerings, and rebukes.

Ava and Jude made small talk; he asked her to move the hassock in front of him so he could braid her hair. Meanwhile, Harriet studied each painting, lifting some off the wall and holding them out from herself, turning them at an angle as though to see the texture or application of the paint. The air conditioner kicked on with its familiar white-noise hum that Ava loved so well; she stole glances at the dark woman's seasoned face.

Harriet lifted a painting off the wall, ever so slightly turning to Ava but saying nothing. She held a seascape canvas, and it was one of Ava's favorites. Mountains of dark foreboding overlooked either side of the ocean, and a woman with long blonde hair stood on the apricot-colored beach. Her thin silhouette was visible beneath white flowing clothing, and she stretched both arms to the ocean with her head tilted back in yearning.

The water was saturated with Aegean hues, and the sun on the horizon sat buoyed by sedimentary layers of orange, gold, rose, and gray, even amethyst, toward the top of the sky.

The ocean was tumulted by breakers. In the first was the silhouette of a well-formed man—tall, understatedly muscular, presumably unclothed. In the second, one could see the faintest markings of a house—trileveled, ornately-columned, existing in its cloud of current. And beyond the surf—just above the water's break but below its murky surface—was a shadowy, oval, infantile form, centered and bathed by the light of the universe but far beyond the reach of anyone.

"You paint a lot of babies." Harriet's intention upon Ava's face was steady.

"Yeah…I'm sorry, was that a question?"

Harriet shook her head but smiled. "Not really." She replaced the painting and, moving to the long table along the wall, picked up a photograph of Mrs. Rhymer—the wife of old-man Rhymer—who helped him run the general store. The woman sat on a stool. It was one of the wide plastic stools with sides like hospitals used for people who were of excessive size, who had trouble getting up from a seated position. Mrs. Rhymer looked into the camera from behind her ancient counter as if she knew why Ava had wanted to take her picture but had resignedly allowed it anyway.

"Who is this?" Harriet studied Ava's face.

"Just a store owner. The general store, down the street a bit from Jude's." She fingered the tail of the braid Jude had finished and laid in front of her shoulder. "She…I think she's one of those people who makes the best of things. I wanted to capture her acceptance and contentment…in the midst of…having problems or…being ordinary."

Jude looked from Ava to Harriet. "She's a wonderful lady. She—"

"She's how life is." Ava held Harriet's gaze. "They all are."

Harriet replaced the photograph and hesitated a moment before returning to a wall and lifting another of the paintings, holding it out to Ava, eyebrows raised in silent query. It was of a big blue-and-green tree, full of yellow birds and tiny babies sashed in coiling yards of white; but except for a few in the tree, the others appeared flung out into the atmosphere—risen but falling over backward; wings, arms, legs, tails, loosened and splayed in the air.

Ava shrugged. "That's how life is, too, I guess. Everybody learns it eventually."

Chapter 39

AVA STILL HATED Halloween.

Paper pumpkins and ghosts dangled about Divine Chevrolet; dishes on desks overflowed with caramels, while candy corn pooled in others, with plastic spoons and tiny paper cups alongside.

"Ava Jane, how're ya doin', little lady?" Chuck asked in his baritone drawl. His dark eyes danced as he leveraged his crooked smile on her; and she hated that she had, some time ago, recognized that's where Scott had gotten his.

"I'm okay, Daddy-O," she said with a gaiety she didn't feel. "Here to do my due diligence."

Ava had arrived only minutes earlier than he and was still at the coffee station. The fluorescent lights glared down on the showroom with impunity, and she had turned to face him only after she felt the light pressure of his hand in the small of her back. As usual, she maneuvered to regain her personal space.

This Halloween was on Thursday, and Thursday was the day on which Chuck and Kimberly had their scheduled affair—when Ava could work in her office undisturbed—when she, figuratively speaking, had the whole dealership to herself.

Ava wasn't supposed to know about their weekly rendezvous, and neither was anyone else, yet they all did. Sometimes, sporadically, Chuck and Kimberly would both be "off" for the weekend; but every Thursday when Kimberly clocked out, she and Chuck drove off in her blue-black Trans Am, neither to be seen again until Friday after lunch.

This day, Chuck wore a black suit and orange tie with pumpkins adorning it; Ava thought it hideous. Kimberly, who was just strolling in from the parking lot, wore black jeans and a body-hugging orange cashmere sweater. As she swung through the doors, Ava could see she sported a flashing pumpkin pin.

"Ava. Kudos on the red suit. You're such a little rebel." She smelled of something spicy and oriental that went with her stature, her black curly hair, and her lips, which today were thick with a dark coral lipstick.

"Yeah. Halloween, Halloween…no biggie for me." Ava stirred cream into her coffee and took a sip, propping her elbow on the arm crossed against her waist. Kimberly made her feel small and slight and childish. "I'm more of a Memorial Day, Labor Day, Groundhog Day kind of girl."

Kimberly looked at her with appreciation. "You're funny, Ava. No wonder Scott loves you."

That took her aback for a moment—that Kimberly assumed Scott loved her. And maybe he did, still, and she just forgot sometimes, in light of the distance growing between them.

"Kim and I are gonna take off, Aves." Chuck had made his coffee and stood looking from one to the other. "We'll prob'ly do a good business today, so tell Franny to call me if things get squirrely…they workin' ya over at the bar this afternoon?"

"Yeah. I mean, I'll go, I hate to get behind. It's only a couple of hours, you know."

"Well. Take care. Try to have fun, honey. You look worn out, you know. Go out with your boy tonight or something. Halloween's not all bad for the grown-ups." He cut his eyes to Kimberly, but Ava looked away.

At her desk, she opened the ledger Kimberly had left for her—along with the invoices and receipts folder—with Franny. In one column, headed "Money In," were rows where she entered car sales, parts sales, and service charges. In the "Money Out" column were rows for cars bought, parts bought, and paychecks written. Then Ava took out the second ledger.

She knew her role well, and she knew the way Chuck had set things up would most likely stand up to scrutiny. Thus, her only salvation was that after Kimberly altered records to allow Chuck to cheat on his taxes, Ava did the end-of-the-year audit; *she* was the one, who, for the last two years, had checked the bank statements against the receipts, invoices, and bill payments. Here's to trust and family.

At first, it had been sickening to do but not so much anymore.

She didn't dare take cash from the safe; it was logical, and just good business, for Chuck or Kimberly or both to keep a running record of what was put into it every day. But Ava had access to the mimeograph machine. She had Liquid Paper. She had an artist's touch and an eye for detail. The ledger and invoices Ava now recorded and kept every day had alterations of her own.

She did everything with precision but removed only the smallest amounts. She would only deal with cash, for the checks in and out had to be reconciled to the bank statements. Also she would only alter handwritten invoices, for a typewriter would never align properly. Every figure entered had to be meticulously recalculated by the same percentage, and the ink, always, from the same trademark Divine Chevrolet pens. But it was easy, shockingly easy for her, with her head for numbers and her obsessive eye for detail.

She sat, her door locked, and worked; and she reminded herself often she would never take that much. But it got easier—it did—as little by little, her security grew, and her fear and disgust diminished. She began to feel less and less like one of the bad guys, more and more like someone owed.

Afterward, she tried not to think about it. Ava looked forward to Thursdays now ever since she'd realized the affair had a scheduled format, and with the same alignment toward routine developed as a child, followed the same procedures she'd always followed before going rogue. Everyone knew their roles at Divine—the receptionists and salesmen, the thieves, forgers, and adulterers.

Her work record had been and still was, immaculate, her reputation impeccable. She knew it was those qualities in part—and also by virtue of her being Scott's wife—that she was offered this job in the first place. She could barely believe it when, her stomach turbid and her heart in her throat, she had made her first alteration: 3 percent diminishment off car sales; 2 percent off service charges; and 5 percent off parts. It would take a while. But it was unnoticeable, wasn't it? And Chuck had so much; and he was a scuzzbag. And

Scott's problems—well, *their* problems—with money and emotional intimacy and time shared or spent in isolation were not getting her closer to a baby. Adoption would cost money. So much money. But adoption was her only chance, anymore, at a family.

She did leave the dealership early, tucking her altered invoices in her briefcase, along with the money deposit for the day. The sun was so bright in the October-blue sky, and the clouds so white that she almost felt exposed—the integral beauty of that perfect day juxtaposed against her stricken integrity. But a conscience long-salved loses its resiliency, and something along the line had chiseled down the strength of her will to be good. She decided to go to the bar early that afternoon and leave the bar early as well. She wanted to go home and call her contact.

Chapter 40

IT WAS A stunning Saturday, the first in November, and they rode in easy camaraderie.

Scott sat a horse like an equestrian. His broad shoulders were lean and capable; his back straight; and his dark hair, unusually long and windblown, crowned his elegant head. Ava loved to ride slightly behind him; it was almost an act of courtship. How scary the world where futures could be determined by half an hour in a hospital or by machinery fails and spoken words. He was strong, she would tell herself because she believed it. There was never a need to worry.

He always rode Duke, of course. Duke was Jimmy's massive black stallion, whose white snip was his only aberration from the rest of his color. It was Duke's speed and assurance in Jimmy's beloved fox hunts that had won them both acclaim in local newspaper articles from Virginia, as well as amongst Jimmy's fellow hunters.

Ava rode behind on Wallis, Corrine's equally beautiful but smaller and more demure bay mare and on whom Ava had grown to feel competent as a rider. She had come to look forward to these outings where Scott took her along, days when he would phone Robin and tell her he and Ava could work the horses that day. They would race the pasture outlying from the cabin and ride surrounding trails, alternating pace and terrain until the horses were sufficiently tired and the demons of each of their riders were subdued. Scott had dark circles under his eyes this day, made darker perhaps by the slate gray of his shirt. His eyes had the storm color too; he had been up late and risen early.

They neared the gate at the far end of the pasture; Scott dismounted to unlatch it, tossing the reins around the fence rail. "We'll take 'em down the Canterbury side but come back up through the fields. I want to run Duke a bit on the ride back. Is that okay with you?" He swung the gate open and shielded his eyes from the late-morning sun as he squinted at her.

"Mmmhmm." She nodded. "Can I run Wallis?" She had been galloping the mare in small spurts of late but never trying to keep pace with Scott. "I'm ready for a big, bold move, I think." She grinned at him, and he grinned back.

"Oh, I'm sure you are. You're a natural, you know," and Ava's heart grew warm from his words. Compliments came naturally to him.

After crossing a gentle hill and its ensuing valley, Ava knew they would come to the Canterbury trail, a narrow pass through the forest that meandered down to a cool tributary of the Tarrymore. They would follow this creek for a while, cross it, and emerge onto the wide part of the property for the run home.

When they reached the Canterbury, they rode in silence for most of the way; sauntering on a single-file trail didn't lend itself to conversation. She alternately watched his back and swept her eyes across the surrounding hilly woods. Sometimes she would throw her head back and see the cold white clouds through a break in the canopy of trees, trying to imagine how far they were in the great, great distance. What a world it was, in such minute and grand extravagance; what a contradiction, with so much right and wrong.

Ava loved this ride. The days she would accompany Scott, the random Saturdays when she missed him excessively, and her heart was stagnant with nameless black stones, she would ask to take the Canterbury. He would know she would want to dismount and lie beside that creek, freezing time while the tethered horses drank. Their tails swatting a random fly now and then, the horses would offer her their soft breathing and the rustling of the layered leaves with their hooves, adding to the brook's gurgle and forest's murmurings, the timeless yet unique "syncophony."

"That's not a word," Scott said but didn't open his eyes. They had come to "their" spot, and he lay on his back with his hands resting on his stomach.

"I'm sure it is. It has to be. Like, a melding of things that go together to make something grander but aren't much on their own." She was propped on her side, fingering the curls behind his forehead.

"You're thinking of *cacophony*. Which, of course, means the opposite."

"No. Yeah, I mean, I know. It's not *cacophony*, it's *syncophony*. It goes together. All the sounds. To make something new." Maybe she was thinking *symphony*…

He didn't speak. Some moments passed, and she wondered if he was slipping into sleep, for his breathing was soft and even. She lay her head on her folded arm and traced the dark hair of his arms.

"I remember when I first saw you, Ava."

She almost held her breath—such was the unexpectedness of his voice and her anticipation of what he would say.

"You had on that pink sundress, that soft one, remember? You don't wear it much anymore." His eyes were still closed. Before she was about to speak, he continued, "And those white sandals, the ones that lace up your leg. I thought you were so beautiful. But you didn't even know it."

He opened his eyes and laced his fingers behind his head as he turned to look at her. His eyes, in the sun reflecting off the water, were the magical color Ava only saw in certain light, on certain days, from certain angles—a pristine blue, still with the gray rims but not clouded within. Those eyes were the windows to the Scott she loved; those eyes showed the soul of the one she'd married. She looked down and found a leaf with which to toy.

"Maybe I did know I was beautiful. Maybe I was setting a lair for you."

He didn't smile but continued to stare at her face. "No. You weren't. And you didn't know. You still don't." His voice had a forlorn sound.

As if he had an appointment, he rose and reached for her hand. "C'mon. Get Wallis. I want to ride up to the Point."

The Point was the rock face overlooking the inlet from which Kenneth Mullins fell, the site officially named Outlook Inlet. It was a high crest above the river, rising from its depths like a sea god, and afforded an incredible view. It was second highest only compared to what everyone called the "mountain," which was visible a mile north in the distance and from which Mr. Mullins dove not that many years before, proving once again to the world that he was no longer a coward.

They followed Canterbury Creek to the river and turned their horses north toward the Point. They had to hug the shores well to stay out of the woods' entanglement but not so close that the horses might skid into the shallows and get swept up by the white cresting current. The river from the north poured through two ranges of rock face; and visitors learned that loose, slippery jagged rock, sucking mud, or a misplaced hoof could send a horse and rider down to a stone-laced fall. It was fortunate that equestrians had worn a trail for years, and Ava knew Wallis would follow Duke without a problem or misstep until they arrived at the Point.

Outlook Inlet had what appeared to be scaffolding abutting its top half and extending above its rock face. Ava knew its story. The county had drilled and hammered the geometric structure of metal pipes and bars into the stone, shielding its precipice, for a reason—to prevent tragedies such as the one met by Beatrice's father.

They once again secured the horses, this time to some scrub at the rock base, and began climbing its eastern face. It wasn't steep, but broad, and Scott knew the crevices well in which to place one's feet; he stayed close behind Ava and directed her. It wasn't long before they reached the flattened crest, and Scott walked to the iron grid and propped his riding boot upon one of the lower rungs. Ava did the same, grasping the vertical bars as if peering out of a cell.

"When was the last time we were up here?" Scott asked. He looked across the river to the horizon, a mélange of tree ridges in varying shades of greens, the slate-colored ripples in between shimmering in the sun.

"I don't know. A couple of years? I've only come that one time—with you." She put her face between two iron bars, trying to see down the cliff face to the rocks below. There was no beach there, just a rock outcropping that stretched out at an angle, just large enough to catch a body.

"I don't like it here, Scott." Ava turned and found a space upon which to sit, both mossy and flat. Silently she watched his back, and it was a moment before he spoke.

"You know what I always think, Aves? About Kenneth Mullins?" He still stared out over the water and didn't wait for her to answer. "He didn't fall. Well, he did. But he did it on purpose." A minute passed—she didn't know what to say—but he turned then from the grid and came to stand in front of her.

"I don't want to have children." It was only six little words.

It was always the same: she heard the words first in her stomach. Fear, her old friend, the sickness of imminent uncertainty.

"This life. Yours, mine…I'm just getting it less and less." He pulled out a cigarette and lit it, dragging and exhaling.

"You shouldn't smoke up here." Her voice shook. She watched his face, believing he hadn't registered her words; but after a full minute of silence, he knelt in front of her and stubbed out the smoke.

"Listen. Aves. I've been thinking a lot. I know you think adoption is going to be the way to go, but…what if we just changed everything?" He searched her eyes, and she felt tears at the back of them that she didn't want him to see.

"You said you sold a couple at the gallery, and you also sold some at that show. I think you're as talented as Harriet, and she actually calls herself an artist." Scott had gone with her to the gallery on a Saturday to take in five of Ava's canvases and had seen her new friend's work.

"She is an artist."

"So are you. But you're spending your time on accounting. And this is what I was thinking: you know I leave Saturday to cover that hunt—"

"I wanted to talk to you about that. I don't want you to go."

He squinted his eyes at her as if he couldn't quite comprehend what she was saying. "I have to go. I'm covering the story."

This was true. The last two seasons—that Scott had been seeking his writing opportunities in earnest—had given him eight published articles, and two were for *Fox and Hound.* The other six for *Men's Health, World of Golf,* and *Planet Golf* had rounded out his portfolio. Now he wanted to focus on fox hunting fall and winter, maybe even traveling to England and Wales and writing of those exploits for American audiences and covering golf during spring and summer, touring the states. She knew his big dream, still, was to travel and write and someday leave insurance sales behind altogether.

"I know you are." Ava forced herself to breathe. "But you leave me. And you know how hard I've been working, and I still have to help Mom. I have to make sure she gets to the doctor and takes her medicine, and there's always stuff to do around the house. *And* there's Bea…" She felt her voice break. "She's really sick, Scott. She needs more help too."

He didn't speak for a moment but then moved to sit on a rock perch a few feet away. He leaned forward, appearing to study her, his elbows on his knees, hands clasped.

"Ava. Listen, baby. There's us. Jeanette is manic-depressive, so what. You got her help, you and your friends, and she takes her little pill. She goes to work—God bless Jude is all I can say—but you can't hover waiting for her to screw up so you can rescue her." He pulled another cigarette from his shirt pocket. She said nothing as he lit it.

"You didn't want that house in the first place. It ties you down. It's a good investment, and we can work on it for thirty years, and we can live there. But with no kids, there's no pressure to get it done. We can travel. You can quit The Fox and Ale or the dealership or both, and I can keep going with insurance as long as I have to. But we don't need all that kid stress, and without kids, we wouldn't even need that much money. And my god, look what Bea goes through with those two. And now the cancer and another one coming…" He shook his head.

She felt the sob coming up from her throat. "But I *want* kids, Scott! What about what I want? What about everything I *always* wanted—to have a beautiful home, with lots of friends, and a family? Doesn't that count in any of your plans?"

Her voice was raised and strident to her ears. She wanted his arms around her. She felt fluid and unglued like she might leak through her skin and puddle on that hateful, rocky ground.

Instead, he sat, and with the coldest stare. He sucked on his cigarette long and hard and blew it out hard to the side. "Why? So you can have the family you never had? You think you can do it right, don't you? Don't you think Jeanette and your daddy—John, right?—don't you think they thought they were going to get it right?"

She held her arms around her waist and spoke to the ground, "Jeanette couldn't have more children. And Daddy died of cancer. I was only four, so there was no time—"

"That's crap, Ava." He said it in a normal tone, dropping his cigarette and stubbing it out with his boot. "I'm sickened by the way she's lied to you."

It was Ava's turn to stare. "Lied to me about what? If she could have had more kids, she would have. She's told me that her whole life. And if Daddy had lived, we could have been happy. We wouldn't have been poor, and Mom could have gotten help as soon as she started acting weird. Daddy would have known she was sick."

He had gone back to the iron grid and was facing it. He said nothing.

"The cancer took all the money. And Mom just started drinking too much, and everything just went wrong. You know that. Kids would have helped, I think. She would have had something to live for and keep her busy. We would have had insurance… She's never had much to love—"

"She had you." He faced her. "Weren't you enough to love? But she spent her whole life drinking and either neglecting you or smothering you—which is a real trick, by the way—and guilting you and looking for answers in a church she goes to just to have people to talk to. Ask her how much in her life she's done for her Jesus."

Ava was crying now. "Why are you being so mean?" They met eyes. Another moment passed as he stared at her.

"I know why Mullins killed himself." He spoke almost too low to be heard, and she didn't respond.

"You would know, too, if you thought about it. You said you read the book."

Ava pictured the book's cover again in her mind—a young, tall Kenneth Mullins sitting cross-legged far out on a bluff that overlooked a treeless canyon behind him. His auburn hair glinted in the sun.

"I did read the book. But since it was written when he was alive—"

"Use your head." Scott turned and faced the iron grid again and spoke his words out over the receptive water. "It's because he didn't believe in God."

Silence. After a minute, he came and sat again on the rock, boring into her face with his eyes.

"It's in there, at the very end. He begins with an exposé about his cowardice and how it gave him life while the bravery of his fellow soldiers cost them theirs. This is also his confessional. Then he narrates his attempts at redemption through the daredevil stunts. It's all about proving to his family that he can become worthy by cultivating bravery. He thinks if he does this, he'll be okay because family is all that he can see that matters."

Ava said nothing. All she could think of was what he'd said about not having children.

"But it doesn't work. He still can't figure out why he, the coward, lived when the 'good' men died…and then he ends it all by saying that though he's driven to overcome, to make recompense, it doesn't work. Not in so many words, but…he says he will never be worthy of the love of his wife and how he can't make himself good enough to earn his kids' respect…or anyone else's either. And most importantly, how he can never bring back the men who never saw their families again or could never have families of their own."

Ava wiped her eyes and stood, brushing the seat of her jeans. "God, Scott, you're always talking like a writer. I don't remember the end being that tragic. He said being brave and teaching his kids to be brave was the best he could do."

"Exactly. A couple of lame paragraphs that say, 'Yeah, here's my best,' but it's riddled with self-loathing and the realization he can never do enough."

Ava turned to look down the steep craggy path up that they'd climbed. She could see the horses below, standing quietly as ponies at a fair, except for their swishing tails. "I don't remember him saying he didn't believe in God."

Scott stood again and spoke to her back, "He didn't. He said he 'didn't know how'...didn't know how 'a' god could do this or why 'a' god would ever do that. It was Robin—remember, she did the report?—who found out he didn't believe in God when she researched him. I read it, you know. It was Susan, the oldest, who told her. And it explains all his unrest while he was alive and all his angst when his wife died. She was all he was living for, I think. To prove himself to her."

Ava had forgotten that Robin had interviewed Susan. The assignment was to report on or interview a local celebrity, so Robin had not only researched Kenneth Mullins but also interviewed his daughter, postmortem.

She turned and looked again at her husband, who was thoughtfully fingering a weed he'd pulled from many that sprouted from crevices. He met her gaze for a moment.

"What he did say, of course, said it all." He cast his eyes to the distance. "All his doubts and unrest..." He looked once more to her. "They found him on his back, you know."

He moved to stand beside her then while the words settled in her bones and hardened. As if on cue, they cast their eyes at Duke and Wallis grazing.

"Really?" she said, as the barest of whispers, for she understood his point immediately.

"Yeah. Flat out, arms and legs splayed like a snow angel." His arms went around her, and he sighed. "Ending it all—free-falling."

They rode back through the fields as they'd planned, galloping most of the way, and except for the wind in her ears and the echoes of Scott's statements earlier, in a more profound silence than the state in which they had ridden out. Ava saw Corrine's red Corvette pulled to the side of the gravel drive, allowing Scott's Blazer room to exit.

"We'll just put 'em in their stalls for now," Scott said to Ava over his shoulder as they walked the horses to the barn. "I'll get a drink and come back out and clean them up, and you can rest for a minute if you want." Ava mumbled an okay.

The cabin inside, after the bright outdoors, was dim—so dim Ava almost missed the surprised look on Corrine's face as her eyes adjusted to it. But she heard her voice, no problem.

"Well, hey, gorgeous!" Corrine offered her Pearl Drops smile from her recline on the worn leather sofa. "Robin didn't mention you were ridin' with your man today."

Ava nodded. She didn't expect to see Corrine either. She didn't relish her boss—this woman to whom she still didn't feel superclose after two-and-a-half years—seeing her so soon after she'd just been crying those tears.

"I'm just gonna pop into the restroom real quick," she said and then veered right while Scott wordlessly went left toward the kitchen.

In the bathroom, she could hear Robin and Naomi a few feet beyond its cracked window. They had a little garden out there, and today they were planting garlic. Naomi's low bubbling laughter melded with Robin's, high and tinkly, cascading over the sill. *That's crap, Ava,* she heard in her mind, and *I'm sickened by the way she's lied to you.*

Lied about what? Yes, Jeanette had lied about money and her drinking or what she'd eaten for dinner. Ava washed her hands and looked out the window. Both girls were kneeling in gardening clothes, twisting up clumps of dirt and tamping with gloved hands.

Ava fought back tears as she stood watching them. Did they want kids? What would either of them do with that ache, that void? Or was it different for them? She tried to steady her breathing. She would not accept this, she thought. He was not going to take this from her.

She came out almost soundlessly. That's what she realized later. She had removed her riding boots on the porch so her feet pattered as softly as an Indian's, and she'd even opened the bathroom door, unintentionally, as silent as a spirit.

She felt as if she had drifted toward the kitchen and, from its doorway, saw Scott facing its sink, head bowed, arms braced against it like a man facing great odds. Corrine, at his side, leaned back against it, her face tilted sideways and back a little, seeking his face; her left hand was cradling his cheek.

Ava stood a moment.

And Corrine, turning her face toward the doorway, met Ava's eyes like a thief caught in the act, her mouth open slightly and stupidly. She slid her hand from Scott's face in a moment—and it slipped to her side like water.

Chapter 41

SHE LAY IN the narrow single bed and listened. She needed silence, but there was always murmuring. There were always footsteps, and whispers, clinically-soft voices ever-mingling to a hum that made it impossible to be truly alone.

She ignored the knock at the door. She had ignored them all, as she had since she'd arrived at the psychiatric facility Monday afternoon, but as usual, it opened anyway.

"Hi, Ava. How're you doing today, honey?" Ava didn't answer, but the nurse continued, "I wanted to tell you Dr. Caffey is going to come in here in a moment. He wants to see if he can help."

Ava turned on her side to face the wall and looked out the narrow single window closest to the corner. A row of bushes, tall and spindly, bowed in the breeze, then straightened, then bowed again, showing silver underbellies. Dr. Caffey could do what he wanted.

"I told him you're still refusing food. He knows you've been here almost three full days and that you wouldn't talk to Oalman or Jeffries, but he knows only the barest of circumstances."

Ava raised a moment to lift her hair from behind her back but didn't turn from the wall as she spoke. "Well, I'm sure you all have told him the juicy parts."

The nurse was the same one she always saw on the day shift—thirty to thirty-five, she was chubby and delicate, with flax-yellow hair and white childlike hands. "He should be in in a few minutes," she said and shut the door behind her.

Ava lay still, watching the swaying bushes. They had multiple stalks and leaves from dirt to sky. *Who did this?* she couldn't help but wonder. *This simple row of foliage, multiplied by nature's other phenomena, by factors of an infinite numbe*r.

She decided not to answer the second knock of the day either but turned over to look at this new doctor. He was a tall man, gangly, with burnt-orange hair rusted by gray. He brought in an aroma of some manly scent, and he sported a blood-orange mustache. He introduced himself from the door.

"Ava, I'm Dr. Caffey. Dr. Oalmann asked me to stop by. May we talk for a minute?"

Ava studied him for a moment. It was funny how all her previous predilections to manners had vanished since she'd come there. She felt an odd sense of control that she now believed she'd been losing for a long time. People were chatting, bringing food, a helpful little pill every evening, and small chilled cups of water. But no one could help her if she didn't allow it, which gave her great satisfaction.

"I haven't talked to anyone," she said, meeting his smiling face with her unsmiling one. "So I'm not sure I want to talk to you, either."

Dr. Caffey sat in one of only two chairs, made of a sparse metal frame and nylon seat and back. He crossed one ankle on top of the other knee, resting a clipboard atop his thigh.

"I understand. But I also know you're smart. You don't want to stay here—so I've been told—and I feel it's only fair to tell you we can't release you until you eat and until we feel we've made some headway conversationally. We need to make sure you're no longer a danger to yourself."

Her heart thundered in anger. "I was never a danger to myself."

The doctor looked down at his clipboard. "It says here your husband took you to the emergency room Saturday night in what was described as a semiconscious state, and blood tests were positive for exceedingly high amounts of alcohol and methaqualone." He raised his eyes to hers. "Is that not being a danger to yourself?"

She glared at his calm face. "I got drunk. I took something to relax. I had never had a drink, and I didn't know what the pills were. They were my husband's. He'd always taken them at night when he needed a way to relax, and nobody ever accused him of being a danger to himself."

Dr. Caffey remained unfazed. "Your husband guessed the missing amount was somewhere in the range of six tablets. If that were accurate, at 75 mg. each, you would have had 450 milligrams of the drug in you. That, combined with your blood alcohol level from the vodka, was potentially life-threatening for a first-time user and non-drinker, particularly of your size. Why did you feel the need to take the pills and to drink? Especially when, as you said, you never had, and your husband confirming that fact."

Ava sat up in the bed, pushing the hospital gown into her lap; she was furious. "Oh, my husband confirmed that fact for you, did he? What else did my husband tell you? That he's a liar? That he's having an affair with my boss, a woman I was *friends* with? Well, of course, you're going to look to him for corroboration of the truth!"

The doctor watched her. "Actually, he did tell me you had had a terrible fight. That he had hurt you deeply, but he didn't say how. And he also told me you found out that day you did not belong biologically to your parents."

Ava's body was rigid with its contained fury—only her hands were shaking. "Rich, isn't it? Did he also tell you he only pretended during our marriage to want children?" Dr. Caffey only looked at her, not speaking. "Yeah. It was a banner day."

Dr. Caffey adjusted his crossed ankle and lay the clipboard upon it. "Did he tell you he was having an affair?"

She said nothing.

"Ava, I can leave. But until you eat and until you talk, you will remain with us, okay?" He waited only a moment before he rose to go.

"Wait." She pushed herself further up against the vinyl-padded headboard and took a deep breath. She needed the pain to come out. The doctor watched her a moment from his standing position but then resumed his seat.

"I do the books for the bar this woman and her husband own, Corrine and Jimmy. Scott's been friends with them since way before I moved to Tarryton, and he lived in a cabin they owned. He took care of their horses. They all go on trips together, especially fox hunting trips. Now his sister and her girlfriend live there since he and I got married, but he still rides, and sometimes I go with him."

"Go on."

"Scott and I had been riding together Saturday, and she was there when we got back."

"Corrine?"

Ava nodded. "And I saw something weird. When I came out of the bathroom, she…was touching him. She had her hand on his face, and something just clicked in me. I remembered when I started working for her and Jimmy at their bar, and they were laughing about this big crush she had on Scott. And I hadn't thought much about it. I thought it was a joke. But she—they're always talking and laughing, and she's really pretty and superconfident. And he does drugs, and she does drugs, and they all drink a lot, and…sometimes, he doesn't even come home. But I always thought he was at Chet's. That's what he said, anyway. That's his best friend."

She was crying. She reached over to the rolling table beside her bed for the tissues.

"So it's still going on?"

Ava blew. "He swears not. He still says he's at Chet's and doesn't want to drive. But why should I believe him? If he lied about the past, he'll lie about the present."

The doctor was writing on the clipboard lying on his propped leg. When he finished, he asked, "Can you tell me about your family?" He lowered his leg to the floor and crossed his hands over the board on his lap. She wondered if they were taught nonthreatening postures in medical school to use on all the crazy people.

"Why not? You said if I eat and talk, you'll let me out of the ward, right?"

"It's part of it. We have to believe you're on the road to recovery. That you value your life and wish to move on. And agree we can follow up with you."

She would agree to anything. She could eat and talk because she needed to leave. She blew her nose again and took a deep breath.

"We were fighting. It started because of that touch. By the time he admitted they'd slept together, I was going ballistic. I brought up other things I'd kind of seen and knew but didn't think much about until I saw them on Saturday. Like the way he's always gone to stay at Jimmy's daddy's plantation house to ride in their fox hunts, and the way he has his insurance meetings mostly at their bar."

"The bar you do the books for."

"Right. The Fox and Ale. It's where I met Scott after I started work there. He used to work there, too, a long time ago, and then when he started to sell insurance, he would meet lots of his clients there. And not only would he go to Jimmy's daddy's, but Jimmy and Corrine would sometimes go on these little trips with him. Like, a couple of years ago, after we were married, they all went to the Masters tournament in Georgia and some other stupid golf thing the year after that. Scott's trying to be a writer, too, just so you know."

"Really? What kind of writer?"

"For magazines, mostly, like about riding and golf. And lots of times Jimmy and Cory would go, too, for no good reason that I could see. Of course, their little clique makes more sense now."

"Why didn't you go?"

"I was busy! I work two jobs!"

"Right. Doing what?"

Ava sighed. "Does it matter? I'm the office manager and accountant at Scott's daddy's car dealership. And we bought this old house that I work on, and I was trying to have a baby. Plus, right after I'd moved to Tarryton, my mom had kind of a nervous breakdown. So my best friend and her husband helped her move to Tarryton, too, and stay in their guesthouse, and then another friend gave her a job, but she's not stable. She's supposed to leave her keys with us when she's not at work and let us help her manage her money, but she doesn't do either and gets drunk any chance she gets. We have to take her to the doctor a lot because she's manic-depressive, and she's terrible about her pills. She'll get depressed or have little temper tantrums. She's a bit of a nutjob."

The doctor nodded. "I see."

"But I've been…so overwhelmed. And I didn't care that much, really, about Scott's stuff, I just…I missed him a lot, and I wanted him to stay home more and help and help me make a family. And I thought Corrine and Jimmy were really in love."

"Are you still planning a family?"

The tears welled. Ava shook her head. "I can't…I can't have any."

Dr. Caffey's eyes were kind when Ava's met his. "I'm sorry, Ava."

"Yeah. Well, anyway, all this truth just came spilling out. I told him how ruined I was, how all I really wanted was love—his, and then to recreate it with children. And he'd been absent or working upstairs at night with his coke and drinking—did he tell you he does cocaine? Probably not. But anyway, this fight, he's getting so angry and defensive because he doesn't have a leg to stand on, and then he screams at me, 'Why would you want a family when you don't even know who yours is?' He says, 'You're an effing orphan, Ava.' But he says the word. He says his family is effed up, and mine sure as hell was because my stupid mother didn't even have the guts to tell me the truth. And then he showed me the letter."

She couldn't stop crying.

Dr. Caffey asked her if she wanted to take a break, so they did. She asked for a glass of water.

When the doctor returned to the room in a couple of minutes, he brought her a tall Styrofoam cup of ice water and a straw—luxuries no one had, as yet, afforded her. As she drank—calmer, then, no longer sobbing—she saw the envelope in his hand. It appeared just as she'd first seen it—the flap not sealed but tucked under and the familiar artless script of her mother spelling out "Scott Divine" on the front, under which she'd written, "Give to Ava if I Die."

"When Dr. Oalmann called me, he said you've refused any visits from your husband. He also said Scott wanted to pay for me to see you because Dr. Oalmann told him you weren't eating or talking, even though your insurance doesn't cover a private psychiatric doctor without a prior evaluation."

Ava sipped her water, staring at the floor.

"So Scott met me outside the building an hour ago and handed me this." Caffey lifted the envelope. "Is this the letter?"

Ava nodded.

"He's very upset, Ava. I believe he loves you, and if it's any consolation, he looks worse for wear."

Ava set the cup on the bedside tray. "Scott's a beautiful man. He never looks bad. Not on his very worst day."

At this, the tall man, who was still standing and not far from her bed, laughed. "Well, though a man, I can see how you would see him attractive, but I imagine he's had better days."

She stared at the letter he held in both of his hands. She lay back on the bed and covered her eyes with her arm.

"I haven't read this, Ava. Your husband made me promise I wouldn't read it unless you permit me. I'm ethical enough to respect that, and I need you to trust me. I only know this is why he said you had taken the pills and vodka. He said when he showed it to you during the fight, you—and I quote—'lost your mind,' so he left so you might calm down. He thought his presence was making it worse because you were so angry about the woman. But when he returned in about two hours, you were passed out with the drink, pill bottle, and letter by your side, so he called the ambulance. That's all he knew and all I know."

Ava uncovered her eyes and shot up in bed to face the doctor, her face an illustration of scorn.

"He only gave it to me to take the focus off of him! Don't you see that? He's a liar! My mother's a liar, too, but oh, I'm sorry, she's not even my freaking mother! Nor was my father my dad, and nor did he die of cancer! It's all lies! Nobody ever loved me enough to tell me the truth!" She pressed her hands against her face and cried.

He was silent for a couple of minutes before he spoke again. "Ava, in a moment, if you'll allow me, I'm going to read this letter. Even before I read it, I realize it contains some hard truths. But I want you to consider that people are inherently messed up, and though many do love each other, they don't know how to do it properly. Whatever the truth is about your mother or who you believed was your mother, she must have wanted you in her life because she's raised you as her own. And as for Scott, the very fact that he asked for my word that I wouldn't read your most vulnerable truths without your permission should be some evidence that he wants to undo some of the pain of his previous deception."

He let the words sink in, and Ava uncovered her face. When she didn't protest, he raised the letter, seeking her assent. "May I?" he asked, and after a moment, she nodded.

Chapter 42

Dear Scott, hey, it's Jeanette, of course! This is the story I was trying to tell you last week when y'all came and moved me out, and no Ava does not know a word but she is so sweet she cannot know. If I die I think she should know, but I don't want her to know if I am alive because she might hate me and I waited too long to tell her, I just could not stand it every time I thought about it and well, but if I die she deserves to know and I know she loves you so much and if something ever happens to me you can help her through it I hope. P.S. I will give you this tomorrow when I come for dinner but you have to hide it because I'm serious Scott, she will hate me so bad.

When I met John I was so in love with him, yessir! But I alway*s* knew he did not really love me that much even my parents told me, Jeanette you love him but he does not love you he will meet someone he loves and it will not be you and so that is why I did what I did.

I pretended I was pregnant, and my parents guessed I tricked him. They still don't want anything to do with me because they said I was a blight on their good name and Ava was a bastard. But John was a decorated marine. He fought in the Korean war and worked at prosperity finance a bank and had a good job. But we dated only a few times, and I knew he did not want to marry me and my parents knew he did not want to marry me he only liked the way I looked and I gave him what he wanted and I wanted to get out of Bright Point where my parents sent me to live with my great aunt because I was so hard to manage so they said. I did not like the catholic church they went to either and I just could not concentrate in school so I was going to go to school to be a secretary but I met John at a dance and well the rest they say is history.

So he married me but he was not really happy. I know. I pretended to lose the baby but in the meantime I was trying to get pregnant but when I said I lost the baby he would not take any chances he said he did NOT want children and I think he was thinking about a divorce but he did not say that. He was really smart and he wanted to be rich and I know he wanted to be in love but I could not make him fall in love with me I tried and tried.

John was a orphan. He never had a family. Of course I couldn't tell Ava that I just said I didn't know where they were so she wouldn't feel so alone. But John was very closed off. But I know he wanted to find a woman to love but here was the thing he would see women in Atlanta. They were the ladies of the night. I don't think he did it much because he tried to be a good husband and he went to work and was nice to me but the thing is he fell in love with this one girl her name was Sapphire. She was a dancer and she was really pretty because I found some pictures in his wallet. She was really tall and had long dark hair and really pretty eyes and a pretty smile and I remember it hurt real bad but I knew I had been bad by tricking John because I knew he didn't love me even my parents said so. So I tried to not get mad.

But Sapphire quit seeing John and he couldn't find her nowhere and then one day she called him he said and told him she had a little baby that was John's and she wasn't going to keep it and did he want it or she would give it up for adoption. Well that just about drove John crazy, because he had lung cancer we just found out and he didn't want kids but he wanted Sapphire. One time he got drunk and told me he was in love with her and wanted to marry her but he would not and Sapphire did not want to marry him she just used him to buy her nice things because she was in love with another man.

But John said no don't give the baby away and he asked me if we could raise it. I was real hurt he had made a baby with her when he was so careful not to make one with me, but I said of course! Because I always wanted babies and I knew John would love it because it was Sapphire's and I would love it because I wanted a baby and John wouldn't let me have one. But I said YOU CAN'T EVER TELL THE BABY IT'S NOT MINE and he agreed.

So he named the little girl Ava and she was the sweetest baby and so smart and real pretty like her mama, tall, and graceful and strong and slender, and the prettiest big grey eyes and we got to be kind of happy and John was doing pretty good but then we got a letter from someone who said they knew Sapphire and she had got syphilis and took enough heroin to kill herself and wanted John to know he really wasn't Ava's daddy and she had asked that friend to tell him but the friend wouldn't tell John his name but said just know she felt bad but wanted the baby to have some money and a nice life and grow up with someone who would love her but she had to clear her conscience before she died.

And John just lost it, but he loved the baby but he was not going to live too long, the doctor said, because probably of some chemicals from the war because he didn't smoke only me. So he hung himself in his friend's basement, Allan Green.

We had a good doctor who said he died of cancer so I could get John's life insurance because it wouldn't pay for suicide but the doctor said he was going to die anyway and it would not be long and he was so sorry for us. And I just couldn't ever tell Ava because I loved her so much and I just can't seem to get it together sometimes and I know, she wants me to go to the doctor to find out what's wrong with me and maybe I will. But I don't want her to feel bad. I just want her to know the truth if I die someday, that's fair. But I can't tell her while I'm alive because sometimes she seems so angry and just fights the world so hard and I don't want her to hate me and fight me too because I love her so much.

But she loves you Scott and you are the one she has to take care of her now and not me so take care of her and if something happens to me and I don't get to tell her just tell her the truth thank you Scott.

Jeanette

Dr. Caffey put down the letter. His eyes looked red and tired when she looked at him.

"It won't help you to tell you I'm sorry. But I am. And you will get through. We can help you, and I want you to believe that."

She said nothing. There was just too much, or maybe nothing at all, to say.

She watched as he began to put the letter back in the envelope. He instead reached in and pulled out a small newspaper clipping. "What is this, Ava? Do you know?"

She stared at it, her face registering nothing. "Something else Scott kept from me. That night—the same night I took the drugs—he told me my old boyfriend sent it, and he just put it in the envelope with the letter instead of giving it to me. She was someone I used to live with."

"May I?" the doctor asked for the second time that afternoon, and Ava nodded her assent.

He opened the clipping and read:

Police Arrest Suspect in Killing
of Young Atlanta Woman
By Clarence Barton
September 21, 1983

ATLANTA—Police have arrested Willie Francis, 44 years old, in conjunction with the murder last month of Alice Gayle Horne, 23, of Dothan, Alabama. Mr. Francis and Miss Horne were last seen checking in to the Westin Peachtree Plaza Hotel on the evening of August 27. Miss Horne's body was found the following morning at approximately 9:15 by a member of hotel housekeeping staff.

Mr. Francis, who has confessed to the killing under police custody and questioning, said he knew of Miss Horne from a previous visit to Atlanta and that they had spent time together by mutual consent.

Mr. Francis admitted to getting angry when the victim "kept asking" for money that he confessed he didn't have and to killing her after she

> "started making a scene" and "threatening to call the police." Coroner reports ruled the cause of death was asphyxiation, and Mr. Francis is being held without bond.

Dr. Caffey rested both pieces of paper in his lap, rubbed his eyes, and rested his face in his hands for a moment before raising it to look at Ava. She lay curled on her side, facing him, her legs almost up to her chin. Tears streamed sideways down her cheek.

Chapter 43

THEY RELEASED HER on Saturday, exactly a week after she'd overdosed on vodka and pills. She had legal drugs now, a prescription for the first time in her life, and paperwork that included an appointment on Tuesday with Dr. Caffey at his psychiatric office in Olympus, only two miles from the crazy ward where she'd met him. She had no plans to fill the prescription.

She had eaten dinner Thursday night, three meals on Friday, and an early Saturday breakfast. She'd conversed again on Friday with Dr. Caffey, as well as with Oalmann, and again with Caffey early on Saturday morning. She was being a very good girl.

Jude met her in the parking lot, giving her a hug that must have lasted a minute. She stepped into the cab of the Ford Courier, and Jude began coursing out of the parking lot, barely containing his exuberance as he told her Bea was coming to dinner.

"So don't go straight through Corinth, please. Take the back roads, will ya?" she said, as soon as he'd pulled onto the highway.

"You're the princess, Princess," Jude said in return. "Your wish is my command."

They drove without talking much. Ava, mostly to break the silence, asked for the exact time; and Jude, after answering, asked if she wanted anything special from the store.

Along the city's outskirts, they passed pristine housing developments, and Ava stared out the window at virtual mansions angled upon emerald-green lawns and enshrouded by carefully preserved trees. Eventually, she began to feel the silence was worse than a lame conversation.

"Do you ever look at all these houses, especially the really big, nice ones, and wonder where they get all their money?"

Jude laughed. "Yes! I work my tail off, and I'll never have a hundredth of that kind of dough."

"I know. I wonder if they're happy. I wonder if they all sit around the table—husband, wife, and kids—eating dinner, talking about their day."

"No. They're miserable, just miserable. They're in debt up to their ears, overweight, and alcoholic. I'll put it in writing if you want me to."

Ava smiled. "Yes, please."

"You know what, Avis? I don't think wealth is in the cards for me, but I'm so okay with that."

"Are you really? Because it seems money sure would fix a lot of problems."

"Oh, honey. It seems to me it causes at least as many as it fixes."

They rode in silence for a while, in easy camaraderie.

"Listen, I don't want to get all mushy, but thanks for everything. For picking me up, for offering the room. I just need to figure out what to do…and, of course, I'm not going to ask anything of Bea right now."

Scott had called Jude after he'd called the ambulance. It was not so long ago when it would have been Bea that he would have called, but everyone had tried to protect Bea since the mastectomy. And now there was this third pregnancy, already at seven months, along with the recently begun chemo and the other two exhausting little ones.

"Think nothin' of it, darlin'. I know you weren't trying to do yourself in…you're too gorgeous and fabulous. But you do know how close you were, right?" He looked first to her, then back to the windshield as he shook his head. "Thank Jesus for Scott and that he loves you. You can't play with that stuff."

She stiffened and fell silent. "I just want you to know I won't stay long, at your place, I mean." She looked at her hands in her lap.

"Ava," Jude spoke low and gently enough for a child, "I want you to stay as long as you need. You'll go home to Scott, of course, but when you're ready. Y'all can work this out. And Jeanette would be lost without you."

"Jeanette's been lost her whole life," Ava said, her own voice flat and sunken with bitterness. "My whereabouts aren't going to change that."

The apartment was unchanged from when Ava had last seen it in the summer—modern furniture in steel and leather, a few pillows and lamps, a TV (an orange cat blinked at her when they entered, disturbed from its nap). She heard a car pass through the parking lot just beyond the patio doors, but the long drawn curtains hid the view.

They entered the large bedroom closest to the front entrance. It contained a double bed with a purple-and-spring-green-quilted spread, an easy chair, two nightstands, a wood captain's chair, and another small, higher table opposite the bed with a TV. On the floor beside the bed was Ava's old Samsonite.

"Scott brought you some things." Jude watched for her reaction. "I promised him I would tell you he wants you to call." He set two brown paper bags alongside the suitcase filled with the clothes and necessities Scott had brought to the psychiatric facility last Monday and which Jude had retrieved from the staff at the front desk where he had checked her out.

Ava wordlessly pressed the two pillows against the headboard, and after removing her sneakers, sat cross-legged against them, taking a long, overdue breath. She couldn't imagine what to say to Scott. Just as she had felt in the hospital, three words were too much, and a thousand could never be enough.

"I'm going to make us a sandwich—grilled cheese. And we're having spaghetti tonight, and Bea will be here at six." Ava nodded. She desperately needed to see Bea. Toby and Gram, who had moved in last month to help while Bea was enduring the chemo, would stay with Heidi and Wesley. "Do you want to nap for a while?"

Jude had the kindest face. He went to a tanning bed in the fall and winter, and his face was perpetually golden, juxtaposed with beautiful white teeth.

"No. But I'd like to lie down a little while. I didn't sleep well at…that place."

"I imagine not." He began to move the bags and suitcase to the corner opposite the bed.

"Jude…can we talk for a minute?" So he lowered himself into the captain's chair, and Ava took another deep breath, pressing back against the pillows. "I don't know what to do."

He waited. It was almost comic that he had thought there would be more.

"Do you love Scott? Because I know you did."

She didn't hesitate to nod. "I loved him the minute I saw him. I can't even describe it. When I met Eric—it was at the grocery store, of all places, did I tell you that?—he asked for my number. He was *so* together. He was brilliant and nice, and he kept asking me out, even though I was sure he was going to wake up one day and see I wasn't worthy. And I thought I loved him. But I think I picked him because he was responsible, and I thought I could finally be secure. I thought I could be safe."

"And what about Scott?"

Ava thought a moment.

"When I first laid eyes on Scott, it was different. It was like… I'd found a puzzle piece missing from my body…or more like from my heart. I'd never felt anything like it." She shook her head in afterthought.

Jude nodded. "Yeah. I get that."

"I've always felt so fragmented, like something was lacking. I was always trying to measure up. And it was like, at first, he couldn't care less, but then…he shined on me." She leaned her head back on the pillows and breathed out a sigh. "Ever since we first started going out, he's brought me little flowers…did you know that? Little weeds, sometimes, actually…that he'd pick from some field or beside the road. Sometimes he writes down a piece of a poem that he's found when he's been reading, just on a piece of an envelope or something, and he'll leave it in my purse." She lowered her head, then, but raised her eyes to Jude's. "And he makes love to me like an artist. Like he's painting me with tiny, perfect brushes."

Jude watched her but didn't comment.

"He tells me I'm the prettiest girl he's ever seen, even though it isn't true. I told him I'm sure he's had prettier girls, and he insists not, and even if it ever were true, that my beauty came 'from inside.'"

"Then why can't you forgive him, Ava? I mean, I know you're hurt. He kept the truth of your family from you, and he slept with this woman, but if you look at both of those from his side, I don't think it's so bad." Jude and Bea were the only two who knew the story. Ava had talked to both of them, but only them, from the hospital.

"How can you say that? Those are two of the most horrible things that can happen to anybody."

"I know, baby, but listen. He married you. Why would he do that if he didn't love you? Men are dogs, honey, and they're always going to sleep around if there's nothing stopping them. And it's in the past."

"That's just it! How do I know that? I mean, that's what he insists, but if it were, why wouldn't he have told me about it? I worked for them, for her! I feel like such a fool."

"Because he was ashamed. On some basic level, even people who don't live by the highest moral code, they still know it's wrong. He didn't want to be the guy to sleep with a married woman or any of the other women, but he was that guy. Even if the husband did know about it."

"That's what's so disgusting. It's sick. He was in on it. And a long time ago, it was around Halloween, and Scott was having a party, and Corrine was there, and she was telling me how she and Jimmy met. And she was all giddy about it, and all the time, they just act like they're in love, and so happy…it's one reason I never suspected."

"Maybe they are happy, darlin'. It takes all kinds. And…you know what…I know you don't buy into the whole Jesus thing—"

"And you do."

"And I do." He smiled. "But we believers—when we look at the world—it's easier to understand when you realize most people don't have any reason to do things differently."

Ava had begun to get teary again; she grabbed a tissue and dabbed at her eyes and nose. "And keeping my lineage from me—not to mention the clipping Eric sent about Chantal—that just added so much salt to the wound."

"Well, since you asked Dr. Jude, I have explanations for all that as well. Jeanette didn't want him to tell. She didn't want you to know. And, by the way, she's been a basket case, not that you've asked, and I told her don't bother coming to work until she feels like it. But your husband thought he was doing the right thing by honoring Jeanette's wishes."

"But it was just another secret! As huge as any one I could imagine."

Right. But it couldn't have been easy to keep. Even though it would've been difficult to tell you, it had to be a million times worse keeping it inside. He's had to hold that in for over two years from the woman he loves more than anyone." Jude leaned forward, resting his elbows on his knees, hands clasped. "It doesn't mean he doesn't love you. It kind of means he does."

"A real man would always tell the truth. Always, always, always."

But the words had barely escaped her mouth before her mind flashed the image that most defiled her statement—the money she'd been "lifting" from Divine, the secret bank account, and the post office box. She felt the guilt and fear she carried in her gut like a wrecking ball tethered by a cable, ever-at-the-ready to wield its destruction.

Jude leaned back in his chair. "And as far as Chantal, can you really not figure that out? Eric sent you that clipping. To Bea's house, which Scott just happened to receive from her one day when she handed off your mail. Of course he opened it to see why your ex-fiancé would be writing you after all that time! And when he saw what it was, well, as far as he was concerned, it was out of sight, out of mind. Why open that wound again? And why give you a clipping your ex-fiancé had taken the trouble to send to you as if the guy still cared about you? Especially when he—Scott—who is undoubtedly struggling with his own issues, sees himself as the husband who keeps letting you down?"

Ava pictured Scott's office upstairs, with its little white-dusted mirror and straw in the desk drawer, the bottle of vodka and a few small plastic cups, a bottle or two of pills. She scooted down in the bed and lay on her side, facing the wall opposite the door.

"Jude…Bea said…well, are you just not gay anymore?" She lay with her hands curled under her chin, not looking at him. "And is it because Bea tricked you into going to church and because you had already slept with a bunch of guys you got scared because they said you were going to hell?" She peeked back over her shoulder at him, her lips pressed together to suppress her amusement at her own wit.

Jude gave a little laugh. "Oh, darlin', not exactly. I wasn't magically cured of all my feelings. But that world was so dark. And I've got something so much better." He rose and came to sit on the bed beside her. "I'm gonna tell you a little story." Ava resumed her curled position; Jude settled against the headboard, let out a slight sigh, and began to scratch her back.

"When I was a little boy, I don't think my daddy liked me very much. I wasn't big or tough or sporty. I hung out all the time with my mom, who adored me and wanted to protect me from everything, which, let me tell you, was totally fine by me.

"So when I was twelve, my dad insisted I try out for football. I had never watched football, even, and had never wanted to play. I wanted to try out for tennis in the spring."

Jude did have a tennis player's build, and Ava couldn't imagine him on a football field.

"So when I came home the afternoon of the tryouts instead of staying at school, Dad was furious. And he whipped me." Jude began to knead the muscles above her shoulder blades with his fingertips. "When it was over, I ran away. I ran all the way to Bea's."

Ava knew he was being facetious; Jude's parents' house was within four miles of the Mullins's. But Ava had never heard this part of Jude's and Bea's history, knowing only that they'd met at school in seventh grade and had become friends.

"You might already know some of the kids at school teased me. I was shy and gawky. I'd never really had a close friend before Bea, and she treated me as if there wasn't anything wrong with me."

Ava rolled onto her back and moved further toward the bed's edge, turning her face to her friend. "What was wrong with you?"

Jude scooted down beside her and, lying on his back as well, lay his hands on his stomach and looked at the ceiling. He gave Ava the impression of someone who had come in for therapy.

"Nothing that I knew of. I mean, I knew by then some of the boys were starting to have crushes on the girls. On the playground, they would snap their bra straps and run or write them notes asking them to be their girlfriends. I didn't feel any of that. I just felt very alone, and I felt like I wanted the boys to like me more than the girls. Also I would go in the woods behind our house and have these adventures, where I was an explorer of the Wild West, or I was an actor—it didn't matter—it was always imaginary play, and I was always by myself. I didn't know, but I assumed none of the other boys I knew did stuff like that.

"But Bea and I hung out at school. We would eat lunch together. She was the only person who acted like she wanted to hang out with me besides some kids who were nice because I was the brother of Normal Steve."

Ava knew Steve was Jude's older brother. Jude called him Normal Steve as a self-deprecating joke because he was straight, very nice looking, and had gone to college on a football scholarship.

"Anyway, she always made me feel like she liked me, and I thought the others just tolerated or accepted me to be nice. So sometimes I'd go over to Bea's house, and we'd hang out—take walks or draw or something. We both loved to draw, of course. And Mr. and Mrs. Mullins just treated me like a regular kid, but then, she died that year, and then he did, like, two years later. So the grandma came and stayed, and it was all super sad for a couple of years…and Bea was crushed, you know."

Ava nodded, holding her arms, then stared at the ceiling as Jude was. "And yet she turned out kind of perfect, anyway."

Jude laughed. "I know! Anyway, by that time, I'd realized I was more attracted to boys than girls and had no idea what to do about it except that it was *not okay.* School became so painful. So especially after her parents died, Bea and I just kind of clung to each other like best friends. And even after she started dating Toby when she was fifteen, we stayed close."

"So when did you start dating boys?" She turned to watch his face again.

"I was sixteen. I'd gotten a license and a car, and I started driving into Olympus on Friday and Saturday nights. You can always find what you're looking for, you know, if you look for it hard enough."

Ava was silent. She didn't want to hear any details, but Jude didn't offer any, either.

"Anyway, that went on for a while. I met Bryan in Olympus at one of the dance clubs, and when he turned out to be from Corinth, we just took up together. Got a place together when I turned eighteen. His parents even backed me in the salon, at first, while I was still going to cosmetology school. Of course, they looked at it as a business investment, and didn't know we were 'involved.'" Jude formed air quotes with his fingers.

"Yeah. Bea told me that. And then you broke up and got a loan."

Jude nodded. "Yep. That's true."

"And you broke up just because you went to church, and they said you shouldn't be gay?"

Jude turned to her and smiled his crinkly smile.

"Are you serious? No! You're a silly goose, Ava Rush." He removed his leather cuff and turned it in his hands, tracing its embossed cross with his fingertip. "I just heard the gospel. And I gave my life to God." A few seconds passed. "I was so lost…" He shook his head slightly. "I thought I'd be so happy, getting to do what I wanted, but I was miserable."

Ava waited, but he didn't continue. "So what happened?"

"Well. Bea was home from college. It was Easter Break, and she invited me to church. That was…gosh, five, five-and-a-half years ago? She'd asked me before, but of course, I thought I was not church material."

"And you found Jesus." Ava didn't even try to hide the cynicism in her voice.

Jude sat up against the headboard and hugged his knees as he smiled at her.

"Yeah…I found Jesus." He leaned toward her and whispered mischievously. "I think He was looking for me."

She pulled her gaze from Jude's face and stared at the ceiling again. Someone—Jude?—had glued up plastic glow-in-the-dark stars. She listened to a car pulling into the lot just outside, its engine ceasing, and two doors opening and closing, and voices murmuring before dying away.

"What did you do?"

He said it simply, low and plain. "I went to the altar." The silence sat laden between them, and he seemed removed like he wasn't there or maybe wasn't aware that she still was. She heard more voices, this time rising, then falling away beyond the bushes that grew at the fringes of the window, as people passed on the walkway beside them.

"At the end of the sermon, the preacher read a verse, and something in my heart just knew it was true."

Ava knew what a verse was, but she wasn't sure how something so antiquated, that the Jews had written down, could convince anybody of much. Jeanette had been going to church since Ava went away to college, and hearing them hadn't seemed to do much for her. "What verse did he read? Do you remember?"

Jude lifted a finger to an unassuming plaque on the wall, one Ava had not yet noticed. In the corner at the edge of the curtain, on a piece of sage-green board and hanging by what appeared to be a hemp string, she saw the words. And below them, "John 20:31."

Apartments are so different from houses, Ava thought, suddenly. *Compressed air. Everything moved inward and in possibility of discovery or surprise. Even the people felt closer but more transient and vulnerable, as well.*

She sought his face again. "And what did it feel like?"

Jude's eyes were soft and tranquil. "Like going home but better. One I'd never had before."

Ava sat up and hugged her knees to her chest as well. "Well, I can't believe it was that easy," she said to the wall and then turned to him with her chin raised in slight defiance. "Plus, I don't believe in God."

"I know." She heard the heater click on.

"And I can't see how you're happy. Now you're all alone."

"No, honey. My life isn't magically perfect. But I'm not ever alone."

She could fairly taste the bile of her misery, so she swallowed, then squinted her eyes at the tanned, kind face. "Why did you change your name? Bea said it was after you got saved."

Jude turned and reached into the nightstand drawer to his left, removed a notecard, and handed it to Ava.

On the first line was printed: "Julian. Origin: Latin. Meaning: Youthful, Downy." A couple of lines down was printed: "Jude. Origin: Greek. Meaning: Praised."

"Jude was one of Jesus's brothers, too, you know. And I didn't think it was such a stretch."

Ava handed the card back, and he replaced it in the drawer.

"Probably not. And it suits you."

"I didn't legally change it, of course. Not yet. But I asked to be called that and began introducing myself that way. And it's what I seek now from God."

Ava had nothing else to say. It didn't make sense, none at all. It was thousands of years ago and miles away, and yet here was everybody now, still grieving over who was probably just a man. Plus it was hard to believe anyone could be so good so easily, forever, as Jude was trying to be—one only had to look at her situation for reference, which showed everybody turns out to be a dog in the end.

"Whatever happened to Bryan?"

Jude replaced his cuff, stood, and held his hand out to Ava, smiling. "You'll be happy to know he survived."

Chapter 44

Dear Scott,
11-12-85

I used to think everything I did mattered, every thought and action, and then I thought last week that maybe nothing did. Maybe nothing mattered, even that we weren't going to work out, but that isn't quite right either. So like many other facts that make life so hard to figure out, I've realized that both of those things are true.

You told me once—at Elkland Falls, when we eloped, remember?—that you fell in love with me because I was good and brave. Well, I think maybe I used to be… But now I'm a scared little girl full of evil.

All I ever wanted was to be happy. I thought a family would do that. I thought love—you, the funniest, deepest, most kind and beautiful man I'd ever known, and children—would do that.

But you blew it up. I have never understood what you were missing or chasing with your drugs and booze and women. But I've been drunk now, and I get it. You just can't lie with the pain in your belly and do nothing about it, can you? Life doesn't work out as we plan, so we have to fill the leaking places with something.

I tried. I studied and worked hard and tried to save money. I tried to be a good person, and I thought the gods would reward me. I thought Jeanette's life was in the gutter because she never tried, but even though I have, my life is garbage too.

When you confessed about Corrine, I felt like I'd been shot. I couldn't imagine anything feeling worse. And when you left that night, all I could think about was how to take that pain away. The liquor (the quaaludes I found were a bonus) worked, so I guess I should have more sympathy for you, especially because now I realize you had two extra dirty little secrets that you've been carrying all alone.

You say your affair meant nothing to her and less than nothing to you. You said it was Jimmy's idea—you didn't want to take much responsibility, did you? But let's admit it. Cory is a beautiful woman. And as Jude says, if you have no moral reason not to…why not? I guess I trusted you instantly, and I guess I trusted too much.

I expected you to be honest and faithful.

I also expected my body to behave like most normal women's bodies and give me the children I wanted.

And I expected my mother to be who she said she was—my mother—and that what I'd grown up believing about my father and my life was the truth. I tried as hard as I knew how to take care of and love Jeanette even though I never understood one ounce of what lay beneath her skin or behind her eyes or why she has taken from me and used up almost every ounce of my goodwill since I can remember. I tried to be loyal to both of you. I tried to be loyal to cons.

I do owe you both for one gift, I suppose. I finally understand why I have felt like an alien in my overly-shrunken family since my first awareness of my separate sense of self. Why I've felt so different from my "mom," and why I felt like my "dad" dying was my fault because, hey, guess what? It was.

What I don't understand was why it was so hard for anyone—Jeanette, John, "Sapphire"—or whatever her real name was—or you to love me. Why couldn't I be loved enough for anyone to tell me the truth? Or be faithful? Or even—like my "dad"—to want to stay around?

All I ever wanted, Scott, was to feel, and to be, normal in this world—and I really, really wanted to be special to you. Now I understand I must have never been worthy of either.

Best wishes,
Ava

Ava read the letter twice.

She went to the kitchen, Jude's kitchen, and found some matches above the stove before standing on the counter and removing the battery from the smoke detector.

She held the letter above the sink, lit it, and watched it turn to perpetual curly ash, then washed its remains down the disposal. The rushing water and grinding of the machinery satisfied her to her very core. She replaced the detector's battery.

Taking another piece of paper from the composition book she'd found in the nightstand, Ava wrote again:

Dear Scott,

We could have had it all.

Ava

She folded the page, wrote "Scott" on the outside, and lay it on the pillow of her bed. Beside it, Ava placed a letter she'd written to Bea, telling her she was going away for a few days to think and to please not worry and that everything would be better when she returned. Lastly, she placed a brief note to Jude alongside these, in which she'd thanked him for everything he'd said and done. She left no missive for Jeanette.

It was after three o'clock in the afternoon on Tuesday, and Ava knew that after the salon closed at six, Jude would be bringing Jeanette home with him. Ava had agreed to talk with her "mother" for the first time since "that Saturday," nine days ago, as her tiny circle now called it. She was certain Jeanette would be giddy with relief at the prospect of unburdening herself on Ava. How wonderful to absolve oneself by sharing one's guilty trash with one's victims.

The day outside was overcast and cold, and it was chilly now in the living room. Ava decided to wait with the curtains opened just a sliver, just enough to see the cab as it pulled up beyond the patio doors. Long before Jude arrived, she would be at Hartsfield airport. Although Ava had never flown, Starr had told her it was a "no-brainer" and that she would be at the Jacksonville airport to meet Ava by six thirteen, the plane's arrival time. No one need know where she was, Starr had promised, and Ava could stay as long as she liked.

Chapter 45

THE JUNKYARD WAS smoky and rank. Where the walls of The Fox and Ale were decorated with hunting scenes and paintings of horses, with trophies and framed fox-hunt newspaper and magazine articles, the Floridian dive sported mechanical art and memorabilia—vintage hubcaps and photographs of horrific car wrecks, remnants of disemboweled engines, sometimes spray-painted and mounted on display boards in configurations of heaven-knew-what.

Ava wanted to press her fingers against her eyelids but knew it would smear her mascara. She looked at her watch: 12:16 a.m., and that was too late. She'd promised herself she would look for a job in the morning, one into which she could fit this unexpected turn of events.

"I don't think you're going to stay. Not that you asked my opinion."

She looked at the well-groomed tall man seated across from her. His skin was the color of well-creamed coffee, his hair was cropped closer than black men were typically wearing it those days, and his eyes were a kind of pine-tree green. Ava had never seen any like them.

"Well, Smitty, you're right. Nobody asked." She took a sip of her Jack and Coke, not caring that she sounded rude. She was drunk.

A smile lingered on his lips. "Why did you call me Smitty?"

"I don't know. I wasn't thinking. It's something my roommate started a long time ago."

Her companion took a slow drink from his rocks glass before he spoke. "You don't know why I said that?"

"I don't care why you said that."

"Because I think you still love your husband."

"I do still love my husband. I just can't trust my husband. Life's a pickle."

He signaled for the bartender. "Are you hungry? The kitchen closes at one."

She looked down and shook her head. "Don't want to lose my high. I'm thinking of quitting tomorrow."

He laughed. "Well, I don't think there's any danger of you coming down anytime soon. You might lessen that nasty hangover headed your way if you get something on your stomach, though."

"Get something on *your* stomach." She lay her head on her arms on the table.

"Hey, come on now. C'mon." He reached over and patted her forearm.

She raised her head and squinted her eyes at him. "Are you married?"

It was his turn to look down. "I'm afraid so."

She gave a short, derisive laugh. "Unhappy, huh?" She took another swallow. "Where are the happy couples, you reckon? Probably not in some scuzzy bar on a Friday night."

"Probably not."

"You know the worst part? There's no beach here. I asked Peter—remember he's my brother-in-law, soon to be *ex*-brother-in-law, why they would live in Florida, not even at the *beach*? And ya know why? Because Starr's family is here. And his isn't!" Her laugh was dry, jaded.

The waitress set down another Jack and Coke and a Glen Livet, rocks, for her companion.

"The beaches are not too far, you know."

"Whatever." She wanted to put her head down again but didn't.

"So your father-in-law, your mother-in-law…Marilyn? They're pretty screwed up, huh?

"Yeah. Don't you think?" She'd already told him "everything"; she was still telling him everything.

"Sure. But I told you, too, we all are. In my opinion."

"Well, we both know you love your opinion." If he were bothered by her offenses, he didn't show it, and she was feeling increasingly brave. "You know I stole, too, don't you? A lot." Had she told him that already? She had no idea, no idea how long she'd been sitting there, nor everything she'd drunkenly blurted. She scrutinized his face for a reaction, her own face hovering just above her glass, but she knew she didn't care what he thought.

He was unfazed, looking straight at her eyes as he sipped his scotch. "How?"

"Same way she did—the girl, I mean—by being selfish and smart. Of course, she did it for Chuck, the daddy—the owner—all part of the tax fraud. He must be some great lover or *really* taking care of her because that was like a second job for her."

"What was the first?"

"Who knows? Office helper? Owner's pet? Office slut? But she had a whole system. It was fascinating."

"What did she do? I mean, what was her system?"

"Oh, jeepers, it was like…like one thing I found, she'd sold some used car and had them make the check out to Kimberly De Luca. Of *course* she didn't report the income. The invoices for parts we bought showed we'd paid more than we had, and the sales receipts showed we sold them for less. She has a whole other folder of the accurate invoices that don't get turned in with the taxes."

He continued to study her. The candlelight from the votive on their table danced in his eyes.

"So what did you do? To steal, I mean."

She shrugged and looked toward the jukebox. A girl was swaying to Lynyrd Skynyrd as she pored over its lighted display. "Little stuff. Until the end." She knocked back another swallow and waved her hand around. "I need some french fries or something." She could feel the room beginning to tilt, and she needed to go to the bathroom. He signaled for the waitress again.

All of a sudden, she wanted to talk. And, anyway, who was this guy, in the grand scheme of things?

"I altered invoices. I took things too. Bits of cash…for parts and services… I'm not proud of it. In fact, it haunts me. But they're cheaters, too, so…"

He was silent a moment. "What about his family? Chuck's. Do you feel bad you're taking from them?"

"I already told you. Robin does great. She's the trainer. She and her girlfriend live like...I don't know...like Thoreau. Real hippies, in Corrine's cabin—she's the slut, remember—and from talking with her, she could care less about her daddy's and mother's capitalistic lifestyle. And then Peter—the one I'm staying with—he's always come across like his dad could fall off the planet, and he wouldn't give two shakes. And the mother...well, she gets paid off too. I didn't tell you that. Or did I? Her husband gives her hush money for his cheating on her, and she literally puts all this cash from *his* cheating at both of his dealerships—he has two! I know, I didn't know either, at first, but that Kimberly girl goes there too, and she puts it, the mom does, in a home safe behind a picture in her art studio."

"Because of the Kimberly girl."

"Yeah. Because he sleeps with her. I took that money too."

He smiled that slow smile again. "Really." He swirled his scotch and ice. "Aren't you riveting. A modern-day Bonnie Parker."

"Oh, man, I love that movie! Okay, well, whatever."

"How? How did you take that money?"

"It doesn't matter." But it swam under her, from beneath her guts, to her tongue. "It wasn't hard, but it was scary. The day I left—last Tuesday—I called his mom, Marilyn. I told her I needed to talk, and she was practically falling all over herself to meet me for lunch. And I told her to ask Scott because I hadn't talked to him, still, you know, all this time. I still haven't, of course. But anyway, I was all, like, 'Okay, I'm ready, meet me for lunch at Malone's with Scott,' and she was like, 'Oh, yeah, of course, love you, Scott loves you so much, we all do, he's just been a wreck,' blah blah blah.

"And so I go to the house and take some out of the safe. While they're at the restaurant. And then I took the cab on to the airport, and here I am."

"And you weren't worried about anyone seeing you?"

"Nah. They don't have cameras. They have Dobermans. And they know me, so..."

"How did you know the combination? Did she tell you that too?"

"No. Why would she? But when she showed me the safe, she showed me inside. When I first got hired. She told me some mumbo jumbo about not running to tell her a bunch of stuff when I started working for them. Said she already knew. 'Course I think she was trying to make sure I knew she was *well* aware, and *well* taken care of, so we'd never have to talk about any yucky stuff, you know…that she'd made her peace with it. Anyway, she left the door open when she got a phone call, and I saw the combo."

"And you memorized it?"

Ava waved her hand away. "Wasn't hard. It's my husband's birthday."

They were quiet.

"I didn't take a lot. Just a few thousand. They are so completely loaded. I'll pay it back. I'm sure I can, one day." Even in her drunken state, her own words didn't make her feel better.

He studied her. "You took it for the baby."

"Yeah. What'd you think I took it for, makeup?"

The waitress set down their fries. The man asked for the tab.

"I already forgot your name. I'm a pretty terrible pickup." She was ravenous all of a sudden and shoved the ends of three fries in her mouth.

He laughed. "Remy. And who said I was trying to pick you up, Smitty?"

Her turn to laugh. "Touché. Hey, I'm gonna pay for my own stuff, okay?"

"Not necessary, I've got it. You've had a hard time. Not counting all the pilfering and plain old grand theft."

"Right. Do you know what it costs to adopt a baby?"

"You mean buy a baby. You're going black market, you said."

"Only because a single woman stands zero chance of adoption in the legal world. It's hard enough as a couple."

"Maybe I'll get a quickie divorce, and you and I can marry and adopt. I don't have kids yet. Not that you asked."

"I already told you I'm a terrible pickup. But we'd be biracial, so we probably couldn't make it work either."

"I'm half white. Still no go?"

"You're too old."

"Just forty-two. I'd be good to you too. I bet you were a good wife."

She took another bite of her food before answering. The fries would make her feel better, though she knew tomorrow was going to be a bad one.

"I thought I was a pretty good wife."

He took her home at two. The lights were off in the small ranch house Peter and Starr shared, and she was grateful no one turned one on when his Lincoln pulled up in front. Starr had given her a key.

"I'd like to see you again." Remy rested his hand on Ava's thigh, and she watched it lay there. He had smooth beautiful hands; and his nails—she noticed for the first time—were clean, trimmed, and painted clear. She imagined them lifting her shirt, his fingertips trailing up each of her sides.

"That would just negate everything I'm running from, now, wouldn't it?" She picked up his hand and laid it gently on the seat beside her. "And make me part of the problem."

Chapter 46

HER HEAD *DID* hurt, just as Remy had predicted; but the coffee, water, juice, and aspirin were slowly helping. Peter had gone to the lab at eight—once a month, he worked a Saturday for overtime. Starr, who had an assistant at the shop she managed, had stayed behind for the morning.

"I appreciate the ride to the bar last night." Ava and Starr sat on love seats opposite each other with a glass coffee table between them bearing a plate of mini muffins Starr had made with a Jiffy mix. From what Ava had gathered in her three days there, Julia Child she was not.

Starr shook her head. "Not a problem." She placed four muffins each on her and Ava's plates. "I was kind of thinking you'd call for a ride home, though."

Ava nodded, took a bite, and mumbled, "I know, I know, but it was really late. I got a ride from a nice man. I think he may want to marry me, too, so that's good. We have to get me and him all happily divorced first, but that's okay… Good things take time."

Starr set her plate on the love seat and picked up her coffee, curling her legs underneath her. "Seriously, Ava, things do happen. Strange men, and it takes them two seconds to find out you're *not* local but you *are* drunk."

"How do you know I was drunk?"

Starr looked at her over her mug without saying a word.

"Fine. I was drunk. I don't know how people do it, though." She shook her head. "Seriously. It feels like one long bad car wreck."

"I know. I think it's overrated." Starr paused for a moment. "Just don't drink so much. Or go back to not drinking. You must have stayed away from it before for a reason." Starr polished off the last muffin on her plate; she ate fast. She was small-boned, short and round everywhere like she'd been drawn out of bubbles.

"Yeah. But look at all the fun I'm having." Ava ate two muffins and nursed her coffee.

She had always liked Peter and Starr. Ever since that first Thanksgiving, when Marilyn was doing her best to present her husband, home, and children as Norman Rockwell prototypes, Peter had respectfully operated above it by deigning not to impress. Starr—quiet, agreeable, and unobtrusive—had integrated with it all, being polite and humble and kind.

"I'm not going to stay long. I don't want you to worry. And I can explain more later about the adoption—it's just complicated. Plus, but I'll have to go back soon, at least for a little while, because of Bea. She's sick, you know, and she's my best friend."

"You can stay as long as you like, Ava. Peter does his own thing. You won't bother him. Plus, he's always respected you. You were different from Scott's…other friends."

Ava let that go.

"You know I'm off Sunday and Monday, and you can even go in with me to the shop on any of the other days if you'd like. It's slower now, of course, but not bad. We do a lot with the holidays. Especially Christmas. You'd like it."

Ava shrugged. "I don't know. I don't care that much about it. Christmas, I mean. Or any of it, really."

Starr didn't pursue it, just pursed her lips together and nodded.

"But I appreciate it. I might." She went to the kitchen and refilled her coffee cup before sitting again on the loveseat opposite Starr's. "Frankly, I don't know what I'm going to do. I don't see how I can go back to Tarryton to live. You know my bar job was with the woman Scott has been seeing, and, of course, the other was with his dad, so…and then, there's him, *and* my mom, who did all the lying on top of all the other ways she's screwed up both our lives. Anyway…I'm thinking I need another plan."

Starr pursed her lips again over her mug and took a deep breath. The dryer hummed in the small back room to Ava's left, and she wished she could listen to it and sleep for about eleven hours.

"I've always liked you, Ava, and I want to tell you something, but I don't want to step out of line."

"Good. I'd hate for you to offend me and mess up this opportunity I have to mooch off you."

"Me too. But I just think you're making an awful lot of serious decisions based on very little information."

Ava's heart quickened with anger, even though she knew Starr meant well. "Okay, well, no offense to you, but I think finding out I'm a bastard orphan whose husband is having an affair with one of my bosses is not 'very little information.'"

"But you don't know he's having an affair. You only know he was sleeping with a married woman before you were married. It just hurts worse because you worked for her, and you guys were friends and he kept it from you. And also, according to you, her husband, who was also your boss, was kind of 'there,' and so you feel foolish and disgusted on top of being hurt. But Scott said it wasn't happening anymore. And, yeah, he slept around before y'all got married, but you knew that, right? He was young, single, good-looking, charming…of course he's going to play around."

"I didn't!"

"You're unusual. Were."

"Oh, not anymore, huh?"

"No, I didn't mean that. I mean, I don't know what you do or did… I don't know what you've done."

"Nothing. I've done nothing."

She thought of Remy and how she so easily could have broken her vows, how no one would have known, and yet she didn't.

But she also thought of the money taken from Divine Chevrolet for almost two years, in sordid, small but steady globs…and then, just four days ago, when she lifted seven thousand cash from the Divines' safe. Well, *nothing*, as everyone would agree, could be a very ambiguous word.

"I only bring it up because I know some things, and I think you're being rash."

Ava raised her ice-water glass to her lips and drained it, then lay back and put her feet on the armrest. "Do you mind? I feel pretty lousy." She studied the popcorn design of the ceiling.

"Of course not."

"How old are you?"

"Thirty-six. Why?"

"The skank is forty-two. But she doesn't look it. Except in her heart. There, she looks about a hundred and nine."

Starr sighed. Ava still stared at the ceiling.

"Ava, listen. Ava, when Scott met you—I don't know exactly when, but after we found out about you—he called us. Well, Peter. But he wanted us to make sure to come for Thanksgiving because… well, you know Peter, he didn't care about it that much and he'd thought we might just stay here, but Scott was kind of excited, and it was about you."

Ava threw her arm over her eyes. The sun was climbing over the patio from the glass doors to her right, and she wanted nothing to do with it. "I can't believe he was *that* excited. He knew me for weeks before Thanksgiving. He barely spoke to me until one night when Bea and I went into The Fox for her birthday."

"I know, but that's just it. You know he had these girls, that he did what he wanted with anybody he wanted to, but he kind of went on about you. Peter was kind of naughty and told me to get on the extension… Scott had never spoken to either of us about anyone.

"He just kind of goes on about how you were so classy and so beautiful, but you didn't act like it—like you didn't even know it. He said you were brilliant and funny, and every couple of weekends, you drove all the way back to Atlanta to take care of your mother."

Ava didn't move, but she knew she wanted to hear what Starr was saying.

"Then—and yes, I remember this too—he said one day you came to work telling how you had jumped in the river off a cliff at your friend's picnic and what a rush it was. And as he was listening, he realized he'd never ask God for anything else if God would give him you." Starr paused. "He'd never talked like that."

Ava could barely feel herself breathing. The dryer was still humming, and her elbow still occluded her vision. She didn't remove her arm when she spoke.

"Well, I know for a fact that Scott is not a praying man." She sat up suddenly, then, and looked at her sister-in-law. "Do you know he has a drug problem?"

Starr nodded. "I know he does blow if that's what you mean. A lot of people do, though. Especially in his circle."

"What circle is that?"

"Bars. Sales. Writers. Rich people."

"That's a lot of circles."

"You knew that when you met him."

Ava picked up her cold coffee cup and drank. "Maybe. But I didn't know it was going to be a problem."

"Honey, I don't know of anybody who does drugs where they're not a problem, do you? I think you were just naïve."

Ava let that settle in. "Well…I didn't know he wouldn't come home sometimes. Or that he would stay in his office all night, many nights, even when he was home, just working or writing and getting high. Sometimes he stays up all night. And that's not a way to help a marriage."

"No. But all marriages have their problems. Did you talk to him about it?"

Ava sighed and placed her cup back on the table between them. She didn't see how any of this was doing much good. "We argued about it sometimes. For the most part, I let it go. At least in the beginning. I thought a baby would give us a normal rhythm too. I thought we'd start to feel like a real family. And after all that went down…well, I just went to work and worked on art a little—you know, Bea and I, and our friend Jude, we do those festivals, and…I did a painting show with this woman, Harriet…and he just kept selling and writing and traveling…" Her voice gave the tiniest waver. "We just never got it together."

Starr got up and went to sit beside her. Ava's hands rested in her lap, and Starr placed one of her own on top of them. "I'm just saying he loves you, Ava. He always has, but you didn't know it for so long because he protects his heart. I think it's too soon to give up on him, don't you?"

In a flash, Ava saw Corrine with her tight coral top stretched against her bust as she leaned slightly backward, her clear green eyes searching the face of Ava's husband, her hand laying like a caress upon it.

"Actually it's feeling a little late," she said and rose to take the tray to the kitchen.

Chapter 47

AVA HAD CALLED Starr the Monday after the hospital released her. She'd called while Jude was at work, booking her ticket for the following afternoon. When she had first asked to visit, she'd realized Starr and Peter both might find the request odd, but they weren't *that* far from the beach, of course; and yes, they understood Ava needed to get away. And, of course, they knew money was tight.

Two days after she'd arrived, Ava had told Starr her purpose was not to "get away"; she was there to adopt a baby. She'd left out the part about the setup being illegal, of course, but explaining she'd be going back to Tarryton soon to tie up loose ends, to see Bea, to make some decisions about Jeanette but not to live there again. In due time, Ava planned to leave it all permanently to find another forever home that would still be close enough to Bea.

Starr acted surprised—she'd thought it took years, and well, of course, Scott had never mentioned it. Ava was vague. She'd gotten lucky, she'd said. Would Starr mind if she didn't share details right now? It was all so new. It wasn't even certain, of course. There would be plenty of time to explain it all later.

Ava mentioned nothing to Peter. With his "superhuman" intelligence, she believed her words would trip her up, and he would smell a rat. If he asked Starr any details, though, his wife would have to say she didn't know; and Ava was counting on his usual aloof unconcern to prevent him from asking questions at all.

The "service," as the voice on the other end of the line always referred to itself, was only thirty minutes from Peter's and Starr's—which, of course, had been part of the plan when Ava had asked to come. How fortuitous that this black-market opportunity that Kimberly De Luca, of all people, had mentioned to her—jokingly, no doubt, at the time, two years ago—was rumored to be on the outskirts of Jacksonville. And how ironic and poignant it was that the journey she'd first planned to share legally and lovingly with Scott—to raise a child—was now her unlawful secret mission, alone.

She'd found a room in a boarding house that very afternoon, that first Saturday, as close as she could get to the St. John's River. It had a view, and already she'd arranged for a month's stay. Starr offered to take the whole day off, after all, to drive her to look at the place after Ava had found it that morning in the paper. She was adamant about Ava not spending for a cab for a thirty-minute drive one way. Grudgingly, Ava accepted.

The room inside the little house overlooking the river was clean and spare—duck-yellow walls with white wood and white wicker furniture…so close to the nursery Ava had created at home, so close to what she considered perfect. She would be adopting a baby, she told the owner, a wizened widow no bigger than a minute with a cotton cloud of hair and faded chambray-colored eyes. Mrs. Fenwick cooed and fretted; she couldn't wait to see the wee thing and was so sorry Ava's husband was away on business and couldn't be with his wife during this magical time. Starr stood by the room's door and listened, sober-eyed, quiet, and neutral.

Ava spent the week living as frugally as she could; every penny counted. Most nights, Starr invited her for dinner, insisting she enjoyed the drive to pick Ava up; and some nights, Ava accepted. Others, she ate apples and peanut butter in her room, tuna fish and celery, and tiny assorted bags of chips.

Peter had declined to drive to Olympus this year for Thanksgiving, opting instead to pick up holiday pay at work. He had no interest, he said, in covering for Ava and very little interest in the holiday, anyway. Starr called Marilyn two Tuesdays before—the very day Ava had flown down—promising they'd drive up in the spring. She listened uncomfortably as Marilyn relayed Ava's disappearance, how her best friend had repeatedly told her mother-in-law not to worry, and though Bea had no idea where she'd gone, she was honoring her friend's request for "space."

It was on a Monday, the twenty-fifth, when the service told her they would meet her that afternoon at one. Her initial call, precisely two weeks prior, from Jude's guest bedroom, had revealed a mini miracle; and right before she'd called Starr to invite herself down, she'd been instructed to call every day using a code word. This she did, first on Tuesday from her in-laws' house, and then each successive day from the payphone at Surfside Pizza.

It was that same Monday, two weeks ago, that the voice had told her she could pay a little more than the couple ahead of her and have her "miracle" baby; they had a pregnancy almost full term. With her two years' worth of stolen cash and her visit to the Divine safe, she'd made sure she could pay for a break in that line.

She'd sat on that phone number for two years. For two years, she'd imagined Scott's surprise when she told him she'd managed to find an adoption service that helped women who couldn't keep their babies and who didn't want to abort. He would be amazed she'd been able to save the money, and he would forgive her insistence on keeping both jobs. He would applaud—of course!—her quiet, persistent attendance at festivals and fairs to market her paintings and photography instead of ever traveling with him on golf trips or hunting events as he strove to realize dreams of his own.

"We can do this, Scott!" had played melodiously on her imaginary tape; and in her fantasies, he would warm to the idea of having children after all. All the savings and hard work, and especially the stealing, would be done. He'd want to get off the drugs, then, too, and stay home more; and it would only be logical to lighten up on his drinking. He'd see the baby and fall in love. Of this, she was certain.

But that had been a million years ago. By the time the marriage blew apart, when she'd called in utmost desperation and been told how to go to the "head of the line," she had not had all of the money even with the skimming from her job. Well, Marilyn's excessive conviviality and carelessness had fixed that, and she had no more tears to cry about any of it. Nothing was constant but change.

The building was one-story and L-shaped, built of cement blocks painted sky blue. The metal window frames with their crisscrossed bars and the metal door were painted royal blue, and the door was thickly barred across its middle. A simple white sign out front, swinging atop a pole, read "Langley's Tax Service." Ava would meet a woman named "Angie" at nine, and she'd be meeting with her alone. The voice gave no other details.

Remy pulled up and eyed the scene for a moment before parking. "I don't like the idea of you going in there by yourself."

Ava inhaled and exaggeratedly released it. "Of course you don't. Because you have to be big ol' you, and I'm just little ol' me, but you knew those were the terms before you drove me."

"And you still can't be sure it's not a creep preying on women."

"No. I can't. But you're right here. And I'll make sure to mention that—that my big mean boyfriend is in the car outside, and there will be no hanky-panky because he won't stand for it."

She squeezed his hand to mollify him further; they'd already agreed she'd take nothing in with her but ID.

"If you're not out in a reasonable time, I'm calling the cops, though. And I'm serious, Ava. You can tell them you were answering what you thought was an ad for a job. That's even believable because of the sign." He gestured a finger skyward.

"Fine, whatever, but Remy, I swear, don't mess this up. I mean it."

He reached over the broad leather seat and smoothed her hair. "I hope it works for you, baby."

"Okay. And don't call me baby. Sheesh, your poor wife…" And she exited the car.

A stout woman answered the bell. She appeared to be in her midfifties and had dyed orange hair. "Yes?" she asked as if she wasn't expecting any callers.

"Wednesday Green," Ava stated, and the woman looked around the small parking lot before allowing Ava in. She gestured to a metal mesh chair on the other side of her low metal desk, and they both sat as Ava's eyes adjusted to the darkness empowered by the small windows and closed blinds. "You're Ava," she said without inflection. "I need your ID."

"That's correct. And I guess you're Angie." She smiled and passed over her driver's license, but the woman ignored the smile and began writing on a clipboard.

Ava looked behind the woman's bowed head to the cement walls beyond, painted the same light blue as those outside and devoid of decoration. Apparently, baby sellers felt no need to provide an inviting atmosphere.

The woman finished writing and passed the clipboard to Ava. "I told you most everything on the phone. This is all we need from you. You're getting no guarantee of anything. We give you a child, and you give us twelve thousand dollars. In cash."

Ava's heart railed against the walls of her chest; her palms were damp. She wished Remy really could have come in with her. "I understand." She used her professional voice.

"We want you to know this is a service the doctor provides to women who don't want their babies and could use some money. He is not stealing babies from mothers like you hear about sometimes. These are usually young girls whose families have either kicked them out or tried to force them into abortions. Sometimes they're older or even married, but they don't want it or just can't keep it. And some of them, especially the young ones, think they're going to keep the baby and realize after it's born, they can't take care of it. We're doing them a favor. Do you understand?"

Ava felt herself growing nauseous, but she nodded. Why wouldn't the girls, or the women, just go to the hospital and go through the usual channels? Give the baby up for free? How did she know—what difference would it make, though—but what if these people were selling babies for money?

The clock to her right, the only adornment on any of the four walls, ticked its incessant annihilation of time.

"We don't guarantee you anything. The doctor delivers the baby and gives it as good a care as he can before we give it to you. We don't know the heritage, and we tell you nothing about the parentage. Are you okay with these terms?"

Ava nodded. "Yes. Of course."

"It's up to you to provide for this baby from here on out. If you can't, you can take it to a hospital, but if you try to come back here or contact us in any way, you will find this building closed as if I was never here because this is a temporary situation. Any questions?"

Ava tried to breathe deeply. "You said you had a baby now but wouldn't say how old or what it was. Can you tell me now?"

"You didn't need to know before you came out," Angie quipped, no kindness in her voice. She looked down at another paper on her desk and wrote some more.

"You can come to this building at five in the morning. We won't be here, but we'll watch when you get here, and we'll come over then. Come alone, and bring cash, clothing, a bottle, formula, water, diapers, and wipes. You'll also need an extra blanket and a car seat. Do you understand?"

Ava nodded.

"What're you driving?" Ava could barely speak for the knot in her throat. She gestured beyond the blinds of one barred window to the parking lot, and the woman rose, peeked through the slats, and nodded before resuming her seat.

"Fine. Answer those questions there." And she jerked her head toward the clipboard in Ava's lap.

Ava licked her lips and wished for water. The paper took no more than three minutes, and she slid the clipboard across the desk. Angie examined it, scowling, then stood, sliding her chair back as she did so. "I'll see you at five in the morning… And don't be late. You're getting a boy. He's four days." And just like that, they were done.

Chapter 48

HE'D DRIVEN HER to Jacksonville Beach, and Ava knew that the man liked her.

The beach was cool but sunny, and Remy walked beside her, hands stuffed in khaki shorts, a thin polo pullover sweater hanging loosely on his tall frame. He had strong, even features and a thin, neat mustache above his upper lip. He walked closest to the water with his head bent toward his feet, unspeaking; she kept her head turned somewhat toward him so the breeze blew her hair away from her face.

"Where does your wife think you are?" They hadn't spoken for about five minutes, and her question served to call him back from some deep reverie or introspection.

"Hmmm? Oh. Her name is Nan, by the way."

"Okay. Good for you. It's harder to ignore them when you use their names, isn't it?"

He smiled. "She thinks I'm at work. Which is where I should be."

"Right. Your construction job."

He smiled again. "Construction *supervisor,* if you please."

"Oh, perdón! Aren't you worried something may go wrong while you're away? I mean, you're the big ol' hairy boss and all."

"A little. I'll go in tomorrow. After I get you settled."

They were silent again for a while. Ava had asked him to take her to the site. Her original plans had involved cabs, but in the last ten days, she'd found Remy comforting in the way she'd always been attracted to strong men. Plus, she needed to save money, awakening almost every night with anxiety about where—after going to see Bea—she would live and work and how she would raise this child alone. It was all doable, and she was confident; but she was tired, strained, and overwhelmed.

"I've enjoyed getting to know you." He spoke those words to his feet as well.

She thought of the dinner she'd allowed him to buy her once and the time they'd gone for monster margaritas. "And I, you, sir," she replied. "We can stay in touch, you know. I mean, I owe you. And especially since I'm not forking over my body, I'll have to find it in the budget for chocolate milkshakes or something down the road."

A couple was approaching, holding hands. Ava reached for Remy's hand and swung it a little bit, smiling at the couple, who looked a little too long but smiled back as Ava refused to look away from their faces.

When they'd passed, she let it go.

"What was that for?" Remy asked.

She shrugged. "I don't know. Shock effect. Kick things up a bit. Have you ever dated a white woman?"

"Once. It was a lot. Most people just try to look without you noticing, but others…they say things."

"I guess it's hard. Not worth it, huh?"

"Oh, no, it would be totally worth it. We just didn't work out. I fell in love with my wife."

"But not anymore?" Silence. He offered her a gentle smile. "How long have you been married?"

"Twelve years. I was thirty, and she was twenty-five. But things…I don't know. She's not much interested in me anymore. Maybe she never was, who knows."

They'd left their shoes in the car and walked with their feet in the cold surf. Remy picked up a tiny perfect shell and put it in the pocket of her rolled-up jeans. "To remember me by," he said.

"Oh, please. I told you, we'll stay in touch. And I'd never forget you anyway. Nobody knows his way around a baby supply store like you, my childless friend."

He had helped her. For almost two hours that afternoon after they'd left the dismal blue building, Remy and Ava had scoured Babies R Us. Remy's trunk was now full of everything "Angie" had required, as well as baby-boy gowns, blue onesies and a gray one with ducks, and outfits with sailboats and bears and footballs. He'd bought her a carrier and some burping cloths. He'd bought her an ice cream cone and passed her his extra napkins without being asked when she'd teared up midcone as they'd been talking.

"Maybe. Maybe not. I doubt Nan would understand."

"So…you're saying she's *not* a swinger?"

"Yeah. Come up here with me." He took her hand and veered, then, and began walking away from the surf and back up the sand toward the road. He found a knoll shaded by the towering beach houses and lay back against it, gesturing to Ava. She leaned against a bank of sand beside him at a respectable distance, crossing her ankles and cozying her hands under the edge of her cable-knit sweater. The water glistened beyond them as seabirds circled and cackled, a few coming to land on some dead sea creature just a few feet downwind.

"Are you sure you want that baby?" The question took her off guard.

"Of course I want the baby! That's the whole reason I'm down here." She remembered so clearly when Kimberly had mentioned it, and even later, when Ava had asked for details—of the friend, who had a friend, who was a nurse, who worked for a doctor not even thirty minutes from where Scott's brother lived, who helped young girls "start over."

"Because, I've been thinking—and don't get mad—but what if this is some kind of black-market thing for real, that it's not just for people like you who don't have twenty-five grand or for girls to get a little money to restart their lives or, you know, for girls whose babies aren't going to have a daddy."

"They're not all like that. Some are married, but—"

"I know, I know what they said. But what if it's some crime ring, and the babies are taken. There was that doctor in Georgia and another in New York. They told the mothers their babies died. I went to the library and looked it up."

Ava felt her insides grow cold; she sat up and faced him. "Why would you do that? Why would you be that cruel? I know you don't know me well, but you know me well enough, and I would never—"

"Listen, I know you wouldn't. Don't get all upset. That's why I bring it up. You're going on their word. Why wouldn't a reputable doctor tell these girls to go to the hospital and give their babies up through the proper channels? And why wouldn't the girls do that?"

"Probably because their parents have kicked them out. The doctor finds them places to live or maybe gives their families a little something. And then they get some money—my money—to start over."

"And how do you know people like you aren't encouraging a girl to have a baby for money? Or to give away a baby she may have wanted if she didn't need the money? Don't you see some problems here? And there are more."

"Well, haven't we turned into Mr. High Horse all of a sudden?" Ava rose and began to stride away, but to her surprise, when she looked behind with the pretense of tossing her hair to gather it against the breeze, he wasn't following. Like the practical coward she knew herself to be, she got fifty feet down the beach and stopped. She had no car, no shoes, and no money on her. She continued walking and sat on another knoll, and when he still didn't come to her but lay there with his arm thrown over his eyes, she trudged back.

"You're lousy for a person's self-esteem." She plopped beside him again. He didn't remove his arm.

"You need me to get home."

"I know, wisecracker."

"Look who's calling whom a cracker."

That made her smile. She couldn't fight with the only friend she had in the state. "Why are you trying to talk all proper-like, anyway? Whom?"

"Well." But there wasn't much to say, so he said it again. "Well."

She lay again with her back against the uprising sandy knoll. The surf was higher, closer, louder.

"What do you make of everything, Remy? Like the ocean and the world and stuff?"

He removed his arm and sat up beside her, blinking at the new brightness. "What does that mean, sweetheart?" And the term of endearment felt odd, even as it added to her perception of the reality that this was an older man. Maybe, she pondered, he knew things. Maybe he had some things figured out.

"Like…do you think there's a point? A purpose? How did we get here, and is there a plan? I want things, and I used to think it was going to be easy to go along in the world. I just needed to have certain little things."

He gave a small laugh. "You're asking the million-dollar question, Ava. 'Why are we here, and how can we be happy?' Everybody thinks they just need a few small things, but when they get those, they don't want them. Or they need more. Or they need things taken away."

She felt defensive again. "I don't ask for too much."

"I didn't say you did." People walked in front of them—an old couple, the man's belly round as a beach ball in a neon-yellow sport shirt and a couple of kids kicking the water as high as they could as they ran.

Remy spoke again. "When I was growing up in Detroit, I was the youngest of four. I imagine there were days when my momma wished she had a couple less of us and a bit of money instead. And my daddy tried to be a good man, but he let her down. He never brought home enough money, and he drank. And it didn't help that he was a white man."

"What does that mean? You mean prejudice?"

"Yeah. People judged him. And her. And yeah, even in Detroit."

Ava already knew Remy had grown up poor, much poorer than she. Living with segregation, through the Depression and two or three wars, and then the Civil Rights Movement—and with little education—it wasn't hard to imagine his parents struggling and beaten down, even without the judgment of others against them.

"I still don't get what you're trying to say."

"My mama had some things you want—kids and a husband who loved her—but she wasn't happy. My wife doesn't have kids and doesn't want kids, and we've got some money, but she's not happy. Maybe if you get some of these things you think you have to have, you're not going to be happy either."

"So are you saying I shouldn't try? Accept a husband who doesn't love me enough to put me first or be honest, a lying mother, a childless home?" She breathed deeply to calm down. *The complete nerve…*

"No. You're not looking at the big picture. I have a little crush on you, in case you haven't noticed. I've already seduced you and run away to Key West to build a life with you and your new baby, in my mind. But from what you've told me, I think you've got it wrong about your husband. And your mother, for that matter. You're just too stubborn and hurt to consider that."

"Wow." She squared her face against his. "Wow." But she waited for him to go on, and in a minute, he did.

"Your husband bought you a house. He wanted to take time and spend time with you to fix it up. He was willing to try for a baby with you immediately and then adopt with you, even though he doesn't need kids to be happy. He wanted you to quit your boring jobs and do the painting and photography you loved and travel with him. And he told you he never slept with that woman after you came on the scene, but you completely refuse to believe that might be true." He paused, but when she made no defense, continued.

"Your mother accepted a child she thought belonged to her husband, who'd, supposedly, fathered it with a beautiful woman he loved and slept with on a regular basis. She could have talked trash about your daddy to you, but she didn't. And despite her mental illness, she loved you to the best of her ability, even after her husband killed himself. And with very little money. Because to her, you belonged to her, no matter what." He hesitated again. "I just wonder if there might be another way to look at these people you've learned to hate, who have drug problems and mental problems, but…who seem to love you anyway."

The sun was setting behind them. It had grown colder in the shade of the buildings. She sat with the constraint of a new awareness in her gut; she sat with a possible truth. What would it be, she wondered, to be able to forgive? Or what would it feel like to go back just a couple of years to a time when she was smart, good, and kind Ava Rush, daughter of Jeanette and John, wife of the loved and loving Scott Divine?

She took a deep breath and stood, dusting the sand from her jeans and offering her hand to the tawny, kind man beside her. "We need to get going, you know. Tomorrow's a very big day."

Chapter 49

THE SUN WAS rising in the astronomical dawn. Ava sat on the front seat of Remy's Lincoln, wearing jeans and her favorite sweater, a fine yellow cashmere. She wanted to remember the outfit in which she picked up her new child; maybe she would even include a piece of the sweater in a keepsake box.

Remy's Rolex read 5:13 a.m. Ava wondered if his wife knew where he was, but she realized she didn't care. She was feeling anxious and selfish and wanted him by her side.

There was no indication anyone was aware of their arrival, and with each passing minute, she became more and more anxious, the butterflies of her stomach in panic mode. She pressed the padded small manila envelope of cash against her chest and breathed.

It was five twenty-seven when lights appeared behind the narrow, barred, and blinded windows. *There must be a back road, a back entrance,* Ava thought. The morning was cool and windy, and the "Langley's Tax Service" sign swung recklessly from its transverse hanger atop the pole. Ava breathed deeply again and looked to Remy, placing her hand on the car door handle.

"Here goes nothing…" She opened the door and began to rise from the seat.

Remy put his hand on her arm. "I think I should go in. I mean, what are they going to do, refuse you the child?"

"Yes! Yes, that's exactly what they could do! They don't know you—you could be performing a sting or something. You could meet one person, and they could signal another, and it could all be over!" Again, Ava sucked in air and exhaled. "Like I said, I think they're trying to do a good thing, but it's still illegal, Remy. So, no." And she exited the car before he could say anything else, taking the cash and the diaper bag with her.

Timidly, she knocked. Someone must have been watching from another vantage because the blinds never moved before the door opened; Angie stood in its frame like a solid fortress, then moved aside, shutting and barring them inside as soon as Ava had taken two steps inward.

Against the far wall, on a folding table, was a car carrier. Inside was a blue-swaddled bundle, a tiny motionless face above the folds. Ava stared.

"You have your own car seat, of course," Angie said and, after Ava nodded, began rummaging through the diaper bag without permission. "This is good." She pawed away. "This is fine. Do you have the compensation?" So Ava produced that, as well.

Angie walked behind the desk and removed the cash from its envelope while Ava stared in the direction of the infant. Before she began counting, the older woman gestured with the stack toward the baby. "You can go pick him up if you want."

Ava crept to the table and peered into the tiny face. He was beautiful, and she knew newborns often weren't. But he was rosy, with the palest pink circles airbrushed onto his bisque cheeks. His lashes were black; his lips, in repose, were like a soft, fresh rosebud. Her inner artist imagined painting that face but knew any rendering would come up short.

"Can I…may I take this off?" And she gestured to the baby's blue cap.

Angie's face appeared softer than Ava had seen it, and she pursed her lips and gave a tiny nod in response. She slid the money back in its envelope and placed it to the side.

Ava reached forward and lifted the cap as if she were picking up a fly by its wings. His head was round with a soft brown down that reflected gold from the harsh fluorescent light. He stirred and brought a tiny porcelain fist to his mouth. Ava felt her breath start. He looked as if he could have been born to her.

"Go ahead and pick him up, honey. He won't break," the woman said as she watched her, so Ava did.

The office was warm, and she lifted him out of his blanket. In just his onesie, he felt like a puppy, just flesh and soft bones; and as she settled him against her chest, he stretched his neck backward and yawned. He smacked his lips a couple of times, curled his hands against her collarbone, and tucked his warm downy head under her chin.

The sob that rose in her throat was feral and frightening. It was a terrible intake of breath, a cry that cracked the air and caused the baby's dark-blue eyes to open as she removed him away from her neck. The baby-powder smell dissipated as she put him down; the room spun as she held the edge of the table. She turned to see Angie—her face startled and stricken and clutching the clipboard on which she'd been writing in a frozen, suspended manner—and Ava knew it had not been her imagination that she'd emitted that coarse and frightening cry.

Stumbling, she reached for the diaper bag and then the envelope of money that lay on the desk in front of the transfixed woman. She had a vague, fleeting perception of her new nemesis coming to life and issuing from behind the wide low desk to come toward Ava as she exited, but Ava didn't look behind her at all. She retched as she reached the door of the Lincoln, struggled to pull a burping cloth from the diaper bag. In a heartbeat, Remy came beside her; she sobbed as he helped her into the car.

The sun was a fiery ball of surety behind them as Remy turned the car onto the road that headed back toward the harbor. Ava, in sudden afterthought, looked over her shoulder only long enough to see Angie's black silhouette braced against the doorway's golden backdrop. It could have just as easily been Jesus standing there—still, unreadable, perhaps full of judgment or reprobation—or He could have stood there in appraisal and found her worthy of something.

Chapter 50

THE SUN ALSO *rises,* Ava thought, *on the blessed and the damned.* It began to show its imminence once again beyond the strong, clear Coke-bottle green plate glass windows of The Fox and Ale, declaring there were still some things on which the world could count.

Ava sat at one of the small square tables facing it—the one where Scott had sat when she'd first laid eyes upon him three and a half years ago. She held a sweaty glass with a few ice cubes, a splash of orange juice, and a lot of dark rum. Behind the bar, ten dollars rested on the stainless-steel shelf from which Ava had lifted the bottle of Bacardi. She planned to take the bottle, and she would not be beholden to either of the owners of The Fox and Ale for anything.

She'd fallen asleep on the short flight home—still holding her rum and Coke on the tray table in front of her—but it was fitful and disruptive and brief enough to feel as if it hadn't even happened, for the total flight had lasted less than an hour and a half.

The cab arrived at the bar before dawn was even a suggestion, and though it had cut deeply into her personal money stash—the money that truly belonged to her—it was worth it. She wasn't ready yet to see Jude or anyone, though more liquid courage was helping. There was much to do.

Corrine would be there early, and on the days she opened, Ava knew she arrived by eight and didn't stay long past eleven. Corrine liked her daily pleasures, and hanging out at the bar was not one of them.

She would talk to Corrine. She would have no peace until she forced herself to talk to Corrine. Then she had to see Bea. No matter how tired, grimy, drunk, or hungover; no matter how hungry, angry, sick, or afraid, she had to see Bea. The chemotherapy was brutal. It had been two months now, and Ava had not even been there for the last one.

She could shower there—eat, sleep, and then figure out how to return the money to the Divine—to Marilyn's—safe. She knew what she'd taken from there and from Divine Chevrolet both, recording the exact amounts lifted and embezzled, even though she wasn't sure why she'd kept track.

Stolen, she said to herself; she needed to use the word. She knew exactly how much she had stolen.

She poured several more glugs of rum into her glass, then walked behind the bar to refresh it with ice and juice. She swilled, enjoying the sweet heaviness. How smooth it had been on the airplane, how satisfying in its Styrofoam cup when Remy drove her that evening to the airport, and they'd toasted farewell in his car. Her companion didn't suspect, as he pressed a kiss on her cheek and another, quickly but deeply into her neck, that she would spend the rest of the night drinking and dozing in the Fox and Ale. His eyes glistened when she'd left him, and she sorrowfully realized she never planned to see him again in her life, and she didn't even understand why.

I owe allegiance to no one, she thought, *but, of course, to Bea.* Maybe with Bea sick, she would give all her allegiance to Bea.

Her head hurt. She was hungry and tired and hungover, nauseous with anxiety, and drunk all at once. She wrapped herself in a hug, hands on each shoulder, dropped her head, and closed her eyes.

She missed him—Scott. She missed him terribly and wondered what he was doing right that moment. She realized, with sudden clarity, that the totality of everything she loved, had loved, and hated in him was contained in that one constellation of cells and spirit. And though only God knew where he existed right then, she knew—even as she'd realized with Heidi and Bea—that that constellation was pitifully small—his existence so tenuous—and how easy it sometimes was to be separated from a person by space, and life, or death.

She thought of Bea again, too, and ached.

Ava knew Scott would be at Jimmy's parents' plantation house that weekend for one of their hunts. Jimmy would be there, too, but Corrine would stay behind to babysit the bar; Ava kept her calendar well. After seeing Bea, she could go home—HOME—and sleep and think until Scott returned on Tuesday. Maybe she would even be gone again by then. Who knew?

Ava watched as Corrine's Corvette convertible eased into a space directly beyond the glass, and she swigged her drink to calm her turbid stomach, even though she knew she was overserved. Ava hated that car—hated it because it was ostentatious and sexy and because it was Corrine's and hated it even more because Chantal had owned a blue one. Chantal may have done some questionable things, but she would never have slept with Ava's husband.

Corrine stopped on the threshold, holding the square gold key with which she'd opened the bar's heavy door. Ava enjoyed her old boss's initial alarm at discovering Ava's shadowy form, her subsequent discomfort, and maybe fear, as Corrine must have tried to discern Ava's intentions.

"Well, fancy meeting me here," Ava murmured and was surprised to hear her words sounded somewhat slurred to her own ears.

"Good grief, Ava. Scare a body to death." The bar owner turned to slide the door's locks into place behind her.

Corrine wore a white sweater—as typical, it was low-cut, showcasing her magnificent bust—and tight black Jordache jeans with boots. Her shagged blonde hair shone yellow gold in the ever-increasing sunlight from the windows. She wore makeup, always, with a stain of pale-red lipstick on her mouth.

"So sorry. So sorry. Wouldn't want to make you uncomfortable." Ava saw no reason not to just dive right in.

Corrine strode behind the bar and deposited her handbag. She put a tiny silver key into the register and began to key it out. The drawer popped, but she gently pushed it to again, being careful not to close it all the way.

"Go ahead and count it. I haven't taken anything."

"Well, of course I'll count it. We always count the till." She pulled out the drawer and counted its bills and coins. Ava assumed it was correct because Corrine pushed the drawer closed without comment.

"I never stole from you guys, you know." Ava rose from the table and lifted the rum bottle, hoisting it in the direction of Corrine, saying, "And I paid for this. Up there." She nodded her head toward the empty spot where the bottle had been and where the ten now lay, then set the bottle back on her table.

"No one ever thought you did, honey. And you can have the rum, we don't—"

"I don't need your charity. You don't get to sleep with my husband and buy me off with some fake charity." Ava stood in front of the table where she'd been sitting, arms crossed, face glaring.

Corrine, who'd begun lifting bottles of beer from the cooler and putting them in the bin where she would then surround them with ice, turned; the expression on her face, Ava presumed, was supposed to register that she'd had no idea this was coming.

"Is that why you're here? To talk to me about Scott?" She dared to stand with her hands on her hips in a show, no doubt, of indignance.

"No. I came to give you these." Ava reached in her jeans pocket and retrieved her own set of keys that opened the bar's black double doors, her old office door, and her copy of the silver register key. She shoved them across the bar in Corrine's direction and stood there, on the patron's side of the bar, staring her betrayer down with every bit of courage—no doubt fueled by anger and alcohol—that she had. "And to tell you that you make me sick."

Corrine, who had been reaching for the keys, stopped and flashed her eyes at Ava.

"Just to get the record straight, I didn't sleep with your husband, little girl." She snatched up the keys, turned and dropped them into her purse, then pulled a bottle of beer from the ice and popped it. "I slept with the man who *became* your husband, way before you were ever a breath or an idea here in Corinth."

Ava, upon hearing *little girl*, could have gouged Corrine's eyes out; but with that next statement, the monster inside her froze. Just for a moment. Just long enough to listen—for a moment.

Corrine turned her back, and Ava watched her breathe in deeply as she walked around the bar and sit on a stool two seats away from where Ava still stood, resting the beer between her legs. "I'm not going to fight with you, Ava. I get it. You're young, and you still think you can move your little chess pieces around the board of the world and have the game—your life—turn out like you planned. You'll get over it soon enough." She gulped from her bottle and propped a leg on her stool rung, watching Ava's face.

Ava stepped the few feet to the low table where she'd been sitting and retrieved her drink. She returned to stand at the bar but said nothing.

"Would you sit down a minute? Can we talk a minute?" Ava noticed for the first time Corrine had three faint lines across her forehead. Her eyes had lost their fire and looked like two placid pools. Ava sat, leaving two barstools between them.

"Where have you been? It's been a month." Silence. Ava focused on staring her down. Corrine took another long swill of beer before she continued.

"I don't expect you to understand this. And I don't know if it will help or hurt, but it's the truth. Maybe it's time for all that." Corrine looked down, inhaling and exhaling before raising her eyes again. "I loved Scott."

Another punch to the stomach. How many before one just fell over dead?

"I loved him, and…I love him." Corrine placed her bottle on the bar and began twirling it. Ava forced herself to breathe. *Maybe it's time for all that…*

"It…I love Jimmy too. I always have, I always will, but it's not like you think it is when you're married a long time. It's not so black and white, so cut and dried. You love other people. And Jimmy, he's a wildcat…he likes to play. You can do things like that, you know, in spite of what you think, to have fun, to create excitement… It doesn't have to mean anything."

"It doesn't have to mean anything? It doesn't have to *mean* anything?" Ava's words came out shrill and grating.

"No! It doesn't. It didn't mean anything to Scott."

Ava's heart was pounding out of her chest, but she couldn't run. She had to listen. She had to find out the truth, and by that, she believed, all of it. "He said it didn't mean anything to you, either." And she watched Corrine's face for every trace of a reaction.

Corrine brought the beer again to rest on the seat between her knees and stared at it. "As far as he knows, it didn't."

Ava drained the dregs of her glass. There wasn't enough rum in the world.

"I'm doing you a really big favor right now—" Corrine began, but Ava slammed the fist holding her drink on the bar in front of her.

"Oh, please, you piece of—"

"Listen to me! Ava." Corrine propped both legs on the rungs of her stool and leaned forward toward Ava's face. "I never told Scott. Or Jimmy. I always…I just always loved him. From the minute he came in here, the whole time he worked for us, and after. You did too. I saw it right away, so don't even bother. All the girls love him." She looked down again at her bottle and said, almost to herself, "Who *wouldn't* love him…"

Ava didn't speak. She needed to hear what had to be said.

"The thing is, he was just a player. He had girls. You know that. He was discontent, though, and…well, Jimmy and I were there… but he didn't like it. I knew. But I loved him. I never thought about doing anything…you know, dramatic. You don't throw away your marriage, with a man you love, for that… And he was so young, but…but it was always there. And then you came along."

Ava had begun to cry. "I need to know what happened."

"Nothing! That's just it! Nothing, really, that meant anything. It's been a very long time. And then…then, when you got here…he didn't even see anybody. Not seriously, anyway. And I was jealous of you. Because I knew."

A glance at Corrine's face revealed the tiniest shine in her eyes, but Ava looked away. She dared not risk emotional intimacy with the person she hated most in the world.

"He barely noticed me. He barely spoke." Ava hated the tremor, the cracks, in her voice.

A weak smile. "I know. I watched him. Scott was watching you. Checking out how you rolled, who you were. Becoming totally taken with you."

Ava wanted to believe. She wanted to believe they had had something special and still did. She'd been holding a wadded cocktail napkin in her fist and began to pick it apart.

"Ava, why do you think Scott proposed that you guys elope less than three weeks after dating you?" Ava remembered telling Corrine and Gwen the story later, back when life had been perfect and clean. "Because he already knew. He'd been watching you so long. Learning you. Falling in love but making sure. That man never does anything halfway."

Ava thought of the way Scott poured himself into his life—beginning his writing career because he'd decided to believe in himself without looking back, traveling at every opportunity to get material, writing at all hours, pitching stories to prominent publications even with so little experience; and how he'd bought the house, so decisive, because she had wanted a house. Even—and this was true, wasn't it?—how he'd tried to make a baby with her right away and furnished an entire nursery, even though babies, it turns out, weren't important to him at all.

"So…there is no affair…now?"

Corrine shook her head. "Ava, there was never an affair. Not on his part. And here's another bone—you already hate me, so what the hell—it isn't because I didn't offer. And your husband said no." She drained her beer and set down the bottle with a thud.

Ava was afraid to move. "You offered *after* we were already together? After we were already married?"

Corrine didn't meet her eyes. She looked embarrassed and defiant both, somehow, and older than Ava had ever seen her. "It's just sex, for God's sake. I don't understand why people make such a big deal…" And she got up to move behind the bar as Ava studied her.

But she was wrong. It was a big deal. And Ava may have been young and half-blinded by ignorance or innocence or whatever the cause may have been, but one thing she knew was that the woman was utterly wrong.

Chapter 51

THE UPSTAIRS OF the Mullins house was six large rooms, three on each side, separated by the broad, varnished hall upon which the end of the two opposing staircase ascensions emptied. Bea's and Toby's master bedroom was in the back-upstairs corner, on the left, if one were facing the house; her mother's and father's had been, before Louise's illness had relegated to her to a one-story existence, on the right.

Bea lay in the window seat, which was long enough to stretch out upon, its window overlooking the same view Ava had studied from the back porch on so many occasions of her visits there—the yard, the field and pasture, the duck and chicken houses, and the blue-hazed ridge of pines beyond.

"First, you have to tell me everything Jude said."

Bea wore one of her signature looks—a navy bandana knotted at the nape—but today Ava knew it covered her thinning scalp, for her hairline was showing, and it was sketchy and patchy and tragic.

"Well, he began by saying what a scoundrel I am for not telling you guys where I was going. But then we talked about Jeanette because I asked him about her right away. I've been afraid she's been living in Crazy Ville while I was gone and y'all have had to deal with it. But he said except for crying a few times at work—'cuz, you know, he had to tell her to stop, bad for business, and all—that she was doing okay."

Bea nodded. "We make sure she's heavily medicated, of course." She was smiling as if Ava were sharing stories from a delightful date or a party.

"Of course. Then he said his father had gotten in touch because a family friend wanted Jude to help her son stop being gay."

Bea leaned her head back and laughed aloud. "Oh, my heavens, I can't *stand* it! What did he say to that?"

"He said he told his dad he loved him and he'd love to come talk sometime."

Ava loved watching her friend's familiar grin, the crinkles of her soft blue eyes, and the heft of her ever-increasing belly with each chuckle.

"Oh, my goodness, oh my goodness…I wish I could have heard Jude tell it. He can turn the darndest things into something funny." Bea turned her gaze out the window. "Toby should be back up soon. He kicks off a little earlier these days, especially on Friday."

Heidi, who had been playing in the corner with a bin of Legos, came and sat in Ava's lap where she'd curled into a bean bag chair close to the head of her friend's makeshift chaise. The little girl reached for Ava's purse and began rummaging through it.

"She's missed you." Bea reached to dab at Heidi's nose with a tissue. "She rarely wants to cuddle in anyone's lap anymore. Always has so much to do."

"I've missed her too. And Little Man, of course, but…this is my homegirl, you know." Heidi was almost two and a half. She had screamed and run at Ava after Clara had opened the door to her a little before noon; while Wesley, at almost fifteen months, had watched Ava thoughtfully from behind his great-grandma's Bermuda shorts. Heidi had insisted on staying with Ava after Gram had walked her upstairs to see Bea, but Wesley had just gone down for his nap.

"Still no words?" Ava stroked Heidi's fine yellow hair and steadied a little notebook as the girl waggled an ink pen across it.

Bea shook her head. "No. And the doctor still says there may never be." Bea kissed her own fingertip and placed it on Heidi's tiny pucker as her child had spontaneously tilted her head back to look at her mom. "Isn't it amazing to think she may go her whole life without the gift of speech?" she asked, but there was no rancor in her voice, not a trace. It was more like wonder.

"She'll do okay." Ava kissed the top of Heidi's head. "She'll have you. And your whole annoying family. Plus Toby and his whole annoying family and crazy Aunt Ava."

A silence passed, and Heidi left Ava's lap for a pile of wooden blocks by the door. The bedroom was awash with blocks and coloring books, Barbie dolls, and Matchbox cars. It was apparent Bea was spending a lot of time here, and the kids—every minute they weren't being wrangled by Clara, who lived there full-time again, or by Susan or Laura, who alternated two days each, a week—a lot of time, too, by default.

"What did Gram say when she saw you?" Bea hoisted herself higher against her pillows and reached for a water glass on her bedside table.

"She said, 'Ava! I can't believe it! You missed Thanksgiving!' and I said, 'I know, Gram, but you *know* it's highly overrated.' Then she hugged me and told me you were lying up here worthless as a cat."

"Did not." But Bea was smiling.

"No. You got me. She did not. But she did tell me they were going to take the baby in a few days. On Scott's and my anniversary, actually." She watched her friend's face, but Bea turned and resumed looking out the window.

"Bea," Ava said, but the other girl didn't speak or move. "When they take the baby...she said the eighteenth...they can start the radiation right away. That's right, isn't it? And that, along with all the chemo you've been getting, that will...you'll probably be okay after that, right? That will be enough?"

Bea did turn then and smiled at her friend. "Are you trying to ask if I'm going to die?"

Ava sighed. "No. We all know you're not going to die. But... I'm just saying...I'm asking...Dr. Larimore, he probably said you'd get well after that, didn't he? The radiation will kill what the chemo hasn't? Stuff like that."

"Yeah." Bea was grinning at her. "Stuff like that. We're hoping for the best."

But Ava didn't feel better. Bea would tell her—she'd have phrased it differently—if the doctors had promised a recovery.

"And they're not 'taking' the baby. They will deliver it early, and she—or he—will be in an incubator. But in time, hopefully, they'll give her to us. Maybe for a ransom, but still." Her voice was light, and her eyes were twinkling. "Unless, of course, you want her."

Ava smiled, hopefully covering for the still oozing but healing hole in her heart. "I don't want no stinking baby. They're vastly overrated also, even more than Thanksgiving." She turned to watch Heidi put Barbies in the plastic refrigerator of a play kitchen by the wall.

Upon arrival, Ava had told Bea the barest skeleton of a story—that she'd been "in Florida" trying to think and figure things out without having to face anyone who knew her or who would ask her questions, and that she'd flown in only that morning. (For the time being, Starr had been sworn to secrecy concerning the abandoned adoption.) She said she hadn't been to sleep but had gone straight to the bar from the airport. And after the whole sordid exchange with Corrine, she'd called Jude to pick her up and then walked two storefronts down to a Baskin Robbins to wait for him, shedding Corrine Woodham cootie vibes as she went.

"I know you needed time to think," Bea had said, as gracious a counselor. "But please, Smitty, don't do that again." After looking upon Bea's pallor, her balding hairline, and after a moment of the worst guilt and self-recrimination she'd ever felt in her life, Ava knew she wouldn't.

"You'll be seven and a half months?" Ava hopped up to help Bea adjust the pillow she was repeatedly nudging behind her back.

"What, when I deliver? Almost eight. That's their best guess." She smoothed the top of her pink flannel nightgown. "They're sure it will be healthy enough to…give me a fighting chance, so…as long as it's healthy, I wouldn't mind a fighting chance." She stole a quick look at Ava as if she may have inadvertently corroborated, after all, that there hadn't been the promise of a stellar, successful race to the victory of her getting to live.

"You need to quit thinking it's going to be a girl. You may get quite a shock, you know, and won't your face be red."

"Aw, posh, I'll adjust. But I think a mom can tell these things… sometimes."

Clara came up the stairs just then, looking damp around the headband holding back her silver hair, and cajoled Heidi to accompany her downstairs for a snack. The child went to Ava first and put both arms around her neck, mashing her face into Ava's. Ava felt like crying.

It was a minute or two before either girl spoke again. Ava could hear Gram clinking plates and running water, the refrigerator door opening and closing. Her musical soliloquy to Heidi wafted to the bedroom—the inflections, lilt, and pauses synchronized to allow for the little girl's mind to register whatever it could and form whatever isolated mental response it had for itself. Bea heaved herself sideways to a sitting position and faced Ava with her legs angled out to allow her belly to rest a little between them as she took a deep breath.

"Do you know what you're going to do?" Unlike her grandma's, her voice was low, level, and firm, as if it was time to figure this stuff out. "Because I have to know you're going to be okay. We *both* have to decide to be okay. You know that, right? A lot of people are depending on us."

Ava nodded, fighting back shame at leaving her best friend like this, and for so long, with no word. "I have to get some sleep. Scott isn't supposed to be back until Tuesday morning—at least that was the trip he planned in September. Then I'm sure I'll know."

Bea stared at her with intensity but also love. "Ava, I want you to listen to me, okay?"

Ava had known it was coming. Bea stayed out of people's business better than anyone she knew, but there were times…and she knew, if ever there had been a time for her best friend to talk to her straight, it was then.

"I told you before you disappeared that Scott had called me a few times. At first."

Ava knew what her friend meant by "at first." When Ava had first come home from the Crazy Ward—as she'd referred to it since her dismissal—Bea had told her that first night, when she'd come to dinner at Jude's apartment that Scott called her several times to see if she could get Ava to talk to him. During their visit today, Bea hadn't brought him up, and Ava still hadn't asked if either had been in touch with the other.

"After Jude called us to tell us you'd taken off for your little mental health holiday and no one had any idea where—and I'm still not prying, just so you know, you'll talk about it one day, I'm sure—Scott called just twice more. Then he said he wouldn't call again because he didn't want to cause me stress or bother me, especially with all I was going through."

Ava had moved from the bean bag chair and had taken a more comfortable seat in the rocker. This one was the mate—upholstered in green fabric but sprayed with white lilies instead of yellow—to the one Bea had given Ava for her nursery, for the baby that never came, so many light-years ago. Ava chewed a thumbnail, watching Bea but wary.

"The first time, he told me to please just call if you called me or told anyone where you were. He insisted he had no plans to follow or find you, only that he wanted to make sure you were okay. And, just so you know, I believed him, though of course, I had nothing to share. But the second time, he said he wanted me and Toby to think of him as our ace-in-the-hole: the one who would 'be there' for us, day or night, rain or shine, when no one else would or could. *And* that he was mailing a letter." She shifted to one hip and lay back against the opposite side of the window seat, propping pillows behind her. "My back…I've got to walk this afternoon…"

"I'll come back. I'll go home and shower and sleep, but I'll come back tonight. I can take care of everything so Toby and Gram can rest—"

Bea was shaking her head. "Susan's coming tonight. And Jeanette will be home, and you won't be able to avoid her knowing you've shown back up. You have to see her, you know…you have to promise, the very next thing…you have to see her, Ava, and deal with it, or the poor woman's going to have a heart attack or go completely insane…got it? That's what I need from you." She looked at Ava as if she were unwilling to go on until she got an answer, so Ava forced herself to nod her head.

"But back to Scott. He *has* helped. He drove me to the doctor last week, and he's the one who goes to the store twice a week for Gram. He took Heidi and Wesley to the park three times and twice with Alex, just to give everybody some breathing room. And probably so that *I* could help *him* by giving him a place to work off his guilt. Do you get that?"

And Ava realized she did. Bea didn't have to call Scott to help, although it probably really did benefit her and her "crew." But just as Ava had always worked through her own guilt for "burdening" her mother as a child—even though she rationally knew, even before she knew the truth, that it wasn't her fault—by continually trying to manage Jeanette's unmanageable life, Bea had given Scott a place to serve to work out his own emotional and mental demons. And Ava realized it was true, although she'd never realized it any way but subconsciously, that giving someone a way to give too is sometimes the greatest of gifts.

"He actually mailed you a letter?"

"Yes. But he made me promise, if you came back, not to show it to you. And also, that I couldn't discuss with you what he said. But, Ava, if you ever loved me"—and she stopped, her voice just on the cusp of emotion—"you will go home and think about what you're doing with this wonderful life that God gave you. And promise me you will be there—after you go home and get yourself together—promise me you will still be there, at least talk to him, when he returns on Tuesday."

Ava sat utterly still. Bea was white, and she'd reached up and slid her bandana off her head in one wearying gesture before she lay back against the pillows. Her head was almost bald, reinforcing what the scattering of dark hair filmed across her pillow had already conveyed. By accident, Ava met Bea's eyes before casting her eyes to the window. *Where are you, God?* She silently screamed, and her mind's eye shook a theoretical fist at the heavens.

"Of course I'll be there on Tuesday."

Chapter 52

THE HOUSE SAT as if it had been waiting for her. All the life, all the generations of toil and mirth and normalcy, all the mediocre and calamitous events and emotions that had gone on or been felt in the occupants before her had drifted away on the currents of Tarryton's winds years before. It was gone—all of it, instantly, seconds after it happened—existing only in the memories of those who had lived it, and undoubtedly most of it remembered, for better or worse, with varying degrees of error.

Even after the cab dropped her off, it took her a moment to see his car. The Blazer sat in the dusky shadows of the backyard cottonwood tree, parked where Scott always parked it when he left on a trip and Ava drove him to the airport. Of course, for this trip they would have taken Jimmy's truck and trailer; they always did when they had to haul the hunting equipment and carriage the horses.

Ava went up the bottom two steps, sat down, and dropped her head for a moment. She had never been so tired in her life. But still, she sat, for she knew when she went into that house, her heart would go one way or another. She had not seen the inside of her own home since that night a month ago when they'd carried her out on a stretcher. She wanted so badly to erase that memory but even more to erase the occurrence. The horror that done things could never be undone was surely God's cruelest trick.

She sat a moment, feeling only her shallow breath. *It isn't over till the fat lady sings,* her mind tittered; and pressing her palms into the hard rock steps, she rose. *Sing, fat lady, sing.*

Inside was cool, and the scent was real. Every house, with its particular occupants and the dirt of that plot, the particular trees, foods, and a dog or cat make up the smells of that particular union of lives; and this comforted Ava beyond description. No matter what would happen in these upcoming days, no matter what had gone on before, at least for now, November 29, 1985, she was here; she was alive, and "here" was home.

She heard him—no, felt him—before she saw him. He stood in front of the sofa as she entered, and she could tell he'd been sitting but must have stood when he heard the taxi or maybe when she came in; but he stood, his hands casually hooked in his jeans' pockets, his dark-blue shirt unbuttoned exposing a white T-shirt tucked in at the waist.

He looked at her. She put down her suitcase and purse and leaned against the wall just inside the door. Then he said her name, "Ava." But that was all.

She took the steps to the living room, and still, he didn't move. She sat, perched on the small hard ottoman in front of the corner easy chair. Scott sank again to the sofa against the wall that was catercorner to her.

"Of course, I thought you were gone." She looked at his face, trying to read it but afraid. What was he thinking? Feeling? For that matter, what was she?

"Yeah. I didn't go."

"Why not? Because Corrine stayed here?" She knew he would know what she meant.

He sat down, with his legs apart, hands between his knees and leaning forward. He appeared to be studying her face for clues, her words not engaging him in the slightest.

"I need you to listen to me, baby, if you can. I need you to give me that gift."

She was taken aback. She was not used to Scott talking like this. She'd expected a strong retort, a denial, or a lashing back but not a request; not to phrase her attention as a gift, not for him to lead with the word, *baby*.

She wanted him to hold her. She wanted to forget Corrine, forget the absence of her womb, forget the drugs she took on that Saturday night, the horrible throbbing of her head, and the thousands of dollars layered with greed and desperation and deceit at the bottom of her secondhand alligator handbag. So she said nothing.

"Ava," he paused, "Ava, I don't expect anything from you. I want to make that clear. But I'm asking something of you. I'm asking for your merciful forgiveness."

What? Merciful. Forgiveness. Asking.

"My whole life has been a joke. Always looking for the answers in the wrong places. Building a house of cards." He looked down at his hands and back up at her face before continuing, "When I saw you, I just…I wanted you. Not only physically, but that was there, but I wanted the whole you. I believed you were what had been missing. You were so…brave and strong and good."

She couldn't hold back the tears. She was so wiped and tired, so strung out and hungover, so full of recrimination and guilt that she felt like she was going to explode. All she'd been holding back—the loss of a family both past and future, hatred for Corrine and Jimmy and probably Scott as well, terror for the life of Bea and the future of her children, even angst for the struggles of Jude's being gay, eight-year-old Alex on a diet, fat Mrs. Rhymer…how could she take it? How could Chantal be murdered and Eric lay with some slutty classmate? How could Liz steal the only good job Ava ever had, and Kenneth Mullins throw himself off a cliff after letting his comrades get assassinated and his wife suffocate to death in their bed?

She sobbed. "I'm not good, Scott. You don't know. I've done some really bad things." He came to her. He took her to the sofa and pulled her to him. "I know what you've done, and it doesn't matter. We can fix it. All of it."

She felt instantly sick, and she pulled back from him and searched his face. He knew? What part? The embezzlement or maybe the money taken from the safe? The intention to, truth be told, buy a baby? She began to tremble, but he pulled her again against his chest as the crying escaped without her consent, as all the grievances of creation purged through her. She thought of her daddy hanging on a rope, Jeanette dragging all her possessions to the street gutter in the middle of the night, and Toby, probably crying alone on so many days on his tractor as he plowed his daddy's interminable rows of corn.

"I'm so sorry, baby." He rocked her. "I'm so, so sorry." The clock on the wall ticked off seconds of portentous silence, while Scott's hand, gentle but firm and methodical, stroked her hair and her shoulder.

It was minutes before she could talk. Curled against his chest, her eyes fell on a book on the coffee table, a book she hadn't yet noticed. "Alcoholics Anonymous" was printed in bold yellow letters on its blue cover. She picked it up and raised her eyes to his. "Almost thirty days," he said, and he held up two crossed fingers. "Twenty-seven, to be exact."

She studied him. "You…don't drink? Anymore?"

He seemed tentative. "Not for today, at least. They tell you one day at a time. Or it can feel pretty overwhelming."

She was speechless—almost. "But the coke…do you…?"

He smiled. "No, baby. You can't do any of it. You can't pick and choose." His smile grew broader as if to say, *Silly girl.*

"Listen, Ava. We can adopt…or not. We can work our regular jobs or pursue our art, sell the house or not. We can work out whatever we need or want to do, but you're not to worry about any of that right now."

The words…so hopeful, so soothing, but…

She sat up straighter, then, and pulled slightly away. "Scott, do you love her? Or did you love her? You have to tell me. Even if it was…or is…just a little bit." She forced herself to stop talking so he'd have to fill the space with an answer.

He leaned forward, took her face between his hands, and they were cool and dry, unlike her own damp soft uncertain fingers that gripped the book like a rescuing piece of driftwood in a sea. These were the hands she'd fallen in love with—mixing the drinks in his cabin that first Halloween, holding his cigarette, guiding Duke and Wallis along the rocky trails beside the Tarrymore, playing along her skin like a symphony.

"No. And I want you to listen to me, okay? Not. One. Drop." It was a moment before he let his hands fall.

The wind blew outside. It would be dark soon. Scott got up and lit two lamps, went to the refrigerator, and poured two glasses of tea. She was surprised how her heart lightened as she realized she'd subconsciously expected him to bring back a beer.

"Babe." He sat down but turned slightly to her as if he were getting ready to tell her something important. "I've been looking for something. I don't think I've ever been sure what it was, but it was something I was looking for in girls and alcohol, even riding and golf and making money. I wanted to find it in cocaine, and it even felt like it worked for a while. And the 'ludes, the acid in college, and even in writing, and in you—as odd as that sounds—I was looking for it in you."

She waited. She'd never heard him talk like this, even though they'd had discussions about important things before—life and philosophy, economic systems, social programs—but she waited, for he was intense and he was opening, and she wanted him to let her inside.

"It isn't there. I love you, Ava, and I want you forever. But even loving you and having you didn't fix it."

That hurt a little. A part of her wanted to hear that she *had* fixed it, that *she* had fixed it, had fixed whatever it was. But she waited. *Please, please... let him make me understand.*

"It isn't in us, baby. And it isn't in our control. It's bigger than us, but it includes us, and best of all, it's for us."

He turned then and picked up a book behind him. It had been lying on the end table the whole time, but Ava hadn't noticed it, either, so intent was she upon everything he'd been saying and on her own emotions. But it was beautiful, its suggestion of glory and import different from every other book she'd ever seen. Scott laid it on the table in front of them, picked up both her hands in his, and kissed them, holding them like a precious goblet of something completely new—life-giving but reciprocal—and able to give something magical and full in return.

Then he began to tell her about Jesus.

END

But these are written that ye might believe that Jesus is the Christ, the Son of God; and that believing ye might have life through His name.

—John 20:31 (KJV)

About the Author

SHELLY DIXON VAN Sanford is a bona fide Jesus freak and a native Atlantan who now makes her home in some of God's best country, a.k.a. the Piedmont of North Carolina. Although her alma mater is her beloved Berry College, and she's a former teacher of Exceptional Children, she considers her best education to have emanated from the University for the Hard of Head. It was there she discovered answers to some of life's big questions, the beauty of multiple chances, and the support of her current tribe.

Shelly started her writing career in ninth grade with some pretty bad seagull poetry, moved on to lovelorn song lyrics, and dawdled with way too many treatises on possible meanings for our existence interspersed with some tragic short stories.

Her favorites are turtles, lemons, family, bodies of water, Collective Soul and Joan Armatrading, hymns, the written word, dancing, and a husband who tells her she can do anything.

As grateful as she is for those who love her, she also appreciates those who harmed, for she's learned at least one secret: it's the dance of sinner and sinned against through which we find our rhythm.

This is her first novel.

Printed in the USA
CPSIA information can be obtained
at www.ICGtesting.com
LVHW092200301223
767812LV00007B/85

9 781685 175511